Milestone Road

Robert P. Barsanti

Copyright © 2012 Robert P. Barsanti

All rights reserved.

ISBN: 0615649904
ISBN-13: 978-0615649900 Rocqua Publishing

The following is a work of fiction.

DEDICATION

For my Uncle, Father James O'Rourke

Acknowledgements

This work would not have been possible without
The encouragement and patience of many women:
Jen Britton, Meri Lepore, Kathy Lepore,
Queen Catherine Stover, Nancy Day,
Kirsten Mugnai, Sydney Fee,
And Ruth Burday.

CONTENTS

Epigraph

Milestone One   1

Milestone Two   90

Milestone Three   176

Milestone Four   272

Milestone Five   360

"Death to the Living, Long Life to the Killers..."

(Written by Whaleman Frederick Myrick on a whale's tooth while aboard the Nantucket whaleship, Susan.)

Milestone One

CHAPTER ONE

A father and his son stood on the top deck of the Nantucket ferry, the steamship "Eagle." They rested their hands on the railing, looked out over the sound to the small sliver of land visible on the horizon. In the last half hour, the boat had trudged out of Hyannis harbor and its collection of sailboats and cabin cruisers, meandered along a breakwater lined with fishermen, and now trotted south across Nantucket Sound on its way to the island.

The older man wore a short-sleeved checked shirt, tan shorts, and a green mask that connected to an oxygen tank. The tank looked to be the size of tall, narrow bottle of soda. To the crew, it was a bomb; they suggested as strongly as they could that the tank and its human host spend the trip outdoors. As it was the middle of a warm September afternoon, the father and son found sitting outside to be no burden and remained on a nearly empty top deck.

Both men attracted the eyes of the other passengers. Not only did they drag around an oxygen tank, but they also were huge specimens of mankind. The father, David, resembled a ruined and exiled king; he stood at 6'7 with broad shoulders, powerful arms, and a kettle of a belly. Disease had ravaged his face and skin, though they had left his physique untouched. Regrettably, his skin was yellowing, pocked, and splotched. All of his hair had fallen out. The scalp lay pink under a Red Sox hat.

His son, Elvis, stood an inch or two shorter than his father. He hadn't developed the arms, the hands, or the belly of the older man. He still had an edge of baby fat that thickened his face, neck, and body. But he was bursting from his clothes. Lightning had paused in him.

His father rested more of his weight on his arms and hands. He sighed and pulled the mask down. He drank in several long sea breaths.

"How do you feel?" his son asked.

"Just lovely."

"Do you want a pill?"

"No more pills." He muttered. "I want a beer."

For all of his size, the son was only fifteen. "They won't sell one to me."

"Sure they will. As long as you look normal, they will look normal. Pretend you are buying a Coke."

"What if they card me?"

"They won't."

"But if they ask for identification…"

"They won't."

The boy went into the snack bar and bought a Molson. He handed the cashier a twenty. The cashier returned the change without looking up.

His father drank half of the bottle in a long swallow.

"The island is a good place. It's a good place for us." he said. "Good people in a small town. Lot of work to be had. No one to make trouble." He touched the bottle to his lips. "You'll like the beach. You might even start surfing."

"I doubt it." Elvis did not know how to swim.

"I tried it. Years ago. Loved it."

His father sat down, gently, onto a blue bench. He futzed with the mask for the oxygen. "Your Aunt Shannon is a good person. Tough. But she is our sort of people."

"Is anyone coming after us?" The boy had thought about this more than anything else.

"No." came the slow answer. "No one is going to come for you. As long as you lay low and don't bust anyone up, you're all set."

His father brought the mask over his face. He closed his eyes and let his head rest back.

Twenty-four hours previous, his father had returned from a chemotherapy treatment late at night and was glowing with determination. "Pack." He commanded. So the boy had packed. He had brought a laptop computer, a duffle bag full of clothes, two trash bags full of sheets and pillows, shoulder pads, his winter coat, and his one and only swim suit. His father put three spare tires in the trunk.

Then the boy drove. He was at the wheel all eighteen hours from Chicago while his father slept in the front seat with the oxygen tank on his lap. Even a fender bender would have blown them into small chunks. The boy drove very, very cautiously. He drove five miles over the speed limit, stayed out of the passing lane, and panicked.

As far as he could tell, no one was following them.

His mother had named him Elvis partially out of pride, partially through the muse of Percocet, and partially with the same parenting logic of having a "boy named Sue." Within a year, his mother was back inside and the young Elvis grew alongside his father. He didn't know what his father did. He knew it involved cash, cellphones, unexplained weeks away, and long showers. At wrestling meets and football games, the other men stayed many feet away from his father, as if they needed time to escape. Elvis didn't know what his father did, but he knew what he didn't do. He didn't have a parking place, a washroom key, or a pass word.

His mother reappeared two years ago. She had discovered that, in fact, Jesus still loved her and wanted her to help spread the good word one white plastic set of rosary beads at a time. She made several phone calls to the house, and then, finally, showed up one afternoon at the door. She didn't apologize.

Since then, Elvis visited her on Sunday afternoons at Starbucks. He bought his mother coffee and a piece of cheesecake while she tried to bring him to her personal savior. Elvis, however, had learned many things from his father. He could see the demon behind his mother's eyes. It sat back, pricked its thumbs, and smiled. When the coffee was done, he had to go to "practice" and she had to go home.

Otherwise, his life was as normal as a 6'7", 290 pound high school freshman could be. He could dunk a basketball standing still. He wore sweatshirts and jeans more often than not. He had a bad effect on chairs. One night, down at the 7-11, a group of older boys shoved him around. Elvis grabbed the biggest one by the jaw and drove him into a pay phone. That gave the bully six quality weeks with a physical therapist and gave Elvis a parole officer. Who, this afternoon, also wasn't aware that the boy had left Chicago, driven to Hyannis, and was on the boat to Nantucket.

As his father dozed and his beer warmed, Elvis looked out over the water. Fifteen hours before, he had seen farmland pass the same way. Except that you could stop by the side of the road, walk into the corn fields, and walk back out. Nobody walks out of the ocean.

He felt the rise and fall of the ferry as it eased through the water. Behind the boat, the wake stretched out for a hundred yards before settling back into the lapping waves of the sound. Their trail disappeared behind them.

Nantucket slowly emerged out of the ocean. The radio towers poked over the horizon, then the bluffs and the palatial summer houses grew. Eventually, the rest of the island emerged: green, tan, and gray.

Elvis woke his father after the ferry passed the mouth of the jetties and was slowing. They stood and watched as the boat rounded Brant Point, and then settled into its slip.

Every other boat on the water was going the other way.

His Aunt Shannon lived in her ex-husband's family's summer home. He was a New Yorker who came from a family of white shoe lawyers who in turn worked at a law firm that had the family name on the stationery. And yet, he did not have a pre-nup. So, when her husband left Cos Cob for a hunting trip with his "associate," Alexander, Aunt Shannon carved out what she wanted. What she really wanted was the island house.

It was an odd house in an odd place. To get there, Elvis drove out of town, past the gray shingled sailors houses, gas stations and pizza joints, to where he turned into the parking lot for a store. Marine Home Center is a long, low series of wooden buildings. The garden section separates from painting by a road, that splits two small lumber yards, a parking lot for delivery trucks, and an industrial laundry. After he drove down that road to a hedge, he found a house with one of the most spectacular views on island. Perched over the creeks, a two story house looked over the harbor, the town, Monomoy, and Coatue beyond it.

Elvis parked their Corolla next to his Aunt's Cadillac Escalade.

He stood and looked around. They had no close neighbors, save for the back wall of the lumber yard. Across a half mile of marsh, a dock and a warehouse stood empty. In the other direction, one other house was perched above the marsh, but was more than a half mile of marsh and a salt water stream away.

It was a great place to hide.

His father rose from the passenger seat. He stepped around the SUV, and began to climb six steps. Elvis, remembering himself, moved to his father. The son cradled the oxygen tank in one hand and put the other around the older man's waist. Weeks ago, the old man would have pushed him away. Now, at the end of a long journey, his father dropped his weight onto his son. His son, as he had been taught, carried it without a word.

At the door, they knocked.

"Does she know that we are coming?"

"Of course."

Elvis took his own counsel. Knowing they might come and believing that they were going to be knocking on the door were two entirely different things. Further, his father pounded on a door as if he had Fate and the host of hell behind him.

When he paused, they heard nothing but wind.

His father knocked again. This time, they heard steps and the door opened.

"David." She heaved. She took a step back. Aunt Shannon had strawberry red hair, a white pantsuit, and the shocked expression of one who meets the dying.

"Shannon, how are you?" her brother smiled at her, as if it all was some strange joke.

She didn't laugh or smile or say anything. Her eyes had grown gray.

Then, too quickly, she blurted "Come in."

Like her brother, she stood well over six feet tall, with broad shoulders and powerful arms. She was dressed for cocktails and conversation, although make-up and evening clothes looked odd on a woman her size.

"Thanks. Just let me walk in for a bit."

His Dad stood and took several familiar steps into the kitchen and through to a living room with a glass wall. He eyed an easy chair, took careful aim, and dropped himself into it.

Shannon and Elvis followed. His son set the oxygen tank next to the chair.

"Can I get you anything, Dad?"

The son looked worried and confused. It was more energy than he had seen in a month.

"Shannon, do you have a beer?"

"Of course."

Elvis slipped into the kitchen, found a can of beer, opened it, and put the can inside a coffee mug. His Dad nodded his thanks, and drank off half the beer. Shannon had settled onto the sofa, although she remained pale.

"So," she said. "How was your trip?" The hostess had slipped in and had taken control of her head.

"Sucked."

"You look good." She added.

The father snorted. "Chemotherapy agrees with me. You look nice."

"Thanks. Nice to see you after all of these years." She tried to make the comment sting.

"Nice to see you." Although abrasive, his father said this with affection. "Shannon, this is my son, Elvis."

"Elvis?" It was involuntary. The boy was used to it by now. When most people heard his name, they looked at him as if he was missing an arm.

"I wasn't there when his mother named him." His father said.

"I assume you don't dance or sing." She said, looking at the boy. "But you have the family curse. People probably don't say much to you about your name, do they?"

"No, ma'am. They don't. Not anymore."

"He's a good boy. He's a good man." His father said.

"Obviously." She turned her best hostess face to the boy. "Elvis, it is a pleasure to finally meet you."

In the brief moment of looking at the boy, and then looking back, her brother, David had fallen asleep.

The boy looked to his Aunt. Then, the two of them eyed the sick man.

"He does that, ma'am. It has been a long trip." Elvis stood and arranged the oxygen mask over his father's mouth and nose, then hissed it on. Within a minute or so, the old man's color improved.

The light was still strong, but turning golden in the room. The house, and the room, had been decorated as if it were the common room to a woodsy prep school. A gigantic refectory table filled one half of the room, with one bench on the far side and a collision of chairs on the other. Two leather wing chairs flanked a leather sofa and beset a coffee table before a fieldstone fireplace. One, now occupied, La-Z-Boy reclining chair faced a plasma television. The walls had prints of old regattas, fish, fishermen, boats, surfers, and a large, signed print of rowers pulling up the Charles. Five fishing rods lay across the rafters as did a mass of signal flags. The rest of the walls were covered in bookcases filled with sagging and fading paperbacks. Opposite the fireplace, a row of glass framed the harbor.

Aunt Shannon looked to her nephew.

"How long will he be out?"

"I don't know. Could be twenty minutes. Could be an hour. Could be all night." Elvis stood

"What did he do?"

"I don't think he did anything."

She looked at him hard.

"Do I look like a dumb bitch?"

"Ma'am?"

"Don't fucking treat me like one."

Elvis found his head spinning. Shannon kept speaking in her low voice. "We both know what your father did. For a living."

Elvis didn't say anything. His Aunt looked carefully at him.

She continued. "You left Chicago in the middle of the night. You drove 15 hours with him sick in the front seat. You don't have a license. You were carrying a tank of Oxygen that could have taken out ten cars around you."

Elvis nodded.

"And he's dying."

Elvis didn't nod. He just stared.

"Where's the cash?"

"In his wallet."

"No, he brought cash. I bet he took a lot of cash." She said. "Your father is many things, but first of all, he is an excellent thief. So, there is money. Somewhere."

She looked at her brother. The mask was over his mouth, his cheeks were slack with sleep, and his body had collapsed into the chair.

"Why?" Elvis said. "Why do you want to know?"

"Because when they come here, looking for him, they are going to want the money back. And I want to give it back."

"No one followed us."

"They'll come." She said. "They'll come and they will kill him, then they will kill you and I and then they will take the money. He thought he was giving you a new life, but he just took away the only one you have."

Elvis stared at his Aunt. The room swam on him. She had transformed in the instant that her brother had fallen asleep.

He did not know, precisely, what his father did for a living. Or who his father had worked for. He knew that his father didn't talk about it or enjoy it. He didn't bring too many of the guys over for the Bears game.

He was a boy who had lived in the house. He knew enough to know that he didn't build roofs, haul trash, or run the commodities desk for the Bank of America. He knew that whatever is father did, it was illegal. And there were three spare tires in the trunk of the Corolla.

"We're not going to die, ma'am." His voice had lost its strength.

"Well, we will need to be lucky."

Shannon looked on her sleeping houseguest, not quite untenderly. Then she turned her eyes to Elvis.

"How old are you?"

"Fifteen."

"Does your mother know you're here?"

"No, ma'am."

"I wouldn't think so."

Elvis didn't say anything. His father had taught him the trick of silence.

"Did he tell you what his plan is?"

"I would say he came here to die."

"Do you want to die with him?"

"No."

Milestone Road

"Then we better make a plan."

CHAPTER TWO

In the morning, his Dad was in the same chair. Aunt Shannon, still dressed for the party, was asleep on the sofa. Elvis found his shower slippers and padded out the front door silently, then started to bring in their luggage. With both adults asleep, he began to perform the physical calculus. His father would be on the ground floor, probably in the guest room that Elvis had slept in last night. He silently shut the door and began hanging up shirts.

It occurred to him that his father may never wear the shirts again. The pants that he was folding, the shoes he lined up; all of them were probably just for show. As the thought rose in his head, he tied it down firmly. Such thoughts did not help him. Not now.

When his father's material was unpacked and the room resembled the bedroom Elvis had carried him from in Chicago, then the boy slipped back into the main room. He carried a Nike shoe box filled with medications. Shannon had awoken, puffy faced.

"Did he sleep through the night?" Elvis asked.

"I think so."

"He missed his medications last night. Today might be bad."

She nodded.

Elvis began lining up the pill bottles on the counter. He had made a special chart on the inside of the shoebox lid.

Shannon touched her brother on the neck. Elvis knew that his pulse was strong and slow at this hour.

She came over, pulled up a stool and sat next to the medications.

"So…" she said.

Elvis looked at her.

She sighed, then stood up. "Let me ask you some questions." The sunlight lit the floor by the big table. "I may have a plan."

The coffee maker had begun brewing coffee automatically an hour before. She poured herself a cup and one for her nephew.

"We have an advantage." She said. "We will be on Nantucket. I am a known person out here. And you…"

Elvis nodded.

"Are you in high school back home?"

"I would be a freshman."

She rubbed her eyes with both hands. Some make-up smeared.

"So, we have to enroll you in school."

"You don't have to."

"Yes, we do. You need to be visible and public and impossible to miss. You have to go to school."

"Yes, ma'am."

"And you are going to play football." She said. "You will be the talk of the town. You'll be in the paper, on TV, everywhere."

"My Dad…"

"No longer makes these decisions. And we are no longer in Chicago where he has protection and respect. He isn't in the shadows out here; he's in the bright sunlight."

Elvis nodded, but he didn't understand.

"Look, son. The men your father worked for would kill you, me, and him. If we were in Chicago."

She searched his eyes for understanding.

"In Chicago, no one would know us and no one would miss us. The police would think that we had left town, if they thought of us at all. Our bodies would be growing Zebra mussels deep in lake muck."

Elvis nodded. He understood what she said, he just didn't understand how it involved him.

Shannon continued. "But we are on tiny little Nantucket. We can't disappear. The more visible you are, the more secure we are. Our deaths—your death---would bring about a lot of interest."

He nodded.

"So Nantucket, and Nantucket High School, and the football team, is the safest place for us."

Elvis was about to speak.

"This isn't an argument. My house, my rules, my plan." She said. "You are about start playing for the Whalers."

"Yes, ma'am."

She looked at him. She wasn't sure if he was making fun of her. She decided that he probably wasn't.

"Okay, Elvis. This is how it is going to work today. You are going to go up to the school and introduce yourself to the guidance department. Then you go out to the football field and see Coach Palumbo. Tell him you want to play football. Tonight, you have to be here for the night because I am going out to dinner at seven and I may not be in until late and I may not be all that steady. Are we clear?"

"Yes, Ma'am." He said. "What about my Dad?"

"What about him?"

"Let me at least lay out his pills for the day."

She allowed that.

Elvis left his father asleep in front of the Today show, picked up his workout bag, and silently left the house.

The morning was surprisingly loud. Starlings clustered in the over grown hedges near the front of the house. The 6:30 ferry churned its way out of the harbor, the low rumble of its diesels underscored the harbor sounds. Within ten steps, the trucks were idling in the woodyard.

At each step, more of the workers noted the huge young man. No one said anything, no one stopped working. Ten minutes later, they all looked at each other and shook their heads.

Elvis wanted to turn around. The web of the new world was wrapping itself around his arms and legs. When he was with his Dad, it seemed as if they could just repack, load the car, and drive away. Chicago was still there and in a moment, he could be back at school, playing Madden with Ted and getting ready for Mount Carmel Prep. But it wasn't. That world had drifted away and was floating off into the stream.

CHAPTER THREE

Maria DeSalvo sat on the toilet in the upstairs bathroom with the pregnancy test in her hand. Downstairs, her mother and father went through the motions of barbecuing steaks and steaming corn. Her brother James was in his room, sending his Lego Jedi into battle against the Sith Lords of his mind. The noises, rhythms, and smells of her house were the same as they had been for almost every day for the last few months.

With her jeans and panties around her ankles, she watched the blue cross slowly reappear. Again.

In her mind, she saw the fences set themselves in front of her in a cascade of Lego pieces. They dropped down, one piece at a time and built a wall before her, cutting off the ground, then the bushes, the trees and finally the sky. Before her was one long, high wall of Lego bricks. And two doors.

She sighed. It was going to be like this. Not in her own house with a husband. Not in her doctor's office. Not with a baker's dozen of joyous friends on the speed dial. It was here, with her brother's Playmobil whale and boat set in the tub, her father's nasty toothbrush and her mother's gigantic, chocolate-stained bathrobe.

The tears rushed up in her like a tide. She stomped them down.

"Dinner!" her mother called out.

Rosie, her mother, was the school nurse, which was exactly the wrong job for her mother to have. She put her daughter on the pill in seventh grade, just about ten minutes after the boys noticed her. She brought home disgusting pictures of women right after they had babies, of genital warts and herpes, of crabs, and lice, and bizarre third world infections that made everything down there black and pus filled. Then, she brought home the sex toy catalog and left it on her pillow with a note "Better than meat." Her mother once told her that she should think about being a lesbian.

Maria pulled her pants back up, flushed the toilet and, for a moment, almost tossed the stick into the trash. With her luck, James would pull it out and make it into a light saber. Three months ago, she had caught him using Tampon tubes as telescopes and rocket ships. All things were possible for the little man.

She thought, for a moment, about Julian.

So she picked up both sticks, put them back into the box, along with their wrappers, flattened them, then tucked them into her belt in the small of her back. She opened the door.

"Be right down."

She dipped into her room, removed the box from her back and tucked it into her purse, then shut her door. At the top of the stairs, she turned and saw James emerge from his room flying a new spaceship. He didn't notice his pregnant sister nor did he wonder what she was hiding. The two children dropped down the stairs.

Her mother, Rosie, weighed over two hundred pounds and may even be as much as two fifty. The flesh hung from her in drips and folds. It must have been years since her last roll in the hay, her daughter thought. Years. Instead, she must have replaced sex with Entenmann's Raspberry danishes, Ben and Jerry's Coffee Heath Bar pints, red wine, and Newports. She wouldn't know exercise if it hit a tennis ball into a dimple in her ass.

Downstairs, they stood in the kitchen, leaning against the counter. They had set places for both children. James still got his sippy cup with juice and this cheese toast. Maria got the same setting as everyone else, but she liked the look of the cheese toast. The smell of roasting meat was doing something to her stomach. The rest of the kitchen was cluttered with magazines, dead plants, dog bowls, books, radios, tools, a large green bowl filled with a gigantic floating frog named Jerry Lee, and a stack of dirty dishes.

Her father, Rick, was a wiry, hairy ferret who weighed, on a good day, half what his wife weighed. He was also the ADD poster child, in constant motion, whether his hands were swinging, his foot tapping, or his fingers drumming. He had taken to chewing gum several years ago, in order to calm himself, and he chewed several pieces to a thin gruel by nine in the morning. He liked his coffee black.

During most of her childhood, Rick was either on his way to a job site, pretending to be at a job site, or late for the job site. Because of him, they screened all calls. Because of him, there were always worried homeowners calling his cellphone. This evening he had put them all aside for one last family meal for the summer. In honor of which, he wore his Carharts, a t-shirt, and a tennis visor.

Maria sat quietly and calmed herself. Everything reeked of death and spoil. The potato salad was overwhelming her, with its pickles, onions, and smell of three days in the refrigerator. The beef rose up like a migraine. Even the dog food gave her stomach a flip. She couldn't show it.

Her mother would know.

She could sniff it out. Every period, every hangover, every wet fart popped up on her Mommy-Radar.

She would figure out right quick that she had a knocked up teenager in the house.

Then it would happen.

So Maria breathed slowly and drank some water. The family passed the platter of steaks, the potato salad, and the corn around the table.

"So, how was your day?' Rosie looked at her.

"Fine."

"What did you do?"

"Nothing."

"Nothing?"

"Elaine and I went to the beach."

Her father looked up from his steak. "What beach?"

"The usual."

Both parents looked at each other. James poked at his cheese toast.

"Y'know, we wouldn't grill you like a terrorist if you only talked a little bit." Rick said.

Maria sighed.

"Elaine and I went to Nobadeer with a bunch of other kids but it was really lame because Jack, Billy, and some of the football players needed to be jerks because we wouldn't do any coke with them and Elaine wouldn't give them…." She looked at her little brother. "any favors."

"Oh." Her mother said. It was an old dance. "Does Elaine do that?"

"Only when she is out of money, but she stole two hundred bucks from her mother's purse and she was all set."

Rosie looked bemused.

"Well, that's nice." Rick said. "How was the surf?"

"Knee to waist high, but it was building as the tide was going out."

"You gotta get back on the board, buppa."

"Only guys surf Dad."

"Not in Hawaii, not in California. We should go out again. You and me, like we used to."

"Dad, I do too many drugs at the beach to surf."

"Not while I am there."

She cut her steak into pieces small enough for Barbie to eat.

"Must be nice." Her mother said.

"What?"

"Spend the day at the beach. Flirt with boys. Watch the waves."

"Who said I just flirted?"

"Like I said." Rosie added. "Must be nice."

"You could come. It's not like you spent the afternoon cleaning."

"Some people have to work."

"Besides Dad?"

"Buppa, be nice." Rick said.

"I am. I am talking a little bit about going to the beach with my friend, avoiding drugs and alcohol, then coming back here to my friendly, loving family."

"You don't have any homework this weekend, do you?"

"As a matter of fact, I do. Mr. Brody wants us to read twenty pages in *Great Expectations* by tomorrow. And I plan to sit in my room all evening and do it."

"No internet, no phone."

"Of course not."

Rosie stared at her daughter.

Maria decided that she really, really liked corn. She took a second ear from the plate.

In twenty minutes, she was safe in her room. With the computer on, Spark Notes up, and a notebook open, she took her phone from her purse and silently texted her friend, Elaine.

"We have to talk."

A minute later, her phone vibrated.

"What's up?" her friends voice echoed in the silent space.

Elaine had been Maria's friend since Wee Whalers. They had sleepovers together, went to Hannah Montana together, had their birthdays at each others houses, borrowed tampons, taught each other about getting drunk, getting stoned, kissing and all the rest. Elaine had the imagination, but Maria had the action.

"Can't talk right now. The Hindenburg is on patrol."

"Got it. Can you text me?"

"No."

"No?"

"No." she whispered with emphasis. In the past, her parent's had checked phones, e-mail, and, everything else on the computer. She lived her life as if she was an ambassador at war. Everyone could be listening.

"Oh, No." Elaine understood without words. "Pregasaurus?"

"Rex."

"Shit. Oh, Shit. Shit, shit, shitty-shitty, shit."

"Tomorrow."

"Pick you up?"

"School."

"I'm with you, girl."

"Good."

When she hung up, Maria switched the phone off.

Pip had nothing on her for keeping secrets

CHAPTER FOUR

Julian was a set of eyes.

Maria had been at a beach party in July. His stare touched her. He stood on the other side of the fire, rail thin, muscular, and so different from anyone else she had known. He had a grace to him, a politeness, and hunter's eyes. He said the right things, showed up at the right times, bought her little presents, and always, always hungered.

It was difficult to get in touch with him. His father had the only cellphone. She had to know that he had it before she could call him. He didn't have any friends that she knew. There was no planning for him, no communicating, nothing but surprise. She would go downtown to the strip with Elaine, stand in line for ice cream and he would slip in behind her. He would appear at parties or on Sundays at the beach. He always came alone and on a bike.

Later, after they had become a couple, he would appear in her front yard after midnight. She would listen for the bicycle wheels on the pavement, and then she would slip downstairs, and outside. They often went to the old windmill that sat next to her house. Later, they travelled across the street into Dead Horse Valley with its scrub pines, oaks, and thick brush. Somewhere in there, in the heat of August, it happened. They hadn't planned, they hadn't thought. Each time, she said that they weren't going to go all the way and each time they had. Violently.

Tonight, she waited for him in the dark of her room. The house settled to sleep around her. Her little brother, James, first settled into bed. Then her father, Rick, fell asleep as the Red Sox lost another to Texas. Finally, Rosie lumbered upstairs and snapped the T.V. off.

Maria was in close surveillance of her ceiling. It wasn't moving, but she suspected it was dropping onto her a centimeter at a time.

She wished she had seen the Oprah when they talked about informing your parents and your boyfriend that you had decided that you were old enough to become a mother. Maybe by letter from Alaska.

She didn't think about telling Julian. She had already decided that he didn't have a vote in this. Her body, her parasite, her baby. They would talk, of course, and they would discuss. It was her call.

And she knew in thinking that…. that she had also decided on flying to New Bedford and the clinic. Maria tried to see it happen. She tried to see walking the halls pregnant, but she couldn't see sitting downstairs on the dog spotted sofa and spilling her guts.

She heard the bike.

Outside, Julian stood in the moonlight amid James' plastic toys and trucks. She flashed the lights. He disappeared into the shadows.

Carefully, Maria stepped out of her room. She edged down the stairs, picked up a trusty blanket, eased the door open and slipped outside.

The autumn air sucked her breath in. Nantucket had gently eased into the September with cool nights and bright stars. She walked across the sand driveway, through a hole in the raggedy hedge and then up to the old windmill.

The windmill had stood since the seventeen hundreds. Once there had been four mills in a row along the top of this hill. One of them probably sat right where her house now was. Now, the last mill only ran in the summer, when the Historical Association put sails on the arms and ground corn. When she was a little girl, her mother sent her over with a dollar to get a paper bag of corn meal. Now, on a cold night in September, the four arms stood still and the long steering arm stretched back into the darkness.

He waited for her on a bench. He was dark and thin, especially in the shadow of the old mill. She wrapped the blanket around both of them, then cuddled in. His skin was cold, for an instant, then hot beneath it. She drew her hands over the muscles of his chest and shoulders and absorbed the heat.

He kissed her slowly, then with building passion. She felt herself slip into the current of his desire, the rising and pulsing waters, the surge and the race, but. But. But her mind wouldn't let go. She put both of her hands on his shoulders and pushed him away.

"What's up, muy gato?"

"We have to talk."

"We can talk. We can talk as much as you want." He slipped his hand behind her head and brought her to him. She kissed him, and tried to stop the lights and the siren he made go off.

She broke off.

"No, No, we have to talk first."

"Okay." He smiled. "Okay, We talk."

He backed away from her, slightly. Maria put her hands between her legs and squeezed.

She wasn't surprised that she had nothing to say. She was surprised that she didn't particularly care.

"Julian, I'm pregnant."

He smiled. His face cracked open and beamed.

"That is so good. That is so so good."

He put his hands on both sides of her face and pulled her to him, then he covered her face with small bird kisses.

While he kissed her, she reeled. Maria had imagined many other scenarios, ranging from gentle and distancing lies to outright violence, but she hadn't seen this.

"Can I touch him?"

"Well, he…it….is very small."

"It's okay if I can't."

"No. Sure. Go ahead. Have fun."

He lifted her shirt and exposed a remarkable white and somewhat flabby belly. He gently touched with the warmth of his palm.

"I am so happy." He said. "You have made me so happy."

On the far side of the mill, a taxi cab parked. She saw herself at that moment. She sat on a bench in the middle of the night, behind the windmill, holding her shirt up so this Brazilian boy could touch her slightly pregnant belly.

"I am not very pregnant. It has probably been a month."

"That's okay."

"There's no guarantee that I will stay pregnant."

"Oh you will. You are young and strong and healthy. You are going to be a wonderful mother."

"Thanks."

"Do you know what I am going to do? I will come to school with you. I will protect you."

"No, you don't have to. No, it will be fine."

"I want to be there."

"I know, but don't you have to work with your Dad?"

His smile flickered. "What can he do?"

She sensed something in his tone.

"You can't tell him."

"Okay." He said quickly.

"No. You can't tell him. My parents don't know, no one knows but you." She looked at him dark and deep. "It has to be our secret."

"Okay." He raised both his hands up in a manner of surrender. " Gato, I am coming to school."

She rolled her eyes.

Julian bent over and gave her a long kiss. "I have a present."

"I don't need a present."

"It's very special, like you. It's very valuable, like you. It is a special day." He dug in his pocket and dug out a coin. "It's for you."

The sixteen year old held the coin. It looked like a quarter.

"It's a krugerrand. Papa says it is one ounce of pure gold."

"Wow" she said, but she didn't understand.

"It's gold." The older boy said. "It will never turn colors or fade away. Like us."

"Wow." She still didn't entirely understand.

He smiled. "You have made me so happy."

He walked over the cold grass to the wheel at the far end of the hundred foot steering arm.

"Don't go up there!" she whispered.

"Don't worry."

The arm climbed at a thirty degree angle until it came to the top of the mill, twenty or so feet in the air. With his hands on the round wooden beam, he ran up it as if he was a monkey. At the very top, there was a one foot square ledge where the steering arm entered the mill. He raised both hands over his head.

The island slept beneath him. The hospital glowed, but its parking lots held no cars and its beds had no patients. The moors and the summer houses were blue under the faint moonlight. Far off, the surf gently rolled in a faint white line along the entire horizon. Far off to the East, Sankaty light swept over the island.

Home was a world away. The mountains, the trees, the warmth-all were gone now. They had left the houses and the plantation a year ago and came here.

He saw the cab parked under a tree.

Much more carefully than when he came up, Julian inched his way back down.

Later, Julian pushed his bike onto the road.

Maria watched him pedal away in the darkness. She leaned back against the bench and looked up at the top of the mill.

What was she going to do now?

CHAPTER FIVE

That morning, she stood in the shower, alone with her dark passenger. Her breasts were sore and heavy and her stomach was unsettled; neither of these was exactly new to her. Her right foot was itchy. Her ankle was looking thicker and felt different today. Her feet were swelling. The thought settled in on her and fit like a falling leaf onto her back yard. All the other changes lay on the grass; she had to admit that the season was changing.

She couldn't do this.

She could keep these fallen leaves a secret, but she couldn't stop the rest of them from coming down. She couldn't stop anything else that was oncoming: the wind, the cold, or the storms.

Eventually, she would have to stop hiding and pretending. Then there would be huge sweatshirts, special underwear, back supports and open sandals for her fat feet.

She would have to use special desks at school. She would travel on the elevator and carry a fat kid's cup of water around with her.

Then there would be the birth.

Julian wouldn't be around for any of it. She wasn't going to marry him, he wasn't even going to stay on island for her to get big. He would be back in Brazil, or in New Bedford, or picking apples up in Maine.

He was a father, but he would never be a Dad.

She was going to be a mother, a Mom, and everything else.

She knew that it all could be prevented. Summer could stretch on for years-even a decade. Then, when the seasons changed, everyone would welcome the changing colors and falling leaves.

All it would take was a small death.

Downstairs, her father had already left for the day.   Her mother was still upstairs getting dressed.

James sat at the end of the table kicking his legs under the table as he ate Cheerios and read an Archie magazine. He was wearing a shirt with a large yellow frog.

"How is Archie this morning?"

"Good."

"How is Jughead?"

"Hungry."

He didn't want to look up.

"Who do you think I am? Veronica or Betty?"

He looked up from his cereal and regarded his sister. She rested her chin on the back of her hand.

"Betty?"

"I'm not blond."

"But you can fix cars. And you're smart."

He went back to his comic book.

Maria could have cried.

Her best friend, Elaine waited for her in the main corridor of the school. The bones of a large fin back whale hung over the main corridor of the school.

She was cute this morning. Elaine had taken her time with makeup, was wearing a carefully pressed skirt and blouse.

"You look like shit." Elaine said.

"Thanks."

"Are you sick?"

"A little."

"Like, or just morning sick?"

"I don't know. Sick."

"You should get a doctor."

"Oh, that will be good." Maria snorted.

"You need one."

"Maybe I'll just ask my Mom for a recommendation."

They stood at Maria's locker.

 "Do you want to skip first period?" She asked in a more tender voice.

"More than anything else in the world."

The two girls walked out the back door, crossed the parking lot and opened the gate. The football field was down a gentle hill, with two sets of wooden bleachers framing it. The school and the parking lot were beyond the near end zone. An old grave yard lay beyond the far one.

"Are you sure?" Elaine asked.

"I pissed the blue cross. Twice."

Her friend nodded. "You're fucked."

"Well, that did happen."

"At least you like him."

"At least I know who he is."

"True."

Sitting in the stands, both girls relaxed.

"What are you going to do?" Elaine looked at her friend.

"I don't know." The words trailed.

"Plan B?"

"I think I am too late for that."

"How long have you been pregnant?"

"No idea."

"When was your last period?"

She thought. "Six weeks?"

"Really?"

"Like that." She said. "I don't know. I didn't even notice. I just kept having baby dreams and my tits started to hurt. So I 'maybe' and I bought the test."

"And here you are."

"Yup."

Elaine was one of the few girls who still smoked. She pulled a pack of Parliaments out of her purse.

"You can still take the flight. They'll just give you a bunch of pills and it will be over."

"Yeah."

"My sister Ellen had one." Elaine was the youngest of four girls. Her sisters were Emily, Eleanor, and Ellen. They were all two years apart. Emily was becoming as physical therapist, Eleanor was in nursing school, and Ellen had just entered University of Maine.

"Yeah?"

"Two years ago."

"How did it go?"

"Sucked." Elaine shook a cigarette loose and lit it. "She had cramps for a week and bled like crazy."

"Did your Mom know?"

"She made her do it. She flew her over. Ellen wanted to keep it."

"Sucks."

"She's boning frat boys now."

"Still sucks."

"The little one would be a little over two right now and everyone's life would really suck."

Maria sighed. "I know."

Elaine was right. She knew that she was right and she knew that it had to end that way. Otherwise, she would get fat, work the checkout line at the Finast for the rest of her life and make eyes at the boys working the bar at the Chicken Box. However, Elaine didn't know about all the "Mommy" hormones rushing through her right now. The flight to New Bedford made her unbearably sad.

"Who knows?" Elaine had a whole list of questions.

"That's the other thing."

"What?"

"You and Julian know."

Elaine sent out a column of blue smoke.

"Why did you tell him?"

"I'm stupid. I've never been pregnant before."

"He wants to keep it, of course."

"He put his hand on my belly."

"Did he feel anything?"

"He said he did, but he is full of shit. It's smaller than a zit."

"What else did he say?"

"He was so happy. Everything would be great." She said. "And, he is coming to school."

"Great."

"Wants to protect me."

"Wants to put a leash around you."

"Maybe." Maria remembered the joy in his eyes last night. "He is a good guy."

"He is also short, illegal, and poor." She said. "And male."

"So."

"So, he isn't Daddy or husband material. Fatherhood, yes. Daddy, no."

The anger rose, although tempered with affection.

"Why are you being a bitch?"

"Just the facts." She finished her cigarette and flicked it away. "You are pregnant and can't think for yourself any more. First, he's a guy which means he wants to get the fuck out of Dodge as fast as possible. Men just leave. Second, he's illegal. Sooner or later, he is either going to slime his way out the door or get tossed out it by INS. If he really stays, he doesn't have two dimes to rub together. He can't buy diapers." She said. "Don't think of him, don't count on him, don't trust him."

"Where did this come from? You loved him this summer."

"You weren't pregnant then." She said. The rest of their class was coming down the field in shorts and t-shirts. "I thought he was fun."

"And he is."

"Clearly." She said. "But now the fun is over."

Elaine put her arm around her friend and hugged her. Maria felt her friend; her heart reached out to her on the warped wooden bleachers. Elaine would be with her forever, no matter what she decided to do.

Her dark passenger was hers alone. Elaine was no more than a spectator shouting encouragement from the stands. Maria had been tossed onto the field.

The fun was over.

CHAPTER SIX

Elvis stood on the side of the football field that warm afternoon. In the middle of September, August came back for a visit; the air hung hot and wet over the field. The team was stretching under the lackadaisical leadership of three captains. Not withstanding the heat, sixty-five kids were attempting to warm up on the worn grass. The crowd of young men represented more than a quarter of the entire school's population. Four assistant coaches walked among the athletes, prodding at them with their feet. The players talked to each other, the captains counted out, the coaches muttered, and nothing mattered.

Every eye was watching Elvis.

Elvis was in shorts and a mesh shirt. He stood a head taller than the coach and weighed fifty pounds more than any player on the field. He carried his pads and his helmet on top of his workout bag. He dearly wished to be wearing them.

Elvis loved his helmet and all the football pads. They hid him. Inside the helmet and pads, he was just a weapon. Whenever anyone looked, all they saw was pads, uniform, and a helmet. He imagined all of those stares, like laser beams, bouncing off him.

Coach Palumbo sidled up to the boy.

"Can I help you?"

"I would like to play on the team, coach."

"What's your name?"

"Elvis Lowell."

Palumbo looked at him and measured the boy.

"Elvis?"

"My Mom was a fan."

"Is that a fact?"

"Yes, sir."

"Did you just enroll?"

"This afternoon."

"And," Palumbo looked at the equipment. "You have played before?"

"Yes, sir. I played left guard, tackle, and nose."

"Do you have a preference?"

"Wherever you need me, coach."

The man with the clipboard nodded.

"You missed a lot of practice, son."

"I understand coach. I just arrived on-island yesterday."

Coach smiled. "Go get changed."

Elvis jogged off with his gear. The team watched him go. The coaches smiled at each other and the boys got excited.

Coach Palumbo had spent his life in football. He got recruited and played three years at Penn State, including on two Orange Bowl teams. As a player, he was neither fast, nor big, nor skilled enough to either start or go to the pros. Nonetheless, he was good enough to get cycled in to the defense and the special teams. At the end of his time, he had letter jackets, trophies, a handshake from JoePa and a six month old baby girl. The best paying gig at that point happened to be as Football Coach/Athletic Director on an island off the coast of Massachusetts. From here, he had thought, he could climb to be an assistant at B.C., and then the future opened itself to him. He thought, often, of replacing the famous old man in Happy Valley.

That didn't happen. Babies happened instead; Melissa and Meghan joined little Mary. Instead of working the camps and coaching clinics in the summer, Palumbo put his lawnmower in the open trunk of his Dodge Dart and mowed lawns across the island. It worked out well. The girls grew up beautiful and dim, like their mother. Five Hondurans and two trucks did the landscaping these days, while he negotiated the contracts. He had bought three other houses in his neighborhood and rented them out for some very nice bank each summer. At this point, standing on the side of this field, he was worth more money than all but twenty of the Division I football coaches.

But he still looked for openings in the spring. He still got the coaches' films of each Penn State game.

He didn't know what to make of Elvis. He was huge. He ran well. However, he had seen huge men before who enjoyed getting hit in the mouth. In truth, Palumbo preferred the fiery little guys who kept pissing people off. You can coach defense and you can coach techniques, but you can't coach big. Elvis was the biggest high school player he had ever seen.

When Elvis came back to the field, the team had been broken up into drills. The linebackers and the safeties were working coverage drills, the offensive skill players were running plays, and the linemen were doing "Alabamas."

Coach Mike Reinemo ran the linemen. He had come back to the island after three years at Alabama and six months in detox. He immediately took his place pouring cement for his Dad, as if he had never left for school. In the fall, however, he brought his three years of drills, sweat, and sitting in the Alabama heat to the high school and coached the linemen. He did a good job at it. He had a simple philosophy; "No one had ever or will ever put a lineman on a bubblegum card or a video game box, but that the line was where the real men worked." The work in the line was just like the work in cement. Dirty, gritty, unpleasant, unrewarding, and manly to the quintessence of sweat. Assistant Coach Tillinghast, who was older, didn't disagree, although he might phrase it better.

He had the boys lined up on the field. Two tackling dummies lay five yards apart, while two other dummies stood upright, fifteen yards apart; the four of them made a rough rectangle. In the middle of all four dummies, two big kids faced each other. The object was to push one lineman back into his tackling dummy. As with most things for the adolescents, it was part drill, part stage.

"Good morning, young 'un." The coach called to Elvis.

"Coach." Elvis had heard coaches go through this sort of routine for years.

"Would you care to join us in the center?'

"Can I warm up, coach?"

"By all means."

Two other linemen took their place on stage, then fought each other for a full minute before the dummy went down. Reinemo and the two players were the only ones watching. Everyone else watched Elvis. He also viewed the boy with healthy skepticism. Big kids are used to just being big kids; they were farm animals lined up in the grass. They didn't mind getting hit in the mouth. Reinemo also preferred the smaller boys who were quick and angry.

Assistant Coach Tillinghast moved over to where the boy was stretching on the grass. He squatted down next to his head.

"What is your name, son?"

"Elvis."

He started writing the name on a piece of white tape. The old man smiled. "Tough name for high school."

"Usually, it works fine."

"I'm Coach Tillinghast."

Elvis switched positions.

"Take your time, and get loose. Take a moment to put your game face on."

"Okay."

"What grade are you going to be in?"

"Freshman."

He nodded.

"You'll be with me, then, soon enough." Tillinghast put the tape on the helmet.

Elvis didn't think so. His mind went back to the coaches and the players in Chicago. Their practice clicked in precision. Everyone was one minute from contact. Not one of these players would have stood on the field at Mount Carmel. The captains would have run them off.

In a moment, he was finished with his stretching, Elvis jogged over to the linemen.

"Welcome to the group, young 'un."

"Coach."

"What is your name?"

"Elvis."

The coach let loose a short laugh. The rest of the team laughed as well.

"Is that your first name, or your last?"

"First, sir."

"Elvis," he said with a smirk. "I want you to face off against Billy. Billy is our starting left tackle. We went 12-1 last year with Billy."

Elvis nodded to him. Billy wasn't looking.

"You know this drill."

"Knock over the dummy."

"We call it an Alabama, here."

"Yes, sir."

"Okay, get ready."

Elvis dropped into a three point stance, with one hand on the ground. Billy went down on both hands. The rest of the players watched.

Reinemo asked himself, silently, whether this boy really liked to get hit in the mouth.

"Set.....Hut!"

Elvis decided to play defense and hold the smaller boy off. Billy zipped to his right and took Elvis' charge to his side. As Billy fell, he kicked up, hard, between the boy's legs.

Elvis fell.

Billy scrambled to his feet and tapped the dummy down. The team cheered. They bore witness to the oldest of plays.

As Billy walked back to his side, he stepped on Elvis thigh and left a big cleat mark on his uniform.

Elvis stood slowly and angrily. He stared at Coach Reinemo and he stared at his grin. To the other side, Assistant Coach Tillinghast was stone faced.

"Are you ready, Elvis?"

The big boy nodded and set into position.

"Set.....Hut!"

This time, Elvis fired out at the boy. Billy tried to swim around him, but got caught as Elvis slammed into his chest. Still on his feet, Billy grabbed the front of the boy's face mask in one hand and slapped the side of the helmet with other. As Elvis' head rung, Billy slipped away and, again, tapped over the dummy.

With his head ringing and his testicles aching, Elvis breathed hate and murder. The team was laughing and Reinemo had turned his back on him. Billy jogged back to his crowd and the other side of the dummies.

Coach Tillinghast stood in front of the seething boy.

"Do you have your game face on? Now?"

Elvis nodded. Tillinghast leaned in to him. "Use your muckers." He showed him his hands. "Put your muckers on his shoulder pads and drive him over the fence."

Elvis nodded.

Elvis went into a three point stance between the two tackling dummies. Billy looked at Reinemo. The coach turned back to the crowd of linemen. He nodded to his starting left tackle. Billy returned to his four point stance.

"Set....Hut!"

Billy again tried to slip him, but Elvis pulled the smaller boy's shoulder pads to him and drove with his legs. Billy was too close to slap his helmet and began moving backwards so fast that he lost his balance. Elvis kept carrying the 220 pound boy past the tackling dummy, past the other linemen, over the sidelines and to a three foot high chain link fence.

Billy hit the fence in the middle of his butt, flipped, and cartwheeled onto the cinder running path.

Elvis turned his back and walked back to the team. As he passed, he shoved the tackling dummy over.

As it turned out, Elvis didn't like getting hit in the mouth.

The entire team, running backs, receivers, and linemen, fell silent. They had been present, they had borne witness, and they would carry forth the word. They would bring it away at lunch and tell it to girlfriends, mothers, fathers, parents, and buddies. By five o'clock, the word would have settled into stone: Billy Trotter had been beat down by a freshman named Elvis.

After practice, the boys showered in one large room, and then dressed in the team locker room. The locker room featured a loud boom box, a chalk board, and lockers large enough to hold shoulder pads, though most of the players put them on top to air out. The air was thick with talcum powder, rap, and fraternal curses. The naked boys stood hairless, with towels tied tightly around their waists in a show of modesty.

No one talked to Elvis. It wasn't malicious or evil; they didn't know what to say to him. Most of these boys had gone to preschool together, smashed each other's piñatas, gone fishing or hunting with their Dads, and passed out in each other's basements. To them, Elvis was like the tourist that walked downtown or who biked past the practice fields.

Elvis had been in locker rooms like this one for two years. The older boys, be they 12 or 18, would form the leading edge of the wolf pack. Their younger followers would nip at the haunches of those who threatened to stray. For as tall, strong, and violent as they were on the playing field, they all were directed by one forgotten message or one dirty joke.

The boys pulled on shorts and t-shirts. They combed and brushed their hair in the mirror, then walked out in groups of four or five. Billy and Jack left with five other boys.

Elvis pulled on his shirt, then wedged his feet back into his sneakers. Now that practice, and the intricacy of the plays and drills were over, his thoughts turned to his father. Had they still been in Illinois, he would be getting him from those big easy chairs in chemo right about now.

"How are you doing?"

Elvis turned to see a boy nearly as tall as he was, but thin and rangy. He was wearing a green polo shirt and threadbare, tan shorts. He stuck his hand out.

"Good."
"My name's Nick."
"Elvis."
"I heard."
The boy nodded.
"Hey, you put Billy Trotter over the fence. You made a name for yourself."
"Wouldn't have happened…"
"If he wasn't a prick."
Elvis smiled. "Yup."
"Let me give you a ride home."
After the two boys left the locker room, the rest of the team looked at each other and shook their heads at the size of the new kid.

Nick drove a red Range Rover Discovery. It was spattered in mud and dirt, with dents on both front panels, a good sized V in the rear bumper, and a set of purple fuzzy dice on the rear view mirror.

He took a decidedly long way to get the half mile to Marine Home Center.

Nick had gotten tossed from Deerfield last spring, during his junior year there. However, he took advantage of the crack guidance staff at Nantucket to enroll as a sophomore this year. The plan, as he explained it to Elvis, was to work out this year, play lacrosse in the spring, and then re-enroll at a different prep school as an eighteen year old junior and then dominate. Out here, you have to play football, so he tried out for wide receiver. Everyone else seemed so slow.

His parents had divorced; his Mom got the house on Nantucket and his Dad got the townhouse in the Upper East Side. All summer, his mother had hosted parties in Sconset and reveled in her good fortune. Now that her golf and tennis buddies were headed back to Connecticut, Philadelphia, and Hobe Sound, she wasn't so sure. The winter with her photography wasn't looking as promising as it once did. "Of course," he said. "When she starts sleeping with someone else, it will all be good again."

Elvis told him his story; came here with his sick father, staying with his Aunt.

"Aren't there better doctors in Chicago?"
"Probably."
Nick remained confused.

"He wanted me to go to school and have someone else take care of him."

Nick didn't know what to say. "I suppose that makes some sense."

He stopped at the strip. He popped out of the car for dinner. Elvis knew that his aunt was attempting to cook back at the house. Further, he had had enough of people looking at him for the day. Sitting in the front seat of the car suited him just fine.

Nick returned. No one had noticed his passenger or interrupted his quiet. They pulled away and headed, finally, to his Aunt Shannon's house.

Nick ate his sandwich as he drove.

"You better watch yourself tomorrow."

"I'll be fine."

"You don't understand. You embarrassed him. They are going to come looking for blood."

Elvis shrugged. "I can take care of myself."

"No doubt, but they are going to be looking for a way to take you down."

Elvis shrugged.

"Whole school is scared of them. They do some sketchy things. They might come for you tonight."

"I'll be home."

"They would go there."

"Let them come."

"Tough guy?"

Elvis looked into Nick's smile. "You gotta be."

Nick pulled up outside the lumber yard.

"Look at this." Nick pulled out his phone and found the picture. A pale female butt appeared on the screen, with the word "Slut" written on it. "I heard that she insulted Jack in class. They roofied her. Then they did this."

Elvis was aware that he was supposed to feel some fear or at least caution. Instead, right now, he wanted to break someone's head open.

"If they ask, tell them where I am."

Aunt Shannon stood at the stove with a set of chopsticks in her hand. A large wok sizzled in front of her. Lined up on the cutting board were slices of red pepper, onion, green pepper, water chestnuts and three pounds of meat.

"Looks good." He said without enthusiasm.

"It will be terrific."

"I'm sure." Shannon didn't want to approach the stove. The boy tossed his practice clothes into the washing machine, then closed the lid.

"Do you need help?"

"No, no. I'm fine. I just don't know when it's hot enough."

Elvis backed away.

"I'll set the table."

Shannon, in a gesture, tossed everything into the pot and skittered away. The oil screamed for a moment, and then was muffled under the meat and vegetables. She moved up to the wok and poked at the meat with the chopsticks. Eventually, she grew bolder, grabbed a spatula, and started stirring and flipping the contents.

In the end, the meal was pretty good, Elvis thought. Some of the meat was rare, some was blackened and inedible. He had eaten far worse, of course. Shannon kept refilling his plate and a glass of milk.

He had set the table for three, but his father remained in his room. Elvis heard the TV, but trusted that he must be asleep.

"Why don't we save the rest of this?" Elvis said.

"Are you full?"

"Sure. I was full ten minutes ago."

"Aren't you hungry after practice?"

"Well, yeah..."

"You have to be strong."

"Well, yeah, but..."

"You don't need to be polite for me."

"I know."

"How was practice?"

"Fine."

"Did you hurt Billy Trotter?"

Elvis glanced at her. "Did you watch practice?"

"No, I just heard about it."

"It just ended."

"I know." Elvis didn't understand and thought she might be lying. "People were talking at the Finast." she explained.

"People talk about football practice?"

"Oh, sure. Football is huge out here." She said. "Everyone wants to know about you."

"What do you say?"

"Just that you came from Chicago and played ball out there."

"What do they say?"

"They want to know what your plans are."

Elvis looked at her. "I don't know." He said. "How could I have plans?"

"I don't know. You're worried about your Dad."

Elvis didn't say anything. The question still hung out there.

"Do they think I am leaving?"

She looked at him with some surprise. The precarious balance rested on today, but would slip when it tipped to tomorrow or even yesterday.

"They have never seen anyone your size before and you just appear." Shannon poked at the soggy vegetables on her plate and tried to shift the conversation into a brighter corner. "They figure you will go to some bigger school."

The weight of the conversation collapsed on him. "When Dad dies."

Later, he sat in the room with his father. The older man's skin had turned gray, and he had difficulty keeping his eyes open. They had left Law and Order on.

"How was practice?"

"It's all right."

"It's not Mount Carmel, is it?"

"No. Not by a long shot."

"Sorry about that."

Elvis sensed that he had wounded his father.

"That's okay."

"You'll be fine here. You'll do well."

"Sure."

"Champs last year, weren't they?"

"So they say."

"You're not impressed?"

He shrugged.

"They test you out today?"

"Couple guys got chippy."

His father, David, loved that word.

"Your aunt heard," his father said, "that you put some kid over a fence."

"Yeah, that happened."

David smiled. "Good for you."

The two of them watched the rest of the episode. Elvis noticed his father had fallen asleep with one eye partially open.

Robert P. Barsanti

CHAPTER SEVEN

Maria didn't know how she felt about her English teacher, Mr. Brody. He was a lean and muscular middle aged man who had won the genetic lottery. All that had been soft and weak had been boiled off of him. He dressed better than anyone in the school; he always wore a blazer or a suit to class, with pressed pants, shirts, and ties.

He was rich. No one knew how rich or how he got that rich, but he owned an old, huge home in Quaise that sat high on the bluff over the beach.

Her friend, Elaine, knew how she felt about Brody. She would throw herself, naked, into the passenger seat of his car and wait for her happy chopped up body to be found in the harbor. Maria had, several times, talked her out of drunken odysseys to his home.

But.

There was something odd about him. Everyone looked at him and asked themselves "Why?" and no one had an answer. He drove a Chevy Blazer from thirty years before with rust that fell in a constant rain. You rarely saw him outside of school-anywhere: not at the grocery store, not at a bar, not on the beach. He was the only teacher her mother never spoke of.

There were rumors.

He had been a soldier. He had the tattoos. On his shoulder, he had the tat "Death Waits in the Shadows" underneath a parachute and below that, the word "The Mog."

He had been a lawyer. He had stepped in to help another teacher a year before in a rental fight. It all disappeared quickly.

Maria really didn't like his eyes. They didn't move much, they didn't smile, they didn't flash with anger, and they didn't leer. They waited. His voice and his face and his hands all showed one thing, but his eyes showed absolutely nothing.

She had English with Mr. Brody right before lunch. The desks were in a circle but he stayed out of the center as much as he could. Sometimes he just let the argument roll in the classroom and didn't stop it, even if they swore or talked about parties or anything.

But no one went too far off the road. Billy, Sean, Tom Kelly, and Jack sat in their defensive football huddle and said nothing for the whole period. In the first week of school, they had been stealing each other's phones. Brody had said nothing until the end of class when he kept the four of them through lunch. Brody had them put their phones on their desk. The phones buzzed and vibrated constantly as friends, girlfriend, and drug buyers tried to contact them. It had been an expensive and embarrassing half hour.

Brody had handed them all copies of *Great Expectations*. No one in the class had any expectation of reading the book. Brody, for his part, knew this as well.

"Take out a piece of paper, would you?" he said. Brody had his back to the class and was looking out the window at the whitecaps on the harbor. "On it, list five things that your parents do for you."

"Like what?" said Billy

"Like anything."

Sean had a paper ball in his hand and cocked his arm.

"Don't do that."

"Don't do what?"

"You need to go downtown for lunch today?"

"I wasn't doing anything."

"I punish the innocent as well as the guilty," he said. "List five things."

Maria wrote on her paper. "Food, laundry, roof, clothes, presents."

"Now, list five things you expect your parents to do for you in the next ten years. Do you expect them to babysit for your kids, do you expect them to employ you, do you expect them to bail you out of jail and hire a lawyer, do you expect them to pay for college?"

The boys stopped writing. Brody noted this.

He turned.

"Billy."

"Yo."

"What do you expect your parents to do for you?"

"Nothing."

"Nothing?"

"I can take care of myself."

"Really?" he said. "Let me ask you some questions. Are you going to college?"

"Yup."

"How are you going to pay for that?"

"Athletic scholarship."

"You think?"

"Sure."

Brody let it pass.

"Let' suppose that you get busted for possession or worse. How are you going to get bailed out?"

"I lead a clean life."

"You do?"

"Yup." The giggles started.

"Always wear a condom?"

"I'm a virgin." He said. "Not ashamed to admit it."

The boys were letting loose.

"What if you were hit by a bus or hurt your knee on Saturday."

"Scrimmage is on Friday, Mr. Brody. Hope to see you there."

Brody smiled.

"About your knee?"

"Well, I am a finely conditioned athlete. If it did happen, I would be covered by my father' insurance. So, if I was unlucky, I would need my folks."

"Key word there."

"What word is that?"

Brody looked at Jack. He was smaller, rounder, and red headed. "What was the key word that Ryan said?"

"Finely conditioned?" The giggles returned.

"I was thinking of unlucky." Brody said. "Ryan here is lucky, but Pip is unlucky. His parent are dead, his brothers and sisters are dead, he has no money, he has no skills, and he has to live with a sister who seems to hate him."

Brody looked at two other students. "He never had those five things and he will never have the five things you count on. If he's arrested, no one will hire a lawyer and no one will bail him out. If he's hurt, no one can pay for the doctor. When he gets older, he has no one to teach him a trade or hire him."

The class had faded on him.

"So, for homework, write a three hundred word journal entry about what you would do if your entire family were to die."

Billy raised his hand. "Mr. Brody, we could get you fired for that."

"Go ahead."

Elaine waited for Maria at the locker. She wore jeans and her green sweater. Maria used to borrow that sweater, but it had stopped fitting.

"You look like shit." Elaine said.

"Thanks."

"What happened?"

"I got knocked up."

"What else?"

"I think that will do it."

They stood at Maria's locker.

"Let's get lunch?" She asked in a more tender voice.

"Sure?"

"Burritos."

"Oh, God." Elaine made a face. "You know, he won't be there."

"I know." Maria said. "I crave a chicken burrito. I am pregnant, you have to be nice to me."

"Not for long."

"You still have to be nice to me.

Elaine looked at her friend. She read as tired, blotchy, and annoyed.

"Sure. Let's blow."

They walked out the backdoor to her white VW Golf. It had been Elaine's mothers and she had hated it. But her father kept it running years after it should have died. Finally, on her birthday, her mother came home with a new Mustang and the Golf fell to Elaine. She changed the radio stations, dumped the yoga gear into the Mustang, and tucked half an ounce into the sun visor pocket.

Nantucket High School started an open campus policy sometime in the middle of the last land boom. Suddenly, the lunch lines were too long to get through in one lunch, and the cafeteria roared with noise, and it lost money by the carton. So, with the wisdom that comes only from being a superintendent, it was decreed that the kids could go out for lunch. Suddenly, the sandwich shops and greasy spoons downtown on the strip hired new staff.

The strip lines up eight fast food shops right in a row. In the summer, the day-trippers walk off the ferry and pass bike rentals, sandwich shops, ice cream parlors, and t-short emporium. In March, you would only pass one, forlorn, burrito and sandwich spot. They phone in their order before leaving the parking lot.

She had met Luther here. Not at first, but he would be here for lunch often. His brothers and whoever else sat in the King cab up the street while they made him go for their meals. His father, his older brothers, and two of his "uncles" gave him orders and a handful of cash. He waited to the side while the high school kids got their food and chatted with her. He was quiet, and shy, and wolfish.

"Have you seen him again?" Elaine saw her friend's eyes.

"No."

"You won't" her friend chided.

"He told me he was going to come back." She thought for a moment.

"Sure." Elaine said. Maria heard the real answer underneath the word.

"Have you decided what you are going to do?"

"No."

"Clock is ticking."

"No shit. But it is ticking in me, not in you."

They stared at the front door of the shop.

"I'm sorry." Elaine said.

"Me, too."

"I don't know..."

"I know...."

"You're a good friend."

"You, too."

Maria was crying.

"It's the damned hormones."

Maria stepped from the car and stood in line.

She was lost in the past when Jack and Billy strode in. She hadn't seen them arrive. Elaine had remained in the car.

"So, what's for lunch?"

"Go fuck yourself." She snapped.

She still felt rattled and hollow.

"You are too pretty to have that nasty a mouth."

Billy stepped to her. She sidestepped him and reached for the veggie burrito. Jack plucked it from her hands.

"Give me that." She yelled.

"No." Jack smiled at her and held it behind his back.

The room had ten high school kids in it. All of them knew and feared Jack and Billy. They fell silent and made a circle for the three of them. No one stood with Maria.

"Guess which hand?" Jack stood before her, with both hands behind his back.

Maria kicked fast and hard, with every ounce of worry, fear, and love behind it. Her right Nike Cross-Trainer, with pink highlights, sunk into his jeans.

The boy fell and dropped the wrapped burrito, then sent both hands into his jeans.

Maria picked it up and hurled it at his head.

"Don't Fuck With Me!"

The room was silent as she left.

CHAPTER EIGHT

The Old Whalers started to arrive at practice the next day.
Ten men stood against the chain link fence on the home side of the playing field. They wore work shirts and jeans, baseball hats and work boots. They stood with easy confidence together. They laughed at each other and joked, but they watched when he jogged out to the practice field.
Elvis knew who they had come to see.
The captains were slowly lining the team up into their warm-up spaces. Elvis, as both the new guy and the guy who missed all of double sessions, settled into the back row.
Coach Tillinghast and Coach Palumbo were on the sidelines. Both men had their arms crossed. Palumbo called his name out.
"Lowell. Hop to it."
Elvis jogged over to the two men.
"Lowell, Coach Tillinghast tells me that you are enrolled as a freshman? Is that true, son?"
"Yes, sir."
"Is this your first year of high school?"
"First full year."
"What does that mean?"
"I couldn't finish my first year last spring, sir."
"Why not?"
"My Dad is sick."
The answer pulled Palumbo up short. He was used to players with jail time, players moving in with their uncles, their girlfriends, and

their uncle's girlfriend, and players just leaving to play more X-Box, but not to take care of their sick Dads.

Tillinghast stepped in.

"How sick is he, son."

"He has cancer, sir. We are here with my Aunt Shannon."

"Is she taking care of him?"

"Pretty much."

Tillinghast nodded. Palumbo had his hand on his chin. "Lowell, where did you go to school last year?"

"Mount Carmel, on the south side of Chicago."

"Did you play varsity?"

"Yes, sir. I have played varsity since seventh grade."

The coaches looked at each other.

"Why is that?"

"Well, coach." Elvis said. "They figured I might hurt the middle school kids."

Palumbo glanced, with weight and meaning, to Tillinghast.

"How did you guys do?"

"Champions last two years."

Palumbo looked as if he had played his last trump.

"You enrolled as a freshman, didn't you?" Tillinghast asked him.

"Yes, sir."

"Son." Tillinghast said, looking up at him. "We have a problem. Mayflower League rules and MIAA rules state that freshmen can't play varsity sports. Ironically, it's to prevent them, or you, from getting hurt."

"Yes, sir."

"So, we have to apply for a waiver, which I am sure we are going to get." Palumbo said.

"If you would like us to apply for it." Tillinghast added.

Elvis looked at the two of them. He wasn't sure what to say. He looked at the older coach.

"I can play J.V. for a while."

"Okay."

Palumbo's face fell.

"Get ready to play in the scrimmage on Friday."

In normal company. Coach Tillinghast was a big guy. He was blessed with a long, angular frame that had helped him on the squash court, the golf course, and, sixty years ago, on the playing fields of Andover and Yale. Between prep years at Andover and retirement on

Nantucket came a parachute drop into the fields of Lyon, A post war apartment in Rome, a consular stay in Damascus, followed by ambassadorships to Kabul, Tehran, and Istanbul which ended after the Seals broke some friendlies out of an Ankarra jail, and sent him to Foggy Bottom for eight years, then retirement, a spot on the wall, the handshake from a grateful President (grateful he was leaving) and a lucrative retirement in Boston at State Street Bank, The Isabella Stewart Gardner Museum, the Symphony, and the Harvard Club. His memoirs were written, his grandchildren had gotten into the right schools, and the barman stocked the right whiskey.

Until his hands started to shake.

The doctors were full of apologies. Palsy. Rheumatoid Arthritis. They started in with "managing pain" and an "active and successful life." Tillie know what that meant. Squash, tennis, and golf had a season or so left before his hands abandoned him. Writing, typing, and the rest were on a similar clock.

He would finish his life as a pretzel.

It angered him to learn this, but comforted him as well. There would be no long senseless wasting away in an expensive bed. Death waited for him, like another graduate degree. Four years or so down the line, depending on the medicine and depending on his energy, he would have one last cold handshake.

So, he put the other houses into the trust, winterized the summer house, then moved his books and his wife down to the island. No one out here knew his past, beyond that he played tennis well and paid his bills on time. He and Sasha settled into a long winter of dog walking, pleasant friends, and an occasional trip back to Europe.

And football.

While the JV was stretching, Tillie squatted next to his new, 6'7 290 pound tackle.

"Son," he said. "We have some work to do."

"Yes, sir."

"I know, and you know, that if we plunked you on that varsity line right now, the team would go undefeated and win the championship."

Elvis didn't say anything.

"The Mayflower League is Division 5B in Massachusetts which means we play every single weak sister and red headed stepchild in the state. You outweigh any two players on those teams. All we need to do is call one play, over and over, and we win. What do you think?"

Elvis didn't say anything.

"Is that what you want?"

Elvis remained silent. He smelled a trap.

Tillie let the silence hang for a minute.

"I want..." Elvis said. "I want to be good at this."

"That's a good answer. That's a very good answer." Tillie said. "We'll see about helping you get good."

The team practiced. The linemen ran through a set of drills on the sled, then some agility work before they lined up to run plays. To Elvis, this was the most difficult part of the practice. Every play had a name or a number that was completely foreign to him. At his size and speed, and when he was heading in the right direction, Elvis was unstoppable. At his size and speed, running the wrong way, Elvis was catastrophic. More than once, he turned the wrong way and flattened the fullback and the running back.

In the fading heat and light of early September, Tillie called for a screen pass to the right. Elvis was to block the 110 pound freshman defensive lineman for three-seconds, then run out to the right, wait for the receiver to catch the ball, and then flatten everything before him. They lined up, and the center snapped the ball. Elvis blocked briefly, then turned and ran hard. He flattened a slow footed tackle, a doubtful full back, and, tangled in their falling bodies, fell hard as the quarterback got sacked by the 110 pound freshman.

They ran the play five more times before everyone finished it standing up. The ball, however, had fallen incomplete.

Elvis kicked it fifty yards down field.

Tillie had him run two laps. On the first lap, Elvis kept to himself and hid deep within his helmet. Tillie joined him for the second.

"Good practice." He said.

Elvis nodded.

"You don't believe me?"

"No."

"What did you do wrong?"

"Other than kick the ball?"

"That wasn't wrong. You got frustrated. You knew you would run anyway."

Elvis was confused again, and said nothing.

"If I thought you were wrong to do it, the whole team would be running and you would watch them."

They rounded the orange cones in the end zone and came up past the varsity.

"No, you run alone when I want to make you the example."

Elvis remained confused.

"Here is the thing you need to work on. For your whole football career, however long it goes, you will be on teams with people who are not as good or as committed as you are. But you will have to play as a teammate. How do you do that?"

Tillinghast pulled off and left Elvis to finish his laps. The other players stretched and watched. The watchers in the stands stood in quiet judgment. Tillie put his shaking hands inside the pocket on his sweatshirt and kneaded his knuckles.

Inside the locker room, Elvis entered to silence. Every eye on the room was on him.

He had been in enough locker rooms to know that this wasn't good.

He eyed Jack, then walked to his locker.

There was a puddle on the floor in front of it. There were droplets on the blue mesh of the door. Inside, his pants, socks, and shoes had droplets and puddles of water.

Or pee.

Definitely piss.

Elvis exhaled. He felt the rage rise within him, and he let it rise. He inhaled and thought of his father, of his junkie mother, and of everyone at his old school. Then, he let the safety come off.

Billy was closest.

Elvis took two slow steps.

Billy, at the peak of his power and in front of a room of his adolescent friends, stood up to the big freshman.

He didn't stand a chance.

Elvis lashed out with his left hand, grabbed the boy by the neck and bull-rushed him at a cement wall. The skull hit the wall with a firm plonk. The boy was three inches off the ground before he could get his own arms to fight the hand around his neck.

Elvis began slapping the boy. Big, heavy, open faced slaps that brought splashed spit and then blood on the wall. By the third slap, two members of the team held Elvis' right hand. Four others, including Jack tried to peel the left hand from Billy's neck. They seemed to be yelling at the big freshman, but he heard nothing. Billy's face had gone from red to a shade of purple and his eyes had begun to bulge. He had seen stars since the first collision, and now night was falling.

Coach Tillinghast had heard the sound of the skull impact. He stood at the doorway, five feet from the confrontation. He said and did nothing.

Nick slipped next to Elvis and spoke to him.

"You got him. Stop."

Elvis kept the boy pinned. Four hands tried to pull the one hand away.

"Uncle." Nick said. "He said Uncle."

Elvis flinched and looked at his friend. He hadn't heard that playground word in ten years.

The four teammates pulled his hand away for a second. In that second, Elvis saw the faces of his teammates, the faces of his coach, and the face of his friend. He looked particularly at Jack. They were all afraid.

And part of him whispered, "Good."

He backed away and let Billy Trotter, God of Fear and Terror, slide to the floor gasping.

The bruise from Elvis' hand would remain for a week. The left side of his face swelled up and remained swollen for almost as long.

Elvis turned to Jack, who backed up from him.

The room remained afraid.

"Your job, from now on, is to protect my locker. Am I clear?"

"Sure." The boy smiled.

Faster than thought, Elvis slapped the boy and sent him sprawling.

"Really clear?"

Jack nodded

Elvis turned and walked out of the locker room.

Tillinghast remained in the doorway watching. Every member of the team saw him. His silence waved a benediction to the violence. Every member of the team saw that he did nothing to help Billy Trotter rise to his feet.

Jack would get a black eye.

"You best follow his instruction, son." Tillinghast said, then turned and walked away.

The locker room cleared out. Jack and Billy were among the first to go, without shower or discussion. Then everyone else on the team filed out. Each boy stepped clear of the puddle of pee and the locker. Nick remained, until Tillinghast sent him out the door.

Elvis stood in the hall next to the gym. None of the players were going to go back into the school, so he felt that he could have some privacy.

He felt no guilt. He felt no shame.

He should. He was aware of that. He had let the control on his rage slip. His father had made him promise to stay in control; his body was unlike others. He could kill and maim far more easily than others could. The playing field and the wrestling mat were channels. They were the forge where his fire could flare and burn. Not the locker room.

Yet, he had seen what he had seen. He had seen how the team had looked at him throughout the practice. And he had seen how they looked at him immediately after he slapped Jack.

Shock. Relief.

He would try to feel shame. He would not do it again.

But....

In five minutes, Tillinghast stuck his head outside the locker door.

"Elvis!"

"Yes, sir."

He handed him a trash bag. "You're going to have to get your stuff, son."

"Coach, I'm sorry."

"Save it." He said. "Your apology isn't for me."

Elvis, silent, followed him.

"I will be outside. Just put your stuff in the trash bag and meet me out there."

"Sure."

"Be quick about it. I'll be driving you home."

"Yes, sir."

Elvis picked up his clothes carefully, then dumped them in the plastic bag. Afterward, he washed his hands thoroughly and tied the bag shut.

Tillinghast waited for him with his engine and headlights on. By now, his car was the only one left in the parking lot. The boy put the trash bag in the back of the car, then sat in the passenger seat.

The coach was silent for the drive, until they pulled into Marine Home Center. The light at the door glowed down the access road to the driveway.

"How is your Dad?"

"He is okay."

"Is he conscious?"

"Yes."

"Does he eat?"

"A little."

"I am coming to dinner tomorrow night. I will bring some food."

"I don't know if that is…"
"I am coming. I will bring the food. Is that clear?"
"Yes, sir."
"Make sure you do that laundry." He said. "Don't make your Aunt."
"No, sir."
"I will be by tomorrow at seven-thirty. Is that a good time?"
"I guess."
"Tell me tomorrow if it isn't."
"Yes, sir."
"Have a good night, son."
"You too, sir."

Elvis stepped from the car, opened the rear door, retrieved the trash bag, and closed it.

Coach Tillinghast drove away with a wave.

Elvis walked down the pavement to his new home.

Elvis woke to the sound of his father retching in the bathroom. The clock in his room read 3 a.m.

He wrapped himself in a bathrobe, slipped downstairs, and picked up some paper towels in the kitchen. Then he came to the bathroom.

His father was standing, hands on his hips, bent over the toilet and dry heaving.

"Need some help?"
"Thanks."

His father took the paper towels and wiped his face, then the seat of the toilet. His son had seen this before and didn't need to ask any questions. His father heaved three more times, silently, then straightened.

"Ginger ale?"
"Something," he said, "even beer."

The father moved slowly to the recliner. He moved slowly, as if he were an upright ladder inching its way over. Elvis scanned the refrigerator and found no beer or ginger ale. Just orange juice, iced tea, and Clamato. He poured a glass of iced tea.

Shannon had piled the pills in shot glasses. This morning's shot was from "Scenic Reno." He brought both glasses over.

His father smiled. "A beer and a bump?"
"Best we can do, I'm afraid."
"This stuff will mess you up, good."

He shook the shot glass into his mouth three times, then followed it with iced tea. He handed both glasses back to his son.

Elvis told him about Coach Tillinghast, practice, and his laps.

"He sounds like a good one, like one of those blue blood preppy warriors."

"Sure."

"He knows you pretty well, doesn't he?"

"I guess." The boy muttered.

"He's right about technique. And your team. You know that, don't you?"

"I guess."

"He is."

"I know." The boy sounded petulant.

"You won't be with him long." His father's tone changed.

"No, I like him. It's just…." He picked some words from the air. "I played against a kid half my size today."

"You will do that a lot this year." His Dad said. "Even on varsity."

"I know." He continued to mutter.

"It's not Chicago." His Dad added.

"No, but it's fine" the boy said. "Tillinghast is coming to dinner tomorrow."

"I like him better."

The boy sighed.

"You have been given a gift, Elvis. You know it and I know it. 'To whom much is given, much is expected.' And you have been given a lot. A huge amount."

The two were silent.

"I've heard that thing about gifts before."

"You'll hear it again."

"Yeah."

"Look," his Dad said. "Have fun and don't get hurt."

CHAPTER NINE

Elvis' locker was untouched.

The sound drained from the locker room when he entered and Elvis did nothing to replace it. Instead, Lynyrd Skynyrd kept asking for two steps in a room that wasn't going to give it to them. Aware of the silence, the quarterback, Harry Meyer towel-whipped a freshman line man. The cry and the laughter broke the deadlock and time slipped forward.

Out on the field, the coaches kept the J.V and the Varsity apart for the day. The bruises on both boys told the story loudly and clearly. A torch had been snatched. The coaches had seen it on the first day, and now the rest of the island could read it in black and blue. Billy Trotter was only keeping that position warm for a game, perhaps two. Then, he would ride the pine. On a Friday a week or two from now, he would be holding the dummy. The wheel turns, but it stays forever still.

In the minds of the coaches, both boys had already dropped off the team. Some humiliation cannot be pretended away.

The boys, Jack and Billy, of course, did not plan on pretending or forgetting anything. They waited and they remembered.

As promised, Tillinghast arrived for dinner a moment after seven thirty. He carried two pizzas, a six pack of beer and no Ensure. Elvis opened the door for him.

"Good evening, Elvis." He shouldered his way into the kitchen. "Please to meet you, Mr. Lowell."

The sick man struggled to his feet. It took him almost twenty seconds but the Coach was in no hurry and waited patiently. He finally assumed his feet and walked gingerly over to shake Tillie's hand. Even in his illness, David Lowell was an imposing figure at just under seven feet and still broad. He looked down into the older man's eyes.

"I see you brought pizza," he said. "and beer."

"I was told that you liked them both."

"I am not sure if I can eat them."

"What do you think?"

He breathed in the aroma from the box. "I think it will be fun to try."

His father sat, with precision and inelegance in one of the upright wooden chairs at the table. Elvis hadn't seen him in one of those since he came back from the hospital.

"Son," his father said. "I think I might need a straw here."

"Coming up."

Elvis darted into the kitchen and back. Tillinghast popped the cap to a Sam Adams and placed it in front of him. Elvis tucked the straw in. Tillinghast cracked one open for himself. Elvis did not reach for a beer, nor did he feel that he could drink one right now.

His father bent forward and took a long sip. The he settled back in the chair.

"If this kills me, Elvis, let everyone at the funeral know I died happy."

Not knowing what to say, the boy smiled.

"To your health." Tillie toasted.

"Let's drink to something that will last longer than that." His father said. "To the game of football."

"Fair enough. To football."

"To football." Tillie reached over and tapped the big man's bottle. Then he sipped his beer.

"Where did you play?" David Lowell leaned back as gently as he could.

"Yale." Tillie said. "We had a good team, back then."

"I am sure you did." He said. "What position?"

"Tight end."

"Blocking, catching?"

"Did a lot of both, a little linebacker, and some punting."

"Were you fast?"

"I wasn't what you would call speedy." Tillinghast replied. "Quick. I had a quick step off the line."

"Let me see your hands."

Tillie held them out. They were remarkable hands. They had held the ropes to parachutes he wasn't sure would open, they had held babies, they had signed treaties, they had shaken hands with monsters both foreign and domestic, and they had led him to victory on courts and greens. Today, they had not shook.

David turned them over in his own big mitts.

"I bet you caught the ball well."

"If it was near me and I hadn't been clothes-lined."

David let the hands loose. "Would you like to look at mine?"

"Sure."

Tillinghast knew how odd this was. But it was an odd dinner.

The dying man's hands were an inch or so longer than Tillinghast's and disease had made them mottled, purple, and thin. They had seen a life. Unlike the Coach's, these hands had scars, poorly healed knuckles, a broken thumbnail, and a ring finger that bent more to the left than it should. Tillinghast had seen hands like that before, but it had been in war.

"Did you play?"

"No."

"No high school."

"No."

David Lowell, sick with cancer and giddy from three sips of beer, looked at his son. "Elvis, I think you should cut up my first piece of pizza and then we will see."

"Okay." Elvis had brought a knife, fork, and cutting board out to the dinner table for just this purpose. He began slicing a piece of pizza into large postage stamps.

Tillinghast let loose the man's hands. The father had made a decision. It was late but not too late. Dark, but not too dark.

"I didn't have much of a choice back then. I dropped out of school in my sophomore year."

"What did you do?"

"I lived on the South Side of Chicago and someone my size was always useful."

Tillinghast sipped his beer and nodded. He didn't know how much the father would say. "Sure."

"I did a lot of that work, for one fellow or another. By the time I was twenty, they could have sent me to Vietnam for a break."

"It was a hard time, then."

"It always is. It always is a hard time when you're poor."

"True."

"I remember Dick Butkus came into a place that I worked. Brought Rosie Greer with him. Two tough guys, big guys. Maybe they had retired. Maybe they were about to. Rosie was the first black guy to walk into the door of our place, but everyone there knew who he was. For his sake, he knew where he was. And I was a head taller and fifty pounds heavier than either. But they had come in Cadillacs and they wore fur. They wore these huge, ankle length fur coats. It was Joe Namath's time and all of those athletes wore crazy clothes. You remember."

"I do."

"And I saw that and thought, I could have played that game and made that money. That night they lost more money playing cards than I made in two years. Then they got up, tipped everyone serving them and walked out the door."

Tillinghast smiled. He understood exactly what the sick man was asking of him. David smiled back at him. The sick man had only one thing in his life. There was only one thing that would last beyond his days and hours. In the silence of men, he had passed it on.

"To football." He said.

"To football." David returned.

So they talked about football. Two sick men drank their beer and ate their pizza as the ferries measured out the hours. By ten, David Lowell was nodding in his chair and Elvis gave a warning look to his coach. When the father woke up, player and coach lifted him up and brought him into his bedroom. The son dressed his father while Tillinghast stood in the kitchen with a glass of water and waited for the all clear. When it came, he arrived with the glass and the evening's pills. David got them all down before he drifted off again to sleep. Elvis covered him up.

Later, he walked his coach to the door.

"You're doing good work here."

"Thanks."

"It's not easy."

"It's not hard."

"There's nothing harder, son."

Elvis stopped, but he did not fully understand it. "Okay."

Tillinghast looked at him. "Get some rest. You have a game tomorrow."

CHAPTER TEN

Maria walked out of the driveway, across Prospect Street, and into the park and Dead Horse Valley.

Dead Horse Valley was less then fifty yards from the windmill and the DeSalvo house. The valley was covered in scrub oak and small pine trees, save for one sandy road cutting through. Back in the early years of the island, when the windmill was on the very outskirts of town and whale ships filled the harbor, Dead Horse Valley was the burying ground for horses, blacks, and the poor of the island. Now, the valley provided the steepest hill on an otherwise flat island. The other, best sledding hill was in the Quaker Cemetery. One way or another, children were going to sled over the dead.

At the top of the hill, the Nantucket Historic Association had built a small shed. In it, they stored the sails for the windmill, lawnmowers for the grass, a host of poisonous paints and weedkillers, and a toilet. With the humor of historians, the summer millers referred to the shed as 'Fred': "Gotta go visit Fred" or "Probably should check to see how Fred is doing."

Now, in mid-September, the windmill had become skeletal; the doors were shut, the sails put away, and Fred was locked up tight.

Maria sat on the bench overlooking the sledding hill and next to the shed. The last light of day was draining to the West, taking with it most of the day's warmth. The cars coming up Prospect had their headlights on. The glare flashed through the gaps in scrub, but, mostly left her in the dark.

Which was a relief to Maria, because she was a mess. The tears started while she was walking out the driveway, the sobs began as soon as she crossed the street, and now, in the shadows, Maria let it all go shudders, sobs, and gasps. She let it all rise up and let it all flow from her.

For ten minutes or so, she pulled her knees up to her chest and cried. Then, when the current seemed to slack, she wiped her eyes, stretched her legs out, and looked down into the darkening valley.

For a moment, she re-examined the cards she had been dealt. Maria shuffled and re-shuffled them, but she still had very little. A hand you would fold on.

Damn. She thought. Damn, damn, double donut damn.

In the quiet of the evening, as her ears adjusted to a silence without tears or sobs, she heard wooden creaks. They were faint, but sure and clear, after a moment.

Maria stilled herself and listened.

She heard a board creak again.

"Who's there?"

She stood up.

"No fucking around. Who's there?"

"Don't run." Came a faint, familiar voice. "Wait a second."

The door to the shed slowly opened. He had taken the hinges apart, so that the door opened backwards; the deadbolt and the door knob stayed flush against the wall. Julian edged out the hinge side of the door.

"Oh my God!" she cried. "I thought you were gone."

"Oh, no. I am here."

She ran to him and squeezed him. He smelled the same, he felt the same, he looked the same. She ran her hands up and down the familiar back and buried her face into his chest. His heart thumped away beneath her ear. He held the mother of his child tight and bent his head to her hair.

"Muy gato." He whispered, over and over.

Her heart rose. She was surfacing from days underwater, to fresh, clean pure air. She clung to him as if he floated.

She looked into his face and kissed him once.

His lips were swollen and he flinched.

She backed away, slightly. He had been beaten, badly. One eye was almost swollen shut, his nose was twice the size as usual. He wouldn't smile.

"What happened?" she whispered.

"I ran away."

"How did you get so hurt?'

"My papa," he shrugged.

"What happened?"

"It doesn't matter, does it?"

"Tell me." She said. "Please."

"I told him about his grandson."

"And he beat you?"

"He was angry for a moment." Julian said. "He will love our baby."

"Look what he did." She said. Maria touched the side of his face.

"Everyone gets a beating. It is nothing."

"It looks like something. It looks like you need an emergency room."

"No, no," he said. "We can't go there."

"We have to."

"They are looking for me."

"You're hurt." She said.

"If they find me, they will take me away."

"Where will they take you?"

"I don't know."

"You're father can't just take you."

"It's not just him." He said. "We have to be very careful."

She kissed him, gently. The feel of his skin, no matter how bruised, warmed her.

He pressed her to him.

"Muy Gato, I have to ask you to do something very hard."

"I am already having your baby."

"I know." He said, with a brief smile. "Muy gato, I want you to come with me."

"Where?"

"Anywhere." He said. "We can go anywhere. I took a bag full of those gold coins. As many as I could carry. I have them all inside."

She drew away. Maria hated herself for it.

"Where will we go?"

"Wherever you want. We can go to Las Vegas. We can go to New York. We can go to Los Angeles, Miami…anywhere."

"I don't know."

"Muy gato…." He said. "They are going to take me away."

"Where could they take you?"

"I don't know."

"Who is going to take you?"

He looked scared.

"We need to go, Maria. We need to go tonight."

"Can't we just bring the money back?"

"It isn't the money." He said. "We need to go. Tonight."

"I can't go tonight."

She sat on the bench. He slipped over and sat next to her. The night was now dark and starless. She heard the breeze rustle the leaves and branches nearby. She tossed and heaved on the ocean.

He sat beside her, silent.

Without him, she would drown. She knew that.

And there was a baby. Pink and happy.

"Yes," she said. "Tomorrow night. I will meet you after the game. At the party. Then we can go."

His face blossomed, after a moment.

Rosie saw her come in the back door. She was sitting at the table, over the ruins of a Sloppy Joe dinner. Rick had put the plates in the sink; she had done that much to civilize him. The table still had post-dinner mess, as did the kitchen. For Rosie's part, it could wait until she finished her beer and Broom Hilda. The old witch was off in a whole other part of the paper.

Maria looked flushed but happy. Happy was not the emotion she expected out of her teenaged, cop-bait, daughter. Tears and worry and even depression, but not zip-a-dee-doo-dah happy.

She certainly wasn't happy two hours ago.

She must be getting laid.

The idea has a certain awful logic to it. It fell into place like a puzzle piece and the picture coalesced. It looked like a boy. A bad boy. The skips. The attitude.

The gold coin she found in the laundry. The Kruggerand.

Maria waved and climbed the stairs.

Rick came out of the TV room and started to go upstairs after her.

"Leave her be."

"Did she talk to you?" He waited at the base of the stairs.

"Leave her be."

"After what you found?"

"Rick, leave her."

"It's from a drug dealer."

Rosie did not look up at her enraged spouse. He was often angry and she had tired of it.

He paused.

"Rick, we'll find out sooner or later."

"You're pretty calm now. You were downright pissed off two hours ago."

"Sit down."

Rick, with twenty years of marriage under his belt and an advanced degree in American Political Theory, sat next to her. Rosie whispered into his ear.

"She has a boyfriend."

He looked at her darkly.

"He's a bad boy," she said. "So, let's let it run its course."

"Did she tell you this?"

"No." she said. "But I guessed. It makes sense."

"But," he sputtered.

"You're Daddy." She said. "And you are a good Dad, but this is Mommy territory here."

Rick looked angry enough to spit.

Rosie held his hand for a moment.

Later on, it was only one of many regrets Rosie had.

Upstairs, Maria looked at the room she would be leaving in a few hours. Then she looked at the shed hidden in the brush of Dead Horse Valley. He was just a few yards away, sleeping on the windmill's sails. A cab was parked on the far side of the windmill, but otherwise the night was quiet.

They had a plan. She would wake up one more time in this bed and then she would go to school and say her goodbyes. At midnight, when the whole house was asleep, she would slip out and meet him at the football party. Elaine would get her there.

Then the two of them would sneak down to the Steamship Authority, hide in the back of one of the 18 wheelers, and then leave on an early morning freight boat. He was afraid, she knew, and his beaten face spoke volumes. So, even if she thought they could just walk on the morning boat and sail away, they would do it this way.

She looked around her room. There were some things she would miss, but they would be there. She would be back. She didn't know when or how, but she would return to the Celtics posters and her old surfboards.

James was busy with Lego Island 2 in his room, sending the beeps, twirls, and whistles around her desk.

She slipped across the hall.

"Am I too loud, Maria?"

He didn't look away from the game as he spoke.

"No." she said. "Pause the game, for a second."

He grunted, but the action stopped.

His older sister nudged him from the chair, and then sat him on top of her lap. The solid boy weight trusted back into her.

"Okay, go ahead."

Without a word, he unpaused the game and send Pepper back on his Lego adventure.

He didn't notice her tears.

One hour later, Rosie stood in the open doorway of her daughter's room.

Even now, with all the wars they had fought and would fight, she felt her heart rise into her chest. Even a little heavy, even teenaged awkward, even sneered into a pout in her sleep, she was heartbreakingly beautiful. She lay atop her duvet, still dressed in jeans and a t-shirt. In her one sleepy pose, Rosie saw her in the crib, in the princess bed, curled up next to her in her own bed, and at almost every other night of her life.

It would not last long. She knew this.

Her time was closing. High school, then, god willing, college. The moments had dwindled down to a bare few, cut off by time and hormones. She guessed ten years of Demilitarized Zones and Cold Wars before they could see each other again.

While Rosie was mentally going through her recipes, Maria's eyes opened.

"Mom."

"Hi, honey."

She sat up in her bed. She looked out the window to the mill.

She felt all of the emotion build in her. Even though he was out there, waiting, she began to cry again.

Rosie saw this. She stepped into the room and sat at the foot of the bed. The mother put one hand down on her daughter's feet. The girl rose and hugged her.

Rosie knew all the wrong things to say, so she didn't say them.

After a moment of absorbing tears and sobs, she tried.

"What is it, dear?"

The girl shook her head.

Rosie patted her on the back. "You'll feel better."

Maria continued to cry. It was too heavy for her to keep carrying.

Rosie patted her daughter again. She went through the list of all of the wrong things to say, "I'm sorry." She finally said.

Her daughter remained against her shoulder.

"I'm sorry, dear." Rosie said. "It'll be okay." If the boy had broken up with her, things would be a lot better.

Her daughter shook her head.

Rosie repeated herself. 'It'll be okay. Eventually. You'll see. There will be others."

At this moment Rosie understood that she had hit another land mine, and that she had no idea what her daughter was crying about.

Maria rolled over and faced the wall. Rosie continued to sit on the bed, holding one of her daughter's feet.

After two one hundred counts, the mother stood, leaned over, and kissed her daughter's cheek.

"Good night, Maria."

But she was asleep.

CHAPTER ELEVEN

On that schoolday, Maria skipped Phys Ed with Elaine. They drove downtown to the Bean. Elaine went inside, bought a coffee for her, a water for Maria, and then they headed out to Brant Point.

Two hundred years ago, Brant Point had been a tree lined marsh that protected the harbor. A salt shaker of a lighthouse was posted at the very end, at the opening to the harbor. Then it became a boatyard where some of the largest and most expensive whaleships had been built. Then it burned. In the years that followed, the Coast Guard built a house, then there was a hotel, then some more houses, and now it was the home to bond traders, hedge fund heroes, and Senators.

. They drove past the Coast Guard base to the tip and the miniature lighthouse. After they parked, the freight boat rounded the point and headed back to Hyannis.

"So…." Elaine asked.

"Do you think I could just move to Alaska?"

"It's cold up there."

"I can deal with cold."

"It's where the rejected men go to play video games and fart."

"I thought they were here."

"Only the best of a bad lot."

"Christ."

Maria stared out into the water.

"I want to get stoned." She whined.

"I know that is bad for the baby." Elaine mocked.

"Shit." She said. "You can get stoned, if you want."

"Not with you in the car. I don't want your baby to get born all fucked up and shit and know that it was my fault."

They laughed.

"I miss it."

"Getting stoned?"

"Yeah, and…"

"It's not that cool. You've done it a hundred times."

"I miss it."

"Don't you get those cool Mommy hormones soon?"

"I hope so." She said. "You want some?"

"No, thanks."

"I'll let you know."

"You do that."

Elaine sipped her coffee and Maria cracked the seal on her water.

"Julian came by last night."

"Good. How was it?"

"Weird."

"I read that your orgasms get more intense when you get knocked up."

Maria looked at her friend.

"That wasn't the weird part."

"You did fuck him, didn't you?"

"No…."

"Okay, that was weird."

Maria swallowed hard.

"He wants me to run away with him."

"You're kidding."

"No." She said. "His father beat the shit out of him because of the kid, so he ran away. He has all this money he took from his Dad, so he wants to take me somewhere."

"Where?"

"I have no idea."

"And you'll have the baby."

"That's the idea."

Maria was silent.

"You know how this sounds."

"Yeah." She said. "I do."

"Well," Elaine looked at her. "What are you going to do?"

"I don't know."

"When are you supposed to leave?"

"Tonight."

"Fuck."

Elaine looked at her friend as if her IQ was draining out her nose. Both girls were silent in the car. Finally, Elaine spoke.

"You know what you should do."

"I think so, and then I don't."

"You know what I think. You don't even have to ask what I think."

"Don't say it."

"You know it, though."

"Don't say it."

"It's easy enough."

"Please stop talking…"

"You get the rest of your life back."

"Don't."

"All right."

Elaine had the urge to turn the car on and take her back to her mother.

"What are you going to do?"

"I don't know."

"Do you think you should tell your folks?"

"I just don't want to think about it."

"That sounds like a good plan."

Maria did not look at her. Elaine swirled her hair around her finger and she weighed her words.

"My Mom was seventeen when she had me."

The sentence did not dance.

"I didn't know that." Maria spoke.

"It's true."

"She married him?"

"For a couple years. Then he left. She says that was good." Elaine looked away from her friend. "My grandparents were more important to me than either of them."

"They did a good job."

"You think?" She looked out at the water. "If you're lucky, you can be like my Mom. You can still be hot for years and introduce your little boy to his new Daddys."

It was quiet in the car.

"That's not going to happen."

"Where is he?"

"Fuck you."

"Where is he going to be in two years? Five years? He has no college diploma, high school diploma or even a green card. Where is he going to be?"

"I. Don't. Know." Maria snapped.

Elaine sighed. "I'm sorry."

Maria looked at her old friend and thought that this would be the last time.

"I'm sorry, too."

"I'm just saying."

"I hear you."

"You do?"

"Yeah." Maria said. "I still don't know what I am going to do."

"Then you know and you don't want to say."

She started the car and put it into gear. A large blue cabin cruiser rounded the point. A tall boy at the bow waved goodbye to them.

Later, in math class, Maria started hating her friend. She felt it build within her, rise up, and overwhelm her.

Maria felt like a big, docile cow (with swelling feet) that was being led around by the nose. First, to the school, then to the abortionist, then back to Mommy.

She shuddered. Abortionist. No reason not to call it what it was. Scrape, bleed, and wipe. Painkillers for a month. Mind the cramps.

It had to be. She knew it had to be. She couldn't sit in the kitchen and have that meeting. And if she couldn't do that, she couldn't be a Mom. Her way was the coward's way.

She dipped into the mathematics for a moment. All of the equations settled nicely down to "0." Mrs. Ronzetti kept asking everyone to "solve for 0." Like a river, the long formulas all finally ended there. For fifteen minutes, she rode the rivers down to the sea. Everyone else faded away.

Then her stomach lurched and the day and the hour came back to her.

Even though she ate nothing, it still came up on her.

She made it out of the classroom and into the bathroom just before her stomach exploded.

She knelt on the floor by the toilet, put both hands on either side of the seat and heaved until nothing came up but a long line of spit.

Maria heard the door open and close.

She looked under the stalls. Billy. Jack.
"Well, look who is on her knees."
"That's convenient."
"Listen honey, while you are down there…"
Billy snorted
"You know you are in the girl's bathroom?" Maria barked.
"Oh, is that what this is?"

Maria tried to rise to her feet. Billy kicked her legs out from under her. The shock of the hit and the pain of it bent her over.

"Hey." She started to say before two hands covered her mouth. A knee forced her face down into the toilet. Her butt got slapped. They jammed a wad of paper towels in her mouth.

Inches from the strings of her own thin vomit, she stared into the water and felt it all fall apart. Time slowed to a series of slides. A heavy knee was in the middle of her shoulder blades and she couldn't keep her neck from crushing against the toilet seat.

The boy who was kneeling on her back was breathing hard and fighting to stay on balance.

Two hands tugged at her jeans.

The porcelain remained cool.

She smelled ammonia and her own vomit. A drop of blood fell out of her nose and into the water.

Someone said something about bitches.

Her jeans slid halfway down her butt.

Sparkles and black bubbles appeared at the edge of her vision.

And a door opened.

"Stop that." It was a young voice, but deep. He was unsure.

The knee left her back and she could roll off the toilet. The cool floor rubbed up against her exposed butt.

Elvis Lowell, all 290 pounds of him, stood in the center of the bathroom facing his two teammates coming out of the stalls.

"You shut you mouth, cow." Jack whined.

"Get out of here." Elvis said.

"What if we don't?" Billy looked up at him.

The anger broke through the boy's nerves. "I will put you through that wall."

Jack did the math fast and it didn't look good. "Let's go."

Billy took a moment to stare at Elvis, then he slipped past.

As they walked out, Billy said. "We'll see you later, honey. You know what snitches get."

Elvis watched the door sigh shut behind the two.

Maria had scootched her pants back up. She sat on the seat of the toilet, feeling her neck. Time was only now starting to move in jerks and starts. She looked up and saw the massive freshman. He not only filled the doorway to the stall, his neck and head rose above the green partitions.

"How are you doing?" he asked.

"You're huge." She blurted out.

He backed up. "Sorry."

"No," she said. "No. I'm just, surprised. That's all." She checked her neck again. "I'm fine."

"Do you want me to get someone?"

"No. God, no."

"How about the nurse?"

"Please, No." She stood and stretched. Her brain felt scrambled with everything that fell about it today. It was time to go.

He looked doubtful. She could sympathize.

"Look," Maria said. "I am going down to the front office and they'll take care of it."

"Do you want me to walk with you?"

It was a confused chivalry for him, she saw. But all she wanted to do was to leave. If she could run without half the school running after her, she would. Now, it would be enough to slip away.

She stepped up to him and kissed him on the cheek.

"I'll be fine." She said. "Watch yourself."

She slipped out, took the back stairs, and was on her way up the hill to her house in under a minute.

Elvis stood still in the girl's room and touched his cheek.

Nothing made the slightest bit of sense.

CHAPTER TWELVE

The sun was still high at six in the evening, when both teams took to the field to stretch and warm up. Summer hung in the air, suspended in salt air and beach grass. The shadows lengthened nonetheless. The dark of the school stretched across the parking lot and the shadow of near goal post poked out to the thirty yard line. The polished stone in the old settler's cemetery flashed as the sun hit and moved.

Elvis stretched with the team. Coach Tillinghast hovered protectively ten yards away. No one watched him.

Elvis sighed.

It wasn't Chicago and Mount Carmel. Their games, and their scrimmages, had over five thousand fans decked out in blue and gold. Thirty cheerleaders on the field, a hundred member band in the stands, baton twirlers with the batons, a flag corp, and live television and radio coverage. Rap music pumped through the stands for warm up, the roars of the crowd deafened, and the stadium lights blinded you to everything but what was on the field.

That was a team, he remembered. He remembered them well. They would have put both of these teams into the hospital. No one could have stopped Dice, nor Johnson at fullback, nor Grant. Grant outweighed Elvis by twenty pounds, got triple teamed, and still lived in the backfield. The only person on Nantucket who could have stood on the same field with the Mt. Carmel team was Elvis.

But he wasn't in Chicago, and he wasn't going back. His mother had moved to her own Dreamland, his father was here on Nantucket, and

McVent, his parole officer, was the only one in Chicago. The team would miss him.

The spectators filled in the wooden stands. The old men, former Whalers all, lined up against the chain link fence against the field. The freshmen and middle school kids went to the top of the bleachers. In between, the parents, friends, and teachers settled into the middle of the home stands.

Coach Palumbo looked at Coach Reinemo and smiled. They broke the team up for drills, ran through them quickly, and then jogged the team into the field house.

For most of the year, the field house doubled as a secret frathouse for Billy, Jack, and their friends. With the help of a master key, they gathered here before school, got high, and went on their merry way. A space heater, some candles, a mattress and the judicious placement of the tackling dummies helped the room be more useful later in the day, and into the evening. In August, the lawnmowers, snowblowers, lacrosse goals, and flat soccer balls were dragged off and replaced by benches and chalk boards; the boys gave up their frat house for the football season and found wilder, sandier haunts.

Now, before the scrimmage, the offensive starters sat on the benches up front, the defense sat to the side, and everyone else moved to the back and sat on the tackling dummies. One of the dummies had a series of initials written in ball point pen down the side, followed by hashmarks. A.M. had picked up a round dozen, and a star.

Tillie drifted over to Elvis.

"How are you doing?'

"Good."

"I don't know how much time you are going to get."

"That's fine."

"Stay ready."

"Yes, sir."

"Put your game face on."

"Yes, sir."

The coaches led the team, one more time, through the game plan.

Outside, the shadows stretched still further at game time. The light burnished the old stands, the grass and the players. In that light, the stones flashed like headlights. The school had crept down the hill, to the edge of the running track and the goalposts poked out to the fifty yard line.

During the first half, the Massachusetts Division 5B Superbowl Champion Whalers didn't look particularly sharp. On offense, the timing was just a little bit off. The running back would hit the hole just after it closed and would get gang tackled for a loss. Passes were a little bit wobbly and a little bit behind, although one memorably bounced off of Nick's chest and onto the ground. On defense, they got fooled by simple counters and reverses which led the whole team into running a long parade down the field. The mighty Whalers were not a particularly disciplined or intelligent team.

But they were fierce. Jack Mitchell, in particular, scared the beejeesus out of the other team. At corner, he was frequently heading the wrong way with a receiver when the ball crossed the line. He changed direction like a bird, sprinted and collided with anyone around the ball.

As long as the game was a street fight, the Whalers held their own. Coach Palumbo knew his team well and called plays that insured collisions. Whenever a running back or a wide receiver broke free, the Whalers floundered. In the scrum of boys and grass, they did quite well. The crowd knew what to look for and they cheered each violent crash.

The Whalers would have gone into halftime with a scoreless tie, had it not been for an unfortunate fumble from Ryan Crowell. With five minutes left to go in the second period, he took a lateral and turned to run upfield. The ball, however squirmed in his hands, before breaking free. One linebacker flattened Ryan while another scooped the ball up like a cat and ran it twenty yards into the end zone.

At halftime, the crowd was uneasy and unhappy. It may have been a scrimmage, but this had not followed the pattern. The team was also quiet and uneasy. In the field house, the starters slammed their helmets and swore in a convincing fashion.

To Elvis, they appeared to be acting. However, he had not been in that many losing locker rooms and wasn't sure how they acted. Elvis took his seat in the back and listened to the offense.

Coach Tillinghast slipped up to him. "I don't know, Elvis."

"That's okay, coach."

"We'll see."

Elvis nodded.

"Put your game face on."

"I will, Coach."

It had ceased to be a scrimmage. Had the Whalers put three touchdown on the board, the J.V. and freshman would have dutifully soiled their uniforms on the field. As it was, they only had grass stains on their butts from stretching, and gleaming, pristine, untouched helmets.

Losing had gone from impossible to likely in a fumble and thirty minutes of offensive futility.

The Whalers emerged from half-time to one of the saddest cheers Elvis had ever heard. The fans weren't cheering on the impending victory or thirty minutes of passionate play; they were trying to will their sons into playing better.

He stretched again before he returned to the deep end of the sideline.

The sun had slipped behind the school; its shadow buried the stands and the field. A glowing summer sunset of red skies and violet clouds spread over the western horizon. To the East, three quarters of a moon rose in a curtain of dark blue.

Elvis was watching the sunset when he saw the car.

His aunt's Escalade had come through the chain link gate close to the school and, guided by police, it had parked in the grass at the far end of the football field, next to the ambulance. An E.M.T ambled over to the passenger side, talked through the open window, and then walked back to his coffee. None of the fans particularly noticed. To them, it was a common occurrence for someone's grandmother, grandfather, or even pregnant mother to park near the field.

But, to Elvis....

He knew who was in that car. He knew why he was here. A golf ball rose in his throat.

Elvis wasn't going to play.

The dizziness flooded the boy's mind. He saw his father, gray and sick in the morning, his breath rattling and flapping and gurgling in sore lungs. He saw the car and the sheer force of will that had put the old man into it. He knew that car would go to the hospital immediately afterward.

And he wasn't going to play.

Elvis walked as calmly as he could to Coach Tillinghast. Tillie stood at the far end of the sidelines with the special teams.

"Coach."

"Yeah."

Tillie saw the young boy's eyes.

"What is it, son?"

Elvis nodded to the end zone. "My Dad."

Tillie saw how it was.

"Stay here, son."

He walked slowly, but with purpose to Palumbo. The head coach looked at the older man, then over his shoulder at the 280 pound freshman and the car in the grass. He nodded.

Coach Tillinghast returned.

"Fourth Quarter. For sure."

Elvis nodded.

"Son, you have got to put your game face on. You have to focus on this field and those men on the other side. You have to hold everything else outside of you and focus on your work. Hold onto your emotions. Hold them still and focus."

The boy nodded.

"Game face."

The rest of the quarter passed by him, like water around a boat. He saw it happen in front of him, but the minutes held no meaning. Both coaches kept their starters in and both coaches kept slogging in the twilight. The crowd had fallen silent as the mighty Whalers stopped the opponents but could do nothing to move them. By the end of the third quarter, the scoreboard glowed in the darkness: "6-0"

Both teams jogged to their sidelines. The starters formed a circle and squirted water into their mouths.

"Trotter!" Palumbo shouted. "Switch to center. Sylvia, grab some bench. Elvis, you're in."

The team turned to him. He saw no one from the inside of his helmet.

He joined the group. A half dozen hands slapped his shoulder pads. Palumbo looked at the team.

"You got one quarter and you're down a touchdown. Whose house is it?"

There was a shout. "Our House."

Billy led the second call "Whose House?"

"Our House!"

"Whose House!"

"Our House!"

Elvis said nothing. He felt rage inside him. His engine was running on a new high powered fuel and he felt it roll.

"Let's Go!"

Coach Tillinghast took a step back and whispered the name of an old Greek warrior to Palumbo. "Watch what happens when Achilles takes the field."

"Who?"

"Watch what happens."

The starters, dirty and grass stained jogged back to the ball along with one, huge young man in a clean uniform. They noticed. The crowd held its breath for a moment. The opposing coach and the players saw him, but they thought little. If he had been good, why didn't he start?

The quarterback, Harry Meyer, huddled the team and called the play "Trips left, 38 sweep on three. Break."

Decoy.

Elvis lined up against 58, who was low to the ground, dirty, and small. The guard, Ernie Calkins was to his right. Nick lined up to his left at tight end. From the sidelines, he watched the boy dive low and under Billy's legs over and over again. This wouldn't take long.

On three, the ball snapped and 58 dove low. Elvis hit him a glancing block to the side and sent him spinning into the ground, then he went hunting for linebackers. One turned to follow the play. Elvis took three quick steps, blocked him under the shoulder pads, lifted him up and dropped him to the ground.

It felt good. Both hits kicked him into the game. The collision hadn't been particularly hard, but he found himself settling into a familiar world of violence.

Unfortunately, the rest of the linebackers had guessed Elvis would be the decoy and had attacked the tail back, Ryan Crowell, just after he got the ball. They dropped him for a five yard loss.

The team jogged back to the new huddle.

A wide receiver ran in with the play.

"Twins left, tango on two."

Pass.

Elvis jogged back to the line and looked at 58. He was looking right back at him. "Fatty, you get out of breath running five steps. You and your Mom fight over the last cupcake?"

Elvis ignored him and looked at the linebackers. He guessed that there wasn't going to be a blitz.

On two, the ball snapped and 58 shot to his outside. Elvis hit him hard again, just to the side of his pads and sent the boy sprawling in the grass. One down, Elvis backed up two steps and looked for someone else to hit.

By the time 58 was back on his feet and Elvis was back to the pocket, the noseguard had shoved Billy back into the quarterback. Harry took the bump, then heaved the ball out of bounds.

Nick came running in with the play.

"Center Screen."

"Huddle up." Harry said. He took one knee inside the circle. "Okay, we have one more shot here. Center screen on four…"

"Follow me." Elvis said.

"What?"

"Give the ball to Ryan. Crowell, follow me."

"Shut the fuck up. I'm the quarterback. They just sent in a play. We're doing the screen."

"Just. Follow. Me."

Elvis weighed seventy pounds more than anyone else in the huddle. He was a head higher than any player on the line. But he had a voice. Slow, steady, direct. And powerful.

Meyer looked at him.

"Who died and made you Queen?"

"Think about it. Last shot."

Somewhere, deep inside Meyer's head, a penny fell. Perhaps because Elvis was so huge. Perhaps because he had deposited Billy Trotter over the fence. Or because he had the voice of gravity.

"Fine. Dive left on one."

Elvis jogged over to his position and put one hand on the ground. He looked up at 58.

"Going right over you, cupcake."

"Give it a shot."

The ball snapped. Elvis brought both hands to the other boy's chest and heaved him. Off balance, the boy stood up and took one step backwards. Then Elvis drove him two more steps until he saw a linebacker flash to his right. He slipped from the one boy and collided, face mask to face mask with the linebacker. The boy lost his footing and fell away. No whistle.

Then Elvis started looking for the safeties. One came sprinting into view; it was as if an oil tanker hit a Boston Whaler. It would be a lifesaving hit.

Ryan had been shocked to find an open hole to run through. He sprinted through it as if it would disappear, then followed the big tackle down the field for ten yards, until he swerved to the outside, dodged one other tackler and made the fifteen yards for the first down.

Behind Elvis, three boys were down in the grass. They started to get to their feet. He turned and jogged past them. His teammates looked at him with a certain surprised awe. Nick patted him on the butt.

"Nice work."

The team huddled up.

Mike Sylvia, the starting center jogged out onto the field. "Elvis, go to the sideline."

"No."

"Elvis, Coach P is pissed."

"No. I am staying right here." Elvis spoke with a voice he hadn't heard before. In Chicago, it would have been inconceivable to do this.

Meyer, the quarterback, spoke up. "He stays, Mike. Jog back."

Mike looked at all of them. "You're nuts."

"He stays." Meyer repeated.

Sylvia shrugged and ran.

"You got one more play before he calls a timeout and reams me."

"Same again." Elvis said.

"Your funeral." He said. "Dive left on two."

Elvis jogged back to the line. The defensive tackle was on his knees, ready to go on all fours.

"Cupcake." Elvis said. "I'm coming over you again."

"Like hell."

"As a matter of fact, just like hell."

At the snap of the ball, Elvis had both hands on the boy's chest and drove him into the path of another tackler, then left him as he fell. Elvis slid into the path of one linebacker, and then a second. Still, without a whistle, he saw Ryan flash to the sideline. Elvis sprinted after him, lining up one last safety who didn't have a prayer of catching the fleet runner. The big man sent him spinning as Crowell crossed into the end zone.

He jogged in, but did not celebrate. There were eight minutes left and now they were tied. Crowds cheered, but the roar stayed outside his helmet.

He did see the car, of course.

Both Tillinghast and Palumbo walked over to him. They set him on the bench, away from the other players. For the first time today, the ball went where it was supposed to; deep and through the end zone.

Tillie spoke first, before Palumbo could get started.

"What did you do wrong?"

"I changed the play." The boy hesitated.

"Why?" Palumbo snapped.

"Because I thought we could score with that."

"Don't think." Palumbo snipped. "I get paid to think. You don't get paid, so don't think."

"Yes, sir."

"Why didn't you come out?" he snapped each consonant like a whip.

"I thought we could score."

"And…"Tillinghast interjected.

"I shouldn't think."

"No." Palumbo said. "No, you shouldn't." He looked up at the field. Coach Reinemo had the defense well in hand. Palumbo surprised the boy and sat next to him. He was aware of the situation and the car and all it meant. His rage seeped out of him and into the bench.

"Son, I know you have a lot on your mind." The coach sighed, then changed direction. "I also know that you were right. If I had pulled you out, we wouldn't have scored. This is just a scrimmage. What happens in the next game if Crowell wants to change the play. Or if, God forbid, Sylvia does. You just showed them that changing the play is okay. You can't do that."

Elvis nodded.

"Get ready to go in."

"Yes, sir."

The coach stood up and popped on the helmet with his clipboard. His ears rung.

Coach Tillinghast stood leaning his hands on his knees.

"Son?"

"Coach?"

"You know he is right."

"Yes, sir."

"Would your father be proud of changing the play like that?"

Elvis looked at the older man and was honest. "Probably."

"Well, then I guess it's a good thing he saw it," he said. "Game face, son. Game face. You only scored one touchdown. We need another."

Reinemo's defense held Lee to three downs and a punt. The ball wobbled up into the air, landed nose first and spun to the fifteen yard line. Elvis looked at the coach. The rest of the offense stood near him.

"Trotter, this time you sit. Sylvia, get in there. Run the plays I send in, and we win. Okay?" he looked at Elvis. "This game is ripe for the taking, boys. It's our field, our home, and our time. Go!"

The offense ran onto the field.

Meyer looked at his offense. "We have the time. We are in control here. We are going to score."

The players looked to him, then they looked at Elvis. "32 Pull on three. Set."

"Wait."

Sylvia looked over. "You pull and get the outside linebacker."

"Got it."

Crowell looked at him doubtfully.

"Break."

Minutes later, they scored. Everyone on the field stared at the still bouncing ball. It began waddling along the cinder track and came to rest in the center of an old puddle. Around him, the team was celebrating. Coach Palumbo and the others began rolling up the wire to their headsets. They weren't in favor of all the celebration, but there was no need to stop it either.

Billy and Jack found Ryan and gave him a good natured hug, but they stayed by his side.

It was a scrimmage, Elvis thought. It was a scrimmage win for a Division 5B team in Massachusetts. He ignored the post game line up and hand shakes. Instead, he jogged to the end zone, crossed over the fence, picked up the football and went to his father.

The engine was purring and the headlights were on. Elvis approached the passenger side. The window hissed downward.

The old man was gray. He wore sweaters and was wrapped in two blankets. His eyes looked yellow. He smelled bad.

"How are you, Dad?"

"Oh, y'know." He smiled. "You looked good."

"Not much of an opponent."

"They know who you are, now."

Elvis wasn't sure that was a good thing.

His Dad continued. "The coaches will play you."

"Sure."

"Good."

His eyes closed for a moment. Elvis glanced at his Aunt, who held the steering wheel with both hands.

His father opened his eyes.

"I'm tired, big guy."

"I know."

"Shannon wants me to go to the hospital."

"You should."

"Okay." He said weakly. "What can I do?" he smiled.

"Get some rest, Dad."

"Elvis."

"Yes."

"Elvis, this is important."

"Yes."

"Elvis, don't let them fly me off island."

"Okay."

"Under no circumstances."

"Absolutely." He said. "Dad, get to the hospital, will you?"

"Okay."

"I'll be right there."

"Okay." He said. "I'll wait."

Shannon nodded to him. She put the car into gear and inched forward. Elvis felt a presence behind him. Coach Tillinghast and Nick stood five yards back.

No one spoke for a long moment.

"Go get changed, son. It is going to be a long night."

CHAPTER THIRTEEN

After he left the locker room, Coach Tillinghast crossed the parking lot, walked through the school, came out the front door, jogged through the post-game traffic on Surfside Road, continued running a hundred yards up Vesper Lane, and arrived at Nantucket Cottage Hospital minutes before Elvis father, David Lowell, did.

He walked up to the charge nurse and told her that she needed to get ready for a sick man. She picked up the phone, looked at him, and began paging Dr. Tupper. The door hissed open on Shannon before she finished dialing.

Tillie found a wheelchair and pushed it out to the car. He gently pulled and placed the large, unconscious man into the seat and then pushed him. Diane and another nurse waited just inside the door.

David Lowell disappeared inside the Emergency Room. Shannon followed to the desk. She opened her purse to a flurry of papers. In a moment, she also disappeared.

Tillie rested his elbows on his knees.

The new waiting room glowed and buzzed. Larry King lived with the spiders on the TVs in the corners of the room. The chairs felt as if they had been rejected from an airline terminal.

It was at least clean, now. Watermarks, dark stains, and shadows of grime had decorated the old waiting room. It had smelled of bleach, mildew, and wet plaster. It was no place to die.

His father had died almost twenty years before. The old man had been seventy-five, still a partner at the law firm, and racked with cancer. He had weighed under one hundred pounds, his hands shook, and they had found a tumor on one of his thigh bones. There was a Swiss clinic that they had hope for. They had considered laetrile and the rest of the herbal remedies. His old man had another answer. On a gray Monday afternoon in late September, he set sail on his Alerion, "Orion" with his Labrador. He sailed out the channel, cut out behind the steamship and headed out passed Great Point Light. Tom Mleczko saw him when he came in with a tuna charter. His father's last public act was to wave goodbye to a stranger.

    Tillie understood why he had done what he did. Especially now. But he never forgave him for taking the dog.

    Elvis came to the hospital fresh from the locker room. Nick Koch came with him, although he didn't entirely know why. What he did know was that the kid looked haunted and drawn. He moved through a happy locker room like a janitor. So he got dressed and walked with the kid.

    Elvis slipped behind the counter and into his father's room.

    Nick watched him go, then turned to the waiting room and saw Tillinghast. The old man was still in his coaching clothes: blue pants, Whaler jacket, and N hat. He sat with his elbows on his knees.

    "Evening Mr. Koch." The older man looked up.

    "Coach." He said. Nick sat one seat away from him.

    "Any word?"

    "No."

    "What did he look like?"

    "Not good." He said. "What do you know about him?"

    "Elvis?"

    "His Dad."

    "Nothing."

    "Nothing?"

    "I've never seen him. Elvis told me he was sick, he came here to recover, and he couldn't drive."

    "It's going to be a tough night, you know that?"

    "Yes, sir."

    Tillie reached for his wallet, opened it, and rooted through it. For a moment, Nick thought he might hand him money for some candy. Instead, Tillie found a business card.

    "Call me when something happens. At any time."

    "Sure."

    He stood up slowly.

    "That was quite a win this evening."

"It was a scrimmage."

"A win is a win. We don't get to win all that often." The old man walked away. He moved stiffly.

Nick remembered going 11-1 last year and winning a championship.

For an hour, Nick sat alone in the waiting room. His phone was jumping around in his pocket. There was a victory party, of course, out in Quaise. Everyone wanted to go and half of them needed rides. He should go. He felt their pull on him.

He thought of Tillinghast and of the silent, huge boy that he came over here with.

He would give it another hour.

Nick's father had remained in New York. There was still an apartment uptown and, he was sure, a girlfriend's apartment somewhere else. When he visited his father, the weekends were very scripted. He arrived at Salomon Brothers in the late evening to find his father in an office, at a desk awash in paper and computer terminals. He would get up and they would leave for barbecue. The old man knew of a fantastic barbecue spot about ten minutes away by cab. Over beef ribs, Nick would download the details of his weeks at Cardigan Mountain School or, later, at Deerfield, and his father would listen and nod. Then, they would take a cab back to the apartment, nod at the doorman (the largest man Nick had ever seen, until he saw Elvis jog onto the field). Then, within a half hour, the phone would ring and Dad would leave for the office.

When he was younger, he would just get stoned in the living room and watch TV. Now that he was passably older, he would slip out of the house and go to some clubs.

Nick didn't hate his father for this. It was how he was; the life of numbers consumed him. When he went to the city, he always felt as if he was visiting him at the zoo.

He has no idea what Elvis was feeling.

After a half hour, Elvis emerged. He moved slowly, with his head down and his shoulders hunched. He looked up for a moment, found Nick, and shuffled over to him.

Nick stood.

"How is he doing?"

"Not good. We'll see."

"Are they flying him out?"

"No." Elvis was firm on this.

"Really?"

It seemed that for anything that needed more than three stitches, the med flight helicopter flew in and took you to Boston.

"Yeah. He's here." He said. "Do you want to see him?"

"Can I?"

He shrugged.

The two of them walked through a maze of corridors, then climbed a set of stairs. His Dad was in the only occupied room: Room 22.

The bed was a sturdy, old wooden queen-sized bed with a spindle headboard and footboard. There were homey lamps on both sides of the bed, an oriental on the floor, and the usual hospital wall mount up above the headboard. Four chairs were lined up on the near side of the bed. On the far side, a breathing machine hummed. It wasn't a room for healing, it was a room for dying.

David Lowell had been a big man. His feet barely stayed on the bed and his head pressed up against the headboard. Nick could see the bones of his arms and shoulders through the blanket. His cheeks were reddened, but the breathing tube probably kept him looking fresh.

Shannon sat at the foot of the bed. She was wearing jeans and a "Hampton Beach" sweatshirt. She looked exhausted.

"You can go home, Auntie." Elvis said.

"No. I'll stay here."

"We can do shifts. You can handle tomorrow."

"I can do this." She muttered.

"We'll take care of him tonight."

Shannon, with her eyes sore with exhaustion, stood. She picked up her bag. "Okay." She said. "Are you sure."

"Yes."

"Really?"

"We'll be fine."

"Then I'll go. Thanks, then."

"Yup."

"I'll be by tomorrow morning."

"I'll be here."

She hoisted the bag onto her shoulder and stepped away. Elvis sat in one of the chairs. Nick sat in the other.

"They wanted to fly him up to Boston." Elvis said.

"Sure."

"He said he didn't want to go."

"What's wrong with him?"

"Cancer."

"Besides cancer."

"Well, he has pneumonia." Elvis said. "That's what they are worried about now."

"What can they do about pneumonia in Boston?"

"That's what I asked."

Nick has switched the ringer of his phone off, but it kept vibrating in his pocket. The ventilator drowned out every other sound.

"He's a big guy."

"He used to weigh 350."

"No shit."

"He weighs about 200 now." Elvis said, absently.

"Holy shit."

Nick leaned back and the silence came up from the bed. For his part, Nick was pretty sure he didn't want to stay. At the same time, he didn't want to leave him, alone, next to his dying father.

So he stayed.

CHAPTER FOURTEEN

Elaine was drumming on the wheel. Techno was angrily sputtering from the poor speakers in the car-but it was enough to start the party. Maria joined in, half heartedly, but then let her friend roll on without her. Elaine had very effectively pre-gamed the party.

Maria couldn't pack. Instead, she sat on her bed for an hour and cried into three clean panties. There were a stack of her favorite jeans. A stack of her favorite blouses. An old backpack. And the stuffed animals stared at her. Paddington's black plastic eyes pierced her soul. She couldn't do it.

So she would buy new. They would go wherever they were going to go and she would stop at a mall for underwear and jeans. It was going to be an adventure.

They had driven through the rotary and were heading out the Milestone Road.

Maria turned the music down.

"Elaine, I need you to do me a favor."

"Sure. Whatever you need."

"I need a ride."

"I am giving you a ride right now."

"No." Maria said. "Julian and I are going to need a ride to the boat."

"Tonight?"

"Later."

"Sure."

"Great."

Elaine didn't turn the music up.
"You're not actually going to do this, are you?"
"I have to."
"No, not really."
"You don't know."
She sighed.
"Elaine, please." Maria asked. "Just give us a ride."
"Fine." She said. "It's your funeral."
She turned up the Polpis Road.

They were in a huge, sweeping estate on one of the points that prodded into Nantucket Harbor. The party started in the media room, with a gigantic television screen showing football, then spread throughout the dining room, kitchen, and living room. In September, the Nantucket High School Senior class were gypsies in the palace. They drank Budweiser out of Simon Pearce handblown goblets, felt up their middle school girlfriends on hand-rubbed leather sofas, and gazed with stoned and uncomprehending eyes at Picasso and Pollock.

The owner was one of the principal in the Carlyle Group. He had made a bad choice in caretakers, and the caretaker had made a bad choice in sons, and the sons had made the right choice in keys. At least he had the money to fix it. Unless they messed with the Pollock.

Maria stood in the kitchen on an island of pregnancy. She tried to fit in, she tried to relax, she tried to have fun.

He wasn't there.

She watched both doors constantly. She even went outside and walked around. No Julian.

At midnight, Elaine came to her with a cup in her hand. Maria thought that she might need another ride to the boat.

"Where is he?"
"Not here."
"Is he coming?"
"Yes."
"Did he call?"
"He can't call."
"He could."
Maria felt the tears build. "Fuck"
"Go get a drink," she said.
Maria shook her head.
"One drink won't make your baby the Elephant man."

Elaine led her into the kitchen. Tommy Kelly, one of less obnoxious of Jack and Billy's friends, was playing bartender.

"I need something sweet. With light alcohol."

He nodded, then he reached for a bottle of strawberry margarita mix.

"Margarita?"

"Sure."

He filled most of a cup with the mix then let the briefest splash of tequila in.

"Thats fine."

Maria sipped it. It tasted like extra sweet lemonade.

"Thanks. It tastes disgusting."

"You're welcome." He smiled. We were all laughing now.

She watched the door. Elaine slipped away.

In a minute, she felt really tired. The sleep crept into her thoughts and Maria looked for a chair that she could sit in to rest her eyes. It felt so strange.

She had been drugged.

The sign flashed in her eyes for a second, as if it was a road sign that she had just driven past. A road sign like "Welcome to Medford, Home of the 2007 Girl's Basketball Champions." and "Beware Slow Children."

Jack and Billy came to help her before she fell.

They led her upstairs to a bedroom.

She was so happy to fall on the bed.

Milestone Two

Robert P. Barsanti

CHAPTER ONE

They were searching for him.
They were in a jeep. He had seen it.
They were pissed. He had cut one of them. Maybe more than one, but he had definitely slashed one of them right across the stomach. Enough to hurt. Not to kill.
They had Maria.
Julian pedaled a rusted ten speed Schwinn across the access roads to the Milestone Bogs in the center of Nantucket's Conservation land. A nearly full moon lit his way and highlighted his profile. Every squeal of the chain echoed across the flooded bogs. At the sight of his moon-shadow, seven deer went leaping into the brush.
So far, he had been lucky. The cops had missed him and he had avoided the boys by staying on the sand. He could feel, however, the hem of Old Man Luck's cape. The minutes were dwindling before that old man would heave him off into the bushes.
For now, he was safe. Julian darted into the shadow of the great barns, then into the piney darkness alongside Milestone Road. The road had no houses along it, just two lines of thick scrub pines and oaks. Beyond the trees, the moors and the head-high brush went on for miles until it gave way to beach grass and sand.
Milestone road ran a straight seven miles from the edge of Nantucket town to the eastern shore of the island. In the moonlight, Julian would be visible for a mile or more in either direction.
Right now, it was a silent road in the middle of a September night. One cab had passed his hiding place in the ten minutes he had rested there. A half mile away, three deer tentatively stepped out onto the pavement.

If his luck could hold, he could pedal for a half mile before he could duck into the moors on the other side of the road and get to the compound by way of sand. Or he could just wait in the dark. They didn't know where he lived or where he went or even if he had a bike. If his luck had truly held, Jack was standing in front of a police officer and explaining the long slice across his belly. Or he was in an ambulance.

When Julian had arrived at the rich man's house, the party was running fast downhill, but there were looks. Nothing was said (because no one would talk to him) and nothing was pointed out (for no one would warn) but he could sense that the stage had been set for him. He went room by room looking for Maria, but only met stares and silence. Finally, he had looked upstairs.

And there she was, in the master bedroom. Drugged and unconscious, the boys were trying to peel her pants off.

The knife came out and it did its work.

Then he ran.

So now, he and his bike stood in the shadows of the pines. The air was so silent that he could hear the deer step on the pavement.

With one last tug on Luck's cape, Julian pushed off with the bike and pedaled it across the road to the bikepath.

He creaked and wheezed back to the Milestone Road.

Three deer stood in the middle of the pavement, astride the center line. They eyed him as he pushed his way forward. At the last, when he could have flicked a spitball at them, they bounded for the brush.

Behind him, up near Sconset, two lights appeared and swept the pavement.

Julian heard the car and he knew. He kept pedaling and pulled into the shadows along the bike path.

The car accelerated.

He made himself relax.

"Heads!"

A green beer bottle zipped inches over his head and buried itself in the undergrowth. The brake lights of the jeep burned red ahead of him, then the car swung to the right and executed a fast U-turn that brought them onto the bike path and face to face with him.

The jeep accelerated.

Julian swerved onto the roadway and let the jeep pass him on the bike path. Another green beer bottle sailed wide. He heard the music, he heard the boys voices, he heard the clink of bottles. He heard the squeal of tires as they spun around another U-turn.

This time, they wouldn't miss.

Julian ducked to the left and headed for woods. The jeep zipped over the bike path where he had been then it spun around one last time.

The Brazilian knew what was coming. He ran into the scrub oak and low brush.

The jeep squealed to a stop on the grass and two boys sprang from the doors, holding long, black, metal flashlights in the air.

Julian ran through brush, branches and darkness. The flashlight beams would hold him and lose him as he ran and crouched. And he may have made it.

But his foot caught the branch of a fallen birch and he toppled forward. He rose up on hands and knees before the first flashlight clubbed him in the center of his back. He fell forward, then rose to the next blow.

The next flashlight sent him into a world of stars. Then the next, and the next, and one last one. Then the world of stars blinked out.

Jack and Billy looked at the fallen boy. The cut across Jack's belly stung and it still bled. He felt the crest of a wave of rage. It rose up and raced to the beach. And it was still racing to a shore, after the beating.

"You fuck!" He kicked the body.

"We fucked you up!" Billy kicked as well.

"Two times." Jack stomped on his back. The body didn't twitch.

Billy wound up and kicked him between his legs. The body shifted forward.

Jack flashed a light on the body.

He could see a crease on the side of the boy's skull. Blood dripped from the ear.

"Hey," he said. The wind and the night were still rushing by him. He reached out to his friend. Billy put his flashlight on the body. The wave of rage faded away. He felt the power disappear in the glare of the flashlight.

"We really fucked him up." Billy said. His voice dropped.

Jack said nothing. He reached forward and felt the side of the neck. Under his fingers, he felt the beat.

"He's alive."

Billy looked at him.

"What do you want to do?"
"Nothing."
"What if he wakes up?"
Jack looked at him.
"He's not going to wake up for a while."
"Oh." Billy looked at the dent on the side of the Julian's skull. Then he looked at his flashlight and wiped it on his pants.
"Let's get out of here." Jack said.
"What if he got jumped?" Bill suggested.
It took Jack a moment to process the fact that it was actually a good suggestion. The two boys looked at the body. "Let's take his backpack."
"And his wallet."
Jack went back to the body. He patted the butt where the wallet should be. There was no wallet. The muscles in the body didn't tense. Jack stood up.
"Give me your knife."
Billy handed him his leatherman. Jack snapped the blade out and cut one strap off.
They heard the buzzing of a cellphone.
"Shit. Who is that?" Jack snapped. In a second, he realized that it was in the bag. He sliced the other strap off, then pulled the bag away from the body. The body shifted lower in the leaves.
The bag was a thin, black nylon-no bigger than a gallon of milk. It was glowing. Jack reached in, found the phone, and threw it deep into the woods. It landed face up. The light from the incoming call glowed like a star.
"Fuck." He said. "Let's go."
Both boys strode out of the woods. Neither looked back.
Tommy Kelly, the third boy, had gotten out and stood by the side of the car. Deep in the woods, he could see the flickering of the phone.
Billy got in the jeep, turned it around and idled it on the other side of the road. Jack wheeled the broken bike ten yards into the woods. Then he and Tommy kicked the broken glass off the path.
Minutes later, Jack didn't see any difference between this spot and the rest of the road. His own bleeding had slowed down.
Then the light flashed in the woods.
Billy accelerated back to town.
No one talked.

At three in the morning, Orion was climbing over Nantucket's eastern horizon. Detective Danny Higginbotham had finished the novel he had brought out on patrol. He sat silently behind the wheel. Henry Coffin, too, was silent. Humid September air built up on the windshield.

Unlike his partner, Inspector Coffin did not wear a uniform, carry a badge, or have a gun. The habit of the Quakers settled on his shoulders easily and he felt no need to shrug it off. He hadn't put the cuffs on anyone in at least ten years and hadn't even raised his voice. As far as anyone in the department knew, the Inspector never even took target practice.

Yet, Danny was safer with the older man than he would have been with anyone else. The only one who would hurt the Inspector would be the Inspector himself. The black man looked at him over the edge of his book. The older man looked out at the sky and the water.

Henry could be silent for the entire night…or even for a week. It was a silence without expectation. Danny believed that, on any given day, Coffin might say a total of ten words and all of them were addressed to him.

Tonight, the old man hurt. He usually nodded off for two hours when he first got into the car and they waited by the side of the road. Whiskey in the evening tended to have that effect on him. Yet, he stayed awake tonight, with an eye on the stars over Coatue.

What could they talk about? He wouldn't ask about the kids, or the wife, or what happens during the day. They didn't kibbitz about sports, or real estate, or politics, or how the world was going to hell on an express train. So, they sat in easy silence and became each other's mute company. Most nights.

Danny also knew that the only way to learn anything was to ask. So he did.

"What is it?"

"What?"

"You. What is it?"

Henry looked at him. Danny tried to be supportive.

"I have a toothache." The old man surrendered.

"Y'know, they have dentists these days."

"Yeah."

"They use some great drugs."

"I know."

"But you won't go?"

"We'll see."

"How about some Tylenol?"

The old man shook his head.

"How can you drink all of the bourbon you drink and not take Tylenol?"

The older man smiled. "One tastes a lot better than the other."

His teeth had been going for a while. When Coffin fell asleep in the patrol car, Danny could hear the noise of teeth grinding over the sound of the radio. He had also seen the old man wake up, spit something out into his hand, then toss it out the window and go back to sleep.

Danny reached into the glove compartment, pulled out a bottle of Tylenol, and dropped them in Coffin's lap.

"You make the decision."

He shook three tablets into his hand, and then threw them back. He swallowed them dry.

In twenty minutes, he was asleep.

His teeth were grinding again.

Inspector Coffin had been farmed out to the night shift. Pacifists have very few friends in police departments. In fact, the Chief had offered him a no-show job several times. If he wanted to drink himself to death each and every night, the Chief would happily clock him in and clock him out. Coffin had smiled at that.

Everyone knew the man was haunted. One of the few bits of self preservation Coffin did every night was to get out of the house. Danny could imagine why.

Twelve summers ago, there had been a young wife and a younger son in the old family mansion on Main Street. The boy, Pete, played in rooms decorated with Chinese lacquer and British porcelain, underneath paintings of his ancestors' whaling ships. The boy had toys, videotapes, and loving parents who gated off the stairs and cut his grapes in half.

Then, on the Fourth of July, mother and son walked down to welcome the in-laws for a week of vacation and grand-parenting. In the summer time crowd, the little boy had slipped out of his mother's hand on Straight Wharf. Her parents were waving from the deck of the Gray Lady as it backed into the pier. Pete had run to them, leapt off the end of the dock, and disappeared.

In spite of a full Coast Guard search including divers, draggers, and a helicopter, he wasn't found for three days. Finally, his body washed ashore across the harbor at Monomoy and was found by a golden retriever on the beach.

Who would want to spend the night in a house hearing those footsteps?

So, Danny rode with Henry Coffin on the third shift.

A familiar red jeep zipped past them, going ten miles over the speed limit.

"License and Registration, boys."
"Sure"
Danny stood one pace behind the driver's sidedoor of a red jeep. Even here, in the middle of the island, you could still hear the slow roll of surf on the south shore of the island.

The boys fiddled in the glove compartment and Danny unsnapped his weapon. It hadn't been that long ago that Danny had ridden around Dorchester and Roxbury. Nantucket was a lot calmer, especially in the middle of the night. That didn't make him believe that even these rich white kids wouldn't hesitate to put a gun in a black man's face.

He hoped his partner was watching.

The driver stuck the license and the registration out the window.

Danny let his flashlight beam hit the two boys in the front. The driver's pupils stayed tiny. In the middle of the night.

"Be right back, boys"

Danny walked back to the patrol car, but left his weapon unstrapped.

"So, who are they?"

Danny showed him Billy's license. The Inspector nodded.

"Who is in there with him?"

"I don't know."

"Okay," he said. "I'll go see."

The older man walked up along side the jeep. He looked in the grass for a bit, then, he looked in the passenger side door. The window unzipped and a breath of beer and boy came out. One young red head sat in the back, while two older boys were in the front. All of them were quivering with attention.

"Jack," the inspector nodded. "Billy." Billy Trotter was a head and seventy five pounds heavier than his friend. His eyes were also pinholes. He was clenching and unclenching his hands.

A car was approaching fast. Danny slipped the squad car into reverse and crept backwards. Still speeding, the car swung past the jeep and then continued on. It was a cab. Danny got the license plate and the name on the side "Ahab Cab."

"Are you going after them?" Jack asked.

"Later."

"Seems to be an emergency."

"Perhaps."

Coffin looked at the red head in the back. His pupils were wide and dark. "Who are you, my brother?"

"Tommy Kelly."

"Your Dad is a roofer?"

"Yes, sir."

"You don't need to call me 'sir'."

"Yes, sir."

Jack cleared his throat loudly. Billy Trotter kept flexing his hands and staring straight ahead.

"Where have you boys been tonight?"

No one spoke.

"Party?"

"We went to look at the surf, sir." Jack said.

"You did?" Henry smiled. "How is it?"

"Rolling well."

"Storm tomorrow, you think?"

"I don't doubt it."

"Uh-huh." Coffin asked. "Why now? Most people are asleep at three in the morning."

"We wanted to see the break at low tide."

Coffin smiled.

"That true, Tommy?"

The boy nodded vigorously. Coffin looked back at the car. Danny stood by the front headlights. Henry nodded at him.

"Billy, won't you step out of the car please?"

He looked straight at the Inspector.

"Really?"

"Sure."

The boy reached behind himself and unlatched the car door, then stepped out onto the pavement. Coffin crossed in front of the jeep.

"My brother, do you have a favorite?"

"I don't know what you mean, officer."

Coffin smiled. "I like you a lot, my friend. I do." He said. "Why don't we do the old stand on one foot and touch your nose?"

"I have bad balance, sir."

"That's a shame. How about if you walk the line."

"My ADD medication makes me dizzy."

Coffin smiled. "Tell you what. You walk the line and, if I still think you might be drunk, I'll take you to the hospital for a blood test."

"Okay, Officer." He spoke out all three syllables in the title. Billy walked out into the middle of the road and stood on a thick yellow line. With both arms extended, he closed his eyes and flawlessly walked five paces to the East. Then, he executed a neat turn and began walking west when he was lit up by distant headlights. The big boy finished the five paces, then came to the side of the jeep.

"Well done." Henry said.

"You know," Danny said. "I saw some wobbling."

"You did?"

"I did."

Another car approached them. Danny eyed it for a second then looked back at Billy.

"I think you should have a blood test." Danny said.

Coffin looked at the boy.

"Whatever you fellas want." He smiled.

The approaching car slowed and pulled over on the opposite side of the road, then set its hazards. Danny noted that it was Pink's Cab. Lewis Pinkham opened the door.

Pink looked like a defrocked priest. He was a good fifty pounds overweight, middle aged, and should be sitting in a guidance department somewhere helping stoned young men through the difficulties of the ASVAB. He had been born on the island to a long time fisherman and junk dealer, left for UMass and then Suffolk Law, before returning to the island for the last of his father's illness.

Pink kept his cab clean and well organized. He kept stacks of brochures for the whaling museum and the deep sea fishermen on the front seat. He also kept his iPod, his cellphone, and a 24 ounce, insulated mug of coffee. Were you a New Yorker coming from the airport, you would find that the seats were clean, the windows transparent, and the conversation sociable. And if you happened to need an an ounce of coke, or were looking for some friendly female company, he could help you out with that as well.

"Can I help, officers?"

Danny, sidearm still unsnapped turned to face him. Coffin cut him off.

"Good evening, Pink."

"Henry."

"On your way home?"

"Sure. But, I could give this boy a lift if you want."

Henry looked at his fellow officer. Danny glowered, then he shrugged.

"That sounds like a good idea to me. They seem very….tired."
"I'm sure."
"Do you have room for three?"
Pink stood by the side of his mini-van and smiled. "Absolutely."
"Okay, then."

Danny handed the license and registration back to Billy. The boy made sure to maintain eye contact through the whole exchange. Coffin stuck his head in the unzipped window. "Everyone out and into Pink's cab."

Both boys came out the passenger side silently, walked around the front of the jeep and into the open door of the minivan. Jack carried a black backpack and walked stiffly. Tommy walked with the least ease, but he didn't appear drunk to Danny.

Pink sat in his car after the boys were loaded in the back seat.

Coffin crossed the silent road. He passed out of the range of the headlights, but the flashing blues continued to light him and the trees up. He stuck his head in the driver's side window.

"Now, remember to get this jeep tomorrow before we have to send the truck for it."

"Absolutely." Jack said.

"Goodbye, fellas. See you later."

The cab pulled away. As it left, Danny flashed his flashlight into the back of the jeep.

Pink drove while Charlie Mingus played. The boys were silent. He knew better than to ask and they knew better than to tell.

They were good boys, but they were boys. Until recently, the island had been a good place for boys. They could work with their Dads building houses. Before that, they could go to sea and catch fish. Long ago, they were stuffed onto whale ships and sent out on the grandest adventure of them all. Boys weren't going to sit at desks and use number two pencils. Boys needed to run and compete and use their hands and their hearts.

Back in the day, the island made men. Nantucket men went out to sea as their mother's little boys and came back in as bearded, full blooded sons of fathers. Those were the men who built the island and built the wealth. They had lived a life by the time they were 25. They had tales they could not tell and secrets that tied them to shipmates and captains. It made them strong.

Today, they were not strong. Today, they had the shark drained out of them. There were girls and women and Playstations that kept the boys rooted on their mother's couches as their thumbs performed what their bodies could not. They had no secrets and no tales.

Most boys never learned to work hard. When the illegals came, the Nantucket boys couldn't fight back. So they left for the mainland and all the hispanics and Bulgarians who learned how to work hard, took the jobs.

After a mile of driving, he executed a neat three point turn, and headed back to town. Now Pink drove a bit quicker. He passed the darkened jeep. The patrol car had already moved on. Billy watched it.

"They will be up here at the rotary. Don't think about it."

"I wasn't." Billy said.

"What happened tonight."

"Nothing."

"Do not fuck me, boys. Not tonight. Do not fuck me."

The boys were silent.

"We had a slow weekend." Jack said.

"Okay." He said.

"There was a party." Jack continued. "Out at Abram's Point."

"Once again, please do not fuck me, boys. Do not fuck me."

Jack cleared his throat.

"We moved some product."

"How much?"

"Enough."

"Did you get paid this time?" Pink muttered.

"Of course."

The boys snorted more than they sold. Pink didn't care. They could frost cupcakes with it, as long as they bought it from him.

"What's in the bag?" Pink asked.

"Just some stuff."

"Product?"

"No."

"Is it yours?"

"Now, it is."

Jack reached over and tapped the red headed boy. Tommy handed his phone to the older boy. The two older boys flicked through the pictures.

"Is there a problem?" the older man asked.

"No problem."

He eyed the boys in his rear view mirror, but could see nothing.

This business had made sense to Pink two years ago. After the divorce, when Sarah's lawyers and the IRS were going up his ass looking for chocolate bunnies, he appeared to have no money and didn't want any real income for her to steal. His house was in a trust, as was the land, and there wasn't much she could touch. Although she tried. It was a hungry season.

The Russians on Essex Road offered a wonderful way to keep the cash coming in.

He brought them customers. They cut him into some of the cash and gave him some product. Then, he took that same product, cut it, and sold it to Jack. For a year now, it had been a profitable sidelight.

In the end, Sarah pried some money loose, some child support, and a one-way boat ticket. She kept his little girl, Carrie. Pink kept the house and his cars.

Pink also kept the Russians. They were hard to get rid of, as was Jack.

He didn't need the money anymore. Sarah was gone and her lawyers were in hiding. Bruce Poor had come by one day, hat in hand, to ask if he had ever thought of developing those fifteen of scrub oak and Japanese black pine behind the house. As a matter of fact, he had. At a million and a half per acre, he most surely had. And that would be the end of the Russians. And Jack. And Billy.

They would all be on their way to jail and it was time to hop off the bus.

When Pink looked into the backseat, Jack was holding up a coin against the light.

"What's that?"

"I don't know. Some foreign coin."

"What does it look like?"

"Here."

Jack dropped four of them in the front seat. Pink felt how heavy each one was. At a stop sign, he saw the stag on it. Kruggerands.

"South African." Pink said. "Practically worthless. How did you get them?"

No one answered.

He kept the four in the front seat.

Pink dropped Billy Trotter off first, at Newtown Lane. Then he swung down to Equator and let Jack go. The boy took the backpack with him. He backed out of the driveway, then drove back out to Bartlett Farm Road.

"Where do you live, Tommy?" Pink knew

"Tom Nevers."

"Off we go."

Coltrane was playing in Amsterdam. Pink turned the music up.

The red head stared out the window at the passing houses.

"What's on your phone?"

"Nothing."

"Nothing?"

"Just a prank."

"You want a piece of advice? I would erase whatever it is right now."

The boy shook his head.

He stared out the window. The coke still flowed through the boy. Pink had no idea what they did and he didn't want to know. But.

Photos.

Those fucking idiots.

Real estate was starting to look even better.

The boy was silent.

"What happened tonight?"

"Nothing."

"You're sure of that."

'Nothing happened."

"Really."

The boy said nothing.

He stared out the window. Pink thought he might see a tear. Those fucking idiots.

"Tommy, I don't want you to think something happened if it didn't." Pink said. "I wouldn't want Billy and Jack to think that either."

The boy stiffened.

"I would get busy erasing."

Pink dropped the boy off in front of his father's pick up truck, then headed home to bed.

CHAPTER TWO

She dialed Julian's number again.

She felt so stupid. So very, very, very stupid.

Of course, he wouldn't be here. Why would he come to this redneck party? They would've lynched him.

And why would he come at all? He had a different country, a different family, and a father who terrified him.

So she came. Like a fool. Like a sixth grader. Like raw meat.

And that's how they treated her.

Maria was sitting in one of the bathrooms, with the door locked.

The floor was black marble, as were the counters. Three people could stand in the shower.

So stupid.

Someone knocked on the door.

"Is anyone in here?"

"Yes."

"Would you unlock the door, Miss?"

"No."

"No?" the voice said. "It's safe now, Miss. They are all gone."

"I don't believe you."

"I am a police officer, miss."

"I don't believe you."

She just didn't want to have to deal with this right now.

"I can break the door down, miss."

"Don't!"

"Why don't you unlock it then?"

"No."

State Trooper Ranney looked at his partner. "Call Coffin. They should be here anyway. It was his party."

She dialed Julian's number again.

One trooper blocked Polpis Road going east and, twenty yards away, another patrol car blocked it going west. As Danny drove up the dirt road, he didn't see too many other cars. The staties were as effective as ever, Danny noted. Of the five cars that were left around the house, only one of them had a driver. Another trooper, complete in his flat hat, was taking his statement.

Coffin noted. "They must have emptied the barracks."

Danny nodded. He had counted five patrol cars, including the road block. The entire summer complement of State Troopers must have been called out to break up one party.

"What do you think?"

"I think someone knows the governor." The Inspector said. "I think the address matched one on the donor list and someone needed to make a heck of a show."

Henry parked the car behind a sparkling clean state cruiser.

Inside, the house looked as they expected.

It was magnificent. They entered into a main hallway dominated by dark wooden floor and bright walls. A stairway descended to the main floor, studded with inlaid wood and highlighted by two banisters made from candy-striping a darker and a lighter wood. At the head of the stairway, a Picasso nude looked down on the muddy and sticky floor.

To the right, the officers entered a dining room. The table sat sixteen and, like the staircase, had been inlaid with swoops and swirls. Now, in the fall, it held only red plastic cups of warm beer, ping pong balls, and an impromptu net of Simon Pearce goblets. A huge Pollack canvas dominated the far wall.

Unlike the public areas of the house, the kitchen was white and black, with black marble counter tops and white cabinets. Their shoes stuck to the floor as they walked in. One side of the sink had gallon bottles of Captain Morgan, the other had melting cylinders of frozen juice concentrate. A clear plastic trash bag was full of Busch beer cans. Cups, wrappers, empty bags, and a t-shirt lay on the floor.

Both officers paused. For all of the trash and for all of the cars outside, they had yet to meet a policeman inside. Nor could they hear them. Bob Marley boomed through the empty rooms. The house has the cloying smell of spilled beer, warm fruit juice and marijuana.

"Someone had fun." Danny said.

They continued on.

The party had started in the media room, with a gigantic blue television screen, then spread throughout dining room, kitchen, and living room. The Nantucket High School Senior class hadn't stolen anything, broken anything, or even caused enough damage to keep the cleaners busy for more than a morning. Had they known that each goblet would have bought them the best dinner on the island, the hand-rubbed leather sofas would have paid for a semester at college, and the paintings could have let them retire without a career, perhaps more would have been taken.

Henry pressed a cabinet door, then let it swing open in front of him. "No Woman, No Cry" abruptly ceased. Both men felt the silence echo. Henry pressed another button and the blue screen went black.

"That's a quality sound system." Danny said. "Even that loud, you didn't hear any distortion."

Coffin looked at him. "You turn your stereo that loud?"

"Just when the missus gets that look."

"And, when she gets that look, you care about sound distortion."

"Of course. What else am I supposed to think about."

Coffin smiled at him.

A state trooper, new to both of them, stepped into the room.

"You guys local?"

The two officers looked at each other. "Of course."

Danny didn't see much blood on Nantucket. It wasn't Dorchester. People didn't arrange divorces with knives and baseball bats as much as they did with lawyers and sniffy parties.

And yet there was blood. Not pools of it, no arterial spray on the walls, not long drippy lines heading down the stairs, but a set of smears on the sheets, some drops on the carpet, and a red fist mark on the door to the bathroom.

The state troopers were looking at the marks, but didn't appear to be taking any samples.

An older trooper nodded at Henry. "She is in the bathroom."

Maria heard the police talking outside the door. But she kept it locked. Maria seemed to have stopped crying for the moment. She sat on the closed wooden lid of the toilet.

"Hello?" a voice said.

"Hi."

"My name is Henry Coffin. What's yours?"

"Who are you?"

"Henry Coffin." The man repeated.

She thought for a second. She knew him. Her parents knew him.

"You're the guy who doesn't arrest anybody."

"Yes," Coffin said. Danny was smiling broadly. The staties had their own opinions. "Now, you know who I am. Who are you?"

Maria looked at her hands. It occurred to her that it was a good question right now. Who was she?

Coffin waited.

The silence pressed on her.

She opened her phone and then closed it.

She had to say her name and she had to leave the bathroom. When she did, it would all start. There would be questions and comments and stares and payback and it would never end. And there was her dark passenger, deep inside. And there was Julian. There was a secret she had to keep.

But she couldn't stay in the bathroom.

She flushed the toilet again. There was no toilet paper inside.

"Nothing happened." She said.

"If you say so."

"Nothing did."

"Okay," Coffin said. "Why don't you just tell us your name?"

She was silent.

"How many of you are out there?" she asked.

Coffin looked at the troopers. "Four, total. Danny and I, and two staties."

"Ask the troopers to leave." Someone in her French class was the son of one of them, she thought.

Coffin looked signaled and they filed out of the room. When the room was emptier, he looked back at the door. "Okay. It's just me and Danny."

"Fine."

She put her hand on the knob. It would all change, now. It would all be different. She took that last moment for herself. Then she opened the door.

"I am Maria DeSalvo."

Maria DeSalvo had inherited too many of the family traits to ever be beautiful. She was a little short, a little heavy and a little fiery. The Inspector knew her mother, Rosie, very well. He knew her father well enough to have coffee with. He had seen this little girl in her diapers.

At this moment, her face remained pale and the remnants of tears ebbed on her cheek. She was wearing jeans, sneakers, and a Miles Reis trash hauling shirt. But there were no bruises, no black eyes, no ripped clothes.

Coffin looked at her.
"Are you bleeding?"
"No."
"Are you hurt?"
"No."
"Why are you here?"
"It seemed safe."
"The bathroom?"
"Yeah."
"Why did you need to be safe?"
"I don't remember."
"You don't remember?"
"No. There was a party here and I drank a beer and I don't know."
"You don't know?" Coffin asked again.
"No."
"Whose blood is this?"
"I don't know."
"It's not yours, is it?"
Danny looked at his partner and rolled his eyes.

Someone, who didn't have a name, had brought her to the party. Someone else, who also didn't have a name, gave her something to drink. Then, she was locked in the bathroom off the master bedroom with a good sized bloody fist mark on the wall. That's what he heard her say.

Danny let the Quaker handle the rest of the questions. White girls tend to talk more when the black cop is out of sight. The troopers, for their part, cleared out shortly after Maria left the bathroom. No crime. No crime scene. Just a trail of blood.

The two of them emerged from the bedroom.

The three walked downstairs, out the central doorway, and into the squad car. Maria sat up front. Danny put the car in gear and headed back out to the Polpis Road.

She didn't know where to go. She couldn't go to the hospital or to the police station or to the strip. As she thought about it, there were more places on the island that she just couldn't go anymore. After tonight.

Danny looked in his rear view mirror at his partner. Coffin didn't look up.

"So," Danny said. Coffin still didn't look up. "To the hospital."

She froze.

"No." She said. "No hospital. Nothing happened."

"Well," Danny continued. "If nothing happened, why were you barricaded in the bathroom."

"The party was getting crazy."

"When parties get crazy, most people leave," he said. "They don't lock themselves into the master bathroom."

"I didn't get raped."

Danny almost asked if she was sure, but he didn't.

"I didn't get raped." She repeated.

"Didn't say that you did." He said.

Coffin chimed up in the back. "Let's just take her to the hospital."

Danny looked at him. "Sure."

"No." Maria barked.

At the hospital, they would call her mother. At the hospital, they would find out about her passenger. As soon as the nurses get her pants off, the stories would start. Then the whispers would fly like mosquitoes

Then they would come after her. And Julian. He would be deported back to Brazil. Her baby would have no father.

"No hospital. I won't get out."

"Why not?" The Inspector rolled back to her.

Danny backed out of the conversation.

"I don't need to go to the hospital."

"Well, probably not. But, we have this sex crimes protocol. And getting found locked in a bathroom pretty much fits. There was a good bit of blood."

"I wasn't raped."

"Then why were you locked in the bathroom?"

She didn't have an answer. Coffin let the silence dangle.

After a moment, she said. "I didn't feel safe."

"Who was threatening you?"

She shrugged.

Maria had put most of the evening away in a box. There had been a drug and a drink and everything had gone underwater. Then there was pain and it all got put in a box. It was a shoe box, from Bass shoes, and she had forced it shut.

"Hospital it is." Coffin said.

The car circled the rotary and headed up Sparks Avenue. The hospital was a half mile away.

"Nothing happened. I am not pressing charges."

The box was leaking.

"Okay." Coffin said. "We're just going to have you checked out."

"Why won't you believe me? Nothing happened!"

She stared out the window. She saw some packing tape and she wrapped the box up firmly.

"Just drop me off at the windmill." Maria said.

"No." The inspector was calm. The patrol car was in sight of Nantucket Cottage Hospital. They came to the stop sign fifty yards away.

"Because nothing happened."

"Who was threatening you?"

The car moved slowly forward. It crossed through the intersection and turned into the hospital parking lot.

"If I tell you, will you drop me at home?"

"Sure." Coffin said.

Danny looked at him in the rear view mirror. The Inspector took being a Quaker very seriously. He didn't lie.

Maria opened the box. She pulled out two names, then shut it before anything else got out. A smell escaped. Leather and beer and weed.

"Jack and Billy were hassling me."

Danny looked back at the Inspector.

"What did they want?"

"What do you think?" she said. "I am not pressing charges."

"What did they threaten you with?"

She looked at him. The box had slipped open and the whole story lay right there for her to tell. It rose up in her lap...

Then she shut the lid.

"Flashlights. They had those heavy metal lights. Mag-lites. They use the long ones."

"You've seen them before?"

She sighed. "My Dad has one?"

"Okay." Coffin leaned back. "Danny, take her home."

With an audible sigh, he put the car in gear and left the hospital.

Hidden by her leg, Maria dialed Julian one more time.

CHAPTER THREE

After Maria entered her home, Danny looked at his partner.

"She should have gone to the hospital."

"No." Coffin's word were quiet and small.

"Why not?"

He didn't know. Maria needed nurses and therapists and all sorts of people right now. The only way to get those people to her was to bring her to the hospital. But he had made the promise. And it was old man's vanity. He kept his word, even to a foolish promise.

He sighed.

"We probably should have." Coffin allowed.

"Henry, I have a daughter. If it was my daughter, and you didn't bring her in..."

"I know."

"Do you?" Danny sputtered. "You know the family, I know the family, we know the little shits that did it. Hell, we stopped them on the road. I became a cop to lock little shits like Jack up."

He was annoyed, but not truly angry. Danny trusted the old man. He was right far more often than he was wrong.

Coffin let the silence hang. There was always doubt. There were always regreets and mistakes. In the midst of all of that fog, Coffin had only wordless instinct. It lit up his heart as a guttering candle might.

The air remained warm and humid. A hurricane was threatening to come up the coast before it swung out to sea. Ahead of it, waves of humid Caribbean air billowed overhead.

Danny looked at him. "Well, it's too late now."

"Yep." The old man said. "Unfortunately."

Coffin was biting his finger and looking ahead. Both Danny and the Inspector knew a whole set of uncomfortable truths. They would have found some semen. However, there was a long leap between finding semen and getting rape charges. Then, the boys would say that she wanted it. At that point, the curtain rises and the Shitshow Overture begins.

It wasn't supposed to be this way, but that was the way it was.

"This job sucks." Danny finally said.

"Hours are nice." Coffin grinned.

The dashboard clock read four A.M.

"How do you feel about doing some authentic police work?" Danny put the car in gear.

"I suppose we could do that. Where would you like to start?"

"That was a nice house we found back there."

"Sure was."

"You'd think they would have an alarm system."

"I know that they do."

"And it was switched off, wasn't it?"

"We both saw that."

"So, maybe we can get the boys on something besides rape."

Henry picked up the radio.

"Dispatch, this is Inspector Coffin."

"Go ahead, Henry."

"Who is the contact person if the alarm goes off on that house at Abrams's Point."

"Let me look."

The line went dead.

Danny looked at him. "You know that everyone up at this hour, with a police scanner can hear us."

"Yup."

"Including our boys."

"Yup." The Inspector said. "Makes it a lot easier."

"Inspector?"

"Yes."

"All of the numbers are in the 213 area code."

"Great."

"I'm sending them to you."

"Great." Henry said.

Danny regarded him, again. The older man did not look up.

Henry spun the keyboard to the passenger seat. Three numbers popped up, all under the name of H. Field Kravits. Figuring that the top two went to a lawyer and a secretary. Henry picked the bottom number and made the call from the police car's handset.

As the line was ringing, Henry put the call on speaker within the car.

A groggy female voice picked up the phone.

"Pardon me, my sister. I am Henry Coffin and I am calling from the Nantucket Police Department."

"Who?"

"Nantucket Police, Ma'am. Is H. Field Kravits there?"

"He's asleep."

"I understand that, ma'am, but he is the contact person we have on file."

"What happened? Is something wrong at the compound?"

Danny rolled his eyes. Compound.

"I am afraid I have to talk to H. Field, ma'am."

"Is it an emergency?"

"I am afraid so."

"Wait."

On the line, there was the sound of bedsprings, steps, and a door opening. In a moment, more steps preceded a man's leonine voice.

"This is Kravits. Who I am speaking with?"

"Henry Coffin. I work for the Nantucket Police Department."

"What is your title, Mr. Coffin?"

Danny chipped in. "He is an Inspector, Mr. Kravits. I am Detective Danny Higginbotham, badge number 235."

"Inspector Coffin, what is your badge number?"

"I don't remember, Mr. Kravits," he said. "But if you doubt we are who we say we are, call 508 228 1212 and ask to speak with us."

"I will."

The line went dead.

Coffin, as part of his Quaker vanity, rarely used his title and his badge. It created awkward moments with anyone who didn't know him. Danny just thought it inane.

"He's an important guy, Henry." Danny warned.

"Aren't we all?"

"You and I can't bankrupt Bolivia."

"Doesn't make him important."

The handset buzzed.

"Phone call for you fellas." came the voice from dispatch.

"Put him through." Henry said. "Good morning, Mr. Kravits."

"What happened at the compound?"

"Mr. Kravits, we just broke up a hundred person party at your house. Unfortunately, we have to currently treat the house as a crime scene."

"Did the alarm go off?"

"No."

"No?"

"No. We would like to talk to your caretaker, but his name isn't on the file at the station. Who is your caretaker?"

"I don't know. I have all this information at the office." He said. "Listen, there are some valuable paintings in that house…"

"I don't know the extent of the damage." Coffin said. "It is important that we speak to him this morning. Do you remember anything about him?"

"Why didn't the alarm go off? Could you see if anything was taken?"

"I don't know. The caretaker could help us, I suppose, if you could give me his name?"

"I only met him once. We hired him on our contractor's recommendation." The minds of the plutocrats continued to stun Danny. He couldn't remember the name of his caretaker either. "There is a Picasso in there."

"Do you remember what he looked like?"

"Big Guy. Yellow Van. Silver earrings."

The two men looked at each other.

"Trotter?"

"It was a name like that." He said. "On the way up the stairs, up high, there is a…"

"I really couldn't say." Coffin said. "When this sort of thing happens, most people send their insurance guy through to look at it."

"Of course, of course."

"Thanks for your help, Mr. Kravits."

Inspector Coffin clicked off the phone. Danny turned the ignition.

"Ed Trotter?"

"Father of Billy. Driver and friend of cocaine."

"And not of Maria."

"Yup. Let's go see what we can find out."

Danny pulled away from the windmill and headed down Prospect.

"Notice how he didn't ask you about the crime." He said.

"Yes."

"Didn't want to know if anyone was hurt, did he?"

"He is an important person." Coffin said, with an edge. "And no insurance agent will beat him to the island."

"Why's that?"

"Because some museum, somewhere, is missing a Picasso."

Ed Trotter built his house on Newtown Road with his first wife in the late seventies. Then, in the excitement of the next two decades, he gambled on spec houses all over the island. Sometimes he gambled and won, whereupon his ex-wives would get paid. Sometimes, he gambled and lost, whereupon the banks came calling. Through it all, he kept his house on Newtown Road, his Harley-Davidson, and a pickup truck.

Newtown Road splits two rows of Cape Cod Cottages, without the benefit of much in the way of landscaping. The street is an odd suburban glitch in the midst of careful planning, historic recreations, and ancient building. It has never been and will never be one of the glamour addresses. As a result, it houses teachers, firefighters, cops, and plumbers and not the Captains of Industry. At three in the morning, they were all at home and in bed.

Danny parked in front of Trotter's yard.

"Run the lights." Henry said.

"Really?" he said. "The Chief is three houses up."

"He has seen the lights before."

"Christ, Henry." The black man said. "I don't really need another letter in my file."

"Fine." Coffin said. "Stay here and watch my hand. If I go inside, follow. If I raise my hand, turn on the lights."

Coffin stepped up the walk and rang the doorbell. Then he waited. In the still air, his breath rose like a spirit. After he counted to thirty, he rang the bell again. By the fourth ring, the door opened.

"What the fuck?" Ed was a big man, with a broad shoulders and a broad belly, long black hair pulled back, and a Red Sox jersey and sweatpants.

"Morning, my brother. Sorry to wake you."

Trotter cooled when he saw the Quaker. Coffin liked calling people "My brother." It unnerved them and it disarmed them.

"I've been up."

Henry nodded.

"Have you heard about Abram's Point?"

"Yeah. I have a phone full of messages from the guy." He said. "Frigging kids."

"You have your key, don't you?"

"Sure."

"Is Billy here?"

"He's asleep."

"Can I talk to him?"

"Why?"

Henry smiled. No point in hiding anything. "I figure he took your key, got your security code, and broke in with his friends."

"He's been here all night."

There it was. The end of the road.

"I would still like to talk with him."

"I can bring him by the station in the morning."

Henry raised his hand at the squad car. Danny put his book down, rolled his eyes, and started the lights going.

Ed looked at him.

"Why are you doing that?"

To Ed's credit, he truly didn't know. Henry resisted the urge to tell him.

"All I want to do is to have an informal conversation right here. If we go to the station, it gets more formal. We have to keep records and do stuff like that."

Ed saw the bedroom lights switch on in the next two houses.

"You're going to wake everyone up."

"Not for long."

Ed looked at the Inspector.

"Look, he's in bed and I am not waking him up. You can run the damn siren for as much as I care. Either arrest him, or leave us alone. Go away, My. Fucking. Brother."

He slammed the door.

Danny flipped off the lights.

Henry walked back down the steps and came back to the passenger side door.

"Do you want to talk to the Chief?"

"Sure."

"He's on the radio."

Coffin picked up the handset.

"Tom?" To the annoyance of his superiors, Coffin used their first names and not their titles.

"Why did you wake me up?" the voice muttered.

"I needed to put some pressure on Ed Trotter."
"Why?"
"His son may have been involved in a rape tonight."
"May?" he said. "Is she talking?"
"No."
"Is she dead?"
"No."
"Are you sure it was him?"
"No."
"Goddam you, Coffin."
The line went silent. Then, after ten-seconds, crackled back to life.
"Can't you guys go back out to the Lifesaving museum and stay out of trouble."
Danny chimed in. "We will, sir."
"Get some sleep out there."
"Goodnight sir."
The line died.
Danny put the car in gear. Time to visit the wife.

CHAPTER FOUR

By five in the morning, Nick had fallen asleep in one of the chairs. The old man remained unconscious and unaware of the nurse' prodding and poking. Elvis watched them work. They checked it off, wrote it down, prodded a bit, and left. At three in the morning, Sherrie came in and lifted up a bag full of his father's urine. It was a disturbing shade of brown, not unlike Coca Cola. She pinched off the tube, unscrewed the full plastic bag, then screwed another one on. She picked up the bag, turned, and left.

Elvis waited for five minutes. He watched the numbers rise and fall on the various electronic monitors. His father's pulse ticked on, his breathing heaved onward and life crawled onward. Then he got up and walked down the hall to the Nurse's station.

The nurse, Sherrie, stood at the desk, checking off paperwork. Behind her, on a large whiteboard, were the vital stats for the only patient on the floor. Sherrie wore what most nurses on Nantucket wore; comfortable clothes. She had on green crocs, blue scrubs, a blue shapeless top under a floral vest and a white headband. Other than her work clothes, she was a tall, elegant, dark skinned woman.

Elvis slipped up to the side of the desk. She looked up after a second. The size of the boy surprised her, especially up close.

"Pardon me?"

"Yes." She smiled brilliantly. It was a professional, charming, and warm smile that she used dozens of times a day.

"I wonder if you could answer a question." He asked.

"I could try."

"Why was my Dad's pee brown?"

She smiled at him again.

"Well," she paused. It had taken her years to learn how to tell this truth. "His liver is very sick right now. When it doesn't function right, many of the liver cells die and come out in the urine."

Elvis paused.

"Is it a bad sign?"

"Well," she calibrated her answer. "It's a sign that he is sick and his body is fighting off the infection as best it can."

"But most people don't have brown pee when they are sick."

"But your Dad is very sick." She said. "You know that."

"I know."

She had seen the dawning of grief hundreds of times. Sometimes, it popped above the horizon in the cold crystal of a winter morning. Other times, it burned slowly through the July fog then appeared and faded fitfully. More often still, it remained sealed behind a thick overcast. On Elvis, the first red, orange, and green ribbons of dawn glowed on his face. She respected that.

"Elvis," she said, warmly. "He is peeing. That's a good sign for him. That shows that his organs and his body are continuing to work."

"Okay."

"Right now, your Dad is comfortable. He isn't in any pain and his body is doing its best."

"I know."

"And you are with him."

"Yeah."

He turned and looked back down the hall.

"Thanks." He said.

"Would you like a cup of coffee? Or a ginger ale?"

"No." he said. "No, thanks."

He smiled awkwardly, backed away from the desk, and returned to his father's side.

A little less than forty minutes later, Elvis heard one quiet knock on the door.

"Yes?" he said.

The door opened on Officer Danny Higginbotham. Elvis stood for a moment.

"Can I come in?"

"Sure."

The policeman carried his hat. He reached one hand out. "I'm Danny Higginbotham."

"Elvis Lowell."

"Nice to meet you." He said. "Mind if I sit?"

"No."

"My wife." He said. "She is the duty nurse tonight. Her name is Sherrie."

"Okay."

"Who's he?" Danny gestured at the sleeping Nick Koch. Nick had leaned his head back and slept, peacefully with his mouth open wide enough for a tennis ball to go in and out.

"Nick Koch. He's a friend of mine."

"He sleeps like a pro."

"He's a good guy."

"No doubt."

Elvis didn't add anything to the moment. He was afraid he knew why the officer was here. His name had come up on a search, or his father's name. As soon as he was logged into the hospital computers, a flag would go up somewhere. He had to assume that the police knew everything and, if they knew, the Outfit knew. The cop was just trying to be a nice guy before he broke the bad news.

If he was a cop.

"How's your Dad doing?"

"I don't know."

"What's he got?"

"Cancer."

"Any particular type?"

"Not anymore."

"Where did it start?"

Elvis looked at the black man in the dark. The metal on his uniform glinted with the green lights. Elvis weighed just staying silent, but he thought talking was best.

"They found it in his pancreas, but it was probably in his stomach before that."

"How long has he had it?"

"Couple years."

"My Dad had lung cancer for seven years."

Elvis looked at him.

Danny continued. "He didn't tell me about it. He was a bastard like that. He wasn't going to let anyone do anything for him. No sir. He was going to go out not owing nobody."

Elvis wasn't sure where this was coming from or why he had to listen to it.

He spoke, nonetheless. "When was this?"

"Long time ago. Fifteen years. Maybe even more. He left my Mom when I was eight and moved to Los Angeles. I saw him once every two years or so. He flew me out there and put me up in his apartment, then in his house for a few days. Dodger games, Disney Land, Knott's Berry Farm, Universal Studio Tours."

"What did he do?"

"For a job?" Danny said. "He was a cop as well."

Elvis smiles.

"Tells you something, don't it? We don't roll too far away after all, do we?"

"I guess not."

"He was a desk cop out there. Assistant Chief for Human Resources or something like that. His donuts came to him on a cart." Danny smiled. "He pushed paper, which, y'know, isn't a bad life. 9-5, no heavy lifting, no long sits behind the wheel, just meetings, photos, and lawyers. No one shoots at him. Then, all of a sudden, when I am 25, wearing a badge, and driving around Roxbury, he comes back and takes a job in Boston. The old man appears in my squad room, wearing the dress uniform. We all thought someone had died." Danny faded off.

Elvis didn't say anything.

"I knew who he was and what he was and why he was there. We had coffee and we talked for a bit and I was with him."

"Hm." Elvis had no idea what to say.

"He was sick when he was hired, and he got sicker during the year. By the summer, the Chiefs realized that they had hired a pig in a poke, but by then he was dying and there was nothing they could do about it. He went into the hospital, for the last time, in July. I was with him, until he died, in November."

Danny paused. He realized that he had gone down a path he didn't want to go down and he found himself in a familiar frozen swamp. It was a tough year. It had been cold, but snowless. They were still doing the Big Dig, the Patriots were just getting good, Sherrie was pregnant, and life eroded from his father in little green beeps and waves.

"It meant something to him." He lied. "It meant something to have me with him. He had company then."

The boy nodded.

Danny held his tongue. He was about to repeat the wisdom that he had been told: "You only became a man when your father died." But this father was not dead and this boy was not a man. He wasn't sure if it was true, either.

Instead, he said "You are doing good work, here. You are being a good son."

The big boy looked over. "Thanks."

Danny nodded.

Maria also could not sleep. A quarter moon painted the floor to her room in a delicate blue.

Alone in her bed, her mind touched on what she remembered of the night. It was a scar that she couldn't help but touch; an abscessed tooth that her tongue slipped to and poked until pain bled through her mouth.

She saw the kitchen, she saw the stairs, she remembered the bed.

And Julian. For a moment.

The pain pulsed and throbbed.

It was all there. She knew it. The box that she carried on her lap was full of horrible things. There was no good peeking into it.

So, instead she looked out her window at the windmill and watched the stars move past the vanes.

With tears.

He was out there. Somewhere.

CHAPTER FIVE

The phone buzzed for ten minutes straight. Bleary with sleep, Pink looked at it, then pulled it to him.

He knew the number. Well.

"Pink's taxi."

"Hey, Pink."

"Hey, yourself."

"Do you think you could give me a ride this morning?"

"Where to?"

"You know."

He sighed.

"Where shall I take you?"

"Oh. To Essex."

"Be there in ten."

"You're a life saver."

"Have your money ready."

Three hours of sleep hung on Pink. He would need to get the boys to drive this afternoon while he crashed. They owed him that.

More than that, he needed to get his brother on board with the sale of the land. If the two of them could get together, then his sister….

He stood in the kitchen, drank a Diet Coke, then tossed it in the trash. He had stopped recycling after the divorce. He also had stopped the tofu, the lawn mowing, and the TV watching. He didn't care if he saw Law and Order ever again.

He went to his closet, pulled on a shirt, found a pair of pressed pants, picked up his cellphone, his keys, and his iPod.

Within five minutes of getting call, he was on his way. A low level of morning fog hung five feet off the ground. Pink drove under it, until the road rose up into it, and then dipped back under.

She lived on Gray Avenue. At seven in the morning, she stood at the end of the driveway, smoking. She was thin, and could still be attractive if there wasn't an animal in her eyes. When he pulled up, she glanced back at the house.

The kids must have been watching a show.

She knew enough to toss the cigarette before she got in.

Wordlessly, he put the car into drive. The iPod was letting Lady Day live long enough to "Bless the child who has his own." His passenger dropped an envelope on the passenger seat.

The Russian had a great system. Pink tipped his cap to him. Pink pulled his cab into Essex Road and drove 500 yards. At which point, a man would walk off a porch and approach the window and Pink would hand him the money. The man (it could be any of five guys) checked it, nodded, then Pink drove around the corner to the end of the street when someone on a bike or a skateboard would drop a package in his open window. The drop off was so good that Pink didn't need to even slow down. Then, once a month, someone would wordlessly ride with him from Essex to the airport and leave a fat envelope in the backseat.

It was a hell of a lot more efficient than wholesaling to drunken high school kids. And Pink knew who took all of the risk and who made most of the money.

Today, a girl rode by on her bike and dropped the package through the open window. His passenger reached for it before they had traveled fifty yards.

"You have to wait."

"I know."

"You have to wait or I won't ever give you a ride again."

"I know."

"Don't open it."

"I won't."

In the rearview, he watched her stare. If she could inject the heroin through her eyes, she would have done it.

Driving quickly and just legally, he got her back to Gray Avenue.

She left a ten on the seat and jogged inside.

Enjoy Spongebob, kids.

By seven that Friday morning, Maria was having a very nice dream. She was floating on a green air mattress in a big warm pool, spinning in circles and napping. When she was shaken from it, she opened one eye and saw her mother.

"You've got a problem, girl."
"What?"
"Downstairs."
"Let me shower."
"No way."
Maria knew where this was going.
"Well, I'm going to the bathroom."
"Piss and downstairs."

She rolled out of the warm bed and plodded into the bathroom. On the weekend, they generally let her sleep until the clock was in double digits. Not this morning.

She sat on the toilet. She didn't care.

It could be anything, but the matter at hand. She came in late. The police dropped her off. She used her father's razor. Her underwear wasn't folded correctly.

She didn't really care. She had nothing to say.

A tentative knock hit the door.
"What."
"Mimi?" Her eight year old brother, James, stood outside.
"Yes, Pooh."
"My show is about to start."
"Okay."
"Mom and Dad want to yell at you."
"I know. I'll be right down. You go watch your show."

She stood, washed her hands, and hoped for the best. Out the window, the sky had grown overcast. The trees were rattling in the wind and it looked cold.

Downstairs, they stood in the kitchen, leaning against the counter. They had set a place for her breakfast and had put the cereal boxes on the table.

Her mother was wrapped in a gigantic, stained, polar fleece bathrobe. Her father was in a t-shirt, carharts, and a baseball cap.

She knew her role in this play. She stood at the base of the stairs and waited for her cue.

"Is there anything you want to tell us?"
"Good morning."
"Is there something going on in your life that we should know about?"
"No."

She sat down at her place at the table. The list that she could say, this morning, was so impressive there was no need to be scared. Her mother could have found the pregnancy test, a police report, or her English grade. The last time this drama staged, it was because she had shaved herself and her mother discovered the hair.

"You're becoming an adult, Maria. You need to think about living your life honestly. When you lie, you hide from adulthood."

Maria looked up at that moment. It's impossible that she could even begin to believe that bullshit.

"What is it?" Maria asked.

"Your mother is asking you a question." Her father was preternaturally calm.

"Ok. There is nothing going on in my life that you need to know about."

"Should." She said. "I asked if there was anything we should know about."

"No." She said.

"Is there any grand secret that you want to keep from us?" The sarcastic ice cubes clinked in her mother's glass. "Because I don't want to pry into something so secret that it would scar you for life."

"What is it, Mom?"

"No grand secrets? Nothing for the psychotherapist?"

"What is it, Mom?"

"Okay, then." She shrugged dramatically at her husband. "It must be simple."

Rosie walked over to her daughter and sat in a nearby chair. "Yesterday, when I did your laundry, I found this."

Rosie placed a shiny, sparkling, krugerrand on the table.

"Do you know what this is?"

Maria's heart spun. On one hand, it wasn't a positive pregnancy test. On the other hand….

"It looks like a coin."

"Where did you get this?"

"I found it."

"Where did you find it?"

"I found it at school."

"At school?"

"It was on the floor in the main hall."

Her father straightened up off the counter.

"I'm taking your door off." Her father spoke.

"What?"

"You are lying to us and I can't trust you if you lie."

"You can't take my door off."

"I'm doing it at lunch time. Good-bye door."
"You can't do that."
"You're not honest. You're not talking to us."
"Fuck you."
Both parents looked at her. Her rage had slipped off the handcuffs and was arming itself.
"Who gave it to you, then?" Rosie asked.
"No one."
"Bullshit."
"No one." She replied. "I found it."
Harry leaned over the table.
"Do you even know what that is?"
"It's a coin."
He picked it up and held it by the edges.
"It's one pure ounce of South African gold. It was mined by slave labor to prop up a racist regime."
"I don't believe you."
"The only people who use this are drug dealers."
"Bullshit."
"You know what gold is worth per ounce this morning?"
"No."
"About 854 dollars."
He put the coin on the table.
"So, I would like to know who gave my baby girl a thousand dollars of drug money?"
"I found it."
"I have watched you try to lie for sixteen years. You can't fool me." Rosie said. "And you are lying to me."
"I found it at school." She said. "If I thought it was valuable, do you think I would have left it in my jeans."
"Yes. You are a moron." Rosie said. "Especially if you keep lying."
"I am not lying."
For a moment, for the briefest of seconds, she thought of putting it all right there on the table. Julian, the baby, even the party last night. Blast their minds out. A cooler head prevailed and she kept her mouth shut.
"Goodbye door." Rick said.
"Okay, then." Maria said. "Goodbye door."
"Give me your phone."
"No." She said.
"There are too many lies, Maria. You have to give it up."

"No." Her voice shook.

"I'm just going to take it." Her father said. He moved to pull out the chair.

Something slipped and broke inside her. Maria bolted to her feet and scared both of her parents.

"Do you really want the phone? Really?" She shouted. Maria shoved past her startled father and went to the sink. She picked up a cast iron skillet, then put her phone on the counter.

"Okay, you can have it In. Just. A. Minute."

From her waist, Maria brought the pan above her head, then hammered it onto the phone and the kitchen counter.

Plastic from the phone flew against the wall. She let the frying pan fall to the floor.

Then she dropped the mangled phone in the green water with the frog.

For the first time in a day, she felt solid.

James wandered into the kitchen. "Mimi, are you okay?"

"I am going to stay home today, James."

"Okay."

Detective Higginbotham watched Rosie pull into her parking place. She rested her head against the steering wheel. When Rosie finally looked up, Henry saw how blotchy, tired, and wet her face was. With one hand, she wiped her tears, then ran her fingers through her hair. She collected her papers, opened the door, and inched out.

She looked at the Inspector. "Don't say a fucking thing."

Henry shrugged. He took some of the books from her and the two of them walked inside. At her office, a line of twelve middle schoolers waited.

They had known each other a long time. There had been a time when there were no children, no spouses, and no tears. Then they all arrived in a slow procession. Now, Henry Coffin stood beside her and he held a grenade.

"Kids," she said. "I am going to need some time to get myself together. Go to class and come back in ten minutes."

They looked at her, then they looked at the Inspector.

He smiled, but they didn't return the favor.

Rosie opened her office, dropped her bag and books into one of the chairs, then sat at her desk. Henry slipped in and closed the door.

She stared at him. They stood in silence for a few minutes.

"I see her being stupid, I tell her that she is being stupid. I show her how she is being stupid. I will reward her when she doesn't do the stupid thing. Then, she does the stupid thing." She said. "And that isn't the worst part. I see her running to the cliff, jumping off, then turning in midair, at that Wile E. Coyote moment and flipping me off with such satisfaction."

"Does she sleep at night?"

"Like a rock."

"Snore?"

"A little."

"You're lucky."

She sighed. "I guess." She leaned back and thought of the silence that wrapped itself around the Inspector. She thought of the little boy who stepped off the dock and never came back. "I'm sorry, Henry." She said. "I don't know anything."

"It's fine."

"Not really." She responded.

He paused and looked out the window at the incoming middle school kids.

"No, but what are you going to do?" he shrugged.

She sighed and ran her fingers through her hair.

"She's in ninth fucking grade."

"Is that what they call it these days?"

"I grind up her birth control and sprinkle it in her Captain Crunch." She said.

"Maybe you should put it in her beer."

"As long as it gets in her before some wayward drippy dick does." Rosie sipped her coffee. "Henry, let me ask you a question."

"Okay."

"Why does my daughter have this in her jeans?"

Rosie held the gold coin up. The Inspector took it from her and examined it.

"Don't see many of these." He said.

"I wouldn't think so." Rosie replied. "Rick thinks it is from a drug dealer."

"What does Maria say?"

"She says she found it in the hall."

"Okay..." he said. "Did you wash it?"

"Yeah."

He put it on her desk.

"Can't you CSI it or something?"

"There won't be any prints on there that we could use. Yours, mine, maybe Maria's."

"Who gave it to her?"

"I don't know." Coffin said. "I'll ask her."

He picked the coin back up and put it in his shirt pocket.

The Inspector sat in one of the student chairs in the front office of the high school. Four cheerleaders stood in front of the secretary's desk, fine tuning an announcement. Others in jeans, sweatshirts and baseball caps pushed in the door, signed in late with another secretary, glanced at Coffin, then shuffled out the door again. Everybody looked tired and beat after the football game. There was a reason why they usually played on the weekend.

The Inspector picked up the paper. The Cape Cod Times had a full picture of a football player picking up another and about to throw him aside. The headline read "Island Giant" and the caption detailed how "Elvis Lowell, of Nantucket, was tossing aside David Roberto, of Seekonk." And he was. The boy was a good six inches off the ground and Elvis, with a savage leer, was looking into the camera.

In ten minutes, the chronically late had been chronicled, the announcements announced, and teachers substituted. The crowd wandered away and revealed Ginny MacVicar. She had been secretary here for 35 years, ever since the Monday after she graduated. Tides of students and staff had washed up against her desk, and then ebbed out into the corridor and life.

The Inspector knew her well. He had pulled her boys over for DUI more than once, then returned them safely to their mother's house. He had talked her ex-husband into taking a walk before it all went bad. He had brought her the news of his death in a scallop boat. They knew each other well.

She looked up from her desk.

"How can I help you, Inspector?"

"I need to talk to a student."

"And..."

"I could use a visitor's pass."

She nodded. 'You know the drill?"

"Of course."

She pressed a button on her phone.

"Homer?"

"Yes."

"Inspector Coffin is here for a Visitor's pass."
"Would you send him in?"

Had Calvin or Jonathan Edwards envisioned a high school principal, they would have seen Homer. He was 6'3" with a wild shock of white hair, suspenders, dark suits, and eyes that picked up the dark sins of his soul.

.Homer stood in his office confronting a pristine desk. No paraphernalia of any kind was on the desk, other than the standard issue telephone. If he could have the phone removed, he would. One file folder had been placed, then squared to the right hand corner of the blotter. Behind him on a three year old computer, a screensaver bounced geometric patterns over a monitor and several diplomas lined down the wall, all aligned to the center point. The room looked rented.

Homer had retired from a school in New York State, retired to a fishing rod, a golf club, and grandchildren. Then, through the miracle of divorce and the comedy of island living, he began his second stint as a parent and as principal. He claimed to have a suitcase packed and the lease broken, if ever the moment came.

"How can I help you, Inspector?"
"I want to talk to one of your students."
"Which one?"
"Is it important for you to know?"
"Well, yes."
"He hasn't done anything illegal."
"Just so."
Coffin spoke quickly. "Tommy Kelly."

Homer looked at the quiet policeman. He had never been entirely comfortable with him. He also was one of the only men to use his Christian name.

"Your not going to tell me what he has done?"
"He hasn't done anything."
"Then why do you want to talk to him?"
Homer sat in his chair. Coffin remained standing.
He shrugged.
Homer cleared his throat.

"We've had this problem before, Henry." He said. "I don't really like the police in my school. You get everyone just a little bit too jumpy."

"I can stay right here and someone can go get him." He said. "I can talk to him in the hall."

"Shouldn't he have a lawyer?"

"Look, Homer…" Coffin said. "Tommy saw a crime last night. I need to talk to him about it."

"But why do you have to talk to him here?"

"It's a good place. I can talk to him without his friends."

"You could bring him to the station."

"There's absolutely no need for that drama."

"You could go to his home."

"I could, but most parents get pretty jumpy at seeing a squad car pull up. Some fathers tend to have bad reactions."

Homer picked up the hint. He sat back in his chair and frowned.

"Was he at a party?"

"Homer…" Henry Coffin looked out the window at Danny and the squad car. "Do I lie to you?"

"Not directly. But you tend to leave things out."

"Some things I can't say. Just like there are many things you can't say. We both do work that puts us in the way of personal, horrid and mundane secrets. And we both old enough and have seen enough of the world to know how petty and silly these secrets are."

"Sometimes."

"And we know how silly and petty some of the rules we have to enforce are. Like tardies and bathroom passes."

"This isn't about tardies."

"I know."

"You bring chaos, Henry. You always do."

"Trust me, Homer."

"Those are famous last words." The principal smiled briefly. "Why don't you go to the conference room? We'll call him down."

Before school had begun, young Tommy Kelly was outside. He smelled Jack. The sweet marijuana smell came over the field house next to the football field. The smoke hung low to the ground in the warm September air, like a low level fog.

He rounded the corner and there were ten of them standing there. They were all older than he was, all faced Jack and Billy, and all had fallen silent as they eyed him.

Jack inhaled. "Tommy was there with us."

They looked at him, now, with a difference.

"Boy's been blooded." Billy took the joint from his friend and inhaled, then he handed it over to young Tommy. Gratefully, he accepted the gift and sucked in hungrily.

The other boys regarded him with new eyes.

"Show them the pictures."

Tommy took out his phone and handed it over. The boys huddled over its screen and snickered. Tommy felt the weed work through him; his fingertips tingled suddenly.

Then a bell rang in the distance. They all ground their smokes into the grass, then trudged up to the school.

When Tommy settled into his first period class and took out his history book, he realized how stoned he was. And he realized that he no longer had his phone.

The conference room had been assembled from an IKEA catalog. The chairs had orange cushions, chrome rails and the dusty of the disco era. The white walls had been decorated with three rows of team photos and four large plaques that weren't quite good enough to make the main corridor. It was a room for mission statements, budget reconciliations, and department head meetings; it was where good intentions went to die.

The Inspector patrolled the photos of long since defeated golf and baseball champions. He knew many faces.

The door opened and Tommy Kelly entered. He still had his baby fat and hadn't gotten the height that he would have wanted. Indeed, he hadn't gotten much that he wanted. He wore a flannel shirt, and jeans that hung halfway off his butt. He also sported a backwards Atlanta Falcons baseball hat. He sat in the chair at the head of the table.

"How do you feel?" Coffin asked him without turning to look at him.

"I'm fine."

"Really?"

"Sure."

"I am hoping you can tell me something about last night."

"Nothing to say."

"Why were you out at three in the morning?"

"We were watching the waves."

"Don't lie, my friend. Never lie. When you lie, you say to the other man that you are afraid of him and afraid of what he will do when he learns the truth."

"I'm not lying."

The Inspector smiled.

"Why are you afraid of me?"

"I'm not afraid."

"But you lied to me. Why are you afraid of me? As you say, I don't arrest anybody."

"I'm not afraid."

The paranoia started to build in the boy. The inspector could see how stoned he was. He couldn't even sit still.

Tommy was silent for a full thirty-seconds while he thought of things to say.

"Okay." Henry took out his own cell phone.

"What are you doing?"

"I am calling your Dad."

"Why?"

"To see whether you are telling me the truth." Henry said. "What is his cell number?"

"I am not going to tell you."

"Why not?"

"Because…"

"I can just find him out working, I suppose." Coffin said. "Then I can ask what you were doing out late, with the boys you were with, and why you didn't want to tell me his phone number. How is that going to work for you?"

The boy stared at him, flummoxed.

Henry spoke slowly. "I am interested, Tommy, and I like to ask questions. When I get bored, I stop. But I'm not bored right now and I don't really think you want me walking through your life, asking questions."

The truth pressed down against Tommy's chest. The boy saw the pictures on his phone again and the images from that night. And Billy and Jack.

He was one hundred percent aware of what the two of them could do.

So, Tommy swayed and didn't speak.

"Nothing happened. We watched surf." Tommy repeated.

The Inspector sighed. He considered the boy and thought about how old he was.

"Okay, we'll talk later."

"No need."

"Thanks for your time."

Tommy turned and walked back to the classroom.

CHAPTER SIX

In the halls, Jack and Billy walked alone.

Everyone knew. Everyone had heard. Everyone knew there were pictures. Some thought there was a YouTube Video. Some claim to have seen it.

No one really believed it.

No one disbelieved it.

It was crazy.

Jack and Billy were in school. They looked wired and happy and just a little bit greasy.

They collected glances, but no stares. Silence accompanied them like a smell. Feet eased a step or so away.

The boys themselves moved with the insolence of lions and the boredom of sharks.

Mr. Brody eyed the two young men in his fifth period class. They sat together on the far side of the circle. They whispered to each other and nodded.

Brody knew why. Today was a day when he had come to school on straight and hungry, as a result, he was irritable, annoyed, and quite focused on his dosed up Iced Tea back at the house.

Still, he took attendance, collected homework, and glanced at the chapter for a moment.

"What do we know about Pip?" he asked from one blackboard.

"He's an orphan." Said one.

"He's a thief." Said another.

"He helped out a convict." Said a third.

"He's a pussy." Said Jack. Brody, aware of the silence that came from both Jack speaking and the word that Jack said, wrote the word on the board.

Then he turned on him.

"Why do you say that?"

"Because he is."

"Why do you believe that?"

"Because he's called Pip. And he's tiny."

"That's only in the movie."

"He's called Pip in the book, too."

Brody grinned at the boy, but he did not smile.

"Let's think about this. Let's add some other stuff to the list." Brody turned back to the board. "In addition to being an orphan, a thief, and someone who helps convicts escape, he is also." The former Ranger began writing in his very neat style. "An apprentice blacksmith."

He turned back to the class. "This means he spends all day with a hammer, banging metal in a hot forge. He has to walk everywhere, he doesn't eat much, doesn't wash much, and has three changes of clothes. So, think of him as smelly, but thin, cut, and with a set of pythons."

The class smiled.

"Jack, come out here." Brody's voice was lighthearted.

The class stopped smiling.

Jack looked at his friend, rolled out of his desk and stood in the center of the desks.

"You will be the 'Young gentleman' who we'll later learn is Matthew Pocket and I will be Pip."

"Why are you Pip?"

"Because I can put on a gun show and you cannot."

"Please."

"Show us those little noodles you have and tell me about it."

Jack was wearing a short sleeved shirt. His thin arms were visible to everyone.

"Okay." Brody continued. "Matthew Pocket and Pip have a fight, which Dickens and everyone else makes fun of. But you should pay attention to two things Dickens shows you, but doesn't explain."

Brody squared up to Jack. He put both fists up in an old style fighting position. He moved Jack's fists into the same position.

"Jack, are you familiar with Rouchambeau?"

The boy backed up and covered up his belt. "Don't you do that."

"Thought you were."

The class giggled.

"Old school fighting was like that. Two men stood up in a tight circle a little bigger than a manhole cover with their fists up. They couldn't move their feet. If you stepped out of the circle, you lost." Brody pulled Jack back up close to him and set his fists. "So when Pip and Pocket set up for a scrap, there could be a serious beating coming."

Brody and Jack eyed each other over their fists. The moment lasted a beat too long and Jack faked a punch. Brody, using very old training, slapped him gently on the cheek.

Jack stepped back.

"Round one to me." Brody said.

"No." the boy snapped back. "You can't hit me."

"I didn't hit you. A brief tap."

Jack looked at him

Brody said. "Step back in."

Jack came back and set his hands.

"Go ahead."

The boy telegraphed a half jab and the former Ranger tapped it out of the way. Then he faked with his left and swung more seriously with his right. Brody tapped him on the cheek as the boy missed and went spinning.

"Round two, to me."

Billy sniggered.

"Shut up." Jack snapped at him.

Brody slipped back into position. "Do you see how the fight Pip and Pocket had was a lot more serious than was let on? In the book, Pip beats the snot out of the kid. Which I will not do. Ready?"

Jack was ready. He jabbed quick, but Brody moved and tapped him three times on the same cheek. The boy took a step back.

"Round three to me."

More giggles from Billy. No one else in the class would speak.

"No."

"Can't move your feet."

"This is ridiculous."

"Maybe Pip wasn't that much of a pussy, then? Was he?"

"Put 'em up."

Brody raised his hands and watched the angry, embarrassed boy. He watched the boy's weight shift and caught the knee on the upswing. He helped it along and raised it above the boy's waist.

"Only punching in these fights. Kneeing and kicking is how sluts fought. To use a Dickensian term."

Billy loved the word "sluts."

"Round four. To me."

Brody settled the boy back on two feet and stepped back. Then he raised his hands, again.

Jack raised his fists, stood close, and jabbed straight. It was a good, strong punch. Brody slapped that same cheek again and stepped in to let the roundhouse go behind his head. The boy lost his balance and the man caught him.

They were in the ridiculous position of two dancers in mid-tango. Jack was in mid-dip, with his arm around Brody's head. Brody held his partner by the waist.

"You're a wonderful dancer, Jack. You would make a great leading lady."

The man pulled the boy up and stood him on his feet.

Billy continued to giggle, but the boy, Jack, was white in the face.

Brody thought about it. He thought about letting the boy take a swing and then, of course, following up. He felt the warrior within him scream for it.

But not here and not now.

"Sit down, Jack. I am done with you."

He turned his back on the boy.

Maria skipped out of the house for lunch and walked down to Amigo's. She wasn't supposed to leave and someone, somewhere, would find out and tell her parents. It was dumb to leave and she didn't even like burritos.

But.

Julian could be there.

Not today.

She stood alone, waiting and looking. But there was no Julian.

Instead, a thin red headed man with a months worth of growth on his chin stared at her from across the street. He was a working man, with overalls, Dunham boots, and a dirty t-shirt. He smiled briefly and crossed the street.

She wanted to leave the instant he looked at her. Instead, she stayed rooted.

"Are you Maria?"

"Yeah." She tried to give him a look.

"I have someone who wants to talk to you."

"About what?"

"Julian."

She softened for a second at the sound of his name, and then hardened.

"Who wants to talk to me?"

"His….friends."

"His Dad, you mean." She was sharper than she should have been. The waiting line looked at her.

"Can we just step over to the truck?"

She looked at him, and nodded. Each step weighed on her.

The two crossed a crowded Broad Street to a black Toyota half ton pickup, with tinted side windows. The door had a broad yellow sign saying "Steven Graves Caretaking and H.V.A.C." The roof and rack were stacked with ladders, its bed was filled with mowers and parts, just like every other pickup on island. However, unlike every other pickup, the windows were entirely tinted.

"Who are you?" She asked.

"Steven Graves."

She nodded.

"I've worked with your Dad."

"You still owe him money."

He smiled. "No, my father does. He ran off."

Maria crossed her arms.

Graves pointed to the crew cab. "Would you come over?"

"I'm not getting in."

"No. Not at all. You and I will stand outside."

Graves steered her to the front tire while he stood next to the rear window. The window cracked open.

She heard whispered words.

"I am going to translate for both of you, if you don't mind. Julian's friends prefer to stay out of the way for now. We hope that you don't mind."

It was insane. Yet the two of them faced each other as if this was completely normal.

"That's fine." She leaned an elbow against the car and stared into the dark windshield.

"We think you are very beautiful." Graves said.

"That's very nice." Maria didn't have time for this.

"We're wondering if you have seen Julian today?"

Her stomach fell. They didn't know where he was either.

Or they were lying.

"No."

"Did you see him last night?"

"No."

"He did not come back home last night. Do you know where he is?"

She felt the ground swirl. They had no idea where he was.

She shook her head, then, as if pulled by gravity, she fell away from the car and crossed the street. Each step took some thinking.

They were silent in the truck, with their hands on their knees.

CHAPTER SEVEN

In the afternoon, after all the buses had pulled through the school parking lot, Pink pulled up and waited at the front door. Jack had sent the text--"Busy?"--an hour before and Pink had responded diligently. He would, as usual, bring Jack on his own turn up Essex Road and back before practice started. Blow was apparently on the training regimen for many of the Whalers and Jack was more than happy to supply.

However, Pink was a good deal more interested in the coins that Jack had found. They were one solid ounce of gold. They also were, as he suspected, numbered, tracked, and highly illegal. "Illegal" wasn't that much of a problem for Pink, but the attention that these coins got was very much a problem. Pink had absolutely no doubt that everyone in the police department knew what he did on Essex Road. Hell, three cops lived on Essex. They had to know. His crime was well camouflaged. No one really noticed what he did.

But Jack could change all that. Jack believed that he could just turn invisible whenever he wanted. For example, the police would be very interested in what Jack was going to bring to the locker room. Everyone from the Secret Service through the FBI, down to the liberal ladies in the elementary school would be interested in the South African coins.

Pink liked boring. Jack wasn't boring.

When Jack appeared, Pink had yet to decide on how to broach the subject.

The boy slid open the sliding door on the minivan and sat in the rear seat.

"Where to?"

"Essex."

Pink pulled away from the curb and into the school traffic. Jack looked down at his phone.

"How did the day go?"

The boy shrugged.

"How is that kid Tommy?"

"Fine."

"Can he keep his mouth shut?"

"Sure."

In his rear view mirror, Pink looked at the boy.

"Do you want to make some money?" Pink asked.

Jack looked out the window. "I am not going to drive this fucking thing tonight."

"I mean real money."

"Sure."

"I can get you a hundred bucks for every one of those coins you gave me."

"Yup." Jack's enthusiasm rattled on the floor

"Do you have any more?"

"Maybe. I don't think so."

"They're illegal. No one straight will take them in the country, never mind on island. The Secret Service tracks them."

"Who?"

"The Secret Service."

"So I should take them off E-Bay?"

Pink almost stopped the car. The boy was joking.

"They are a federal crime, Jack."

"Yup."

"I can clean them up for cash."

"I'll look in my pants pockets."

Pink looked once more at the boy in the back. They had turned onto Essex and someone was approaching the window.

"You do that."

Jack had other things on his mind. There was the girl who got away. Maria. She was on his mind. He didn't like the look she had in class. And she shouldn't have that look. No sirree, not after the Double Trouble that she almost had. Most girls, after a Double Trouble, keep themselves the fuck out of the way. But there she was.

Perhaps she didn't remember.

Jack smiled. He remembered.

Right after Maria, Tommy Kelly was lined right up. He had talked to the cop today and he hadn't said anything. Jack didn't know, for sure, what Tommy had said or hadn't. There was a lot he could say. He had a lot of stories.

And he had been there.

He had heard that sound. It reminded him of hitting a baseball bat against a rotten tree. It was a sound that you knew immediately as you heard it. Couldn't ever mistake it for something else as long as you lived.

Tommy had taken pictures. He couldn't tell where the pictures had gone. Jack had wanted one picture in particular and he still had that. The last thing he wanted, the very last thing, was that any of the other pictures come out. He had erased them off this phone, save for one.

And that one he was sure to remember.

Tommy might even go to the front of the line. His phone would soon go into the harbor, but Tommy might just go to the front of the line. He might get some Double Trouble of his own.

The biggest thing on Jack's mind didn't have a number or a name. It was lying in the woods off of the Milestone Road.

Pink dropped him off at the front door. Jack was going to complain about the walk to the locker room, but he didn't. Too much was in his head.

Instead, he stuck his head back in the car. "Pink, could you pick me up after practice?"

"Sure. Why?"

"I have to get the jeep."

"Okay."

"One more thing." Jack said. "Could you pick up Tommy Kelly?"

"With pleasure."

CHAPTER EIGHT

Coffin lived in a graceful, brick Federal mansion built by one of his whaling owner forebears. It pushed itself right up to the sidewalk on Main Street, but hid its windows behind curtains and shutters. Every fall and spring, contractors studied the house, created their own home repair projects, then wrote thesis length bills which they submitted to tenured accountants.

Otherwise, the house remained silent. The Inspector didn't know what would happen to it when he died. Presumably, the contractors would still get paid and some cousin would move in for the summer.

Since he had assumed the night shift, Henry Coffin had grown used to sleeping in the morning. He collapsed within minutes of walking in the front door, then slowly rose from the sheets in the middle of the afternoon. It solved the problem of what to do with the day.

That Friday, at three in the afternoon, Henry dressed in a clean shirt and jeans that had another couple days worth of wearing. With a glance back inside the house, he closed the door and entered September.

He walked up a quieter Main Street. The summer had slowed and the fall had ceased. Two weeks ago, the road would have been lined with Volvos and Land Rovers from Connecticut and New Jersey. Now there was the odd Ford Escort and the first fall of leaves.

Three or four people watched him walk up the street, but they did not approach nor did they wave. They were not unfriendly. The Inspector was a marker of the island, just like the Fire Chief and the head of the English department. Henry noticed and nodded.

Otherwise, the buildings on Main Street were dark. Most of the old houses had been bought by hedge fund managers and their clients. They sent the wives, the decorators, the architects, and the lawyers down to throw money like breadcrumbs. When the birds came, the re-modeling and re-visioning were undertaken. When the two weeks in August came, the house was full of happy and entertaining plutocrats, everything whirred, purred and sparkled. By mid-September, the plutocrats had returned to Greenwich on their Gulfstreams and the houses fell to darkness.

Save for one.

Henry made the turn at the Hadwen House and walked down Pleasant Street. Once upon a time, this street had candle factories and rich man's houses at one end, and "New Guinea" at the other. Black, Brown, Portuguese, or Catholic, you lived at the base of the hill. Today, the only difference between one address and the other was the plane you flew in on.

Henry turned right at Mill Hill, passed the windmill, and walked into the DeSalvo's driveway.

Twenty years ago, when Rick and Rosie DeSalvo had first moved to the island, they bought an old summer house, winterized it, patched the holes and settled in. Henry Coffin had been there, with plaster in his hands and paint on his shirt. The house stood the test of time, although the wind had flicked the paint away, chip by chip. The neighbors, however, had brand spanking new cedar shingles.

Rick was planing a door behind the house. In jeans and a bright red t-shirt, he leaned hard into the wood. He was a small, wiry, hairy man with the body metabolism of a ferret. He bounced, moved, shifted, and wiggled. Like several others, he was a PhD carpenter. Long ago, he and Rosie had come to the island in the summer to work while his dissertation stayed on the desk. Then, the desk became a changing table, and the dissertation moved to the bookshelf. When they bought this house, the dissertation moved to the top of a closet as he spent his waking hours swinging a hammer, climbing a ladder, or changing a diaper. He still kept it, of course. Fifteen years too late and deep in the midst of obscurity, he kept it like a road less traveled, hoping that he should go back there one day. He often thought of it as he watched baseball games in the evening.

Rick did not hear the older man approach. Coffin thought of what he should say, and of what he should do. He had had his share of beers on the front porch. Then time broke, Petey died and Beth left. The years built and grew.

There were things he should say, but he did not.

Rick pushed the wood plane up the side of the door. "How can I help you, Inspector?"

"I was hoping to talk to your daughter. She doesn't answer the phone."

"There's a reason for that." He pointed to a beam inside his garage. Six feet up, a Nokia flip phone had been nailed onto it.

"Were you tired of paying the bills?"

"I thought she should get off the grid." He said. "You can find her computer in the back of my pick-up."

Henry smiled. "You think this will work?"

"For today." Rick added. "If it doesn't, she doesn't get the door back on her room." He looked at the older, heavier man. "What do the police want with her?"

"I need to ask her about some kids at school."

"What trouble are they in?"

"I don't know. She isn't in any." Coffin said. What he didn't say hung in the air.

"Is this about the kruggerand?"

"No." Coffin answered. "But I will ask about it."

"Do you mind if I sit with the two of you?" The carpenter tried to hide his concern.

"Yes."

Rick stopped smiling and turned on the cop.

"Henry…."

"If there was a…police…. problem with Maria, I would let either you or Rosie know. I need to know about someone else."

Rick put the plane down. "I think I have a right to sit with her when the police question her." He folded his arms. The years climbed back up between them.

"My brother," Henry said. "She hasn't done anything wrong. She may know something to help someone else out and she probably doesn't even think it is important. But if you, the angry Dad, sit next to me, she won't tell me what month it is."

"How about Rosie?"

"Rick, I need her to trust me."

"And she doesn't trust her parents?"

"Show me the fourteen year old who does," he said. "Especially without her bedroom door."

Rick looked at the old man and held his gaze. Then he nodded.

Maria had watched the Inspector since he first had walked down the sandy driveway.

She sat on the edge of her bed, in her doorless room and looked at the empty place where there had once been a computer.

It meant nothing to her.

The phone, the computer, the door meant nothing while Julian was missing.

From her room, she imagined the glint of gold.

"Maria" her father called inside. "Cop is here to talk to you."

She came downstairs. James was sitting at the kitchen table watching Bob the Builder while her mother was pounding chicken breasts.

Rosie didn't even look up.

Coffin walked her out the driveway to the mill. All through the summer, the Historic Association sent out volunteers to set the sails on and run the mill. As soon as Labor Day broke on the calendar, the sails came in, the vanes became sticks and the mill turned still.

These days, the mill just brought Julian back to her. Standing triumphant atop the steering arm, he waved to her. He wasn't there.

She felt that she should be angrier at the Inspector. She felt that she should throw off a set of adolescent pouts and stomps, but at this point, after this day, she was just tired.

They sat on the bench behind the mill.

"So." She said.

"You lost the door to your room."

"Yup."

"Why?"

She shrugged.

"You lost your phone, your computer, and your door?"

"Yup."

"Why?"

"You'd have to ask them."

Coffin nodded.

"I may have a kid who can tell what happened that night."

"So."

"So, then you could press charges and we could arrest them."

"I am not pressing charges."

"You should."

"Believe me, it is the last thing I want to deal with right now."

The Inspector weighed that. He wasn't sure what could be worse than going to school, everyday, with the boys that raped you.

"What else is going wrong?"

Maria glared at him from behind the castle walls. She had thought of asking him to find Julian. However, asking the police department to find an illegal alien seemed like a bad idea. Almost as bad as bringing her pregnant ass to the hospital for a rape kit.

The Inspector was waiting for her answer.

"It's just a big mess right now."

"That big?"

"That big."

"Is this part of the mess?" Coffin produced the kruggerand.

Maria felt her heart skid.

"No." she said. "I found that in the school. On the floor."

"Don't lie."

"Not a lie."

He sighed.

Coffin leaned back and looked over the top of the mill. The arms formed an "X" against the landscape.

"Well," he said. "See you later."

CHAPTER NINE

Two hours later, Tommy sat in the back seat of the cab. He was sweating.

His father was supposed to be home, but he wasn't. So, he shouted something to his mother about going for a run when he saw the cab drive up his road.

Now, he sat in his shorts and t-shirt in the back of the cab and he wondered what this was all about.

Pink didn't wonder. Instead, he turned Dizzy Gillespie up and let the concert at the Newport Jazz Festival fill the car. The summer hours still lingered on the island. At six in the evening, the sun hung well above the western horizon and the warmth of summer lingered. He even rolled his window down.

Jack and Billy stood at the front of the school. Jack had a backpack with him, but Pink suspected that he didn't do much in the way of homework. The cab had come to a stop when both boys hopped in.

"Pink, you have to see this."

"What?"

"Pull around the back of the school."

"What is it?"

"You'll see. It's remarkable."

"Okay."

Jack was dangerously enthusiastic, while Billy was downright morose. Pink suspected he would see a dead mouse or some girl in a ridiculous outfit. Instead, when he turned the corner, he was a witness.

"Ever heard of a kid named Elvis?" Jack asked.

"No."
"Did you see today's Cape Cod Times? He's on the cover."
"Do I need to?"
"Take a look," Jack said. "That's Elvis."

Elvis was the biggest person Pink had ever seen. If he wasn't seven feet tall, he would be soon. The boy was massively broad across his back and powerful from his legs up. He wore sweatpants and a sweatshirt, with impossibly huge feet.

"Pink, he's a freshman."
"Wow."
"Our boy William here may have a starting problem." Jack snickered.
"Elvis has a problem." the other boy muttered.
"The bigger they are..."
"Did he practice today?" Pink asked.
"He dominated the scrimmage last night." Jack answered
"Last time." Billy said.
Pink accelerated away.

The jeep had remained untouched, in spite of the canvas roof and unzipped windows. Some of the morning fog had settled inside and brought out the aged musty smell of old upholstery, spilled beer, and bong water.

With Pink cruising back out to his house and his bed, Jack stopped joking. Tommy silently crawled into the back seat. The engine sputtered to life. Jack waited for the traffic to clear, then he swung out onto the Milestone Road and headed away from town.

"Hey, do you still have my phone?"
"Yup."
"Can you send it back here?"
"Nope."

Without another word, Jack pulled onto the grass next to the bike path.

"Is this about right?"
"Let me see."

Billy stepped out of the passenger seat and walked along the pavement. Jack rolled slowly up the grass. Two pickup trucks passed them on the road.

"Here we go." Billy said. He looked back into the car.
Tommy didn't understand.

Jack did. He didn't want to walk into the woods and find something lying there. He heard that hollow wet sound again and he knew what would await him. His life would turn then. In the sober light of day, it would turn. Both he and Billy had agreed on Tommy. They would keep his mouth very, very shut.

For this moment, when his friend looked at him. This moment was the last moment when his life was normal. The last moment before something truly ugly would walk in his nights. If he drove away, the question would build. If he walked into the woods, the answer would explode.

"Fuck it."

He switched the car off and hopped from the driver's seat. Without a hitch, he struck right into the scrub oaks and pine. The branches were broken, the bushes were trampled and there was blood on the leaves.

But no body.

He hunted around in a circle. He might have crawled off and died further in.

But all of the blood and broken branches stopped right here, fifteen yards in from the road.

"Billy. Tommy. Come in here."

The bigger boys looked around as Jack had. The relief was as bright on his face as it was in Jack's heart.

"What is it?" Tommy said

"You see anything here?"

"No."

"Do you know what that means?"

The boy thought for a moment. "No."

"It means." Jack said. "That you are going to enjoy your dinner tonight. Your dinner is going to taste better than any meal you have ever had. Your bed is going to be the softest bed you ever slept in."

Tommy nodded.

Before they took him home, Jack and Billy drove him to the end of the road in Tom Nevers. The road takes a sudden left onto new pavement fifty yards before the old pavement goes over the bluff and into the rolling Atlantic. Tonight, with the remains of a tropical storm five hundred miles to the Southeast, the waves rolled in chest high to a surfer.

Jack was all smiles. His grin infected Tommy.

The three of them stood on top of the bluff, fifteen feet above the beach and twenty yards from the breaking surf. The sun was gently settling into the clouds to the West. The orange glow suffused over the moors and the sands.

Jack opened his wallet and handed Tommy a hundred dollar bill.

"You made a mistake last night."

The boy looked at the hundred dollar bill and didn't understand. "What's this for?"

"It's for your phone."

"I can't...."

"You made a mistake. You took those pictures. Pictures live forever. There's a copy on your phone now, a copy at the phone company, and maybe even one on your computer." Jack grinned. "And every one of those pictures has a time and a GPS number on it. Anyone can tell where and when the pictures were taken."

"And by who?" Billy said.

"Well, not quite." Jack answered. "They can tell whose phone it is. Not who held it."

"Phones get stolen." Billy said.

"They do. They surely do. Very valuable thing, this cellphone."

"And with all the new people on island. And in school. Lot of thefts."

Tommy looked at them, with the barest understanding.

"So," Jack said. "Someone stole your phone yesterday. From your locker. You better tell your parents. And the principal. You don't know what happened to it."

"Okay."

"And," Jack said as he flicked through the photos remaining on the camera until he found one from the night before. It was a picture of two female butt cheeks, with the word "Remember" written over the top of them. The letters were a touch smeared. He showed it to Tommy. "And, you have no idea who could have e-mailed this picture out."

"Don't..." the boy said.

"I'm afraid..." Jack said as he thumbed a few buttons "that this photo just went out to everyone in your address book."

Tommy felt the world spin on him.

"So, the phone was stolen, wasn't it?"

"Yes." He said.

"You have no idea what happened to it. Or who took it."

"No."

"Okay."

Jack tossed the phone to Billy. The bigger boy opened it, then threw it like a knife out to the water. It landed just in the last reach of a wave. The next wave tumbled it, and the ones after pulled it, rolling, into the salty and rocky surf.

CHAPTER TEN

After practice, Elvis' father was awake and sitting up in bed. His cheeks were pale and punctuated in gray and black stubble, his hair was a mess, and his upper body looked thinner than it had even this morning. But his eyes were open, lively, and happy.

Shannon sat next to him, with a book face down on her knee. A flash of anger burst in the boy, and then faded. She hadn't called him when his father had woken.

"How are you doing, hero?"

"Great."

"It is good to see you."

"No, it is good to see you."

Elvis felt the emotion rise, unchecked in his chest. Unbidden, he felt his eyes get wet and his chest tighten.

"You're in the paper."

"I saw."

"It's a good thing."

Elvis didn't think so.

"What if the cops see it? What if they have a warrant?"

"You're safe here." David said. "You're safer now."

"How?"

"You're famous."

"I'm in one paper."

"Shannon just told me it got picked up. It will be in the New York Times and the Boston Globe tomorrow."

"It doesn't matter."

Shannon spoke up. "Elvis, now you are known. Now, you can't disappear."

The young man looked to his father. He nodded. "High profile, now. Wait until they start writing articles about you. You can't disappear."

It didn't make sense to Elvis, but it made sense to his father.

"What did the doctors say?" Elvis spoke carefully.

"They gave me a thumbs up."

"That's good."

Shannon looked at her brother. He smiled at her. "Well, it is a qualified thumbs up. I still have cancer." He said. "How was practice?"

"Fine." Elvis said. He focused on the inanities of his life.

Both of them let the word fade.

"You played well." His father said. "I am glad that I came to see it, even if it almost killed me."

"You can stay home next time." Elvis said.

"We'll see." He said. "First, I have to get out of here."

His son smiled with hope.

The old man continued. "I will come to more, don't you worry. I will be there and I will sit in the stands."

Aunt Shannon looked at him in a way that Elvis hated. His father let it pass.

"It was nice to see them use you well."

"Dive left, dive left, dive left."

"And then some misdirection." He said. "Are you going to start now?"

"I don't know."

"Were you with first team today?"

"For a bit." Elvis said. "We'll see."

Shannon cleared her throat. "Elvis, your father is tired. He needs to rest."

"No, I don't."

Shannon looked at him. "You are about to nod off."

"Maybe." He said. "First, Elvis and I will watch Sportscenter. You can go get yourself some dinner if you want."

Shannon looked at her nephew. "Don't keep him up."

"He'll be fine."

"He'll be asleep before I get back."

And he was.

The two of them watched the first ten minutes of the show before the older man nodded off. His father's head leaned back against the pillow, his mouth sagged open, and his eye-lids drooped, but didn't quite cover his eyes. Elvis tugged the oxygen mask up and over his mouth and nose.

Shannon came back to the room with a small plastic tub of pasta salad and a bottle of Perrier. She resumed her seat on one side of her brother while Elvis sat on the other side.

"Well, I am glad he fell back to sleep." She said. "He needs his rest."

"When did he wake up?" Elvis asked.

"Around noon."

"Why didn't you call me?" the boy snapped.

"I'm sorry?" She said.

"Why didn't you call me when my father woke up?" His voice did not shake this time, but his feeling was clear.

"Because you were at school."

"But I asked you to…"

"And I decided not to." She said, bluntly. "He faded in and out for most of the afternoon." She said. "You caught him at his most lucid. You made him very happy."

He caught the edge in her tone.

"You say that as if he is dying."

"He is."

"No, I mean as if he is going to die tomorrow."

"He might."

"No, he won't."

"Elvis," she said. Her voice wasn't unkind. "You have seen the x-rays and the tests. You know as well as I do. He isn't getting up from this bed."

"No." he hissed.

"Look at the room. Look where we are. He is in Hospice care."

"I'll get him out of here."

"How will that help him?"

Elvis looked at her with anger, frustration, and the few last ropes of his self-control fraying. Shannon, with all of her own faults, saw this.

"Look." She said. "No one thought he was going to fight off the infection or was going to wake up, either. If they had sent him up to Boston, he would have died on the helicopter. So." she said, slowly. "He's alive now."

"Yes…"

"You have to look from his eyes for moment. You have to get out of your own head and think about him."

"I always…"

"Then listen." She said, quiet and forceful. "He got into that car yesterday sure he was going to die. He was sure of it. He wanted to see you play. He wanted to see you on the field, in your pads, and kicking ass wholesale."

Elvis said nothing.

"We had to stay to see you win. He made me promise to let him die in the car and not tell you. Can you understand that? Can you grasp that?" she said with fierce urgency. "He demanded that I sit in the car, with his cooling corpse so that you would keep believing he was alive. Just so you would keep playing."

Elvis had nothing to say.

"He's nuts and he has always been nuts." She said. "Imagine how he would feel if you skipped practice to sit with him. Practice. I swear he has dreamed you alive. He closes his eyes and runs wind sprints and suicides with you."

"Okay."

He kept his tongue still.

"Elvis, he is going to die." She said. "Tonight, tomorrow, two weeks, two months, but he is going to leave us. He knows it. You are going to have to let him go. It hurts now and it will hurt worse then, but imagine seeing from his eyes. Imagine feeling his pain."

"Is he in pain?"

"Of course he is." She said. "You think cancer doesn't hurt?"

"I don't know."

"Think about it," she said. "Of course it does."

His anger no longer flared, but it burned steady in his chest.

"You think he should be dead, don't you?" he accused.

She looked at him and took the full measure of the huge fifteen year old with a dying father. She could not lie to this boy.

"I don't want him to suffer." She said. "So, yes, I suppose so." She sighed. "If he had died in that car, with the clock ticking off the seconds and a celebration on the field, wouldn't that be better than months of pain in this room?"

Elvis said nothing. He rested his huge head in his hands and squeezed his tears into his palms.

"I don't know." He said.

"I don't know either." She replied.

In a few minutes, when he straightened back up, Shannon was deep into her Sudoku. She saw him upright and composed.

"We have to talk about something else, now."

"What?"

"You need to call your mother."

Elvis said nothing.

"She is worried, naturally."

"About what."

"Well, your Dad."

"No, she's not."

"Of course she is." Shannon said. "She was married to him for ten years. You don't stay married for ten years if you don't love someone."

Elvis paused. From his mother, he knew what addiction looked like.

Elvis looked at his Aunt. "Have you met her?"

"Of course."

"When?"

"Dear…"

Elvis said nothing.

She looked at him "It must be fifteen years ago."

"Really."

Aunt Shannon looked uncomfortable.

"If we call her, everyone will know where he is."

"Everyone?"

"The Outfit." He said. "They will come."

Shannon looked at him directly. Before her was the enormous adolescent. Not unlike his father, back when they were young and poor. In her mind, she saw the man he would become; protective, aware, and angry. Pity the fatherless child.

"Elvis, they know where we are."

He stopped. "Did you call them?"

"No. I would never." she said. "But as soon as the hospital activated his health insurance, they knew. They are on their way here, one way or another. They might already be on island right now."

Elvis looked through her. She continued.

"They weren't going to touch us. But now that you are on the front page…" she said. "You are safe. They can't touch you without coming out of the shadows and men who work for the Outfit," she looked at his father, "don't like to come out of the shadows. You can't worry about them. You still have to let your mother know that David is dying. She has to know."

Elvis sat silent. "She isn't…"

"Please," Shannon whispered. "Please. Try to understand her. People do stupid things that they regret and can't undo. People… people…" She looked back at her hands. "People imagine a world they want to live in and make decisions based on that pretend world. Then the real world knocks them over. Again. It happens to everyone. Even you."

Elvis looked at her. He was tired of talking to his Aunt. He knew the truth and she did not and he could not tell her. He could not show her what he had seen. Certain smells, certain sounds, certain touches were his alone. There were some things, he thought, that might be forgiven but could never be forgotten. And then, only if the dead could forgive.

There was nothing he could say to her about this.

"Okay." He said.

He got up and left the room. The door closed behind him and his eyes adjusted. It was always three in the morning in the hospital. He walked to the Nurse's station.

"Is there a phone nearby?"

The older woman looked up and pointed to a lounge across the hall. The room had one TV bolted to the ceiling, soundlessly playing Fox News. Otherwise, the room looked out over the parking lot, a field, and then the high school. Even the lights of the football field were close by. They loomed over the school building. The world outside the glass felt a thousand miles away from the world inside. He felt as if he were looking out from inside an aquarium.

He found the old phone, put it on his knee, and stared at it.

It had been a month. Not even.

He had kissed her goodbye on that Saturday and then he had disappeared. There were excellent reasons for this, but that didn't overcome the weight of the handset or the difficulty of pressing the buttons.

The fifteen year old looked out the window. The daylight faded slowly.

He dialed.

"Hello?" Her voice was tentative and nervous.

"Hi Mom."

"Elvis." She said. Her voice relaxed and released. "Elvis," she continued. The tears bordered the edge of her breaths. "Thank God. Thank God. Thank Jesus. Thank God."

"How are you, Mom?"

"I am so happy to talk to you, sweetie. I'm so, so happy." She said. "How are you?"

"I'm fine Mom."

"I've missed you so much. I have been so worried. Everyone is looking for you."

"I know."

"We even called the police."
"I'm okay, Mom."
"You know you have missed some of you appointments."
"Yes, Mom. But I am okay."
"And the team…"
"I know."
"Where are you? Are you playing football?"
The question gave an answer. She knew.
"I'm okay, Mom. I am safe."
She paused.
"Is everything all right there?"
"Well, no."
"What's wrong?" Her voice seized with concern.
"My father is dying."
"Oh, honey." And in her voice he heard surprise. "Oh, honey, I know. It must be very hard."
He thought for a moment. Everything that he wanted to say needed to be studied before he let it leave his lips.
"It is."
"How is he doing?"
"His fever broke and he was awake for a while today."
"Thank God for that." She said.
"He looks a lot better."
"Do the Doctors think they can release him?"
He thought about how odd that question was. "They haven't said."
"Well, I hope he gets better."
"So do I," she said. "What are you planning to do when he gets better?"
Elvis heard the calibrated lie.
"I don't know."
"Are you in school there?"
"Yes."
She didn't say anything. Elvis didn't explain either. After a long moment, she spoke.
"Elvis, honey, you belong here with me. You know that, don't you?"
"Mom."
"This is where you are supposed to be."
"Mom."
"You have no right…"

"Stop." Elvis said. He saw a red tailed hawk circle and he focused on it. "Stop talking about rights. I know what happened, Mom. I know what you did."

"Elvis," she sighed. "There is so much you don't know."

"Not now, Mom." He said. "Not now."

"Please think of your future, honey," she said. "Think of it."

"I am."

"I miss you."

"I need to go, Mom."

"Call me tomorrow, will you?"

"Sure."

"I can fly there in a moment, you know."

"Please don't."

"I miss you, honey."

"I will call tomorrow."

"Okay. Love you."

Elvis hung up the phone.

Aunt Shannon left shortly afterward and encouraged Elvis to be in his bed, at home, by ten. He didn't commit.

Instead, he sat in the plastic chair next to his Dad and listened to him snore. The nurses walked in, wrote down their numbers and walked out. He spoke to them politely.

He didn't know what he would do. Or should do. Or could do.

Chicago, with his mother, was impossible.

Nantucket, with Shannon, was almost impossible.

The Outfit was sending someone.

It was a pickle.

While he was lost in his thoughts, there was a knock on the darkened door. Elvis looked up for a second as the door swung open.

He braced himself.

Nick stood there, with a backpack.

Elvis relaxed.

"What are you doing?" he asked.

"Sitting."

"Are you ready for some football?"

Elvis, for the first time in a week, smiled.

Nick closed the door, turned the TV channel to a college football game played on a blue field, then offered the fifteen year old a can of Busch beer. Elvis took the beer over his sleeping father. The old man, he was sure, would not mind.

Inspector Coffin and his partner parked next to the windmill.

Light had abandoned the island. The clouds hung just out of reach, with a wet north east wind flapping the grass, cracking the pines, and setting the power wires humming.

Danny turned a page.

The old man shifted in his sleep.

Both Higginbotham and Coffin had dressed warmly for the night. Danny was in a dark blue sweater vest that had "Nantucket Police" on the left breast. Henry was in a gray hoodie sweatshirt. Half of the stuff the old man wore, Danny thought, looked as if it had pulled from the "Take it or Leave it" pile at the dump.

A recent model pick-up truck drove up Prospect Street, slowed near the mill and pulled into the parking lot where the police were "stationed." Danny folded the corner of his book and set it down. The truck parked behind them. With his old city reflexes, Danny put his foot near the accelerator and his hand on his gun.

A tall man in a tan work jacket knocked on the window.

Danny lowered the window.

"Yeah?" He growled.

"Officer?"

"Yeah?" Danny was annoyed and professionally worried.

"Is Coffin with you?"

Danny looked at the still sleeping Inspector. Good thing this wasn't an ambush.

"He is a little indisposed."

"I wonder if I could talk to him."

"You can talk to me."

"Well, he knows me."

Danny knew he would always be a black man on this island. For most of the islanders, he was Tonto to Coffin's Lone Ranger.

"Go back to your car and I will send him over."

"Thanks."

The detective rolled the window up.

He took his hand off the gun and nudged the Inspector. Henry Coffin's eyelids fluttered. He sat up, blinked, and was happy for once not to be traveling at 80.

"Man came to visit you."

"Who is it?"

"No idea." Danny said. "All of you white people look the same."

"Where is he?"

"Parked behind us with a shotgun waiting for you to open the door."

Coffin smiled at his partner. "Okay, no funeral, just dump the ashes off the ferry."

"Can I put them in my garden?"

"Sure." He said. "I don't really care at that point. Fire me out of a cannon."

Coffin opened the door, stepped out, and stretched. No shotgun blast. He moved back to the pickup truck and opened the passenger door.

Steven Graves was a young man who had the curse of looking like his father. His father, also Steven Graves, had been a fantastically good heating and ductwork contractor. In the late eighties, he had twelve guys working for him, and six red panel trucks going from building site to building site. He also loved to bet and to snort cocaine by the tablespoon. When the bubble burst, the old man flew to the Cape, rented a car and disappeared. Avis found its Taurus in Tampa.

His son was eighteen; full of piss, Coors, and kind, kind bud. The creditors came calling two days after his Dad disappeared, then the sheriff came, then the banks. Coffin and his partner had stopped the boy on Milestone Road with a zip lock bag on the passenger seat, a bottle of Jack Daniels between his legs, and a shotgun. Coffin had driven him back to his house, broke the seals on the door, and let the kid sleep it off for one last night as a child in his father's house.

In the ten years since, the boy had cut his father loose in bankruptcy court, kept what the old man had taught him about heating and hard work, got his ticket, and just kept working. He bought a house in the Badlands, rebuilt it, and parked his trucks there.

This truck was new and clean. Sand hadn't even built up on the floor. It had a club cab but the Quaker hadn't even glanced behind his seat before he sat inside.

"It's late, Steve."

"No shit. Why don't you work normal hours?"

"I would have to stay awake."

"You could sleep better."

"I would have to work, though."

"I hear that."

They both looked forward.

"My brother, what's on your mind?"

The young man hesitated. "I'm missing a guy."

"What guy?"

"A guy who works for me."

"Maybe he went home."

"No, I doubt that."

Coffin looked at the man, but Graves wouldn't look him in the face. This concerned the Inspector.

"You don't want to file a missing person report, do you?"

"I thought I would ask you about it."

"Why is that?"

Graves looked at the older man. Coffin smiled.

"We haven't found anybody, but we'll keep our eyes open." He said. "What's his name?"

"I don't know."

"Guy works for you and you don't know his name?"

"The guys call him Julian."

"But you don't think that is his real name?"

"It's not like I take W-2's"

Coffin sighed. He wasn't sure how he felt about illegal labor. On some days, he felt that it was capitalism at its best. On the rest of the days, he felt it was two steps up from slavery.

"What does he look like?"

"Tall, thin, curly hair, about 150-170 pounds. Hispanic. Looks like he's 18."

"No photo?"

"Christ, no."

"Well, this should be easy. We must have an entire soccer league full of these guys."

"I know."

"When did he go missing?"

"Last night."

" He's probably with a girl or he passed out in some house."

"You don't know these guys." Graves said. "They don't do any of that."

"What do they do?"

"They work."

A gust of wind rattled the car. Coffin was doing the math, but it wasn't adding up.

"They don't want to talk to me." Coffin added.

"That too."

"Be straight with me, my brother." He said. "It makes both of our lives easier. You come at midnight to tell me about a guy who has been missing for about twenty-four hours. You and I have been missing for a lot longer than that. You could have phoned this in and we could have told you to wait a week."

The younger man was silent for a long moment.

"These guys," Graves said eventually, "They are great, great workers. None of them have missed a day. Not even an afternoon. Hardest workers I have ever seen. Brazilians. But they don't talk to anyone but themselves. I talk to one guy, pay that guy and he pays everyone else. They cook for themselves, don't drink, don't do drugs. They just work, lie low, kick a soccer ball and watch TV."

"Okay."

"They know where each other is minute by minute. Nobody saw him go and they are a little freaked and a little pissed."

"What happens when shows up drunk and without his underwear?"

"Not these guys."

"Show me the eighteen year old guy who doesn't want to be drunk and pantless."

"Honest to God, Henry. Do you think I would be here, talking to you, if that was a possibility."

He was scared. Coffin had missed it at the beginning, but here it was. Graves was deep down terrified at losing this guy.

"So you checked the bars?"

"Yeah."

"And the houses?" Henry knew that there were four or five private houses that would take the boy's money.

"Looked there."

"Is there a girl?"

"I think so."

He nodded to the DeSalvo house.

"Really?"

"They used to flirt with each other when we got lunch."

"Did he tell you he was seeing her?'

"No, but..."

"But?" Coffin said.

A large set of jig-saw pieces appeared on the kitchen table in the Inspector's mind. Maria was keeping her mouth shut to protect him. And he thought of one gold piece.

"That's why you're here outside her house."

"And to see you."

"Luckily we happen to be in the same place."

He nodded.

"Your Brazilian. Is he selling drugs?"

"No. Absolutely not."

"You're positive."

"Absolutely."

"Maybe once?"

"It is scary how squeaky clean these guys are. They are exercise and jiujitsu freaks."

"Maybe they sold them once upon a time?"

"I really doubt it."

He was terrified again.

"How did you get involved with these guys?"

"I don't know. Honest to Christ. I have no idea. They just showed up at job site and killed it in a week…."

Coffin looked out the window.

"Steve, we have been here for most of the night. Danny would have seen someone coming or going from the house."

"Okay."

"We'll keep our eyes open."

"Why are you here?" Steve asked.

Coffin smiled. "Another bit of police business ends up here. If we see him, I'll let you know."

"Okay."

"Let me have your cell"

After keying the number into his phone, Coffin stepped out from the cab, waved, and got back into the squad car.

Within ten minutes, the Inspector had slipped back to sleep. At the end of the shift, Danny had to wake him in order to drop him off at his home.

CHAPTER ELEVEN

At eleven the following morning, a Saturday, Elaine remained in bed.

Nonetheless, she listened intently and when she heard the door slam and her mother step outside, she scurried into her parents' bedroom and swept up the phone. She dialed as fast as she could.

"Elaine!"

"Yeah."

"I need you to do me a favor."

Elaine didn't say anything. Then she spoke. "Don't you think you should rest?"

"I've been asleep for hours." Maria said. "I need to find him."

"Okay."

"So come pick me up."

Her friend paused for a moment too long. "When?"

"Now."

"I can't go now." She said. "Besides you should have seen the look your mother gave me yesterday."

Maria felt a redness grow. The heat grew from her waist and rose to her lungs and throat. Maria, with her eyes out on her mother and the woodshed, knew that she didn't have long.

"You took me to that party."

"Maria,"

"You were there, weren't you?"

"Look,"

"You knew, didn't you. You knew what they wanted, didn't you?"

"No. No.. I didn't I swear. I didn't." Elaine slipped and a sob squeezed out. "I swear. I swear. I had no idea. No one knew. No one."

"But you were there."

Elaine couldn't speak.

"I'll be across the street."

With her eyes still on her mother, Maria pulled some dirty clothes off the floor. She dropped silently down the stairs and passed out the front door, across the yard and Prospect Street, then waited on a bench.

Elaine picked her up five minutes later.

They drove out the Milestone Road because they had no idea where to go. Maria hated to admit how little she knew about him. She didn't know where he lived. She didn't know who he lived with. She had never seen his bed, his clothes, his food.

Elaine didn't want to talk.

Elaine felt horrendous. She had no way of talking about what she knew. She got six e-mail messages this morning. The boys had taken pictures. You couldn't tell anything. There were no faces, just a big butt with the word "Remember" written on it. No one knew, but everyone knew.

"How are you feeling?" Her friend asked, tentatively.

"Fine."

"That's good." She nodded.

In her mind, Elaine saw Jack climbing the stairs with a dopey Maria. She had seen Billy and that red head kid following them. She had done nothing.

"What are people saying?" Maria asked.

"Nothing." Elaine, to her shame, did not show her the picture on her phone.

"Really?"

"They're dickheads. Everyone knows that."

Finally, they went to the one spot where they could find anyone.

Maria DeSalvo stood on the strip in front of Amigo's, looking for the big Toyota pickup. Elaine stood next to her, but no one else talked to her. They stood out front for thirty minutes and waited for something to happen.

The black Toyota crew cab rolled up next to Amigo's.

Her heart flapped its wings and jumped from the nest. She took two steps to the driver's side and knocked on the window.

The truck went back into gear and pulled away.

Her heart plummeted and bounced off the ground. She felt the tears build.

"Let's go." Elaine muttered.

A Honda rounded the corner and slammed to a stop near where she was getting in the car. Jay-Z came blasting out of the driver's side door.

"Hey Maria!" Billy said. He held his flashlight outside the car window. "Remember?"

All she heard was laughter.

The Labrador made a happy sound and rearranged himself at the door.

It had been a short rest, one that ended at 11:30 to the sound of a sad, and full dog. Henry had found his sneakers, an old golf hat, and a light sweater. He arrayed himself, opened the door, and watched the dog bolt for one of the ancient elms that his forebears had planted on Main Street.

Then, man and dog, the two walked up Main Street. The season had, technically, ended three weeks ago, but the current rich who inhabited Nantucket arrived in early August and left in mid-October. Their current car was, ironically, the mini-Cooper. Six of them were drawn up in front of the mansions of Main Street.

Overhead, the thick green canopy of the elms reached to the other side of the street. Starlings were in the air; the dog got the scent and chased around every corner for falling, but hidden snowflakes.

Starbuck and Coffin, like an old Whaling partnership, walked painfully up Mill Street, slipped behind the mill and came to the DeSalvo's backyard.

Rick was in his workshop, with the table saw going. He wore a t-shirt, jeans, and a Whaler's baseball hat.

Henry stood at the workshop door. Starbuck sat behind him, sensitive to the noise.

"She's not here."

"Who?"

"Maria."

Fifteen minutes after Henry had reported her missing to the department, Elaine brought Maria back. Henry, Rick, and Rosie stood in front of his shop. Rick was white, Rosie weak with tears, and Henry looked as he always did.

Maria sobbed without a breath and curled up into a ball in the back seat. Inside all of the pain and tears, she tried to return back inside, to that wonderful, floating, warm baby.

She couldn't get there.

Elaine put the Golf into park and stood outside the car. She opened the back door and helped the girl get out. Maria couldn't stand.

"What the fuck are you doing!" Rick yelled.

"I'm just bringing her back."

"What did you do?"

"Nothing." She said. "I'm sorry. I'm so sorry."

Rick had his hammer. He brought it down on the hood of her car. The echo snapped Maria awake.

Rick swung and shattered a headlight. Then he swung again and got the other headlight.

"Rick…" she said.

He brought the hammer over his head and hit the windshield. It shook and wavered, but did not shatter.

Maria screamed.

Rick hammered again. Now, a star of cracks appeared.

Elaine ducked back into the driver's seat.

Rick hammered again and the cracks ran to the edges. Now, he switched and began to batter the hood of the car.

Elaine started the engine and locked the doors.

She threw the car into reverse and backed up as he hit the hood with the claw head. The car ripped the hammer from his hand.

The girl backed into a bush, switched gears and floored the accelerator. The VW bolted out of the driveway, fishtailed into the bikepath, then sprinted down the hill. After running the stop sign, she slowed to the speed limit and crept back to her house.

Elaine, Maria's best friend, sobbed and left the car.

The hammer remained in the hood.

Inspector Coffin sat at the kitchen table. Across from him, Maria also sat, looking down at her hands. Rosie, still red with rage and terror, kept herself busy at the sink. Rick knew where he could not be. So he fired up the table saw.

Rosie didn't know what to do. The last place she wanted to be was in that kitchen and listening to what was going to be said. However, the only place she could be was in that kitchen. Her hands were tied, her mouth was gagged, but her ears were open and listening.

"So," Coffin said. He spoke with infuriating calmness and composure. "Did anything happen when you were downtown."

The girl shook her head.

"I know you don't want to talk, Maria. I understand. It's too big right now. It has to be killing you. You are carrying all of this around, all by yourself."

He stopped speaking and let the silence sit.

"We care about you. We all do and we want to help you. We want to ease all of this weight. We need you to give it to us."

Maria was deep inside herself and floating.

Coffin eased back. The pain she felt radiated throughout the room. Coffin shielded his eyes and winced for her. She was speaking and, at a basic level, she was thinking about herself and the future.

"Can you tell me what happened on Thursday night? Just what you remember."

She was continuing to cry, although she had ceased sobbing. The tears dripped down her face and fell into her lap.

She shook her head.

Rosie could not breathe. The air would not come into her lungs. The mother looked at her daughter and the policeman at the table and could not believe that it was real. It was and she must bear witness. She would rather die.

"Elaine was outside my window at midnight." She said.

Coffin nodded.

"And I snuck out."

The silence rose up around her words.

"She drove me out to this party."

Neither adult asked anything.

"And I was drinking this punch drink and I started getting dizzy so I sat down on a bed."

"Who gave you the drink?"

"Some red headed kid."

Maria had not looked up at all. Her voice was flat. Coffin wrote a name down.

Coffin counted to ten before he asked his question. "Then what happened?"

"Jack." She said. "Billy." There was a pause. "Nothing happened. NOTHING HAPPENED."

Rosie sighed in her chains.

Coffin dare not look anywhere but at the girl.

Rosie stood at the sink, crying and biting her index finger to keep silent. Her head bounced silently in pain.

Henry looked to the daughter.

"Thank you." He whispered. "Thank you. You are very brave."

She cried more.

Rosie moved from the sink and put her hand on her daughter's back. Maria neither flinched nor welcomed it.

Sensing that whatever else she was going to say would come later, the Inspector stood. Starbuck saw his master stand and he left the sofa.

Coffin caught Rosie's eye for a moment, but the pain was white-hot and his glance flinched. He dearly wished Danny and a squad car was with him.

"Maria, I am sorry to ask this. But I wonder if we could talk outside for a moment."

Two shocked faces flashed at the Inspector. Rosie's flashed stun and amazement that she was getting pushed away. Maria's just held horror.

"Later, Henry..." Rosie said.

"I'm sorry, but I think I need to talk to her now." He said. "And alone."

"Henry."

"What do you think Maria?" He looked at her. She saw the cold glance of winter.

She nodded.

"We'll be right back." Coffin said.

The rage had returned to Rosie. Full and building.

The old man and the young girl crossed the back yard to the hole in the shrubs that circled the mill. She led the way into the historic park and he followed. The two of them sat on a bench. Always the same bench.

"So." Coffin said.

"I told you everything."

"Would you like to tell me about Julian out here or would you like to tell your parents and me at the same time?" he said. "Or would you like me to go around and research it from other people. Elaine, perhaps?"

Maria said nothing

"That's the thing about the truth. It always comes out. It always rises up no matter how hard you try to push it down."

"You don't know."

"I've seen a lot of lies fade."

"You don't know." She repeated.

"I can find out." He said. "You told a great story in there. It was mostly true, wasn't it?"

She nodded.

"But I need to know one thing and I thought I should ask you by yourself. Where you can still have some confidentiality."

She looked at him. Anger, tears, and fire.

"Why did you leave this morning?"

She didn't answer.

"So, I know people are looking for Julian and I know that they have already connected the two of you together. And I know that you have a kruggerand. And I know that Elaine couldn't find him." Coffin said. "And I know that someone who had been raped and couldn't go to school anymore wouldn't just go downtown for lunch."

Maria didn't say anything. She felt like a fool.

"I wasn't raped."

So she told him almost everything.

She kept her dark passenger to herself.

Ten minutes later, Coffin walked to the back door of the DeSalvo's, sent Maria inside to her mother and father, and collected Starbuck.

Maria started showering and scrubbing the writing off of her before the Inspector was out the driveway.

Milestone Three

CHAPTER ONE

The summer had returned to the island on the following Monday. Humidity came in on fogs and breezes. The mist slowed down the airport, obscured the neighbors, and hid the harbor from the school, but it did little else. By eleven o'clock, it had retreated out to sea. The cars, the bicycles, and the surfboards gleamed in early autumn sun. From the windows of the school, you could look out and see dozens of late season vacationers waiting on Sparks Avenue with the golf clubs, swim suits, and kayaks.

Coffin sat in one of the penitent chairs outside the principal's office. It had been a slow and sleepy night out on the roads. Danny was more than happy to let the old man sleep it off and Henry was more than happy to oblige him. Nonetheless, eight o'clock at the school was pushing him away from his bed.

"Inspector?"

At the sound of his title, Coffin rose and walked into the office. The desk remained as clean as it had been on Friday, with the exception of an iPhone centered and aligned.

"So," Coffin said. "What seems to be the problem, Homer?"

"What do you know about cellphones?"

The principal was fidgeting in his chair. The staged calm that he usual draped over himself had been kicked to the floor.

"Enough to keep them from interrupting my dinner."

Homer nodded.

"How about legally?"

"Do you have evidence of a crime on that phone?"

"Let's say, hypothetically," the principal looked out the window for some words. "Let's say that someone took this phone off of a student and, hypothetically, found a disturbing picture on it. What...might...be done about that?"

Coffin grinned.

"Well, hypothetically, that would be an illegal search."

The principal nodded. "I couldn't do anything about the photo?"

"Hypothetically, no."

Homer tented his fingers.

Coffin reached onto the desk and took the instrument from it. He turned the machine on, then pressed the button for photos.

And there it was. Two white female cheeks with the word "Remember" written across the top. The bed sheets visible around the butt were the same as the ones in that house in Quaise.

It was Maria. He knew it without being able to prove it.

"Do you know who it is?" Homer asked.

"Yes."

The Principal waited.

"I can't tell you, Homer, you know that."

The principal rolled his eyes.

"If I tell you, then you will go to the young lady and offer some sort of help. And she will want to know why or, at least, what you know. You couldn't tell them without violating the law, could you?"

"Well..."

"I don't see how." Homer sighed. Coffin continued. "Whose phone is it?"

"A freshman."

"Anyone I know?"

"Can't tell you."

"Okay. Fair enough." Coffin put the phone in his pocket. "I am going to take this with me."

"You can't use it."

"No, Homer," He said. "I can't use it in court. I can still use it."

"What am I supposed to say at the end of school?"

"Tell the truth. Tell that poor freshman that I took it from you. Tell him that he can get it from the police station. Or I could drop it off."

Homer's face pinched.

Outside, in the squad car, Henry took off his professional and pedantic demeanor. He rubbed his eyes. Then he sat back. Danny put the car in reverse, but the old man put his hand on him. Danny put the gearshift back into park.

Coffin put the phone on his lap. Wordlessly, he restarted the phone and showed his partner the picture.

"Well, it's her."

"I think so."

"Who's phone is it?"

"Some freshman. Homer wouldn't tell me. He didn't take the picture."

"No?"

"No. I would guess that it's made the rounds."

"Picture breaks the case open, doesn't it?"

Coffin shrugged. "It might."

"We can get time, location, phone number, everything else."

"Yup." He said. The old man looked at the window into the Nurse's office. "Can't use it without a warrant."

"Not in court."

"No." he said. "That's not my problem."

"Okay."

"My problem is Rosie."

"If you go into her office and tell her, then she freaks out."

"Understandably."

"And you have no answers."

"No." he said. "If you were this girl's father and you knew that your daughter's bum was in every high school phone on island, how would you react?"

"Not well." Danny said. "But I would want to know."

"He has already lost a hammer."

Coffin looked into the gray window. "Let's go and drop this off downtown. One of the young guys can decode this for us."

Rick sat at the kitchen table drinking coffee.

James sat in the living room. Arthur and his rabbit friend were getting on a bus to go to swim lessons. Fourth graders rode the bus in the city, if you were on PBS. Probably not in New York. Not safe. Not on Nantucket, either.

He knew what Rosie had told him. The facts were arrayed in front of him, but he was having trouble believing them. They were bills for something he had not bought. There had been a mistake.

Because he sat at this table with her for breakfast almost every day. He had mashed bananas for her years ago. He used to make Mickey Mouse pancakes for her. The two of them would use the special Vermont maple syrup while Rosie went with Mrs. Butterworth. Maria had gone through an omelet phase as well. Now, she was in the teenage world of Captain Crunch and silence.

So it hadn't happened.

But it did. He knew it.

Someone had raped his little girl. When he felt his rage turn red, and then white, he imagined pain.

He sipped his coffee. Arthur and his friend were asking for help in a diner.

The nail gun figured prominently. If you nailed the legs and arms to two by fours, the body would float face down for a good long time. A hack saw blade seemed appropriate, as did screw-drivers, awls, and even a wide-bit borer.

Fantasies like this were the idle tools of the weak. Strong men act, weak men dream.

There would be consequences, of course. He knew that. But what would the consequences be if he did not act?

Could he look at his little girl if he did not?

Could he tell Rosie that he dare not do what he should?

He sipped his coffee.

There was a bill to pay if he acted. There was still a bill to pay if he did not. A bigger, caustic, burning price that would eat at all of them, if he did not.

Rosie came into the house as he was driving a three inch nail through a thin wrist into a clean piece of white pine.

The two of them looked at each other.

Elvis wasn't talking. He didn't say a word in any of his classes. Mrs. Lind kept him after class to talk to him about his silence, but he just looked at his shoes. Eventually, she just said that if he wanted to talk about anything, she would be there for him.

He just nodded and walked away.

His locker was untouched. This Monday, the team wore only shorts and helmets. They would go out and loosen up, do a set of sprints or two, then jog into a classroom to watch the game film of the last game. Back in Chicago, the coaches would then break up the team into skill sets and have them look at a few plays from the upcoming opponents, but it didn't appear that Nantucket sent scouts out. If scouts actually traveled, whatever they learned, they only shared with Coach Palumbo.

Elvis changed quickly, then locked his locker. Today, of all days, he hoped Jack would piss in his locker. He dearly, dearly hoped he would.

The two boys arrived on the practice field just as the team had split into line and had begun to stretch. Team rules stated that you had to wear a Whaler's t-shirt to practice, but Jack, Billy, and a few other upperclassmen had taken an interpretation of the rules. They all wore the skull and crossbones. Coach Palumbo blessed the t-shirt with silence. They have to have some freedoms.

Neither boy looked at the huge freshman, although he was featured in their minds. They had not forgotten him. Not at all. They had not forgotten the embarrassment in the locker room. They had not forgotten the marks on the neck or on the cheek. They had seen the paper. No, they were one hundred percent aware of Elvis and What Needed To Be Done.

Otherwise, it was the usual Monday practice after walking over a weak team.

Coach Palumbo approached Tillinghast.

"Did you get the fax from the MIAA?"

"I did." Elvis was now cleared to play Varsity.

"What do you think?"

He shrugged. "He has an awful lot going on in his life. New school. Dying father." He paused. "Might be good for him."

Palumbo looked at him and smiled. "I thought you might argue the other way."

"Well, I do think he is young, but he can't play on J.V. He has too much experience and he is too big."

"I agree."

"You won't have him for two weeks, though."

"Why not?"

"Bad news is coming."

Tillie looked meaningfully at the head coach, but Palumbo missed it. Instead he walked down the lines, encouraging and correcting the young men. He stopped at the freshman.

"Son, I want you up with us on varsity today."

Elvis nodded.

"I want you to compete for starting left tackle."

He nodded again.

Palumbo was nettled. "Do you have anything to say?"

"Thank you, sir. I will do my best with the opportunity."

The coach looked at the young man. He didn't know whether this burst of coach-speak was mocking or serious. The boy didn't look at him, so he gave him the benefit of the doubt.

Both Billy and Jack noted the conversation. While they didn't know what was said, they could guess.

After the warm-ups were completed, the team lined up on the goal line for a series of sprints. One of the young coaches, Coach Mackenzie stood at the fifty yard line and whistled the team through a half-hearted approximation of suicide sprints: Race to the 10 and back, to the 20 and back, to the 30 and back, to the forty and back, and then to the other end-zone.

Elvis took these sprints dead seriously. He lined up next to Nick and tried to keep up with him. Today, he welcomed the pain of the run. His world disappeared into a yard line. His only goal was a point in front of him. There was no room for anything else in his brain but running and breathing.

Jack and Billy had lined up to the right of the big freshman.

When they were sprinting back from the forty, Billy made his move. He fell into the oncoming legs of the 280 pounder. His helmet hit just below the knee.

Elvis fell hard, rolled, and missed a collision with Jack. The fleet safety stepped just out of his path and cleated Elvis in the back.

Billy Trotter looked up from the ground. "Watch were you fall, you big oaf."

Elvis said nothing. He stood and jogged back to the goal line where Nick waited for him. His knee and his leg felt secure. The other two boys had resumed jogging.

"Let's go."

Elvis took off at a full sprint. Nick, caught standing, caught him on the thirty-five yard line and beat him by ten yards. He was, however, breathing hard. They walked around the end zone with their hands on top of their helmets. Jack and Billy finished just before the freshman jogged in.

Mackenzie and Palumbo stood at the center of the field. Neither looked pleased.

"Mitchell! Trotter! Could you out-run the J.V. this time."

"This guy tripped…"

"Men don't need excuses or explanations. Run faster than the J.V."

"But…"

"That's it." He barked. "Line up."

Inspector Coffin and his dog, Starbuck, appeared at far end of the field. He leaned on the chain link fence and watched.

Elvis put Nick between himself and his two enemies. When the whistle blew, he ran hard. Fleeing, he sprinted to the ten and back, then to the twenty. Koch was five yards behind him and fighting. The big kid, bellowing and pumping, as serious as cancer, raced away back and forth.

Billy Trotter timed himself better this time. As Nick and Elvis turned at the forty yard line, he launched himself at the side of the freshman's knee.

This time, Elvis was ready and side-stepped him, Jack dove in a second later, but met Nick's legs instead.

The rage burned inside. Elvis felt a nuclear heat released from some boiler and, with a distinctive pleasure, he stepped into its flame. He grabbed the facemask and pulled Billy to his feet.

He said nothing. But he twisted the helmet over to his right, so that Billy's head was almost upside down. Then he twisted it just as far to the left.

When he remembered the scene later, what scared him was the complete silence. Elvis didn't curse him, berate him, or insult him. He just tried to twist Billy Trotter's head off.

Palumbo stared. He moved the whistle to his lips, but Tillinghast put a hand on his shoulder. It shocked him for a second.

When Elvis went back to the right, the whistles started to blow. Nick stepped into Elvis face.

"Let him loose, Elvis."

Elvis did not look or recognize his friend.

"Let him loose."

Jack and other teammates where trying to pry his fingers off the mask. With a stop to the twisting, Billy just unsnapped his helmet and stepped away.

All of the coaches came running.

The team stepped away at that moment. The threat was over and Billy Trotter had jogged away.

"Come on, Fattie." He yelled. "Bring it."

Elvis, without a word, whipped the helmet at the boy. Trotter turned and took the full force of the hit in his side.

Whistles screamed around the field. The entire team jogged over to watch. Tillinghast and Palumbo both reached Elvis before he could push his teammates away. However, the one police officer on the scene didn't move a step.

"Easy, champ. It's over." Tillinghast looked in the freshman's eyes. The boy breathed out, blinked, and started to silently cry.

"Go." Tillinghast said to him. "Run it out. Four laps. Go!"

Elvis, relieved to be running, set off at a pace. No one but Nick, saw the tears running down the freshman's face.

Trotter was sitting in the grass. He took his shirt off and examined the growing bruise.

"I am going to sue him." He barked. "I am going to get that fat ass. And I am going to sue the damn school. Did you see that? It's assault."

Harry Meyer, the handsome quarterback stepped through the crowd. Silently, he extended a hand to his downed lineman and pulled him up to his feet. Once he was up, Meyer half turned, and then delivered a right cross to the left of his jaw. Billy landed on the ground again, but this time he bounced up.

"What is that for?"

"You know."

Jack stood next to his friend. The two of them turned to the quarterback, but found the rest of the offensive line standing between them.

Coach Reinemo, off to the side, nodded.

The whistles continued to scream.

Palumbo, at the top of his lungs, got the team on one knee. He sent Billy and Jack to the showers, and then to his office.

For the rest of the team, he had them run twenty sets of bleachers. Mackenzie and Reinemo led the drill with sadistic pleasure.

Palumbo marched straight at Tillinghast. The two of them stood at the fifty yard line with the arms folded. The head coach was irate, but understood how this was done. He understood that Tillinghast had been an Ambassador and knew a bit more about conflict than he did.

"What. The. Hell."

"Do you think he can start?" Tillinghast offered, jokingly.

"I think I should cut him, get him expelled, and then press charges."

"I wouldn't do that, coach."

"I should."

"You'd have to get rid of Meyer as well." Tillie said. "He punched him, without provocation."

Palumbo recrossed his arms. The boys were starting to slack on the stairs. Meyer barked at the ones not going hard.

"Bastard."

"Hell of a leadership move."

"Still a bastard."

"I'll ask his Mom."

"What the hell do you think is so funny?" Palumbo snapped.

Tillinghast paused. He did need to be more serious. "Coach. Think about what happened on the field today. You found out that your prize freshman lineman won't take any abuse from anyone. You found out that he gives it out a lot harder than he takes it. Right?"

"That would be the same freshman lineman who changed my play in his only game and then refused to get out of the game? The same freshman who could have killed a teammate?"

"The same freshman who is about to lose his Dad."

"I heard that already."

"The old man won't make the week."

Palumbo looked at the old Ambassador. "You sure?"

"Ate with him this weekend." He said. "The boy is barely keeping it together."

"Damn."

Elvis, at that moment, had started his tenth trip around the running track. Reinemo stopped him. Elvis was about to join the bleacher run, but Reinemo made him stand and watch. Tillinghast smiled. It was a good move. Especially since two of the JV kids were retching.

"Coach, think of what else you saw today. You saw your offense and your quarterback step up and unify. They became a team today."

"Of course, I might lose my safety and a lineman."

"You saw what they did?"

"I saw."

Both men knew what Mitchell and Trotter had been trying to do. One severe knee injury and Elvis' career would be limited. Maybe he would return for high school, but the big time college day would never come, nor would pros.

"I think you had a great day, coach. If they had succeeded, you would have lost the best professional prospect in New England, had a split and unhappy team, and no championships. Now, you have three or four championships in front of you, a unified team, and the opportunity to drop two troublemakers."

Both men watched Elvis at the bleachers. His teammates now were just barely getting up the benches. It would not be long before Reinemo sent them for a gentle, cruel jog around the field.

"I can't lose the troublemakers this weekend. I don't have anyone to replace them. And I can't play Elvis."

"You may not have a choice."

Not for the first time, Palumbo looked a question at his assistant.

"You see Coffin beyond the end zone, don't you Coach?"

"Yeah."

"Do you know why he is here?"

"He's bored and drunk?"

Palumbo did not work at the school and was not enmeshed in its net of gossip.

"Rosie DeSalvo's daughter hasn't been in school for a couple days. There is a picture going around of her ass."

"No. They raped her?"

"I don't know."

Palumbo, father of three daughters, fell dark.

"I think you can guess who two of the suspects are."

Coach Palumbo looked at the Quaker and his dog in the end zone. A year ago, in January, he and the black guy had woken him up on side of the road. He had tripped over the line at the Maddaquet Admiralty and had fallen sprawling, in his Toyota Sequoia, into the bushes off the bike path. The old man gave him a ride home, congratulated him on the championship, and tucked the number for a cab in his hand.

He knew who Rosie was, of course. He knew nothing of her daughter.

But he knew her dad. Rick DeSalvo had put the roof on one of his rental houses. It had been a hundred degrees, middle of August, on a Sunday with two of his Ecuadorians. They worked from six to six, then banged the rest of the shingles in the next morning. He was crazy. The rule about crazy was that you didn't even talk to their daughters.

The Head Coach looked at his assistant. "Was it this insane in Turkey?"

"The same. Different language, though."

"Christ."

The team had soaked through their shirts and shorts. Harry Meyer, he of the ferocious punch, spanieled the runners around the field.

They all took a knee in the end zone. Reinemo and Mackenzie looked at Palumbo.

Tillie patted him on the shoulder. "Go get 'em, killer."

A half hour later, Coffin leaned against the rear door of the school. He wasn't sure what the boys were driving. It wouldn't have surprised him if Pink pulled up, opened the door, and welcomed the boys in with cold beers and lit cigars.

But he didn't.

The red jeep was tucked around a corner, near the dumpster. It wasn't particularly hidden, but it was as close as you could get to a side door without wearing a handicap sticker. With the soft-top on and zipped up, most of the windows were opaque. Coffin weighed opening the door. With the identification of the picture this morning, everything was getting very serious, very fast.

The two juniors walked out the back door of the school early. As they hadn't seen Coffin during practice, they were surprised to see him waiting for them at the jeep.

"How are you doing, boys?"

"Okay."

"You took a little abuse out there, today. Didn't you Billy?"

"You should arrest him. You saw what he did. It's assault."

"And battery." Coffin added. "He hit you pretty good."

"Go and arrest him."

"I'll talk to him."

Billy stopped walking in the middle of the lot. Coffin and his dog remained where they stood.

"Oh, I forgot." The boy said. "You don't arrest anyone, do you?"

"Not often." Coffin admitted. "But, I would like to speak to you for a moment."

"Why?"

"We found an interesting photo on the web."

"I find dozens of them a day. They tell me it is healthy to do that."

"This one isn't that healthy."

Jack smiled. "You'd be surprised."

The two looked at each other for a moment.

"You fellas know where I could find Tommy Kelly?"

"Can't say that we can." Jack said. Silence swung through them again. "Anything else?"

"He was with you last Thursday."

"We gave him a ride."

More silence.

"One more thing, boys." Coffin said. "Have either of you seen Julian?"

"Whose Julian?"

"Brazilian kid. Thin."

"Don't know any Brazilian kids. What do they look like?"

Coffin was watching Billy Trotter. Jack was taunting the old man, but the bigger kid was avoiding his eyes. A cold wind blew over Trotter.

"Maybe you want to tell me about it." Coffin said. "Before this gets any bigger."

"How can this get bigger?" Billy asked. "We don't know the kid."

Jack was quicker. "We don't really have to talk to you, do we Inspector?"

"Well, I would think you would want to talk to me right now. As opposed to later."

"Yeah, but we don't have to. Do we?"

"No." Coffin smiled.

Jack smirked again. "Are there any charges, officer?"

"No."

"Well, we need to talk to our lawyer. Next time you want to ask us anything, why don't you talk to our lawyer?"

"Who is your lawyer?" Coffin asked, knowing the answer.

"Pink." Jack said. "Or, Lewis Pinkham, Esquire."

Elvis left the locker room early. His teammates had granted him invisibility and he had gratefully accepted it. No one spoke to him, no one hassled him, and no one talked about him. At the same time, he wasn't stared at and the room didn't fall silent when he entered it. Meyer blasted his music, mocked his pudgy center Sylvia and commanded the attention that would have fallen elsewhere. Elvis slipped out without a shower and was on his way out the building when Nick Koch caught him.

"Moments away from a clean getaway?" he said.

"Almost."

"What's up?"

Elvis looked at him. "Really?"

Nick smiled. "What did the coaches say?"

"Nothing."

"Nothing?"

"No one has said a word to me."

"Which means no one has thrown you off the team."

"Yet."

"If you made it through practice, you made it," he said. "Jack and Billy didn't quite get there."

"They're still on the team?"

"Didn't see them in the locker room?"

"Didn't see their lockers empty either."

"So what? They're dicks." He said. "Everyone knows it. Helps them sell the stuff to the middle school kids if everyone thinks they are so gangsta."

The two of them stepped out into the back parking lot to see Jack and Billy talking to a guy with a dog.

Nick walked a touch quicker to the Range Rover. Elvis tossed his bag in the back seat and sat on the passenger seat. Nick, with an eye on the rear view mirror, started up, and then pulled out.

"You have to shower, buddy."

"I was just going to walk home."

"Now, you have to shower in case I drive you home." He said. "How's your Dad?"

"Fine."

"Fine as in up and throwing the pigskin around?"

"No, he's okay. He's tired a lot."

"Okay."

Elvis fell silent. The effort was difficult. Nick saw him straining.

"Are you going to watch Monday Night Football tonight?"

"No."

"Want to come over my place for it?"

"No. I'm sorry. Not really." Elvis said. "I need sleep."

"You can sleep when you're dead." Nick joked.

Elvis tried to smile, but he had slipped back into the quiet.

Pink picked up Jack and Billy in the supermarket parking lot. They stood on either side of the jeep and waited. When Pink pulled up, they slipped in the back and sat together. Silently.

Practice had ended. Neither looked particularly winded or even sweaty. More to the point, they were still as knives. A week ago, each of them walked as if there was a ten pound weight hanging off their belt buckles. They once strutted with the cowboys and bull riders of the past. Now, the strut was gone. Pink missed it.

Pink knew why. The news had flown around the town. Nothing stayed secret on Nantucket. It may not be broadcast, and it won't be hung around your neck, but that doesn't mean that your sins and failings aren't in the sunlight. No, the island knew. And Pink knew.

The boys in the backseat waited.

"Boys, did Coffin visit you at school?"

"Yup." Jack said.

"He tell you what it was about?"

"He wanted Tommy."
"Why is that?"
"He may have done a bad thing."
"He may have?"
"Yup."
Pink nodded. "If Coffin is involved, you should be cautious."
Neither boy said anything. Neither looked in the rear view mirror.

CHAPTER TWO

When Danny Higginbotham came to pick the Inspector up that night, he considered just driving on. The inspector sat on the steps to his old Whaling mansion, wearing the same shirts as last night, and looking decidedly unfocussed.

Instead, however, he parked the car.

"How are you tonight, Henry?"

Coffin said nothing. He levered himself up into the air, walked three steps to the passenger door, put one hand on to the roof, opened the door, and then collapsed inside.

"Henry, how about a sick day. You look very sick."

Coffin just shook his head and closed the door.

Danny wanted to tell him that they were professionals. They went after bad guys. That they didn't get drunk when bad things happened. They didn't black out. But Coffin had already passed out.

On a Monday night in September, when the island was still full of fools and their gardeners, Danny Higginbotham would be driving alone for a few hours.

Late that night, the big man's voice was hoarse. He called the remote control a "gun." He called the TV, "Emily." He caught himself and smiled and wondered why the city was so silent. He couldn't talk more than a sentence or two without resting, and frequently, sleeping for a few moments. Whenever Elvis stood from his chair, his father would wake and urge him to sit. So he would sit. It was important to the old man.

The TV was stuck on ESPN. The late night Sportscenter kept repeating over and over, watching the Patriots win big, the Steelers escape, the Cardinals lose, and the kick returner from the Bears score twice on long distance runs. Once, at three in the morning, he pointed to Tom Brady getting crushed by a linebacker.

"Football is the bulk."

"Try that again, Dad."

"Football is the bowl. Dead."

"Dad?"

The older man, sick and drawn, stared with a burning fire at his son. "Football. Is. The. Duck. Head."

Elvis, having learned a thing of two, nodded.

His father nodded back at him, then he eased back into the pillow. He sighed. "Football is…."

Then he fell asleep.

Elvis tiptoed out of hospital room, stepped into an empty hospital room, stripped down to his underwear, and lay on top of the sheets.

The son could not sleep.

At 2:30, the old man showed signs of life. By three, he was blinking and licking his lips. Detective Higginbotham had taken the precaution of reloading his coffee in his thermos and of stocking three water bottles in a plastic bag at the old man's feet. He bent down, cracked open the first bottle and drank half of it.

"So…" Higginbotham said. "Why don't you use any sick days?"

"No."

"Why not?"

"Home is the last place I should be."

"Drunk and passed out in a police car has got to be a close second."

The older man glanced at him. "Possibly."

"Definitely. This is not what we do." The edge rose in Danny's voice.

"No?"

"No."

"Why not?"

"Other than being drunk with a gun on your hip?"

"Umm." The inspector, of course, carried no gun. Danny felt his knife of anger get a little blunt.

"You can't solve anything when you're drunk."

"How is solving anything going to help?"

Danny looked at him for a moment. "Justice. Finding bad guys and locking them up. It's what we do."

"Let me ask that question again. How is that going to help Maria or her family? Right now."

"Getting those boys off the street will help them feel better."

"For tomorrow night. Then they plan for a trial. Then for testimony. And for cross-examination. And, in the best case scenario, the boys come out of jail in a few years and she can see them every time she buys groceries."

"We can't think like that."

"Which neatly explains why I am drunk."

Danny, surrounded and besieged, clung to his fairly obvious point. "Cops should be sober on duty" and didn't understand how he had lost that argument.

"You could take care of your deadly breath, then."

"How about some mouthwash?"

"Sounds great."

They stopped at Cumberland Farms, used the badge to open the door, and bought an industrial sized bottle of Listerine. Higginbotham thought that he should keep that in the car. Then he wondered if the old man would just drink it.

"Do I smell better?"

"Infinitely." He said. "Tomorrow, we will need to get deodorant and laundry soap."

Coffin nodded.

"I stopped by Maria DeSalvo's house this weekend. She told me most of the story."

Higginbotham was about to joke, but he heard the tone and didn't.

"She and Julian were going to run away last night. Jack and Billy caught them at the party." He paused. "Everything else followed."

Danny accepted this fact and poked it.

"Can I be police now?"

"Please."

"Where's Julian?"

"I don't know."

"Did she get raped?"

"I don't know."

"What do you think?"

"I think there was a little bit of blood. I think she was locked into the bathroom. I think they took a picture of her butt. I think that the kids are shitheads."

"So you think she got raped?"

"I don't know."

"But you think..."

"Perhaps."

"Good thing we took her to the hospital to get examined." He said. "Really good thing you told her parents that we picked her up from the party and brought her home. Good honesty there."

Coffin sighed.

"Okay." He said. "Be skeptical. Tell me what you think happened?"

"Maria goes to the party looking for Julian. Maybe he's there, maybe he isn't. Jack and Billy see her there, slip her three extra Roofies and have some fun."

"Why Maria?"

"Why not? She's a sophomore, she's mouthy, she was alone..."

"Wrong place, wrong time."

"Something like that."

Coffin sighed. He could see the simplicity.

"Then," Danny continued, "Because they are stupid, they send that photo out. Who took it?"

"Tommy."

"Bet it was Jack."

Coffin felt his brain swell. He drank more water

"I don't like it" Coffin said.

"Is it because I am black?" Danny teased.

"No." he said. "I just don't."

"But it makes sense."

"Yes, but...."

Danny put the car in gear. Coffin put his hand over his head.

"Where's Julian?"

"Scared shitless in the woods." Danny said. " Or New Bedford, New York, and points west."

"How did he get a krugerrand?"

"I don't know," he said. "Do you want to do a little police work?"

"No." Coffin said. "But let's go."

Tom Nevers had been the last large swath of the island to be developed. At the time, the Great Minds of the town decided that it could be the future home of the firemen, policemen, and teachers. But they wanted the rest of the island to get rich, too. So, the left hand side of the road was laid out in one and three acre lots, with several curling, suburban roads. The right hand side of the road was laid out in half acre and quarter acre lots, jammed up onto dirt roads. The town employees were smarter than everyone figured. After they built cheaply, they sold off the right hand side of the street to summer folks as well. Then they quit their jobs and moved to Duxbury.

The Kellys remained. Their house had been tucked in among the scrub pine at the end of Hereford Street. Three green pickup trucks were parked in the driveway, along with one beat up Toyota Rav 4. The house was good sized, with a second story that had distant views of the water and a roof that still had roof jacks and two by fours on it.

Danny crept the squad car down the lane and pulled up next to a stone fence. Coffin had been awake for ten minutes and seemed much more lucid, although the smell remained the same.

"Put the flashers on."

Danny looked at him. "We just got warned about this."

"Have faith, my brother."

Danny sighed and ran the lights. Within thirty-seconds, a shade moved and a light went on downstairs.

"Here we go."

Danny stopped the lights. The two men walked up the path and knocked on the door. It opened within five seconds.

Mike and Ginny Kelly came to the door. She was in a purple sweatsuit. He wore BVD's and a Notre Dame T-shirt. Both looked tired.

"How can I help you, Inspector?" he said.

"My brother, my sister." Henry said. "I was hoping that I could talk to Tommy."

"It's a little late, wouldn't you say."

"I know. I am sorry about that." Coffin said. "I was hoping to talk to him outside of school and without him coming down to the police station."

"It's two-thirty in the morning, Henry." Mike said. "He's asleep."

"I know." He said. "I'm sorry. I can get him at school tomorrow."

Both parents looked at each other.

"What's going on, Inspector?" Mike asked.

Henry hesitated. "He might be involved in something ugly."

"Might?"

"Well, he is involved, but I don't know how much."

Both men were silent in the doorway. Ginny looked to the Inspector. Coffin knew what was expected and what he needed to do but, at this point, he didn't want to push it through. The moment hung.

"Can Danny and I come in?"

"Sure."

The Inspector waved at his partner. Danny switched off the cruiser's engine, picked up the folder, and locked up.

The two officers climbed the stairs to the main floor. The four adults sat at the kitchen table. Both of the Kelly's were tired and red-eyed. Coffee was brewing in the machine. Stuffed cats, spider plants, and "Mommy Knows Best..." filled a clean and cluttered room. The refrigerator still held middle school pictures of the little Tommy. Henry took a cup of coffee in his hands. His was an old Christmas mug. Danny's mug celebrated 25 years of Toscana Excavations. The three men took their coffee black.

For a second, Henry thought of the boy with the sagging pants and the stoned eyes that looked at him in the conference room at the school. He was their boy. Their only boy.

The inspector put his hands on top of the black folder that Danny had brought from the car. He thought of leaving.

"Mike, Ginny, I want to talk to you before we talk to Tommy. I want you to ask whatever you want of me, then we can talk to Tommy. Okay."

"Is he in trouble?" Ginny asked.

"Maybe." Danny said.

"Should we have a lawyer?" She looked at her husband.

Coffin knew that they should. Coffin knew that this would let him get up from the table and walk away. But Coffin also knew that they would look at him, think about it, and figure that no one was getting arrested tonight.

And he was right.

"Let's hear what the Inspector has to say."

Coffin looked at them and reached for a cool spot inside of himself.

"On Thursday Night, we stopped Jack, Billy, and Tommy on Milestone Road at two in the morning. Tommy was in the backseat."

"I thought he was in bed." Ginny said to her husband.

Mike nodded. "He sneaks out occasionally."

"You knew?" she said. "Why don't I know about this?"

"We'll talk..." Mike said. He looked at Coffin. "What happened?"

"Well, nothing." Coffin said. "Pink came and picked the three boys up."

"Pink?" The father glowered.

"Yeah, in his cab."

"He has been hanging out with Pink?"

"Well, he picked the three of them up." Coffin said. "They had been to a party that night in Quaise..."

"We think." Danny interjected.

"Yeah, they said they were surfing." Coffin added. "But we are here because of a picture that has been going around school."

Coffin opened the folder and handed a blow up of the "Remember" photo to the parents.

"What is this?" Ginny asked.

"This a picture taken on your son's phone at 11:47 Thursday night."

"It wasn't his phone."

"I am sorry," he said. "All of those pictures have a digital signature. You can see whose phone, what time it was, what day it was, and even what the GPS coordinates are." Coffin pointed to a mass of letters and numbers at the bottom of the sheet.

His mother looked up. "What did he do?"

His father didn't wait. "Tommy!" His voice ricocheted off the wall. "You get your ass up here right now."

The boy had also been awake for some time. He clumped up the stairs wearing a Notre Dame T-shirt and sweatpants. He looked decidedly more boyish and less punk without his hat and with his sweats pulled up.

The boy's eyes locked on Danny Higginbotham. The Detective thought that this might be the first time a black man had been in the house. It was definitely the first time a black man was in the house with a loaded Glock.

"We have some questions about some pictures."

"What pictures?"

"Pictures from the party last Thursday."

His parents sat and waited.

"I was here."

"No, you weren't." His father said. "You slipped out."

"No, I didn't." The boy snapped.

Coffin looked at him. "Tommy, we stopped the three of you on Milestone Road. You and I were there. Let's not lie. Not now."

"I meant to say..." he waffled. "I mean I wasn't at the party that night."

"These pictures are from your camera."

"It was stolen. It got stolen from my gym locker."

Coffin frowned. "Tommy, then you don't mind if we look up all of your phone records?"

"It wouldn't take much for us to pull that phone apart. We could see everywhere you had been." Danny continued.

The boy stood before them. He paled.

He saw three people run into the woods and two walk out. He saw Jack wipe something off his Maglight

"Right now, we just have the pictures." Danny said. "But the thing about cellphones is that they have everything. Texts, phone calls, locations. They are great little recorders."

Henry shot a look at his partner. Generally, he let the fibbing and the white lies come from Danny. But they didn't have the phone. If the boy pulled it out of his sweats right now and called a lawyer or Pink, it all ended here.

However, he didn't. Instead, he went paler.

"They threw it in the ocean. They said you couldn't get anything from it."

His face relaxed after the truth scurried out. And then he remembered what Billy and Jack do to snitches. He remembered.

His relief paled and shriveled. They would know.

Coffin cleared his throat. "We're not here to get you in trouble, Tommy. We need to solve some problems."

The boy looked at Detective Higginbotham. His eyes were ten miles away and were tracking a cab.

Coffin continued. "Who stole your phone?"

"I don't need to talk to you." He blurted.

"Yes, you do," his Dad barked. "Yes, you absolutely do. We have police in this house at three in the morning and you need to explain yourself."

"I can't talk to you." He barked. "My phone was stolen. I didn't have it. I didn't go to the party. I was right here." He looked at his Dad. "Why don't you believe me?"

"Tommy, look at me." Coffin said. He was tired, gray, and faded; as threatening as an overcoat. "We stopped the three of you on Milestone Road."

His father blazed, but held still. Coffin kept his eyes on the boy.

Danny backed up and away from the table. The boy watched him. He was losing hold of gravity.

"Tommy," Coffin asked. "Who stole your phone?"

The question landed next to him like a life preserver.

"Jack. Billy."

"And they used it?"

"Yes."

"They took pictures with it."

"Yes."

Coffin opened the folder and removed the "Remember" picture.

"Who took that picture?"

"Jack." Tommy lied.

Coffin wrote the name down.

"What was happening here?"

"Nothing."

"Tell me all of it." The old man asked.

Coffin kept himself from looking at the boy. Instead, he glanced at his mother. She had set her jaw and was leaning back, out of his line of sight and behind her husband. The boy was looking at his hands.

"Billy and Jack had brought this girl into the upstairs bedroom." His voice had become sing-song.

"At the house in Quaise."

"Yeah," he said. "And she was real dopey and sleepy. She fell on the bed and sort of rolled over. So, Billy rolls her over and he starts working her pants down. Then he writes on her butt and takes a picture."

"With your phone."

"Yeah." He grunted the word.

"Then what,"

His mother put her hand on her mouth. His father looked into his face.

"Nothing. Another kid came in."

"Nothing?"

"I swear, nothing. Nobody did anything to her."

Coffin looked him in the eyes.

"Nothing?"

"No, this other kid came in. He was her boyfriend. He had a knife and he swung it around and he slashed Jack in the belly."

"Wait. Say that again."

"Before anything could happen, this kid came in with a knife. He held it like this." He picked up a butter knife and held it with just his thumb and the first three fingers. "Then he barks something and he takes two slashes at Billy. When they back up, he gets between them and the girl. Then Jack comes for him and he slashes him across the belly."

"He was bleeding?"

"Yeah."

"Then what happened?"

"Then you guys came." His voice had gotten higher.

"We weren't there. We stopped you on the road, remember?"

"No, the other cops came to break up the party. We all ran."

"What happened to the girl?"

"Nothing."

"What happened when the cops arrived?"

"We ran."

"You left the kid with the knife and...the girl...in the bedroom."

"Yeah."

The boy was still staring at his hands. Coffin knew there was more.

"Then what?"

"Jack was pissed. He was more pissed than I have ever seen anyone. Ever."

The phone rang.

Everyone at the table jumped and stared at it. It was a red wall phone, still with a cord. A wooden message board hung next to it with a spool of white paper and mouse with an apron.

The phone rang again.

"Danny, would you go out to the car?" the Inspector asked.

The Detective was already moving down the stairs.

Billy stared at it as if it would explode.

The phone rang again. Coffin stood, walked over, and picked it up.

"Good morning."

There was noise on the other end of the line, but no words.

They didn't hang up.

Silence was the water that Coffin swam in. He waited.

In thirty seconds, someone said. "Remember."

Then the call ended.

Coffin turned and looked at the family at the table.

Mike Kelly had his head in his hands. Ginny was pale and looked to the Inspector.

Tommy was terrified. The spell had broken and he had remembered. He remembered what happen to snitches.

"Son," Coffin said. "Son, you need to tell me what happened to that boy."

"Nothing."

"What happened when Jack caught him?"

It was a wild guess. Coffin looked at the horror on the boy's face and guessed that something ugly. Something horrible had slipped into their lives and murdered sleep.

The boy shook his head. "They are going to kill me. They are going to fuck me then they are going to kill me."

His father slapped him. Short, violent, angry swing that caught the boy right on the ear. The boy fell from his chair.

His mother did nothing.

His father crabbed sideways from his chair, grabbed his son by the hair, and pounded his head into the floor. Coffin felt the impact in his feet.

"What happened next!"

"I don't know!" he screamed. "I don't know. They caught him on the road and they ran him into the woods and then they came out and wiped off their flashlights and we threw his bike in the woods and we cleaned off the glass and his phone kept ringing and he wasn't there the next day."

"Where?"

"Right near the hill and the Tom Nevers Road. Right near the bus stop." The boy was sobbing. His father maintained a firm control on his hair.

"What did you do?" he asked and banged his boy's head on the wide plank flooring. "What did you do?"

Coffin put one hand on the man's shoulders. He released his son's hair.

"When they were going to rape her, what did you do?" Mike Kelly asked his son. "When they attacked this boy, what did you do?"

The boy didn't answer. He rolled into a ball and covered his head.

His mother sat at the table with the coffee mugs, cream, sugar, and put her head in her hands.

Ten minutes later, Henry sat in the passenger seat.

The first echoes of dawn washed to the East. Coffin still felt the thump of a head on wood.

"She wasn't raped."

"I am not convinced."

"Fair enough." Coffin said. "But we might have a dead boy to look for in the morning."

"Who?"

"Julian."

"What did he say?"

"He said that Billy, Jack and Julian went into the woods, but only Billy and Jack came out."

"Did he tell you where?"

"Pretty much."

Danny looked at the old man. He was staring out the window into the dark.

A car passed by on the paved road.

Henry and his partner cruised the island in search of Pink's cab. While they were in search, they broke up another gathering, pulled over two drunk drivers, and otherwise made a nuisance of themselves for the late night partiers. By the time the Tuesday sun started to make itself known over Sconset, the two policemen were parked outside of Essex Road. Within a half hour, Pink's Cab pulled out of the road. Instead of running the lights, Danny just followed him until he let his fare out at the Stop and Shop.

She disappeared into the store.

Danny pulled up right next to him. The Inspector stepped out of the police car and nodded at Pink. He rolled his window down, but his eyes followed the Inspector as he walked around the front of the car and to the side, where the old man opened the door and sat in the back seat.

Pink turned around.

"How can I help you, Inspector?"

"I need a ride."

"Inspector…"

"Here's a twenty. Take me to Surfside Beach."

"It's a lot less than twenty bucks."

"I will want a ride back."

"Is Detective Higginbotham going to follow me?"

"Should he?"

"I'd rather he didn't."

"Good enough."

Coffin flashed a thumbs-up sign to his partner and eased back in the seat. Pink did not have any jazz playing, which was odd. He was exhausted. His eyes were bloodshot, his skin was pale, and the cab was, slightly, out of whack.

"Pink, you're too old for this, aren't you?"

"For driving cab?"

"No." Coffin smiled. "For driving cab at five in the morning."

"You're older than I am. You're working."

"I am not sure if you would call what I do work."

The cabbie smiled.

"You said it, not me."

Coffin smiled. "You know what I mean."

"No, I don't think I do, Inspector."

Coffin took a moment to examine the back of the minivan.

"There are a lot of bad things that we like Billy and Jack for."

"Why are you telling me?"

"Because I can't figure out why I always see them with you."

"They call and…"

"Pink, I am going to act as if I know everything that I know. I know what the Essex Road route is and, frankly, I don't really care. I would rather have you selling the stuff than someone I don't know. I know that you are trying to sell some land, but your brother is all over it and is trying to squash it. I know that you don't, really, need the money. It would be nice, but…."

"You don't know all that you think you know."

"Fair enough." Coffin said. They pulled into the parking lot at Surfside and surprised some seagulls and their crabs. "Here is what else I know. You and I are old. We have been around the block more than once and know a thing or two. We know how to avoid the bus crashes."

"Is there a bus crashing?"

"Why do you need to ask?"

"For a Quaker, you do like to talk in riddles."

"For a lawyer, you seem pretty obtuse."

"You want me to rein in the boys?"

"Perhaps."

"Well, I can't," he said. "They're just boys. You say that you like them for an assault. I hear that, I think fight. Boys get in fights. It happens. We live in a time when if a kid comes home with a black eye somebody wants to sue."

"Funny thing for a lawyer to say."

"It's true, though. And you know it." He said. "A girl gets drunk at a party and gets it on with a guy, the next morning her Dad wants to yell rape. Do these boys run a little wild? Absolutely. Are they different from boys from a generation or two generations or five generations ago? No, they aren't."

"Nice closing, Counselor." Coffin looked at the back of his head. "I still don't understand why you are with these two?"

"Maybe I just like them? Maybe I want to do something for them? Maybe I want to keep them from crashing?"

"Maybe, Maybe you should hop out while you can," Coffin said. "Or maybe there is something else going on."

Pink had already stopped the car. He turned and faced the Inspector. "What are you implying?"

"Not a thing, my brother. But I will tell you this. There have been mean vicious punks out here for years. We always figured out what to do with them. We sent them out on whale ships or we stuck them out in the farms or they went to war or California or out fishing but we always did something with them. They never stayed here. These kids are sharks. They smell the blood, they circle in, they take a few bites, and then they swim on."

"They're not sharks."

"What are they?"

"Just boys."

"Just boys headed to a bad end."

Pink regarded the hungover Inspector.

"Is that a threat?"

"I suppose it is. I suppose it is."

Without another word, The cab turned around and drove back to the Stop and Shop parking lot.

By now, the dawn pooled up over the Atlantic and a glow hung in the fog along the road. Danny brought the cruiser back up the Milestone Road to the hill that Tommy had described. Wordlessly, he pulled onto the bike path and crept up it while Henry played the spotlight through the woods.

"What are we looking for?"

"A bike or a body." Coffin said. "Or anything."

The woods were not precisely woods. The ocean and the salt air crippled and bent the trees. Scrub oak and black pine were the only plants that grew over ten feet tall, and they only reached that height with carbuncles, blight, and a list away from the North east. Beach grass and bushes clustered at the foot of these trees, as well as ribs and arms of grey branches.

They found the Schwinn on the second pass. It had not been hidden or carefully buried, but, as Tommy had said, was tossed into the bracken. The Inspector caught a reflection of light of the seat post. He stepped out and examined it, careful not to move or touch it.

Danny called into the station and asked for some help gathering evidence. By now the pick-up trucks, work vans, and taxis were driving past at higher and higher speed.

The Inspector continued to prowl through the bushes. He found cans, bottles, and another bike; all of which stretched back decades What he did not find, in each spreading semi-circle away from the bike, was a body.

As their shift was ending and Danny was preparing to leave to pick up his daughter and bring her to school, Henry found Julian's phone.

It was wet and without power. It was, most likely, useless. But it was a recent model Sanyo on top of a wet pile of brown oak leaves. Coffin was careful to take a picture, plant a flag, then pick up the phone in a bag, as if her were picking up his Golden Retriever's poop. He labeled the bag "Exhibit 2: Phone." Coffin tramped out of the woods holding the phone.

The Chief's Suburban had pulled up behind Danny's patrol car. The two men stood by the side of the car with their arms crossed. Danny, when he saw his partner, waved and left to pick up his daughter.

Chief Bramden stayed there.

"What do you have there?"

"A cell phone."

The Chief nodded. "Is it evidence?"

"Could be."

The Chief did not move. Coffin walked up to him and stood before him. The Chief reached out and took the bag. He stuffed it into his coat.

"Inspector, what do you have here?"

"My brother, I think we have a murder site."

"Do we have a murder?"

"Maybe."

"Do we have a body?"

"No."

The Chief recrossed his arms and he nodded.

"Henry, for a man who doesn't arrest people, you have been involved in some fairly odd investigations recently. A week ago, you were running the lights investigating a rape that did not happen."

"The victim didn't press charges. It doesn't mean the rape didn't happen."

"True." Bramden smiled. "Has she pressed charges? Is there any...biological evidence?"

"No."

"Okay." The Chief was enjoying this. It was not often that he caught the only Inspector in Massachusetts out quite so far on the limb. "Now, you are investigating a murder when there is no body."

"Well, I suppose so."

"How can this be?"

"I talked to a boy a few hours ago and he told me about Billy and Jack clubbing a kid in the woods here. I found his bike and I think I found his cellphone."

"Why would Billy and Jack do that?"

"The kid interrupted them with a knife before they could finish with Maria DeCarlo at the party."

"And Maria won't sign a statement that she was raped, nor is there any medical evidence."

Coffin looked at him. "Correct."

"Who was this boy that saved her with a knife."

"His first name is Julian. He's illegal and Brazilian."

"Henry," The Chief looked at him. "You have two stories that neither person will write down, a bunch of guesses, and a rusted bike. You don't have a rape and you don't have a murder."

"Well, not yet."

"Not ever, Henry." He said. "You can't even prove that this kid Julian existed, not if he is an illegal. You sure can't prove he is dead if there is no body."

"Yet."

"You were in the woods, Henry." The Chief said, with a smile. "If there was a body there, I am sure that your keen eyesight and sense of smell would have found it. No body, no gulls circling the body, no blood on the leaves, nothing."

Coffin looked into the woods.

"Let me take you home, Henry. Get some sleep."

CHAPTER THREE

Just past dawn, Rosie heard the saw going. If she heard the saw going, all of the neighbors also heard it.

Rick was out there on the table saw; he was cutting through a four by four of solid pressure treated pine. The saw had the deep rumble of a bear feeding. Rosie put her sweatpants on slipped her feet into a pair of untied sneakers and went padding out to the shed.

The saw was off and he was examining the cut. Rosie stepped up behind him ad tapped him on the shoulder.

"So, what are you doing?"

"A little work."

"What are you making?"

"A crucifix."

"One or two?"

Rick looked at his wife. "Well, I was thinking I would make two, but maybe I should make a third?"

"Why don't we leave it at two? At least until ten."

Rick looked around. "Oh."

"It's fine."

"Anyone call?"

"No."

He set the four by four on the ground. It was about six feet long. She reached out and touched his back.

"Rick, what are we going to do?"

He straightened slowly and backed into her hand. He sighed and pinched the bridge of his nose.

"I don't know." He muttered.

She sighed.

"Can we send her back to school here?"

"No."

"What if the boys are arrested?"

"You know how that will work."

He nodded. Arrests, then bail. Guilty until proven innocent, accompanied by a restraining order and a tutor. Maybe. Maybe a trial or a plea deal or …. But the island would buzz for months. Everyone would wear the robes and sit on the bench. They would get an answer, but not justice. Not really.

"We send her away, I don't know how that helps her."

"I bet I could find a convent in New Hampshire or Canada."

"Nuns would work."

"They would," she said. "I don't know how many of them are around."

"We could go."

He looked at her. "We could…"

"But,"

"We didn't do anything wrong, did we?"

"Doesn't matter," she said. "Does it?"

"No."

She felt his hesitation. She hated it. It was money and it was business and it was being the master carpenter to the Bond Chiefs and the King High Partners. It was having his business card handed around the locker room after a round of golf. It was getting calls on Monday morning after the cocktail party broke up for the weekend. "Really liked the work you did for…"

There had been a time, long before this, when he was going to be the professor who made his own dinner table. There had been a time when there was going to be a book about the history of woodwork among the slaves. There had been a time of historical reconstruction and artisanship and master classes. However, that time and that path had passed.

Rosie could see that he had been happy. She could see that he loved the work and the attention and the money. He used the computer to check the mutual funds and the retirement funds and the college funds. He didn't gamble on spec houses or land swaps or any of the other big time developer swindles. Instead, he came home at five, kept time open on the weekends, and was a decent father. He knew who he was and who he wasn't.

However, the man he once was sat on the top shelf of a closet, waiting for two more chapters and some editing.

He had made his bed.

She let her hand wander up to his tight, sore shoulders.

"If we leave," he said. "Are we running?"

"Maybe." She admitted. "If we stay, who do we fight? How?"

He nodded. "With crucifixes."

"If only." She said. "What if we went and looked at some boarding schools."

He nodded.

"I'll try to find ones with tall metal fences and lesbians."

He nodded again.

Starbuck and Henry Coffin appeared one more time in the DeCarlo's backyard.

Rick was in his workshop, with the table saw going. He wore a t-shirt, jeans, and a Whaler's baseball hat.

Henry stood at the workshop door. Starbuck sat behind him, sensitive to the noise.

Rick looked up then switched off the saw.

"Have you caught them?"

"No."

"Don't."

"You got plans?"

"I not only have plans, I have power tools."

"You gonna build him a hutch or something."

Rick looked cold. "Something."

"How is that going to work?"

"What you don't know can't hurt me."

Henry looked at the angry father. "What happens afterward?'

"Afterward, I sleep peacefully."

"You think?"

"I know more than you know."

Henry nodded.

"Is she here?"

"Yup."

"We'll talk later, my brother."

Rick flipped the table saw back on.

Henry knocked and opened the back door. Starbuck scooted past and skidded to a stop in the center of the kitchen. Rosie commanded his attention.

"Afternoon, Henry."

"Afternoon. You have a fan."

"Good boy." Rosie opened her refrigerator and pulled out several slices of cheese. She folded them over to make one thick looking plank.

"Make him do something for it." Henry asked.

"Of course." She placed the plank of cheese on the end of his nose. "Now, stay. Stay!"

Starbuck looked cross-eyed at the cheese. His tail flapped once.

"Now, go."

He flipped it up and snatched the cheese out of the air.

Thirty seconds after licking up the scraps from the floor, he looked up into her eyes for more.

"Get out of here." She said, without any particular firmness. He stayed in the kitchen, but Rosie didn't look at him. After a few seconds, he starting nosing around looking for scraps.

'How are you doing, Rosie?"

"Just fucking fabulous."

Coffin nodded.

"Is she here?"

"She went back to sleep."

"That's good."

"I suppose."

"Rick is out there making a crucifix."

"Keeps him out of trouble."

Henry sighed. "What are you going to do?"

"I have no fucking clue." Rosie snapped. "How can I sit in my little nurse's office, doling out aspirin and Ritalin, while those little turds are walking around with their hats on backward?"

"We don't really know what happened."

"I know what happened."

"You sure?"

"She doesn't come out of her bedroom. We can't get her to the hospital. Yeah, I know."

The Inspector took a moment to feel for something strong deep inside himself.

"You didn't go to work today, did you?"

"Hell no. I would have poisoned the little fucks."

"I need to show you something." He said. "You're not going to like it."

Coffin sat at the breakfast table. Rosie stopped pacing in the kitchen and sat across from him.

"Hit me, Henry."

Coffin opened the black folder and pushed the picture across to her. She looked down at the word "Remember" written on her daughter's lower back.

She paused.

"They are little fucks, aren't they?" Her voice was small and grim.

"Yup."

She pushed the paper back. "Put it away. I don't want Rick to see it. Or Maria."

"You know it is on the internet."

"Everything is," she said. "They won't see it now. They won't see it today. I can't speak for tomorrow, but I have today by the balls."

Starbuck was lapping up the crumbs under the table. Rosie stood and walked over to her cup of coffee, then came back and sat down.

"Danny and I confronted the young man who took the picture last night."

"Who?"

"I have to do everything by the book if I want to arrest him. Can't tell you."

"As if I can't guess." She snorted.

"He told us that nothing actually happened. He told us that someone else came in and protected her. We found her in a bathroom."

"You found her?" She stopped. "You found her. You found my daughter in a bathroom and you didn't tell me."

Coffin reached for that firm rope and held it tight.

"Danny and I found her locked in the bathroom. She told us..."

"You knew this happened. And you didn't tell me."

"Yes." Coffin said. "We were..."

Suddenly there was nothing to say. Henry saw his sin before him.

"Please leave, Henry. Just go."

Rosie stared a hole in her table.

Coffin stood, collected the dog, and slipped out the door.

CHAPTER FOUR

The Assistant District Attorneys for the Cape and Islands are based in Hyannis. Once a week, usually on a Monday, they come over for the various perfunctory court hearings and pleadings. Generally, the ADA rides the high speed ferry with many of the lawyers she will meet in the court in an hour. They gossip, trade newspapers and, occasionally, cut a quick deal on the defendants. Then, they all go through the dance moves of the court room, break for lunch, dance again until the four o'clock boat, then return to hearth and home.

In the last year, Erica Davidson had come over to do all of the legal scut work on island. The police liked her because she didn't cut many deals with the multiple losers. She was also six foot two, brunette, powerful, beautiful, and as of this October, seven months pregnant with her first child. She should be at home, in bed.

However, at eleven in the evening on this Wednesday, she waited for Inspector Henry Coffin in the one and only interrogation room/storage closet/break room at the police station. Chief Bramden had long since given up the ghost and had gone home to his health club meatballs and posturpedic mattress.

Detective Danny Higginbotham had received the message that she was there for the old man, made the Inspector put on a cleaner shirt, and drove him down to the station. Erica had a series of folders, a yellow legal pad, and a chirping and charging blackberry in front of her.

"Erica. Always a pleasure." Coffin stood and waited for her.

"Inspector. Detective." She gestured at the two chairs.

"To what do we owe the honor? Shouldn't you be home and in bed?"

She looked up. "You know what one of the bitch things about being pregnant is? It's that everyone has an opinion about what I should be doing with my body."

Coffin smiled.

"As it so happens, Inspector, when you get to be my size, sleep is a fairly random event anyway. Since I get to skip out on work tomorrow and sleep alone in a hotel room tonight and get room service breakfast on the taxpayers, I am going to count this a win."

"Well, that's good."

"But I was really tempted to send a few of your colleagues to your house to roust you this afternoon."

"Glad you didn't."

"Inspector, let me ask you some very pointed questions right now. If you want to have representation for this, we can arrange it for tomorrow."

"I am fine, Erica. Ask away."

"Did you threaten Jack Mitchell, Billy Trotter, or Lewis Pinkham?"

"I did not."

"Did you physically threaten or intimate that you would use your power as a police officer and as an officer of the court to threaten them?"

"Absolutely not."

"You did not harass them in any way?"

"No."

"Good. Sign this." She said. "It's a letter to their attorney that affirms what you just said. I will also send them a letter that says that I have investigated the matter and consider it concluded."

Coffin signed it without reading it.

"Now that that is done." She put the letters into a folder. "Tell me what the hell is going on?"

"We like Jack and Billy for a rape and a murder."

She didn't look up. "What have you got?"

"Nothing."

Davidson looked at the Inspector. "Nothing?"

"A touch more than that. We have the rape victim and a witness to the murder."

"Have they given you statements yet?"

"No, not yet."

"Any other witnesses?"

"No."

"How about physical evidence?"

Danny chimed in. "No."

"No body?"

"No."

"How about the rape?"

"There was no semen, just bruising." Danny said. Coffin glanced at him, but he wasn't really surprised at the lie.

"Videotape? Cellphone calls? Message pads where we could do pencil outlines?"

"Not yet."

"Not yet?"

"Well, someone posted a picture of the assault victim up on the internet and it bounced around school."

"But…"

"But they posted it from a stolen cell-phone."

"So…" She said. "You have a victim who can point out these two kids, but she won't write a statement. You have murder, but no body. You have a witness to the murder, but he won't write a statement."

"Yes." Coffin said.

Erica sighed. "Hell of a job, guys. This case pretty much carries itself. I'll bring it to Judge Anastos in the morning and he'll have them in jail by lunch."

"Well," Coffin smiled. "It's a work in progress."

"Let's forget the murder case, because it is a missing person's case for the next ten years. Let's talk rape. Do you know how hard it is to prosecute a rape case?"

"Yes."

"No, I don't think you do." She said. "The first thing the accused will do is deny he was there, then he will deny it was him, and finally, he will say that she wanted it to happen. No physical evidence, no witnesses, no pictures, not even a statement…." She shrugged.

"We have some other leads."

"Well, here is your other problem. The two boys have lawyered up and accused you of harassment. Which we have dealt with here. But you can't just appear at their school anymore. Now you have to talk to their lawyer first. This guy Pinkham."

"Well, that figures…" Danny said.

"Who is this guy? I've never heard of him." She said to the black man.

"He's a native, a cab driver, and he got disbarred about five years ago. And he's a drug dealer."

Henry added. "I would put the drug dealer part earlier, but yeah."

"So, he's a motivated pain in the ass who knows just enough to be dangerous?"

"Yes." Danny said.

"So, you won't use your charming religious talk to wheedle a confession out of the two of them?"

"Probably not." Danny shot in.

"Inspector?"

He sighed. "He's right."

"So," she eased back. "The good guys are going to lose this one."

"There are still some other paths." Coffin added.

"But," she said. "You have absolutely nothing right now."

"Yes."

"Leave the three of them alone until you get a few statements."

Coffin said nothing.

"Am I right?" she asked.

"You're right." Danny agreed. "But he's a stubborn old man." He smiled at the growling Inspector. "It's why some of us still love him."

Fifteen minutes later, they were outside the DeSalvo's house.

Detective Higginbotham looked at his partner in the darkness. They were seated in the squad car, in the shadow of the old windmill. The Inspector respected what Danny thought. And the words from the Assistant District Attorney still dribbled from his ears.

"It's all right Henry. We'll get Pink and his buddies selling coke or something in about a month."

Coffin didn't look at him.

"The evidence doesn't exist, Henry. Nothing we can do about it."

The Inspector remained silent.

"We can get them another way, you know. If we get everyone to put pressure on Pink, he will give them up to us. You know that. You KNOW Pink is not going to let these two boys pull him and his money down. We can get them for whatever drug charge we can think up, because Pink will play ball, and we can lock these kids up for a good long time."

Coffin nodded. He was thinking.

"Henry," Danny said. "Henry, it's a problem we deal with everyday. We don't partial out justice. We let horrible people carry on their horrible lives everyday. Pink sells drugs to school kids, but we don't punish him for that. We're not going out and arresting those folks, are we? We don't do justice, we do peace. We go out and try and get folks to tolerate each other for a little bit. It's all we do. We are just social workers with guns." He said. "And you don't even carry that."

Coffin nodded.

"Let's go in."

Rosie wore a t-shirt and pink sweatpants. She sat at her kitchen table with a cup of black coffee, the newspaper, and an exceptionally fat frog. Henry knocked on the door, then pushed his way in, stepped gingerly over and sat at the table opposite her.

"How are you doing?" he asked.

"Been better."

"I'm sure. Sorry about that."

She eyed him and let the silence coalesce around the man. "How can I help you, Inspector?"

The silence stuck.

"I'm sorry, Rosie."

"Me too, Henry. Me too."

"I wanted her to trust me..."

"Henry, I trusted you."

Coffin nodded.

"And you didn't trust me." She continued.

"Yes." He said. "And that is what I am sorry about."

Rosie sipped her coffee. She didn't acknowledge him in anyway.

"Where's Rick?" Coffin asked.

"I don't know," She said. "And that is really scary."

"He won't do anything stupid."

"Tell me something smart that happens after midnight."

The Inspector nodded to her there.

"Rosie, this is what I believe." He breathed in. "I believe that Maria has had a secret boyfriend for a few months now, a boy named Julian. Julian is Brazilian, and illegal, and doesn't go to school. I think that they made plans to leave the island together last Thursday night and they were supposed to meet at the party. Then, at the party, someone fed roofies to Maria and brought her upstairs. Her boyfriend came in then and sliced up Jack. Then the cops arrived and everybody ran, except Maria who found herself locked into a bathroom."

Coffin paused. Rosie sipped her coffee.

"I believe that the boys chased Julian down and beat the tar out of the kid. I think they must might have killed him." He said. "Nobody can find him or find his body."

The Inspector put the kruggerand on the table.

"Does that mean the case is over?"

"No, it means that I need to find Julian."

"Alive or dead."

"Yes." The Inspector said.

"And, because I know you, you think that he is dead. So this can be something for Maria to have. A souvenir."

Coffin nodded. "That may be a touch brutal."

"But you think he is dead."

"I have no evidence."

"But you think that?"

"Yes."

Rosie put her finger on the coin and pushed it around the table. Then she left it alone.

"And that's the truth."

"As much as I know."

"All things being equal, Henry, I would rather have the lies back."

She sipped her coffee.

Coffin stood up and looked at his old friend. "What are you going to do?"

"I don't know." She admitted.

"I know."

"She can't go back to school here."

Coffin nodded.

"Those two boys…" she said. "They are still there."

"Yes."

"And they aren't going anywhere?"

"Eventually. We will get them on something, eventually."

Rosie looked at him. "Really?"

"We are watching and listening. They will do something dumb soon."

"Good luck with that." She said. "I can't send her back there. I am going to take her out to some school in New York in a few days. We'll check it out."

"Do you have contacts out there?"

"No." she said. "But it is an all-girl's school in the woods."

Coffin nodded. "What are you going to do?"

"Me?"

"Yeah."

"Go back to work. Wipe noses. Hand out drugs. Watch all of those kids who knew what was happening and did nothing."

"You could resign."

"No." she said. "I definitely cannot do that. We still need health insurance. We will need even more money to send her away to school. No, I have to keep working."

"Sorry."

"It's what we do, isn't it Henry?" she said. "It's what you do. One morning you wake up with your heart ripped out and you want to stop the world. But it doesn't and food needs to come to the table, doctors need to get paid, and retirement creeps along. It's a cruel sun that shines every day."

Coffin nodded.

Hours later, The Inspector had been steadily snoring at the Lifesaving Museum. He did not remember his dream, but even dreamlessness is a break.

He awoke, however, as the car was doing seventy and climbing.

He sat himself up in the seat and blinked the sleep out of his eyes.

"Just got a call from Paul Brody."

"Yeah."

"He says Rick has been out to see him."

"Is he still there?"

"He won't say."

"So he is."

"Rick wanted to hire him."

Danny put the car in gear. "Now," Henry said. "Why would he want to hire a former Special Forces soldier?"

"I have a a better question."

"Which is?"

"How much do you suppose he charges?"

Brody lived out in Quaise. He taught school, read books, and enjoyed moderate amounts of prescription morphine mixed with iced tea.

His house had been his father's fishing cabin. Then, with the addition of a gallon of gas and several cigarettes, it became a glassy, two level cape on the edge of dark scrub pines and a darker ocean. When the officers pulled in, they blocked Rick DeSalvo's pick-up truck.

The house was dark. With some experience, the two officers circled around the back to the deck. Paul Brody sat at the edge of a chaise lounge. Three feet away, Rick lay sleeping in his chair. Both of his wrists were taped to the arms of the chair.

"Good afternoon, Paul."

"My brothers." He said. Henry smiled at his little joke.

"So…" Henry said. "He couldn't stay awake, could he?"

"He had some help."

Danny looked. Paul held up his pitcher of iced tea. Somewhere in there were some powerful hospital level pain killers.

"How much did you give him?"

"A couple hours worth. Maybe until dawn. He is breathing long and strong."

"Good." Danny said.

"So," Henry asked. "What happened?"

"He came out here a couple hours ago. Real nervous."

"Had you heard?"

"Yeah."

"So, we sat out here and had a beer. We were polite and civilized. Then he asked me the best way to kill a man. I told him that the killing was the easy part. It was living with yourself afterward that was hard."

"Have any effect?" Henry asked.

"No. He said that he wasn't sure how he could live with himself if he didn't."

Henry did nothing, but Danny looked out to sea.

"So…." Henry said.

"So, he asked about a bunch of different methods and all before I suggested a long range shot."

"Nice of you."

"It's the hardest to do. He wouldn't have the nerve."

"I wouldn't be sure of that." Danny said.

"Ever done it?" Paul asked. He was calm and non-confrontational.

"No."

"You see the figure in the glass and you think of everything you are going to take away. If you are human, you jerk the rifle. High left."

"Rick's motivated."

"'Motivated' is good for strangling or for stabbing, not for a distant shot."

Henry looked at the soldier. "I'll take your word for it."

"So he wanted a rifle." Paul continued. "We talked guns for awhile. Then, I think, he realized that he would never do it. So he asked me."

"What did you say?"

"I told him to tell me when."

Danny and the Inspector looked at him. Both believed that he meant what he said.

"I'd rather you held off on that."

"It's why I called you. Now I can't."

"Good planning." Henry said.

"Let's hope so."

Danny saw the blackness filtering around them.

"We would miss you." The Inspector said.

"You would." He said. "I would have to be so careful that you would have no proof." He sipped his drink. "Luckily, George Bush paid a lot of money to teach me how to do that."

"Don't." Henry said.

Brody lifted himself up and eased back in the chair. Both police officers had no doubt that Brody had been considering it.

"Tell me, Henry. How do Quakers get rid of rats?"

"Same as anyone else."

"Same with bugs?"

"Yes."

"So, how are we to rid ourselves of these two?"

"Well, they're people."

"Not to my way of thinking. Not as I use the word."

"I am not saying that I like them. I am not saying that I don't think a really long spell deep inside a prison wouldn't help them find Jesus. I mean that they are just boys."

"Just boys?" Danny turned on his partner. "After what we have seen?"

"Jack didn't invent rape. Billy didn't create witness intimidation. Go back a decade and find me a Billy. Go back two, or three, or ten. Pick me a town, pick me a city, pick me a country, and I'll find you these two."

"You know what happened to them?"

"Sure. They got whipped on whaleships, sent to war, or dropped into the back forty. I don't care about them that much."

Both men looked at the Inspector. He continued. "I care about you. I don't want you to do something stupid that you will regret for the rest of your life."

"How do you live with yourself if you do nothing?"

"How come those are the two choices: kill them or do nothing?"

"You got another option?"

"Lock them up for a very long time."

"I think you're wrong, Henry." Brody said. "These ones are different. They have no fear, they have no hesitation, they have no shame."

The Inspector looked at his partner. "Nothing like this in Southie?"

"They would do this in Southie. They would do worse. However, ticking away, in the back of their eyes, was a fucked up morality. It was the game, but the game had rules. You never break the rules. If you fucked someone's sister, you could expect a bullet or a baseball bat, but no pity. These kids have no rules."

Brody continued. "They are sharks. They have swum into a placid calm little pool full of fat little fish, and they are feeding."

Danny added. "The rules in Southie would involve these boys getting hurt in an expensive, and likely permanent way."

"Shouldn't be that way." Henry said.

"There are a lot of things that shouldn't be." Danny said. "I want the same island, the same community that you want. I don't want Southie. But, that's how it gets handled there."

"Not here." Henry said. "Not here."

"We'll see." Brody said. "Don't be surprised if those two boys just disappear one night."

"You won't."

"I might."

"You're better than that."

Brody smiled. "Goodnight Henry. Goodnight Danny."

Both men went home to their beds. When Rick woke up, finally, he went home as well

CHAPTER FIVE

Elvis woke to the sound of a thud, a snap, and a heavy sigh.

At the sound, he instantly knew and instantly denied, that the rest of his life had grown much more complicated and much more painful. In the space of a breath, he felt something fly away.

Then he heard a moan.

Elvis sat up in the flashing dark. The lights of every machine began to flash.

His father moaned a second time.

Elvis opened the hospital room door. The nurses were hurrying towards him. His father sat on the floor with his left leg at an impossible angle. His robe was open and all lay exposed. Further, the old man had lost control of his bowels on the floor.

David Lowell closed his eyes and rested his head on the edge of the mattress. The lies and illusions had burned away, as had the pleasant distance of the morphine. He would never stand again. His hours had dwindled to a handful. The granite facts stood before him

"It's okay, Dad," lied Elvis. "I'll call everyone."

The son found a blanket and covered his father as best he could. The nurses arrived.

The father made two swinging turns of his head.

David looked at Elvis as the old man tried to say "Love." But there were no words to rise from his throat and he knew anyway. In his mind, he realized that he had said his final words.

Tears came and continued to flow until the nurses medicated him.

Sherrie Higginbotham walked Doctor Tupper to Room 22. Both were tired, both had been up late, both had found their lives ground down by the specific and personal violence that the island and its inhabitants shipped to them. An eight month old had come in with broken vertebrae and a visible slap mark. Tupper's high school classmate had disappeared deep into the web of Alzheimer's. The rest of the pageant was starting to move.

So, when the two of them came to Room 22 and the dying man, they came with the professional callous of people who walked at the edge of the shade. They knew that some people stood on the line for a while. Some backed away for years, but eventually, everyone slipped over the line.

When Tupper thought of death, he thought of the dark side of the moon. Without any atmosphere, the moon had a clear line between day and night. Astronomers, without irony, referred to it as the terminator. It swept along the lunar landscape with the remorseless speed of gravity. And so did death. You might be able to out-run it for a while, but it would sweep you into the shadow.

So, when Tupper looked at the chart for David Lowell, he saw a man who was too tired to run from the shadow. He was tired and he was down and he needed something for the pain. Tupper knew all about that.

When they stepped into the room, the big kid sat next to his father.

"Son, could I have a word?"

Elvis stood and slowly moved to the door. The doctor's head came up to the boy's chin. Sherrie looked right into the center of his chest.

"Son," Tupper said. "Your father has had a bad fall. The fall from bed snapped his femur in two. We have straightened it out and splinted it, somewhat. Because his bones have become very brittle, they aren't going to heal quickly or well. And, because he is so sick, we can't bring him into surgery."

Elvis heard, but he was not able to understand. He asked. "So, it will take time?"

"Your father, unfortunately, does not have a lot of time. His cancer is at stage 4 and has been for some time. He has tumors growing in his arms, his chest, and his legs. The break occurred at the same spot as a tumor. Further, we suspect the cancer has advanced into his brain. Neither of his pupils appears to focus, which suggests that he can't see."

"Okay." The boy said.

Sherrie looked at him. She remembered how he had been during his father's first night in Room 22. "Elvis, I need you to listen to me. What I am going to say is hard, but I need you to hear it."

"Okay." The boy repeated.

"Your Dad can't see, Elvis. He can't eat, he can't speak. He can't walk, he can't go to the bathroom. If he wakes up, he may recognize your voice and he may not. But he is in pain."

"Okay."

"We can't fix his leg, Elvis. We can't fix his cancer, now, either."

"Okay."

The two medicals looked at each other. Dr. Tupper began a familiar line of questions.

"Does your father have a living will?"

The boy's eye focused. "Yes."

"Who has the power of attorney?"

"I do."

"Son, are you sure?"

Elvis looked beyond the two of them to the wall. "I have it. We wrote it in Chicago when he first started getting treatment."

"Do you have it with you?"

"Of course."

It was a well worn, creased business envelope that the boy had in the front pocket of his backpack. Both nurse and doctor read it, then they turned it over.

"Son, this is very important. Does your father want us to employ extreme measures? Do you know what that means?"

The boy did, but he could not speak at the moment.

"It means that, when he stops breathing, we can't resuscitate him."

For a second, Elvis couldn't think why his father would stop breathing. Then he remembered.

The doctor and nurse saw the boy pale.

"Okay." He said.

Tupper looked at him. "You need to call his people."

Aunt Shannon arrived while he was on the phone with Nick. She settled into the other chair and took out her Sudoku and her knitting. There was nothing to say right then. She left at noon and returned four hours later.

Coach Tillinghast appeared before school. He had worked out, showered, and returned to the hospital before he would go to school and then to practice. He said a few words and shook the boy's hand. He would be back, he said.

The boy said, "Sure."

Nick appeared at lunch. He shook Elvis' hand as well and said he would be back later.

Elvis said, "Okay."

Others came and left. Through it all, his father slept. The machines beeped, the bags were changed by the nurses, and the light was kept low.

There was no bag for his urine.

Elvis stared at the spot where the bag once hung. The absence itched him.

Then, he knew.

His father wasn't pissing anymore, either.

Coach Tillinghast returned with a sausage pizza. Nick carried in two six packs of Sam Adams. Shannon, with an eye on propriety and the stories of the nurses, cast a cold eye on the beer. As Tillinghast opened the first bottle and invited the boys to join him, there was no room for her words and rules in that room. Nor was there time for it.

"So," Tillie leaned back and looked at the boy. "Tell us a story."

"About him?"

"About your Dad. Yes. Tell us about him."

"I don't know."

The enormity of the task lay before him. He remembered moments, glances, and snippets of time. He didn't know a story. He couldn't reduce all the life that had been his father into the narrow channel of a story.

Shannon spied him and waited.

"He loved football." Elvis said. "He loved everything about it. When I was in Pee-Wee, he didn't want to coach it. He wanted to hold the line markers. He wanted to be precise about where the ball was and how much was left for first down. I was…seven? Everyone was four feet high and lost in the helmets and pads, but he wanted the down and distance to be precise. During one game, the ref lost count of the downs and called for third down twice. Then, my Dad yelled his name-"Ted." The ref turned, pissed as hell, saw my Dad, saw the numbers and gave up. He called time out and raised his fist for fourth down."

The males nodded. Tillie looked at the dying man's sister.

"Did he play football as a boy?"

"Not for long."

"No?"

She cast a quick, cruel glance at her nephew. "You never met your grandfather, did you?"

"No."

"There was a reason for that."

She didn't say anything else. She felt that that should be enough. But three pairs of eyes were on her. Their silence pushed her forward.

"He had fought in the Pacific. He was a Marine who survived. He had the tattoos, he had the stare, and he had the silence. Never told us a word, of course."

Tillinghast was of the generation. "What was his battalion?"

"Fourth Marine Raiders. Survived Iwo Jima and New Guinea."

"Meat-grinder."

"So I read. I found his stiletto, a Japanese sidearm and a skull after he died." She said. "And the patch. But he was no hero. He was a mean, drunken, violent man who drove subway cars all day and beat people up all night. He would get started down at Caruso's, then he would walk home and start again."

She continued knitting.

"He killed my mother. Slapped her hard when she wasn't ready. Spun backwards, hit the edge of the stove on the side of her head and fell. He was there." She nodded at the dying man.

"The police came by and talked to him. The priest came by and talked to him. The rain just kept falling on the room. Then, Joe Batters came by. Then the roof opened."

"Who?"

"Joe was very high up in the Chicago mob. Old guy then, with two other men. Everyone was very calm, even happy. They didn't look like mobsters, they looked like lawyers. They knew David Senior, of course. Someone had been in the Marines. Someone else had seen him at the bars. Thought he was down on his luck. Did him a favor. Made my mother's murder disappear in an icy fall. Big funeral. Lots of flowers. Devoted mother. Horrible loss."

She continued to knit.

"But, the Outfit hired itself a new man in Elvis' grandfather and he liked his new work. This was the sort of thing he was good at. The beatings stopped, but he was never home. The boys needed a new mother and there I was: sixteen and ugly. Money was dropped off, food was made, Ms. Racini came over twice a week to help out and keep an eye on things and that was it."

"David got his growth spurt in seventh grade. By eighth grade he was 6'4 and 250 pounds. No one picked fights with him. No one talked to him at all. He kept growing. That fall, he started playing football. The other kids from the Outfit played ball as well, and one of them even made the pros, but David only got to play one game. He dominated another team. He won 6-0 and no more envelopes appeared at our door."

She took the moment to recount the stitches she had knit. She hadn't told Elvis what she was making, but she was using baby blue yarn.

"So, it was me, David, and Mitchell. The food ran out, our father didn't show, and Mrs. Racini only drove by on her way to a bridge game."

"So, a week after the game, someone stops David on the street and offers him a job. He has to carry school bags. So, fourteen years old, 260 pounds, and almost as tall as he is now, David becomes the youngest bagman in Chicago. The envelopes return, along with Mrs. Racini (with Manicotti this time) and we all carry along happily. No one at school looked for Davey, the football team lost the next five games, and I could make him scrambled eggs in the morning."

She looked up from her knitting.

"So that's how Mitchell and I finished high school and how I was able to afford Lake Forest nursing school and my career. When I could, I left for New York. Mitchell felt his father's itch and joined the Marines. Died in Vietnam."

It was a story that glowed with varnish. She had taken it out often and showed it around for all to see. But it was a story and it was hers and there was a victory in living long enough and climbing high enough to tell it with perspective. To the survivors, history is a children's tale.

Elvis had let the words flow into him. He accepted them into various tanks and would look more closely later. Nick surfed the words, hitting moments where the story began to roll on itself. Only Tillie listened. Only Tillie really heard what she was trying to say about herself. There was guilt; deep, old, blackened crimson guilt woven into the blanket of her life.

"How did your Dad die?" he said, somewhat coldly.

"He shot himself." She began a new row. "He lost a fight on a pickup and came home with a separated shoulder. He grabbed his military pistol, stood in the bathtub, and put a bullet through his head and into the pink tile. Davey found him. Then he called me and said, "Dad's dead." No one came to the funeral." She looked at Elvis. "You were four."

The listeners sat back. Shannon focused on her knitting.

Tillinghast looked to Elvis. The boy had drifted away on the stream.

"What was the trip like?" Tillie asked him.

The boy did not move.

"Elvis," he whispered.

"Yeah."

"What was the drive from Chicago like?"

The boy blinked. "Fine." He said. He glanced at Nick and the coach. "Strange. He had told me about the cancer a year before. He had lost his hair. And he was smaller. And quiet." Every word came out with difficulty. "We would sit in the living room with the radio on and some books, but he would stare out the window. Y'know. He was dying."

"I think he decided he wasn't going to die in Chicago. There were phone calls and meetings and visits and, at each one, he got more quiet. Then, in the middle of the night, he wakes me up and tells me to pack. So, I had this hockey bag that I jammed all my dirty clothes into and some of the clean ones, and a few other things, and I tossed it into the car."

"Didn't you ask why?"

"No." Elvis said. "No. I didn't."

He paused.

"I knew that he was sick and I knew that he was…sad. And he mentioned Shannon. And," He paused again. "He was my Dad. He didn't do stupid things. If he wanted to go for a drive, then we would go for a drive. I suppose if I knew that I wouldn't be coming back…"

The others gently smiled.

"He slept most of the way. I kept it at 65, ate at the drive-throughs, and just kept moving. He woke up and was much more lively when we hit the Mass Pike. Then the Cape Cod Canal. I think he was surprised that he was alive."

"Do you know how much money he was carrying?" Shannon spoke.

"No."

"He has $600,000 in cash hidden in the spare tires." She said. "He wasn't only worried about cops."

Tillie looked at her.

"How much is left?"

"Most of it."

"Which is…"

She put her knitting down. "What business is it of yours on this night of all nights?"

"Whose money do you suppose that is, Shannon?" Tillie pushed

"I am sure I don't know." Shannon feigned ignorance.

"Do you think the Outfit might want it back?" Tillie pressed.

"It's safe."

"No, it isn't."

"This isn't the time..." she glanced at Elvis.

Elvis looked up. "Aunt Shannon?"

She looked at the boy, then at Tillie.

"I can hide the money so that no one can get it, without the Marines and a court order." The coach said.

"How can you do that?"

"Who did I work for?"

She reached for her knitting and answered him with her glance. "It's safe."

"Aunt Shannon, it's not your money." Elvis spoke quietly, but with all the rage of the moment.

"Oh, Elvis, dear...."

"He is still alive, Aunt Shannon. It's not your money. You don't get to make that decision."

"Dear,"

"Give it to Tillinghast."

"I can't believe that we are talking about this..."

"Give it to him."

"Why do you trust him?" She snapped. Her mood flipped into a thing with teeth and claws. "What has he done for you? David came back to me. He came limping back to me. I am the one who has to house and clothe you for the next four years. I am the one who always has to be responsible, who has to look out for others. Then I can't get the money? No. No. No. "

The others looked at her.

"What will you say with a gun in your face?" Elvis spoke. She heard the dark, feral tone of his grandfather in the boy's words.

"I'll just say I don't know."

"No, you won't," he said. "You know what they do. You know. You know what my father did. You know what your father did. You know."

"Listen," Tillie broke in. "I can set it up as a trust in the boy's name. It will send you a check every month until he turns 21. And it will be completely safe. There is nothing they could do."

"There is always something."

"No." Elvis said. "No. It goes to Tillinghast. Tomorrow."

She picked up her knitting.

By four in the morning, Elvis was the only one still in the room.

Shannon had left by midnight. Nick and the Coach stayed until one or so. The beer was gone, and the pizza was cold. Elvis stood and shook their hands and thanked them for coming.

Both said it was nothing. The least they could do. Both meant it.

He still ushered them out.

Now, it was just the two of them, again. They had been together in that house on the South side, in the kitchen, in the TV room, at the gym, and in the car.

And now here.

For the last time.

The fact of the old man's body dispelled the sweet aroma of hope. The odd lumps in his arms, his thin chest, the skull of his face. Death had been taking him bite by bite in the last few weeks. Even a man as solid and his huge as David Lowell could be slowly nibbled away by death.

His father knew death. They had worked together many times before.

Although unsaid, the son had understood this about his father's work. It was unsaid and therefore unforgivable. But it was work and it was done and there were mornings that the old man stood in the shower for an hour and then walked to the bedroom and remained inside with his books for a day or more.

Cars waited for him outside, but he did not leave.

Men, even priests, would visit, but he would not answer the door.

Then, after a day or two, he would go to the gym and lift himself hoarse. Then he would sit in the steam room, take a cold shower, and emerge pink, edged, sad, but ready with net and trident for the next animal to be released into the coliseum.

Elvis had always known what his father did. The specifics had eluded him until a boy teased him on the playground in sixth grade. After Elvis finished working on his face, very few kids in school teased the fat kid anymore. By middle school, when the growth spurt was in full, bone-aching glory, no one would dare.

His father didn't punish him for the fight. The two of them spent the next four days putting a new roof on the church rectory with the work crew. No one would tell his father "No" or would shoo his son away. No union boss or foreman pulled him aside. Instead, they all said, "Yes, sir" and "Mr. Lowell."

Elvis understood why.

Elvis understood why they only watched sports on TV. He understood why there were so many books in the house. He understood why they started the car with a remote starter, took odd detours at strange times, and went to Kitty's for dinner and nowhere else.

He also knew why there was a map of Nantucket on the wall. Surrounded by water, a thousand miles away, with a new life and new work. It was the only heaven David Lowell would know.

That was why his father took that map down in the middle of the night, just before leaving Chicago.

It wasn't fair.

He knew how ridiculous that was. Nothing was fair.

But. Still.

When a man died, he lost everything he was going to be. His father would never see him play a varsity game, never see him play in college, never see him in the pros. His father would never be the big guy in the funny hat in the parent's section. He wouldn't tailgate in Happy Valley or at Chestnut Hill or between the Hedges or in the Grove.

He would never stand chest deep in the surf.

He would never bring a striped bass into the boat.

He would never see a wife or a grandchild.

Everything he would see he had seen. Everything he would hear, he had heard.

It wasn't fair.

A four in the morning, Sherrie, the duty nurse, came into room 22 to check the vitals on her patient. In the blinking electric dark, Elvis sat next to his father. She noticed the beard on the father, still growing even now.

She wrote on her chart.

She looked at the man on the bed and made a decision. It was a decision that both of them had made many times before.

"Elvis," she said. "Can I show you something?"

He moved slowly. "Sure."

"Do you see this drip right here?" She pointed to a plastic tube that dropped down to his father's central line.

"Yes."

"This sends the morphine into his body. Morphine is the drug that blocks all the pain that he feels. It goes right to the brain, finds the pain receptors, and blocks them with pleasure. With good stuff. They say it feels like floating on a rubber raft."

"Okay."

"Do you see this blue box right here, on the stand."

"Yes." Elvis was suspicious.

"This regulates the amount of morphine he gets. Right now, we have him getting as much morphine as he can get and still live. There is a huge amount of pain coming into his brain and we have to block as much of it as we can. The problem, Elvis, is that the amount of pain he is feeling is so huge that the morphine can't stop it all."

"It's like something is taking big bites out of him."

"Yes. Exactly." She said. "Exactly, the cancer is taking more and more bites from him, like a shark does, and he feels each tooth. The cancer is everywhere, including in his brain. He can't speak anymore, can he?"

"No."

"He can hear though, probably." She said. "But he can't use his hands or anything else at this point." She turned the blue box towards him.

"Now, if he gets too much morphine, he won't feel any pain, but he will stop breathing."

"And he will die."

"He will." She admitted. "But, he is going to die very soon. It could be in an hour or in a week or even a month. And he is suffering from all of those bites." She stopped for a moment and cleared her mind. "He would die the same way. He will stop breathing and his lungs will fill with fluid and he will die. Without morphine, it will be very, very painful. With morphine, it will be quiet and numb. He will drift away on the tide."

Elvis made his head nod twice.

"Now, Elvis, pay close attention." She said. "If I were to type in the code 143 into the blue box, it would remove the safeties and he would get a straight flow of morphine into him."

"That would kill him."

"Yes, it would kill him."

The boy looked up at her, as if she had just handed him something bloody.

"So, you must remember to never key in the numbers 143 into this pad."

She left.

Elvis, quiet and alone, considered the infernal thing she had presented him with.

CHAPTER SIX

"Danny," the radio called.

"Yup."

"We have a report of shots fired at 44 Somerset Road."

"We're on our way." Danny started the lights, swung the Ford around, and accelerated. The Inspector perked right up. He swung the terminal towards him and quickly typed in the address.

Then he grinned.

"What is it?" Danny said.

"Our new friend, Jack Mitchell."

Somerset Road is one of the few roads on island that once were paths to the beach, or to the sheep. It starts near the cemetery in an optimistic bit of two lane pavement, then turns to one narrow lane of pits of frozen winter sand and deep puddles amid scrub pines and high brush. Older cottages and houses were tucked back into the woods. After several tricky spots, it straightens and runs out onto the Miacomet Road.

When Danny pulled onto the road, he had to slow to a crawl. He circled the big puddles so only one side of the cruiser dipped into the water. After five minutes of careful driving, he pulled into the driveway at 44.

The house was a modest Cape Cod tucked up onto a small hill. Several shingles had blown off the side of the house and the roof had developed a thick layer of greenish growth.

Four cars were parked in the driveway: two pick-ups, a Toyota sedan that looked permanent, and a red jeep. Jack Mitchell, his father, his father's girlfriend, and his younger brother stood in the driveway staring at the jeep. All four tires were flat and a stream of greenish fluid was flowing down the driveway to the street. "Party Wagon" was written on the rear window in dirt.

    Henry opened the door before the squad car had stopped.
    "Morning, folks." He said. "What seems to be the trouble?"
    "Nothing." Jack snapped.
    "Is that a fact?"
    Henry walked forward and looked at the Jeep. He saw two bullet holes in the two left tires. Then he looked up at Bud, Jack's father.
    "So, what happened?"
    "Some guy started shooting at the Jeep." The older man spoke in long, narcotic cadences.
    "Take me through it slow." Henry addressed the father.
    "He's gone now. We don't know who it was." Jack barked.
    "But he put at least five bullets in your car." Coffin said. "Did he say anything?"
    Bud opened his mouth, but Jack snapped. "No."
    "After he fired five or so shots, what happened?"
    "He just drove away." No one else was speaking. Jack appeared to be the only one tied to the earth.
    Coffin took his notepad. "Well, let's start with something more concrete. What are all of your names?"
    "Why do you need that?"
    "I have to file a report."
    "Why do you have to file a report?"
    "It's what we do."
    Coffin smiled.
    "You don't need our names for this."
    "Jack," The Inspector said. "Someone emptied their gun into the Party Wagon. If you want to press charges or file an insurance claim, I have to write a report."
    Jack was thinking. Everyone else was glazed like donuts. The girlfriend had the nods while she was standing.
    "Why don't you just go and catch him?"
    "Who?"
    "I don't know."
    "What was he driving?"
    "A green pick-up truck." Bud added.
    "Anything you remember about the truck?"
    "No." Jack said, forcefully. He glared at his father and his father looked to the ground.

Henry looked at the boy, then at his Dad. "Did you see a pick-up, Bud?"

He hesitated. "We sleep on the other side of the house. Jack saw it and I heard the gunshots. I called you guys."

"And we are glad you did." Henry looked at the boy. "So, what happened, my brother?"

"I don't know."

"Really."

"Yup."

"Where do you sleep?"

Jack's face had contempt, scorn, and outright anger mixed in it. But, he had realized the danger he was in. Reports and names were public. The Inspector, as was his want, smiled at him.

The old man, Jack thought, is going to have to lose his phone.

"Right there." Jack pointed his thumb back at the house.

"What is your story, my brother?"

"We don't have a story."

"What happened?"

"We were inside and we heard shots."

"You were asleep?"

"Sure."

"Then you opened the curtain and saw...."

"Nothing."

"You saw nothing?"

"Yeah, but I heard the shots. My Dad called 911."

"So, was there a pickup truck, or not?"

"I don't know."

"Was there a guy, or not?"

"I don't know."

"Do you know anyone who would want to do this to you?" Henry asked. "Any enemies, my brother?"

"No." Jack snapped.

It had become clear to the boy. If Coffin went and found the shooter, the whole story would break open. Tommy would tell the police everything and on the record. There would be statement and depositions and cross-examination and something ugly would stalk out of the woods on Milestone Road.

Henry didn't say anything. Danny was standing on the far side of the Jeep with his clipboard, taking notes.

"Damn shame." The black man said. "Damn shame that a pretty little crackerjack ride like this got messed up."

"What did you say?" Jack barked.

"A cracker...jack ride like this. Damn shame."

Henry looked at his partner. "Did you call the tow truck?"

"Should be here in ten."

"Why did you call a tow truck?" Jack whined.

"We have to impound it. Evidence of a crime."

"No, you don't."

"Sure we do." Danny said. "You've seen it on TV. We will have our CSI staff dig the slugs out of the radiator. Then we will try to match it up with the right gun. We'll go over the jeep with a fine toothed comb. We'll find your assailant."

"Can't they do what they need to do right here?"

"Oh, no." Danny continued. "Then we will fingerprint all of you, so we can eliminate those prints."

All of them looked at each other. Those fingerprints, they feared, could lead to some dark and ugly things that had been buried by time.

"We're not filing charges." Jack spoke.

Coffin looked at him. "Someone came to your house, shot up the old party wagon here, and you don't want to file charges? Why on earth not?"

"Forget it."

Danny stood next to the Inspector. "Y'know, Henry. These guys might be trying for some insurance fraud."

"No. I don't think they would do that."

"They could be," Danny spoke, loudly. "Y'know, they shoot up the car, file a report, and then claim that the car was shot by an unknown assailant who may, or may not have, been driving a green pick-up truck."

Jack looked at the two of them. Jack's younger brother, who shifted from foot to foot uneasily, was careful not to make eye contact. His head nodded as well. He didn't look older than twelve.

"If I don't file charges, nothing happens?" Jack said.

"Well, reports need to be filed." Danny said.

Bud looked confused and dazed. Coffin had glanced at him early and saw how he stood and how small his pupils were. He knew that look.

Danny looked at the Inspector. "Well, this is something, now isn't it?"

"Yup."

"Wouldn't have thought it."

"Me neither." Henry said, then looked back at Jack. "So, my brother, someone who may or may not have been driving a pick-up truck shot up your jeep and left. You don't want to file charges."

"No."

"Fair enough."

Danny put his pen back inside his shirt pocket.

As they drove away, The Inspector patted his partner on the shoulder.

"Crackerjack?"

"I hate wanna-be rednecks."

"You prefer the real, god-fearing, moonshine-drinking, string-em-up real thing?"

"You always know where you stand."

"You got the gun."

"That's what they do to us colored up north." He smiled. "Give us guns. That's how I know where I stand."

Henry smiled. "Let's go out to Tom Nevers and find our gunman."

Summer had slipped out the door, but left most of its belongings behind. The echo of warmth slipped in on a southerly wind. It obscured the stars, fogged the windows, and dripped from the power lines.

Henry looked out the window at the pine trees speeding by.

"What about Dad?"

"Did Bud look functional to you?"

"Okay, perhaps I am stuck in another century."

"Perhaps?" Danny was enjoying this immensely.

"Why would Dad cover for six gunshots in the driveway and a ruined car?"

"Just a reach here, my brother." The black man smiled. "Perhaps he either can't stop it or doesn't care."

Henry shook his head.

Danny drove at a sedate 45 miles an hour down the Milestone Road. Deer hopped alongside the car, but in the woods. After a few minutes, he eased the car to the right, onto the Tom Nevers Road.

This time, they left the lights off in front of the Kelly house. Coffin, on his way to the door, stopped to put a hand on the hood of the pick up truck. Still warm.

Danny knocked on the door with the butt end of his flashlight.

They heard nothing.

He knocked again.

Still, no sound.

Henry gestured at his partner and they returned to the truck. In the wash of the flashlight, the steering wheel was dripped in blood. Blood smeared on the door handle. Hand prints of blood spackled the seats and painted the paper towels.

"Let's find him."

The front door remained locked, so they circled the house. Sliding glass doors guarded the bedroom, but they were similarly locked. An outdoor stairway led up to a deck.

Henry led. Unarmed, he announced himself before he came into view of the windows.

He needn't.

Big Mike sat on the floor of the kitchen, holding two large bags of frozen carrots to his face. His clothes were covered in blood.

The porch door opened at a touch.

"Mike, this is Henry Coffin. Danny and I are here to see if you are all right."

"You can go away. I'm fine."

"Yeah, you look it," said Danny. "Where's the gun?"

"There's no gun."

"No gun?"

"My hunting rifles are locked up downstairs."

Henry squatted next to the big man.

"Let's get you an ambulance."

"No, I'm fine."

"You're in shock."

"No, I'm fine." He said. "I am going to stay right here in my house."

It was an odd conversation. Danny stood in the living room, looking for the weapon. Mike was talking with both bags of frozen vegetables covering both sides of his face. Henry squatted next to him. The light from the open refrigerator washed over the two.

"Would you like us to call you a Doctor?"

"No."

"You are going to need some stitches, judging from what I am looking at."

"I'll be fine."

"I'll call Tupper. He'll come here."

"Don't."

Henry nodded to Danny. Danny took out his cellphone and called the hospital. The big man heard the call, but didn't object.

"I'm not leaving this house."
"You won't."
"I'm not going."
"Fine."

Henry didn't ask him anything for two minutes. He stood out of his squat, and then sat on the floor next to Big Mike. Both of them had their legs out straight. Danny shook his head.

"Mike, what happened?"
"I had to stop to avoid a deer."
"You did?"
"Yup. Banged my face against the steering wheel. Hurt something bad."
"You did?"
"Yup."

Henry sighed. He locked eyes with Danny, but Danny didn't know what he wanted, if he wanted anything.

"Mike, we just left the Mitchells. They told us that someone in a pick-up had come out and shot up their jeep."
"The Party Wagon." Danny added.
"Don't know nothing about that."
"You don't?"
"Nope."
"Snitches get stitches?"
"Hell of a thing for you to say." Anger seeped out.

Henry looked at the Birdseye bags. "Because I made your boy snitch?"
"Didn't say that."
"Mike," Danny said. "We have these kids. We're building evidence and lining up statements. We will be putting them away."
"When?"

Danny looked at him sadly. "I don't know."
"Not for six months."
"We can arrest them soon."
"When?"
"I don't know."
"You know that Pink and those boys drive up and down Tom Nevers Road and wait for my boy to leave this house."
"I hope we took care of that earlier today."
"I doubt it." Mike said, still oozing blood. "I seriously doubt it."
"Mike, you can't run away. You can't hide. My God, you were the father asking his son why he did nothing?"

He was silent.

"He might have been right." The man muttered. "Maybe you have to walk away from some fights."

"Don't walk away from this one. Don't do that to your boy."

"He can't go back to school." Mike said. "He won't."

"He went yesterday."

"He won't tomorrow. Not after everything we saw. You know kids. They are going to ruin him." He said. "They already have."

Henry Coffin turned to the big man sitting on the floor. "You know what you should do?" he spoke softly.

"Do tell."

"Let us file charges." He said. "Have Tommy give a statement."

"Oh, that would be great." The big man had a sarcastic laugh. "You need to keep drinking, Henry, because you don't make any sense sober."

"How's that?"

"So, let's charge these little bastards, right? They will just take that and smile. They will go hire a lawyer and prepare a defense. Right?" he said. "Look at me. Do you think they go for lawyers? And," he continued with a snort. "I can hear the testimony on the stand. "Did you rape Maria DeSalvo?" No sir. Then, their lawyer will make Tommy out as if he raped girls in the elementary school. Good idea. Henry. Great. That should really solve the problem for all of us."

The big man snorted.

"There's a point in a man's life when he's got to speak truth." Coffin answered.

"What point is that?" Mike said. "Is it before or after they kill Tommy in the woods like they killed that other kid? Or after they rape him with flashlights? That's their new threat. When do I allow that to happen?"

"It would be right now."

"Fine, Inspector. Fine. Allow me to speak truth. I braked to avoid a deer. Someone stole Tommy's phone."

Henry stood up and walked away.

Tupper came to the house twenty minutes later. He came with a black bag, a scowl, and the whiff of a past century. With much cursing, he laced twenty stitches into Big Mike's cheeks and nose. He said nothing to the Inspector.

Henry stood outside on the deck. His partner came out to him. Coffin looked at him, hoping he had brought two beers out of the refrigerator.

"What's happening to us, Danny?"

"You and me, or to the island as a whole?"

"Everyone."

"Going to hell, one step at a time, I suppose."

Henry didn't smile. He continued to look over the bruised eastern sky. "I remember, years ago, when Sam Sylvia was murdered, we got the story right away. Johnny Harrington called me from the Angler's Club and told me Sam got pushed off a fishing boat. Then, even when we had so much evidence the lawyers were rolling their eyes, Johnny still wants to testify. Put some words to it. He says."

"They say Harrington was a first class pain in the ass."

"He was. And he drove drunk and he hit his wife when he got in the mood. When the time came for him to stand up, he stood."

Danny looked at the old man. He knew, from painful experiences, that the most outrageous lies begin with "I remember when…" This was gnawing at the Quaker.

"They all want to live in the shadows. They want to scurry and mumble and stand on their hind legs with their whiskers in the air." Coffin said.

"They are afraid."

"What are they afraid of?"

"Themselves."

The two of them watched the fog lighten

"You know how this shit gets handled in Roxbury?" Danny said.

"Sure."

"Back in the day, someone would get a message to Whitey Bulger." Danny paused. "You remember Whitey Bulger?"

"Sure."

"Maybe it would be a cop. Maybe it would be a bookie or snitch. Might even be a priest. He would get word within six hours. And Whitey would let his crew know and the cops would know when to go get some coffee and look the other way. Then Bulger's Cadillac and two white panel trucks would pull up in front of a house, the kid would get grabbed, and it would end in a mudflat."

"That's a mob."

"That's a community. And it is standing up."

Henry looked at his partner. "Lynchings got handled the same way, my brother."

"Yup." He said. "But Johnny Harrington sold his house, moved to North Carolina, and took his mob with him. Big Mike don't have a posse."

"No, he don't." Coffin said. "You know who is still here?"

"Who?"
"Pink."

Detective Higginbotham tucked the squad car behind a house, turned the lights off, and watched the end of Essex Road. The Inspector, for his part, took a nap. By six in the morning, when dawn was rising through the fog, Pink's Cab appeared at the end of the street. A bike approached it, paused, and then peeled away. As the cab rolled through the stop sign, Danny ran the siren and flashed the lights.

Pink pulled over immediately.

His passenger, an older woman in jeans and a t-shirt, took off running. Neither officer bothered following. As soon as Danny had parked the car behind the cab, the Inspector was out the door.

"Wow, Pink." He said as he stepped to the driver's window. "I hope she paid for her ride when she got in the car."

"Inspector." The cabbie spoke. He looked tired and disheveled, as if he had just been roused from sleep. There wasn't even any music going in his car. "Why have you stopped me?"

"Danny saw you run through a stop sign. He says you didn't come to a full and complete stop."

"What do you say, my dear and ever honest brother?"

"I didn't think you had. Seemed you stopped long enough for a bike to pull up." Coffin smiled. "I lost that argument." He shrugged.

"Are you going to write me a ticket?"

"I was thinking about a warning."

"In that case, I would like a written warning."

"You would?"

"Yes."

"Well, then." The old man said. "License and registration, please."

Coffin brought those back to Danny, told him to write a ticket for anything he felt was appropriate, and then returned to Pink.

"So," he said. "I wanted to talk to you about another matter."

"No."

"No?"

"No." he said. "If you want to talk to me about anything, you can make an appointment. Or call a Grand Jury. Or invite me to the station for questioning. I haven't seen Chief Bramden in years. I'm not talking out here."

"Pink," Coffin smiled. "We can talk today. We can talk tomorrow. We can talk whenever you want. But as to where?" Coffin paused. "It will always be right here because Danny and I will always be waiting for you on Essex Road. Next time, I will come with a long distance camera and a parabolic microphone to see if the kid on the bike says anything."

Pink looked forward.

"And the kid on the bike and everyone else on this street will start to wonder about all of the bad luck and attention that you seem to bring.

Russians, they believe in luck. Latvians, Slovaks, Poles, and most of your Slavic cultures believe in a lot of luck, too. I don't think the Jamaicans do, but they don't seem to live here. And if you bring these people bad luck, they may have to move on."

"Doesn't matter to me." Pink said.

"Good." Coffin said. "Pink, I am delivering a message to you. I want you to listen carefully. Your high school friends are starting to cause the sort of problems that I take an active interest in. They are making me …curious. So, I want you to convince them that they should become a lot less interesting to me. After the last few days, I am very interested in everything that they do. Including everything that they do with you."

"What do you expect me to do? I am not their parents."

"I expect you to give them some fatherly guidance." He said. "I would be willing to bet that you can be very persuasive when you want to be." Coffin said. "And you want to be, because these Russians will cut you loose very quickly."

"You don't scare me, Inspector."

"You shouldn't be scared of me, Pink." Coffin said. "You should be scared of those boys. You trusted your house, your business, your savings and your liberty to them. And they can take it all away in a conference room with me. What stories could Jack and Billy tell, if they were motivated?" The old man paused. "And what would the residents of these houses do if they thought you, or someone you know, was telling stories? What do these Russians do to snitches?"

Pink didn't say anything.

Coffin didn't either. He heated the silence up to boiling.

In two minutes, Detective Higginbotham delivered a ticket for an equipment malfunction. The cabbie took the ticket, his license and his registration without a word.

Coffin stepped away. "I hope I won't have to see you again, Pink."

The cab eased off the curb.

Coffin waved at the empty street.

Twenty minutes later, Danny Higginbotham turned the car onto Spinnaker Drive. He parked in front of his house.

The front door of the colonial opened and Danny's seven year old daughter, Hadley came bouncing down the path. She wore a pink jacket with white fur around the edges and pink boots. She carried a small unicorn and a huge backpack.

Henry moved to the back seat, behind the screen and in the middle of the six month old vomit smell so that the little girl could ride to elementary school with her father in the relatively pleasant front seat.

Hadley turned around in her seat and looked at Henry through the black metal grate. She had four red barrettes.

"Daddy says you look like a bum."

"He does, does he?"

"Yes."

"Do you think that is a bad thing?"

"No." she said with her voice trailing away.

"I like your coat, Hadley."

"Thank you."

"I like the unicorn."

"His name is Oscar."

"That's a nice name for a unicorn. Do you have other unicorns at home?"

"I have lots of unicorns."

"Do they all have names?"

"Of course they do."

"Do you have a favorite one?"

"No. I love them all."

"What do they do while you are at school?"

"They sleep a lot, like Daddy."

"I sleep a lot too," Henry said. "What do they do at night?"

"They run around and play. They protect me from bad dreams."

"Are they good at that?"

"Very good."

They pulled up in the circle in front of the elementary school. Danny got out, opened the door for his daughter, grabbed her backpack and walked her in. He also opened the door for Henry, who moved from criminal to cop. He moved the squad car out of the way of the buses, then he put the lights on so Danny could see it. His partner returned minutes later. The two men drove off into the thinning traffic.

"So I look like a bum?"

"Out of the mouths of babes."

"You think?"
"You could get the coat cleaned."
"Why?"
"It would smell better."
"It doesn't smell."
Danny rolled his eyes. "My little girl wouldn't call you a bum."
"Bums are people too."
"Yeah, yeah. Inner light and all that."
They were silent,
"She has a unicorn for you," Danny said. "It is on her bureau."
"Really."
"Doesn't have a horn, though."

CHAPTER SEVEN

At three in the morning, Rosie had made up her mind. Or, as it happens, she finally made peace with the only path that she could really take. She would take her daughter off island to a school. She would go there every weekend and whatever other days she could spare. The school would be remote, quiet, and free of men.

Maria could check out the rooms and the dining hall. Rosie would take the counseling service for a test drive. If it was manned by someone who was knitting or updating her Facebook page, they would walk out the door. If there was a tough, middle aged lesbian bitch with a softball glove and an electric guitar, that's where Maria was going.

Because the girl couldn't stay here. With the rapists walking the halls and pissing in the bushes, she couldn't be safe. If Rosie could gut them like deer and hang their drying carcasses on Main Street, every shufflebum and drunk would still see her daughter as that girl that got herself raped.

You can't pretend that no one knows. Everyone knows. The only secrets worth a damn were the ones that everyone knew. The whole island was burning. The rumors, the guesses, and the truths were all red embers. Every minute she was on-island was a minute in the grill.

She couldn't do that to the girl.

The whole family couldn't go, either. It wasn't fair to James, it wasn't fair to Rick and it wouldn't work. Every day, that girl would know that the reason they were in a shitty rented house in Belmont was because she got raped. It would drown her. The rape was bad enough.

So, it was water or fire. Or exile.

Rosie chose exile.

When the shifts changed, Elvis remained seated by his father's side. The sunlight poked through the venetian blinds on the East side of the hospital, but in room 22, sunrise nor sunset ever appeared. Sherrie, on her last stop in the room, turned the two table lamps on. She also pointed out the shower and the bathroom to Elvis.

He nodded.

Rosie stood at the door to her daughter's room. Rick had put the door back on, aware of all the barn door irony and pathos in doing so.

They had their memories here. They did at that. Rick had assembled her crib in here and moved the baby into her room an ungodly seven months after she was born.

Rosie remembered all the crap that built up in the room. She didn't think she bought it all, but it wound up in here and could only get removed in hefty bags. American Girl dolls. Polly Pocket. Disney on Ice. Backstreet Boys. Dora. And the jeans. There were always more jeans and pants. Maria was never a dress-up girl. She didn't have a closet full of sun dresses and tea party skirts and high heeled shoes. But there were thirty pairs of sneaker in there somewhere. In middle school, she decided it was her husband. He would go out and buy her little things, or give her some money or whatever and the shit would just flow into the room.

So, here she was. Atop a pile of old presents.

Rosie felt it ache in her heart. She couldn't go. They were going to Disney on Ice. They were going to Elaine's birthday party. They were going to go see the Backstreet Boys. They were going to go on a girl's weekend to Boston and see a movie and eat chocolate and get their hair done.

Those days had hopped away. They worried about credit cards and discounts and making the boat and leaving that bag in the back of the rental car. The days had hopped by and disappeared.

And now, the boys had wounded her little girl and she had to. Had to. Had to. Had to. Send her away.

Tired and with the edges of a tremor in his right hand, Tillinghast appeared at the door to the house behind Marine Home Center at six in the morning. Shannon wanted to argue with him and tried to pick a fight, but he wasn't rising to her bait. After ten minutes, she disappeared into a side room and reappeared with a duffle bag stuffed full of cash.

She assured him it was all of it.

He assured her that people far less polite than he was would search the house.

She assured him that she was smart enough to avoid putting bullets in her head.

He asked her to call him when there was a strange car in the driveway.

With that, he hoisted the bag into the back of his Cherokee, drove to the wharf, and got on the 6:30 ferry. He napped in the car, then rented a car and drove straight to 500 State Street in Boston. He rode the elevator to the 35th floor, stopped in a familiar law office, shook hands with all concerned, waited for the money to be counted, and then accepted a receipt for 597,315 dollars.

He returned to his car, had lunch at Locke-Obers with two old friends from the museum, and then drove back to Hyannis and a three o'clock flight back for practice.

Rosie awoke on the sofa downstairs. She had fallen asleep on top of the unfolded clean clothes. They were still clean, of course, but they were smushed.

She had hoped for another fifteen minutes of sleep. Just to close her eyes.

The horn on the 6:30 steamship sounded as it left the dock.

She closed her eyes and readjusted the pile of shirts underneath her head.

Then, very softly, she heard the sound of someone retching.

It was a cough, followed by a splash. Then another cough, and another splash. Not much of a sound. For most people, it was nothing to roll over to. A quiet trip to the bathroom in the early morning.

Not for Rosie.

Back in those sensitive days, she used to run the water to hide the sound.

She knew that sound. Oh, yes. She knew that sound.

Her heart dropped. She sat up silently and listened to the slow heavy footsteps of another day.

Maria would not be going to school off-island. Not right away.

While Tillinghast was on his way to Boston, Shannon returned to the hospital with her knitting and her books. David remained upstairs, alive, breathing but no longer sitting up and taking nourishment. His son remained by his side.

He was exhausted. The little scruff dotted his cheeks, as it did his father's. With the dust of gray and black, his father's beard had the distinguishing scars of a long fight.

She would do it differently. Had she been in the position, it would have been done differently. And when she is in David's position? She wanted it fast and painless. Have a nice meal, have a martini or two, kiss someone close, fall asleep and drop the curtain. Afterwards, she didn't care. They could chop her up and drop her down the toilet for all she cared.

For a moment, she saw that there was no "they" in her life. She would have a very small funeral. The only "they" in her life was lying on his deathbed with the other one heartbroken next to him. Her ex-husband, Tony, would come, with his new partner Alexander. Probably. If then, only for the house.

There had been many men over the years. Many arms beneath her head, many hungry lips, many heaving hearts. She had kept a list of their names and there was room for many more nice young men. In her heart, she thought that "they" should come to the funeral. What stories they could tell! And they were men now, beyond the frat house ownership and rutting dominance of youth. The laughs they could have! The stories they could tell!

But they wouldn't come. They had wives and lives of their own.

It was left to this boy. When the chips were down and she found herself in Room 22, she knew who she would see. This boy.

Shannon had returned to her seat and taken up her knitting.

"We have to talk."

Elvis looked at her. "Is it about money?"

"No." She said. "Not really."

Elvis knew she was thinking about money. "Okay." He said. "I am sorry we have to talk now."

"What are we talking about?" He asked.

"You need to call your mother." Shannon said. "You need to invite her."

"Oh."

"The Outfit will come, as well. But the money is gone and he will be gone. They will leave us alone. Too many people know us. You were in a bunch of papers last week. Reporters will start calling soon."

Elvis wasn't so sure.

"David," she indicated with a knitting needle "will soon be on his journey and you and I will be left. You are going to have to make a decision, then. You are going to have to decide…" she picked up a stitch, executed a difficult roll, and then continues. "What you are going to do?"

"I am not going to go back with my mother."

"Okay."

The two of them paused. Elvis, in a second, understood how much of an orphan he was going to be.

"My father said I could stay with you. You said I could stay."

"I think I may have said that. And you can. But we are going to have to have some understandings about our relationship."

"Like, what?" Elvis looked at his dying father for a moment. A bubble of rage was building.

"Well, I may not have the same relaxed style of parenting that your father has. You may not like my house rules. It' something you should think about."

The bubble rose.

"Aunt Shannon, you don't have any children. How do you have a parenting style?"

She dropped her knitting.

"Please don't talk to me like that."

The bubble rose. Elvis looked around the room at the various lights, dials, and readouts that came from his dying father. The rage was useless. Worse, it was toxic. All it could do was poison. He caught the bubble against his palm and held it, patiently, underwater.

He thought of his Aunt as if they were wrestling.

"Aunt Shannon, I know that my father could have taken me anywhere back in September. He knew he was dying. Everyone else probably did too. But instead of going to Santa Fe, he came here to his sister. Then the two of you set me up in school and on the team. Surely, he wanted me to stay here with you after he…died." The word shocked him and the bubble he held underwater shook. "He didn't bring me to my mother, he didn't bring me to Lake Forest or Santa Fe or Texas. He brought me here. To you." Elvis said. "And, knowing him, I am sure he said something like that to you."

The bubble held.

She looked at the boy. "I know what he wanted and he can't tell us right now what he said." Elvis noted the past tense. "I told him that it would be up to you. And it is. It is a horrible time for you to think about this. I know and I am sorry. I think you should spend this year here, or at least until Christmas. I just think that you should know that Nantucket is a small place, not a city. It is very limiting and," She paused. "I am not so indulgent as your father. I don't have the money he had and can't keep you in quite the same style. I have barely enough for me." She picked up her knitting. "It's just something to keep in mind."

"To keep in mind?" he said. "To keep in mind?" Elvis swung between violence and tears. "What I have in mind is that I would trade all of his money for one more day with him. And you want me to think of curfews because you are pissed at cash."

Shannon looked at him coldly. "I didn't say…"

"Thanks to him," Elvis said. "There's money. And thanks to him, maybe I can go pro. And you think I am some spoiled brat."

"No…"

"If killing you would bring him back, I would do it. Even for a day."

The bubble dissipated.

Elvis stood, stretched, and walked out into the hall.

Aunt Shannon had nothing to say to him.

He slipped into the lounge at the end of the hall, dialed the number from memory. As he heard the phone ring, he felt as if he had pointed a gun at his own head.

"Hello?"

"Mom."

"Elvis. How is your Dad?"

"He's dying, Mom."

"Where are you?"

"Don't play stupid, Mom."

"I really don't know."

"Nantucket."

"I'll be there tomorrow."

"Come alone, Mom."

She hung up.

Rick had slipped into the empty marriage bed upstairs sometime early this morning,

At eight, he took James to daycare, and then he went off to his new job site in Shimmo.

Maria did not rise from her bed.

Rosie puttered around the kitchen. She cleaned the dishes from dinner and from breakfast, wiped the counter down, and threw out the old food from the refrigerator.

It was a day to take care of business. It was a day to leave the comforting lies and faiths behind and take hold of reality.

She took one of her old pregnancy vitamin pills from the back of the shelves and placed it on a dish. She placed the dish in the middle of the table.

She put the gold coin near it.

Then she made pancakes.

Maria came staggering down the stairs.

"They smell good."

"I felt like pancakes this morning." She said. "With no one else here, I thought we could have them for lunch."

"Sure."

Maria sat in her customary place at the table. Her mother had, thoughtfully, put down a placemat, silverware, a glass, and set her a place.

When she was settled, Maria noticed the pill on the plate. It was brown and, as pills go, huge. It looked to be almost a half inch long. Then she noticed the coin.

"Was the Inspector here?"

"He came by late last night."

"Is he done with the coin?"

"That is what he said." Rosie stood with her back to her daughter and held herself together. Maria picked up the coin and rubbed it.

The mother didn't have an answer and she didn't want the question. She wanted it to slide away into the day. Today would be the day. Now was the time.

She pushed the air out of her lungs.

Rosie came over and put three pancakes on her plate.

"Thanks, Mom."

"You're welcome."

Rosie had already served herself and brought her plate over. She sat at her usual spot. She took the maple syrup from her daughter and splashed it over her breakfast.

"This is nice of you, Mom."

"It is nothing."

"It's still nice."

"Thanks."

Both women took their first bites. Rosie set her fork down in a moment.

"We need to talk. About the future."

Maria looked at her mother. There was no threat and no anger in her voice, but there was no warmth either. "Okay."

"Have you thought about what you are going to do?"

"Not really."

"Okay." Her mother had another mouthful. "I think its time that we do that, don't you?"

The first edges of panic lifted along the back of the girl's neck. Her left hand dropped to the coin in her lap. She rubbed it and nodded.

"What should we do on Monday?"

"I don't know."

"Do you want to go to school?"

A jolt of panic hit the girl. "No."

"What about your friends?"

She nodded. "No, I don't want to go back."

Rosie smiled. "I didn't think you did." She said. "Now, do you want to stay home?"

It was the tone. It was the total, quiet, professional voice. It was the pancakes and it was the silverware and it was the kruggerand and it was the pill in the middle of the table. She knew. She knew. She knew.

"Maybe."

'Maybe?"

"Where else could I go?"

"You don't need to go to school here. Aunt Catherine lives in Newton. Uncle James lives over in Newport."

Maria paused.

"I would have to move."

"You will probably have to move anyway." She said. "But it wouldn't be for good. You can come back here for some of the weekends and we will go up there for the others."

"You aren't coming up, are you?"

"To live, no."

Maria felt that. It felt like a hinge swinging on her and a life she couldn't have anymore.

She slipped back inside herself for a moment.

Rosie watched her.

"We don't have to decide anything now."

Maria nodded. She had slipped away. The girl was in a country that Rosie had never visited. She could not go in and rescue her. She could not send in the Marines and she could not just obliterate the ground. Instead, she had to wait for her daughter to wander out.

And hope she made it.

In that quiet, Rosie tried to see the world through her daughters eyes. She had been raped, more likely than not. She was, probably, pregnant. The baby daddy was gone or even dead.

Who could know this pain?

In that light, what could the mother say? What did she know of pain compared to this? She couldn't talk of Aunts or boarding school or school uniforms. Her daughter had been seared at the stake. Yet, she sat at the table clutching what she could and trying to just stay upright. And, perhaps, take one step. Today. One step.

Rosie realized that she should just put the girl in a hospital. Some place with good therapists and quiet grounds and two hours to visit on Sundays. Arrogance and anger kept her here. Rosie had wanted to punish her for being stupid and spreading her legs. There had been punishment enough. More was yet to come. Any sane woman would run away or hide in her bed.

Instead, Maria was right in front of her at the table.

"Do you want another pancake?" Rosie asked.

The girl nodded.

Her mother swooped up her plate. She also slid away the plate with the pregnancy vitamin on it.

She didn't need to know and didn't want to ask.

The day also passed slowly and painfully for Elvis.

Instead of knitting, today Aunt Shannon read. She quietly turned the pages of "Marley and Me." Occasionally, she smiled at the story. Elvis had somehow forgotten his reading and spent the morning contemplating his sleeping father. Some time, just after noon, she finished the book and set it back into her bag.

It was quite a bag; buttery leather, with two longish handles. Inside, she had brought cookies and crackers in zip lock bags, two water bottles, a bag that looked as if it held toiletries, and an assortment of clothing, also in tinted zip lock bags.

Then she pulled out her Sudoku.

Elvis watched her with growing frustration and anger. He felt as if he and his father were in the zoo, in a cage actually, and she had stopped by on a warm summer day to watch the two of them.

Not for the first time today, Elvis sighed.

"Aunt Shannon?" he said.

"Yes, dear?"

"Did you want to go get some dinner?"

"No, I think I am fine." She said, looking down at her magazine. Then she looked up. "Would you like something?"

"Sure."

"Why didn't you just ask?"

"Sorry," Elvis said. "Could you get me a sandwich?"

"Of course."

She was glad to go.

Three minutes after she had left, Elvis had turned off all the lights in the room. He felt more comfortable in the dark and, he imagined, his father did as well.

The room was silent, save for the mechanical buzzes, clicks, and drips of the machinery and the slow breathing of a dying man. The room, even after a day, had no smell other than the faint whiff of cheap cleaning products.

Elvis moved his chair up against the bed and held his father's hand. It felt cool and dry. Each crease and callous felt distinct.

"Dad, can you hear me?"

He did not answer.

"Just squeeze my hand if you can."

He did not answer.

"Do you want to see Mom?"

He did not answer that question either.

Elvis had the cool hand nonetheless.

"Dad, what do you want to do?"

Neither the older man, nor the bed, nor the curtains, nor the machines, nor the air outside or the sun above or the ocean all around answered the son.

He still held the hand throughout the afternoon.

Tillinghast returned to the island in time for a phone call from Shannon.

"They are here."

CHAPTER EIGHT

Tillinghast arrived in fifteen minutes, accompanied by a squad car holding yawning Danny Higginbotham and an equally tired Henry Coffin.

Shannon looked on the three of them doubtfully.

Danny, for his part, looked at her equally doubtfully. He had known this. The first time he had seen that large young man, that time at the hospital, he had picked up the vibe. Once they had been with John Law up close, they were always a little too aware. Maybe too bold, maybe too shy, maybe too talkative. But aware.

Shannon looked at the Inspector.

"Is this going to work?"

"Sure."

"You guys think you can take them on?"

"We're not going to challenge them to a basketball game."

"I'll stay back here." She volunteered.

Coffin looked at her. She hated the way he gazed. His eyes never left hers. "Suit yourself." He said. "Call 911 if they shoot us."

The Inspector nodded at Tillinghast. Danny put the car into gear and drove down the driveway. At it's narrowest point, Detective Higginbotham parked the car horizontally across the road. Roadblocks are always about psychology.

Tillinghast walked behind the squad car then waited for the Inspector to emerge from the passenger seat. The two old men walked abreast down the driveway, with Danny following behind, carrying the riot gun. Within the last twenty yards, Coffin removed his cell phone from his coat and took pictures of the car and the workers.

By the time they got to the van, all motion had stopped. The eyes were on the police car and on the riot gun.

Coffin put his phone away.

An older man came down the steps to meet them. He was tall, athletic, and had gray, curly hair cut close to his scalp. He wore a brown work-shirt that identified him as "Walter." He stood with confidence of a man surrounded by guns.

"Good afternoon, my brother." Coffin said.

"Afternoon. What do you all want?" Walter replied.

"Well, I was wondering what you are doing here?"

"We have a work order that calls for us to install an entertainment room into this house."

"Is that a fact?"

"Absolutely."

"Could I see it?"

"If you insist," Walter produced it from a clipboard and handed it to the Inspector. At first blush, the order looked genuine. It seemed to have been ordered by Mr. Gotzakis from Chicago.

"Well, Walter." Coffin said. "This looks very good. Do you mind if we go inside to see your work?"

"Don't you need a warrant for that?"

Coffin smiled. He loved dealing with professionals. "I suppose I do, but I happen to know that the owner and current resident of this house is at the end of this driveway and she has already given me permission."

"I still won't let you in unless she is here."

Danny picked up the odd verb. So did the Inspector. Both men stared at Walter as he realized the slight slip he had made. Not that it made a whit of difference.

"My brother," Coffin continued. He folded the work order back into thirds and presented it back to Walter. "You might be here installing a $60,000 wide screen TV and speaker system, but I rather think you are here searching for some missing money. Now, I could go back up the driveway, bring Shannon down here, and then we could have some drama. Or we could avoid the drama entirely."

Tillinghast stepped forward, opened his briefcase on the hood of the van, removed a folder and then removed a photocopy of the receipt that had been handed him 8 hours earlier.

"Walter, I took almost $600,000 in cash up to this lawyer's office this morning. Since then, per my instruction, they have established a trust and invested the money into several lucrative enterprises both in this country and abroad." Walter looked amused, but not surprised. "The cash you might be searching for is quite gone."

"We are just installing a home theater."

"I am sure."

Walter nonetheless, examined the receipt. "For the sake of argument," Walter said. "Could I call this firm and verify the receipt?"

"Of course."

One of the co-workers handed him a cellphone. Walter walked six steps to the side of the house.

Walter had arrived with a curious five man crew. Two of the "men" were boys little older than twelve. They had appeared to be helping Daddy at work. It occurred to Danny what an ingenious idea this was. No one would question a father with his two sons no matter if they were installing Sonys or stealing them. Now, it didn't look quite so ingenious. Not with a shotgun staring at him.

Within two minutes he came back, and handed the phone to Tillinghast. He spoke into it.

...

"Thank you, James." He said.

....

"No, that will quite do."

....

"I am fine, James. Thanks for your concern. There is no need to contact anyone."

....

"Yes, I will call back later."

Tillinghast snapped the phone shut and handed it to one of the young boys.

Walter smiled.

"I don't suppose you would want to get us that money, would you?"

"No." Tillinghast smiled back. "No, I would not."

"That could put you in some danger."

"I doubt that." Tillinghast said. "Not only do I have the police with me to protect me, but I have enough resources to dissuade."

"To dissuade?"

"Sure."

"It could put other people, like say, a son, in some danger."

"Again, I have powers to dissuade."

"You can't dissuade me. I am a finger on the hand."

"I understand that. I can dissuade the man who directs the hand."

Walter, while still angry, was amused at this odd turn. "Will the police be with you always?"

"I don't need the police."

"Really?" he said. "Are you a super-hero? Are you Batman?"

His crew smiled.

"Walter," Henry Coffin interjected. "I think you have two choices before you. First, you could pack up your friends and these nice boys, go out for pizza, go to the beach tomorrow, and then return to Chicago. Or, we could have some unnecessary drama that will put your employer in dire jeopardy."

"My employer…" Walter said with a smile, "Has never been in dire jeopardy in his life." The threat seemed clear.

Coffin glanced at his partner. Danny caught the gleam in his eye and dreaded it. He chambered a round in the riot gun.

The noise distracted everyone, save the inspector. He took his phone back out and took two pictures of Walter. The other man glared.

"Why do you do that?"

"Now I have your picture on my phone and in my e-mail. Should you choose to shoot us, I am sure that someone will look at my e-mail. Don't you think?"

He spat.

"With all those boys behind you, I would think you might want this to stay as peaceful as possible, my brother." Coffin said. "And so do I."

Walter wanted to pistol whip the old man as a teachable moment for the youngsters. But he didn't.

Tillinghast looked at him.

"Why don't you call your manager and discuss with him the problems you seem to be having with this installation?"

"I don't think I need to bother him."

Coffin took his phone out and took another picture. He began to circle the house.

"Hey!" Walter yelled.

"What?"

"Stay right here."

"No."

Danny Higginbotham walked up close. The muzzle of the big shotgun was five feet from Walter's head. "Everyone needs to keep their hands out where I can see them."

Tillinghast stepped forward. "Look, none of us wants any drama here. There is absolutely no need for it. It will hurt everyone long term." Walter, pissed at the Inspector and the shotgun, glared at the coach. Tillie continued. "Call your contact and tell him what the situation is."

Coffin had disappeared around the house and was peering in the windows at the sliced up cushions, destroyed furniture and holes in the wall. He walked up to the backdoor, stepped inside and continued to take pictures.

Walter looked inside at the old man. The afternoon had gone from odd (in coming to the island) to strange (and the house) to downright bizarre (with a receipt, two cops, and this smooth talking old man.) He didn't really have any choice but to make a phone call.

It involved one call to one number, followed by a call to a pay phone. Eventually, there was a connection.

"We have a situation."

…

"No, that has been placed with a lawyer and is probably overseas."

…

"He has a receipt."

…

"I know."

…

"He's not here."

…

"He's not here either. But there are cops here. They aren't doing anything."

…

"It is a huge clusterfuck."

…

"The head guy seems to think he is a threat to you."

…

"Okay."

Walter handed his phone to Tillinghast. "He wants to talk to you."

The old coach smiled. "Sure."

He took the phone and put it to his ear. He didn't say hello.

"Listen, I am Ambassador Paul W. Tillinghast. I am 68. Go and talk to who you need to talk to and figure out who I am."

Then he hung up.

Walter was sure, at this point, that he would be hunting down this guy's grandchildren. Ambassador or not.

The black guy did not move his gun, however.

"Walter," Inspector Coffin spoke from inside the house. "You'll notice that we didn't come here with a SWAT team, state police backup or even a bullhorn. Do you know why?"

"Because you are all stupid?"

"Never underestimate your brothers." Coffin said. "Never assume that your brother in business is stupider than you are. It is usually better to assume that he is smarter than he appears." Coffin said. "Walter, there is nowhere for you to go. You can't leave this island if we don't want you to. And now that I have your picture, you really can't go. You are trapped."

Coffin was not angry or accusatory. Instead, he was instructing a student on the finer points of checkers.

"We really don't want drama. We want Elvis and Shannon and everyone else connected to this left alone. Forever."

"If they give the money…."

"Don't promise what you can't deliver, Walter. As you said, you are a finger on the hand."

"What if we just break the boy's hands? Or knees?"

"You will never leave this island free." Danny said.

"And then I will begin dismantling your bosses business." Tillinghast said.

"Shut up, old man."

Coffin took pictures of the young adolescents who came to help rip things up and search.

"Inspector," Danny called from the front. "Let's just bring the staties in. Enough of this."

"No." Coffin said. "No, that won't end this." He looked at Walter. "Will it?"

"Just a finger on the hand."

"Indeed."

The phone rang. Walter flipped it open. "Yeah." He said.

…

"Yeah." He continued. He eyed Tillinghast.

…

"Okay, here he is."

Walter handed the phone to Tillie.

"Ambassador, you make quite an impression." The voice was cheerful but forced.

"Thank you."

"Not many men hang up on me and collect their pensions. Women, well, they have different rules."

"That is what I have heard."

"I was told that, if I hurt you in the slightest, the Delta Force would whisk me to Guantanamo and make me stand on a box with wires running to my nuts."

"I don't think Delta is that crude."

"Perhaps not."

Tillinghast cleared his throat. "The money that David Lowell took from you is well-hidden and legal now, so you can't get it without exposure."

"Apparently."

"David Lowell is at death's door. He won't be getting up from the bed he is in."

"I have heard that before."

"I can take Walter up to the hospital."

"I think Walter has done enough for me today, don't you?" The voice dropped five degrees.

"He has kept the Special Operators out of your bedroom."

"Is that what you spooks call them? Special Operators? Sounds like the people who call you looking for your credit card payment."

"Can't hang up on those boys in Delta."

"No, I suppose not." He said. "You said David Lowell is dying?"

"Walter will be able to bring you an obituary." He said. "I do not think he will last the night."

"How about his hands? Could Walter bring those?"

"No, not that."

"Fair enough." He said. "I have to ask. It's in all the movies."

"You need to leave his sister and his boy alone."

"How about the boy's mother?"

Tillinghast looked at Coffin.

"I haven't met her."

The voice on the phone paused.

"You're cold, aren't you?"

"I have a very limited set of concerns."

"I'll say." The voice chuckled for a moment. "So," A chair squealed as it turned. "You keep the money David stole, the boy and his father remain unpunished, and I get to keep from seeing sunny Cuba."

"Among other benefits."

The voice laughed.

"Ambassador, you know that I make far more than $600,000 everyday, right?"

"Of course."

"And you know that, in letting this money slip away, I might encourage others to steal."

"And you will have to cut off hands."

"I might." He said. "I haven't yet, but it sounds like a good idea. If it is good enough for the CIA, it is good enough for me." He chuckled again. "Here is what I think. I think the $600,000 is money I paid to you for this conversation. You are a wonder, Ambassador. You are a wonder. You steal my money, you hang up on me, you mouth off to one of my employees, and you still get your way."

"Diplomacy, my friend."

"Russians never stood a chance, did they?"

"No, sir. They didn't."

"Hand the phone to Walter, would you?"

CHAPTER NINE

The day ended slowly, bathed in gold. The October sun was still wrapped in the colors and warmth of summer. It dropped through one thin line of clouds, touched the horizon, and squeezed itself over it.

Tourists ignored their burgers and their lobsters to watch it illuminate the evening. Fishermen paused to watch, as did the dishwashers, truck drivers, and football players. For those two minutes, on this particular evening, the island stopped, soaked all the light in, and counted itself blessed for being thirty miles out to sea. They all witnessed an astronomical miracle that happened every day, more regular than clockwork, but more special.

Hours later, Danny Higginbotham, unable to get back to sleep, annoyed at his own grilling and at the pitifully cool pile of coals he had established, saw the sunset glow against the gray cedar walls of his house. Here he was, he thought, with his wife and his daughter in his house cooking two large swordfish steaks on his grill with his beer in his fist. He wasn't in Roxbury, he wasn't alone in an apartment, he wasn't eating fast food in a cruiser with some gun happy redneck. If he looked up at the scoreboard, he was doing all right.

Henry Coffin had fallen back to sleep, with the help of a glass of bourbon and an old book. The duvet was wrapped tight around the old man and his eyes darted about under their lids. In the glow of a setting sun, he dreamed of a warm lump on the other side of a mattress and a little boy who jumped up and landed between them. The boy carried a Lego biplane which he landed and took off from his mother's hip and from his father's chest. In his sleep and alone, Henry made the sounds of an airplane propeller.

    Shannon was cleaning. Her entire kitchen lay in heaps on the floor. Flour, baking soda, sugar, cereal, oatmeal, and every other dry good that the house had retained for thirty years lay in its own landfill on top of the peeling linoleum. She sat in one of the remaining chairs, although its cushion had been slashed, and considered the landfill of her cooking life. She had made Bisquick biscuits for her husband, years ago. There it was. Irish Oatmeal for special cookies was drifted over near the door. The King Arthur Flour that seemed to breed moths centered the whole mess. The fading light of day illuminated and set ablaze all of these memories.
    She thought of burning the house and starting again.
    Instead, she picked up the phone book and called Topham's cleaners.
    There would be people coming over, soon enough. And she was too old for this.
    She made herself a Manhattan and waited for the girls to arrive.

    After wishing Walter and his boys well, Tillinghast had gone to practice. Afterwards, he had picked another pizza up at Sophie T's and stood outside his Jeep in the visitor's slots at the Nantucket Cottage Hospital. The last minute of direct sunlight reddened the white pizza box, the white skin and white hair of the old coach. For a moment after practice, he had wondered if he should bring the boy something different this time, but the boy doesn't know what he is eating and probably doesn't care.
    Not for the last time, he thought of that last voyage for his father. It had been ego and it had been control and it had placed grenades in the chests of everyone who had loved the daft old man. David Lowell was generous in his death. It would hurt and scald, as all deaths do, but it was clear, irreversible, and without the slightest shadow of doubt. There would be a body to go into the coffin. There would be no hopes about hospitals or islands or New Bedford fishing boats.
    And he wasn't taking the dog with him.

In the moments after the sun set, the sky lit up with one last burst of color. Tillinghast noted it, then hit the automatic door button and walked into the hospital.

The boy sat in the dark with his dying father. The room smelled of sweat, old pizza, medicine, disinfectant, and the sweet dust of death.

"How is he doing?"

"Pretty much the same."

"Is he in pain?"

"He doesn't seem to be."

"No."

The boy took a slice and ate half of it in one bite. He chewed thoughtfully.

"Did you talk to him today." Tillinghast asked.

The boy took his time with the pizza. "Yes."

"Any response?"

"Probably not."

"Probably?"

"He might have squeezed my hand. He might not have. I don't know."

"It's a good thing to do."

"I know." Elvis said. "I know." He looked at his Dad. "They say that the cancer is deep into his brain."

"It probably is."

"He probably can't hear me."

"Maybe not."

Elvis looked at him.

"Think about babies." Tillinghast said. "Their brains aren't really developed, they can't see anything, and their ears can't pick out individual sounds. They know what their mother's voice sounds like. They know what she smells like and what her heartbeat is."

Elvis nodded. He smiled. "So, I am my father's mother."

"Right now." Tillie also smiled. "The child is father to the man."

"He is going backwards."

"In a manner of speaking." The coach said. "But I am sure it isn't pleasant, even if he has morphine. I am sure that he is full of pain, even now."

Elvis sat silent.

"Is my Mom on island?"

"Probably not."

"Probably not?"

"I think she may have left."

Elvis looked at the older man.

Tillie continued. "Your mother inadvertently led some of your father's former business partners to your Aunt's house. Shannon called me. Henry Coffin and I met them outside. They agreed to leave you alone."

"Was my Mom there?"

"I didn't see her."

Elvis had his huge elbows on his hands. He thought about this.

"They didn't bring my mother here to the hospital?"

"I doubt it. Actually, I am sure. I would have seen them here. And they aren't."

He sighed. "She is who she is."

"Unfortunately."

"You can visit her later, if you want."

"Yeah." He said. "That must have been some conversation."

"It was fine. Everyone was fine. They wanted the money and when they saw they couldn't get it, they left."

"Just like that."

"Pretty much." Tillie said. "People are reasonable, in the end. If you make them sit and think for a second, they generally do the right thing."

"Still, it must have been something."

"Everybody has something to live for."

Elvis considered his father.

The two of them sat in silence for an hour. Then, the three of them watched ESPN together.

Maria rose from sleep slowly.

The dream had been bad, but she wasn't crying or even feeling hurt. Perhaps sad.

She had seen him again. Julian had sat with her on the bench at the Old Mill. They had kissed and touched. He had said his sweet things to her, again. He had stroked her belly, then, as he had before, he climbed the long steering arm to the top of the mill.

He raised both his hands.

Her dream had changed and the mill was now perched on the edge of the harbor. Luther waved once more, then he dove. His dive was more of a long glide. His body soared out over the waves and entered the water without a splash. He treaded water for a second and waited for the now heavy and now very pregnant Maria to waddle over to the edge of the cliff. He waved once more to her, and she back at him.

Then he swam out into the channel.

He was gone. She knew it. The knowledge came to her as the word of God. It relieved her and it saddened her.

She sat on the edge of the cliff, watching him swim away, and hoping that that moment would just stretch out into the rest of time.

The boy awoke with a start.

Nothing in his life had changed. The meatlover's pizza had cooled to a scab in its box. His neck and back were sore from sleeping in the chair. The lights continued to wink. No buzzers were sounding, no alarms were going off, no running footsteps down the hall.

There wouldn't be.

At four in the morning, the truth appeared to him gray and resolute. There would be no help. There would be no miracle. His Dad could not come and make the tough decision for him.

And he had thought it all out. The mini-debate did not need to rage in his head any longer. All he needed to do was to look at his father with a clear eye and he knew how this would end. His body was still too healthy. His mind had lost huge chunks in the last attack, but the body continued to labor on in spite of shark bite upon shark bite. So it would go for six months in a nursing home. And then it would end on second shift when the duty nurse was doing Sudoku and his son was a hundred miles away.

So it should be now.

And even after the steep plunge of a decision, a voice cried against it and locked him into his chair. Visions of Christmas, of birthdays, of game days, and dinner in the house, and the long drive, and the last game he ever saw all bound him to the chair. His father would rise, they said. He would rise again and it would all be right.

But it wouldn't.

The huge lumps on his chest, on his arms, on his neck exposed the lying hope. Elvis found that last fluttering hope and held it in his huge hands. Something could happen, it said. Something or someone could help. If only they had faith. If only they searched.

Elvis considered the small bird. It perched on his thumb and looked at him sideways. Then he caught it with his other hand, pinched its neck, and felt the crack of tiny vertebrae.

He stood from the chair, took three painful steps and knelt by the blue control box to the morphine drip.

He pressed a small button that said "Override."

He keyed in the numbers 1-4-3.

Then, the son waited for his father.

The end came like that of a sinking ship. His breathing grew slower, shallower, and more irregular. The alarms and lights began flashing, but no one ran up the hall. Then, there was a burst of short quick breaths, followed by a straining silence. Another burst of quick shallow breaths, and a longer silence.

Finally, the last breaths fought their way into his lungs, and then slipped out. The spirit of the man slipped underwater, and then dropped to the dark bottom. His body only remained along with whining alarms and beeps.

Elvis stood and walked from the room.

As soon as he appeared, three nurses entered. The alarms stopped, the flashing ceased, and they began preparing the body.

No one talked to Elvis.

It was 4:17.

Milestone Four

CHAPTER ONE

The news of the man's death spread like the tide. It crept slowly and inexorably into the background of the island. It was noted and tallied, like a football score. People heard about David Lowell and then paused, but since it did not concern them and was not anyone they had known, they merely nodded and continued to mix sugar in their coffee.

Elvis called his mother, but there was no answer at her phone. He left her a message.

He then called Aunt Shannon. She was on her way.

He called Tillinghast, who thanked him and told him to grab his workout bag.

Which, inexplicably, he had. His Aunt may have dropped it off, or he may have taken it, or it somehow made it into the pile of gear that got transferred to Room 22 with his father. His homework was still buried under the kitchen table, but his t-shirt, shorts, sneakers, jock and socks were clean and in a Nike bag at his feet.

The sun was rising over Sconset. The bright reds and flashes of green and purple burst across the low clouds. Then, the shadows lengthened and the stars faded out in the first light over the island.

The red Cherokee pulled up in front of the main door to the hospital. Tillie just waited.

Elvis was late for the sky. The room and the building was still caught up in the business of the night. He watched his hand key the numbers in. He saw his father's body fight for it's last breath and for the next one that never came. And he saw the final settling.

Tillinghast was outside in the growing light.

He picked up the bag and slipped down the stairs to the waiting car.

Neither man said anything on the way to the gym.

Rosie awoke to her buzzing phone. It vibrated across the surface of the night table like an annoying toy.

She turned it over to see the phone number.

School.

So she flipped it open.

"Morning Rosie."

"Elizabeth. What's wrong?" She was the front office secretary and the source of the important news.

"Do you remember the new kid, Elvis? The kid who was in the papers?"

"Sure."

"His Dad died."

"Oh." Rosie let her voice drift away. "What of?"

"Cancer. The boy was with him at the end."

"Where did he die?"

"At the hospital." She said. "Why?"

"Oh."

"At the end it was fast."

"When are the services?"

"We haven't exactly heard, but the wake will probably be on Thursday night."

"Thursday?"

"Yup." Elizabeth paused. "Homer would like to know when you will be back."

Rosie paused.

"I don't know."

"Homer thinks it would be good if there were some grief counselors at the school."

"And he would like me there."

"You know how he is."

"Yes. He is an idiot."

The silence approved her.

"He feels that we haven't had any deaths for a few years now and he might have some freaked out kids."

"It's not like anyone knows the guy."

"The football team likes him. And Elvis is huge."

"I remember what he looks like." Rosie said. She sighed; she was tired of the eyes and mouths of the island. "Look, we are still not ready and we are supposed to go off island. I will call the counseling service and maybe Reverend Mayhew and see if they can come by."

"I will let Homer know."

"Message received, Liz."

"Have a good day."

"You too."

Rosie clicked the phone shut.

At the wake, Elvis knelt next to his father.

The days since his death had been a parade of mundane choices, repetition, and cleaning.

He had not fought with his Aunt about much. Shannon and he had picked out a simple, silver casket the day before. She wanted a catered party at the house after the burial. He didn't care. She wanted hors d'oeurvres and a roast beef. He didn't care. She wanted open casket, she wanted him buried at Prospect Hill Cemetery, she wanted a limousine to take her to the burial. He didn't care about that, either.

He did care about a Catholic funeral. His father rarely spoke of the church, and when he did, it wasn't anything to repeat. Shannon fluffed herself and looked upset, but Elvis merely said, "No." Steamship round of roast beef and chocolate mousse in wine glasses was fine: communion wafers and airy eulogies was not. If anybody had anything they wanted to say, they could say it at the grave.

He cared about money. If anyone sent money, it was going to the Nantucket Hospice. Nothing to the Heart Foundation, or AIDS network, or any of the charities that Shannon's friends liked. Hospice was it.

Elvis regarded the made-up face before him. He had killed his father. He got to decide where the money went.

Surprisingly, there was money. The bill for the entire funeral went to a lawyer in Chicago. Allied Hauling sent a huge spread of flowers, along with a four figure check. Other Chicago groups, from Unions to Sons of Hibernia to a ski club sent four figure checks. Aunt Shannon saw this as proof of her brother's generosity in life. "Wasn't this nice of them?" she clucked at each envelope. Elvis knew better; tribute was tribute.

At four-thirty on Thursday evening, one half hour before the wake officially began, Elvis was kneeling. He looked into a face that he would never see again.

It was crazy. It was insane that this was the end. His voice was silent, he would not open his eyes. He would not stand again.

Elvis was also conscious that he knew as much of his father right now as he would ever know. It would all erode. Tomorrow, the sand would start to wash away and the shoreline would move more and more inland. Some memories would remain. Some images would stay in his head for the rest of his life. But the daily moments, the small sidelong glance of a man drinking coffee and reading the sports page. That would slide away.

Even this moment, kneeling before this open casket for his last look at his father, even this moment would fade away.

Elvis stood and gave way. Shannon waited for her turn at the kneeler, as did several of her friends. He slowly moved to the back wall with Ricky Whelden, the funeral director. Ricky was normally considered a tall man, but he barely was as tall as the boy's ears. He wore a dull cotton-poly blend gray suit, with a Knights of Columbus pin on one lapel and another indeterminate one on the other side. He moved to say something to the son, but didn't. The boy leaned against the wall, sighed, and watched the group of women standing at the casket.

At five, Ricky pointed to the spots where he wanted Shannon and Elvis to stand. The mourners would come in, walk straight ahead and shake hands, then pause before David, then sit in the chairs.

Except they didn't.

The door opened out on to Union Street. Through it, Elvis could see cars pass, bicyclists pedal back to town from the beach, little kids and their parents stroll, and no one walked in. Shannon sat with her friends nearby and chatted. If anyone entered, she would be close enough to stand up and greet, if she had to.

At five fifteen, Tillinghast walked in. He entered with a smile, shook Ricky's hand, and walked up to Elvis. He rolled slightly when he took his steps; he had not dressed. He stood in his sweatpants and coaches jacket, with a whistle around his neck. Shannon's friends noticed with their silence.

He stepped up to Elvis and put his hand out.

"I am sorry for your loss." Tillie said, meaningfully.

Elvis looked up into his face. "Thanks for coming."

"Happy to be here. For you." He said, then he released the young man's hand. "The team will be coming down in about twenty minutes. They needed to shower and change first. I wanted to come down first. I hope you understand."

"Of course." The boy said, confused. "Thanks. Thank you."

"It is the least we can do."

"No…"

"It is." Tillie said. "Trust me, it is the least."

The coach shook hands with Aunt Shannon, and then met with her friends. For their initial disapproval, they were ready to shake hands with the former ambassador.

Others slowly arrived. His teachers walked in, still in classroom clothes. They shook his hands, muttered their apologies, and sat together before the casket. Several other friends and lunch partners of Shannon's appeared. They knew the traditions, knew Ricky, and knew the arrangements. Each spoke to Elvis with well-worn sincerity while each, privately, marveled at his size. The boy handed the last one to his Aunt, before he saw Maria.

She was both crying and smiling on a face blotched with emotion. He tried to shake hands with her, but she reached up and hugged him around the neck. He bent down and gently reached around her tiny body. The hug lasted seconds longer than he thought and as he thought of ways to disentangle himself, she sobbed in his ear. She thought only of Julian.

The sob touched him. It slipped through his chest and brushed his heart. He felt the organ leap and his own emotion build.

Then she stepped away.

"I'm sorry." She said. "Thank you."

Elvis was flummoxed. "It's okay."

"No, no. It isn't." She smiled. "But thank you."

"Okay."

Rosie shook his hand and took after her daughter, just as confused as Elvis was, although a good bit more relieved. When the two of them knelt by his father, the teachers eyed the two of them with appreciation.

The team arrived in one long line of boys. All of them wore ties and jackets. They moved with deliberate speed and uncomfortable silence. They had been instructed on what to do and what to say, but it was a strange and novel time. They had not been to wakes or funerals before, nor did they believe that they ever would go. The death of Elvis' Dad was the first brief touch of black to enter their lives and, though they knew what to say and how to act, once they finished with the handshake and the prayer, they sat in the chairs like boys and whispered to each other. Reinemo, Tillinghast, and Palumbo-all schooled in the art of the possible-let them whisper and hoped that that was all that would happen.

Nick hung back with Elvis to talk, but Elvis didn't feel that he had anything to say.

Elvis did notice, however, that neither Billy nor Jack made the trip to Union Street. Palumbo noticed as well, with a strong wind of relief. Now, when he asked them to clean out their lockers tomorrow, there was an ironclad and irrefutable reason for cutting them.

Finally, with the funeral home full, Reverend Mayhew arrived. The Reverend was Unitarian and universal. He had been a tall, elegant man now stooped over a walker. His eyes had been clear, his hair short, and his skin permanently burnt. In his youth, he had been a missionary to Peru and Ecuador. As a result, he said the rites with the wonder of a man performing a miracle. Afterwards, he had returned to the lucrative work of guiding the families of investment bankers and trust fund babies in Greenwich, Connecticut. He had retired to the island twenty years ago and lived with his second wife outside of town, on a small plot of land with potatoes, mushrooms, two pigs as deacons, and a henhouse of a congregation. After he arrived, he became the island's de facto chaplain. He married almost everyone, blessed the boats, led the Peace Vigils, gave the invocation at town meeting and spoke over the funerals. Mimicking his wedding patter was a parlor game.

Unfortunately, Parkinson's had made serious inroads to his body. The body and hands that had once climbed Macchu Pichu at dawn and raced sunfish at the yacht club, shook and rattled. Flecks of drool dripped down his chin and his eyes bulged. The cane had given way to a walker and soon, to a wheelchair.

He shuffled his way forward to Elvis, stuck his hand out, expressed his sorrow. The old minister had to turn his head sideways in order to look up into the face of the young man. The boy expressed his thanks.

"My son, can we talk over here?"

"Okay." Elvis looked over at the door, but night had fallen outside. Tillinghast extracted himself from the football team and slipped over to the old Reverend. The three men backed up to the wall. Elvis pulled a chair over for the older man.

"Son," Mayhew said. "I have been asked to say a few words tomorrow at the burial."

"Okay." Elvis has no idea how he would be able to do that.

"I never met your father and I can't pretend that I knew him. It would help me out if we could talk about him a little. Tillie has told me some." He nodded at the coach. "But I would like to add a little more."

"Okay." Elvis said.

Mayhew looked at him. "How do you feel?"

"Okay."

"A little numb?"

"Yes."

"You should be. It`s a good thing."

He nodded. Mayhew with all his physical pain, could see the pain of the boy: the pain he felt now and the pain to come.

"What did your father do?"

"I don't know."

"You don't?"

Talking about him made the bubble of emotion rise in his chest. He did not have the energy anymore.

"He was in organized crime, Reverend." Elvis said. "I think he hurt people."

Mayhew was quiet for a moment. Tillie looked at him. The minister reached one dry, arthritic and knobbed hand over to the boy's. "Don't worry about that, son."

"He didn't want to." Elvis muttered.

"I'm sure not."

"He didn't have a choice."

"Of course."

"He had no education and his father basically abandoned the kids when he was fourteen. They offered him a job. And he had younger brothers and sister."

Mayhew looked over at Aunt Shannon.

"So he helped…"

"Yes." Elvis said. "And then he had me."

"Do you have any brothers or sisters?"

"No."

"It was just the two of you?"

"Yes." Elvis felt that each word was a step on a white hot path.

"What about your mother?"

Elvis shook his head. "I don't know. She's an addict. I don't know."

Minister and Coach shared a glance.

"So," the minister asked. "What are you going to do now?"

Elvis shrugged. "Shannon said that I could stay with her."

"Would you like to?"

"Sure."

Mayhew looked at the boy. From his age and experience, he could see the road in front of the boy. In South America, it was not uncommon and the path was still dangerous, but well-trod. Better here than some other spot, he thought.

"Why did he bring you here?"

"I think he wanted to die here."

Mayhew nodded.

"Shannon was here. I think he wanted her to take care of me." He said. "But he liked the island. He had been here before I was born and he wanted to come back. It was his time."

"And the cancer killed him."

Elvis was silent. He had killed him.

"Yes." He said, finally.

Mayhew nodded. He understood enough about these deaths that occur in the middle of the night.

"Elvis," he said. "Did he have any last words?"

"No."

"It could be really simple, like "change the channel" or "enjoy every sandwich""

"Well, he wasn't making a lot of sense towards the end…"

Mayhew nodded.

"…the last thing he tried to say was garbled. It was "Football is the duck head."

Mayhew and Tillinghast once again glanced at each other. "Duckhead?"

"I know. It doesn't make sense." Elvis said. "He really, really wanted me to play football."

"Did he try to say any other words?"

Elvis thought back to that moment when he would hear the last words his father would ever say to him. It had been a Monday morning after the football scores when he could barely make sense. "I don't remember what else he tried to say."

For a long moment, Elvis was back in that morning with his father lying in bed. The TV was on, the highlights were running and he was desperately trying to say something.

Then he had fallen asleep.

That was all his son could remember.

The emotion rose high in his chest.

James had gone to bed. The boy had waited for his sister to come home, but it was too late for him. He had tottered upstairs after watching all of "Monster's Inc.", including the credits, then trudged upstairs. Rick DeSalvo followed the boy into his room. James cuddled into his sheets, kissed his father goodnight and waited for a story. Rick had no more than opened a book when the boy was sound asleep.

Maria and her mother returned an hour later, during the third inning of the World Series. To her father, she looked tired and blotchy. He came out of the TV room to welcome her back, but Maria glared at him, momentarily, then climbed the stairs.

His wife followed. Thirty minutes later, she stepped back down. Rick got up from his book and the kitchen table.

They had a lot to talk about.

"Nice to see you." She said

"Nice to see you." He replied and kissed her. She was an awkward size and it was an awkward hug.

"Glad you did the dishes."

"We ate takeout."

"Color me surprised."

He sat back down at the table.

"How was it?"

"Fine."

"Fine?"

"It was a lovely wake." She pronounced. "Quiet, calm. The football team came, all but those two." Rick straightened up, as if bone had just ground onto bone. "Shannon had brought her ladies who lunch. Some school folks."

"Nice to see the team there."

"Good thing they were there, or there wouldn't be anyone at all."

"Why did you two stay?"

"I don't know." She said.

"You don't."

"She wanted to stay. She wanted to be there for Elvis."

"Elvis." He smiled.

"Seems like a good kid. He's in a tough place."

"Oh, I'm sure he'll be all right."

"Why is that?"

"Because he probably weighs 300 pounds, runs a 4.7 forty, and can lift a pickup. Some football coach is out there, right now, smoothing the yellow brick road out for him. I saw the photo."

She heard the bitterness. Elvis had won a genetic lottery, but he had to pay a debt. A big one.

Maria had big debts too. They were still waiting for her big pay day. Rosie had spent a good bit of her time at the wake considering the quiet face of the dead man while she concocted scenarios for confronting her daughter. Nothing came to her. Nothing that she really wanted to do right then. If she wasn't sure, perhaps it wasn't true.

But it was true.

And it would be true tomorrow.

Rosie brought herself back to her husband and their kitchen table.

"Elvis tossed Billy over a fence a few weeks ago. Kids say he crushed Jack against a locker and almost killed him the other day. Maria says that he is the only thing that scares those two fuckwads."

Rick settled back. The two of them were sitting in the glare of the kitchen. Someone had scored a run on the TV.

"What do you think?"

"I don't know." She shook her head. "I don't know."

"He's not the mystery boyfriend, is he?"

"God, no."

"Well, what is he?"

"He's the only guy who did anything about those two pricks. He's a high school Dirty Harry."

Rick nodded. "Can't be all bad, then."

"No."

"When are you guys going off island?" He asked.

"I don't know. Not tomorrow."

"No?"

"She wants to go to the burial."

"So, Friday?"

"Yeah." She said.

She decided not to tell him about the pregnancy. It sat there on the table, near where she had put the vitamin, and she decided to put the biggest secret in their marriage into the closet for a while. It might end them, she thought idly. Communication. Secrets. All of those bad things that she taught the kids about.

Nope. She wasn't going to give it words. Not now.

She poured both of them a fresh cup of coffee.

CHAPTER TWO

Danny had not planned on going to the burial. Ten o'clock in the morning remained his prime sleeping time, but Sherrie had prodded him out of bed. Now he stood, among the few mourners, at the burial for David Lowell.

Sherrie had a soft spot for the big kid. He had made an impression on her at the hospital, as had Tillinghast of course. She watched the kid suffer for his Dad on two occasions, and she felt for him when the old man finally slipped away. He had been a good man, she said.

Danny, with his memory of putting a shotgun to a hired killer, didn't contradict her. Danny also knew that terminal cancer patients tended to die in their sleep at the hospital. Sherrie never said why and Danny didn't ask her. But he had a pretty good idea why she felt connected to this young man. The secret to his marriage, he suspected, was in the questions they didn't ask each other.

They parked two rows over from the plot. Without the football team, the crowd of mourners was seemed particularly meager. A large group of older women, dressed conservatively, if not particularly somber. Very few others were there: Coaches Palumbo, Reinemo, and Tillinghast; Nick, Maria, and Rosie from the school, two men in dark suits who represented the quiet rooms on either side of the law, Ricky and his assistants, and Mayhew.

Elvis wasn't particularly concerned about the mourners. Two or two hundred could have appeared, he wouldn't have noticed. Instead, he watched the casket. He walked with it out to the hole, then stood to the side.

His father had never been a prankster. But it felt so strange, so unnatural, that Elvis expected the lid to lift and for his Dad to step out.

Of course, he was dead.

Of course, he had seen him die.

Of course, he had helped him die.

But it was so strange, so out of place, so unnatural for him to be in the casket.

At odd moments, Elvis was convinced he wasn't in the box. Instead, his father was in the small crowd. In those moments, Elvis saw a glimpse of a shirt he wore, his hair, and the barest snatch of his voice. He knew those were mirages. He knew they were coming and where they were coming from.

But he was still holding things in his head to talk to his Dad about. He wanted to joke about Tillinghast. And Shannon. And Maria. He had built up quite a list for when he saw him again.

In the exasperating sunlight, Elvis was alone. On both sides of the cemetery, people were headed off to the beach or the golf course. Overhead, the Cessnas continued to fly people to the airport for the weekend. August's roses retained their color into the early weeks of fall, as had the Queen Anne's Lace and goldenrod. Rolling, puffy fair weather clouds blew over from the mainland. Everyone at the burial, but Elvis, had sunglasses on. Shannon and her friends had re-applied sunblock twice.

Elvis didn't understand any of it.

Ricky Whelden gently guided Reverend Mayhew to the casket. He took one hand off of the walker and laid it on the silver metal of the box. Within a minute, the conversation about restaurants, golf scores, and tenants had faded to silence and the ladies were ready for the show. Everyone came up to the edge of the green Astroturf that bordered the hole. A set of low metal hand rails also bordered the hole, as if people would walk up to the edge and peer in.

While he looked at Mayhew, Nick, and Coach Tillinghast stood behind him. Maria and her mother also moved closer.

Mayhew cleared his throat.

"Friends, I'm sorry."

Whatever lingering conversation, ceased. Instead, the air held a gentle summer wind, the shuffle of brush and grass, and the distant rumble of surf.

Even in this quiet, it was difficult to make out what the old man said.

"Friends, I'm sorry that I can't out-shout the wind anymore or silence the cars, so I hope you all can hear me. I will try to be loud, but my outdoor voice right now was my indoor voice not all that long ago."

He paused. The mourners were eyes and ears.

"We have come here to witness the passing of David Lowell. Much of what he was is in that box right there. The part that you would see in a picture or walking on a street or look at over the dinner table is now in that box. In a few minutes, we will lower it into the ground and cover it with dirt. That part of David Lowell will be gone from us."

"We know what happens then. 'the worms crawl in, the worms crawl out, the worms play penuckle on your snout…" We have all see the movies and the TV shows to know what happens to the body. We return to dust, as the scripture says: "Dust thou art and dust thou wilt become." The State of Massachusetts, modern science, and our own friend Mr. Whelden, prevents both the worms and the dust, but this part of his life is, nonetheless, over."

"There is another part of him, of course. Many of us believe that we have a soul that was imbued into our body before birth and that, later, will rise from our bodies at death. Some believe that at that point the soul will reconnect with God. Others, like the Hindu, believe that the soul will get recycled into the body of some other living thing, like a cow or a scallop or something. Others believe that the soul will enter Heaven for an eternal reward, or Hell for eternal damnation. St. Peter waits at the pearly gates with a scroll that will judge where you go. Or, more biblically, that the dead will rise on Judgement Day, be judged by God, and then get sent to an Eternal Reward."

"Personally, I am not so sure as to why God would wait a millennia or two. God, whatever you believe him to be, has a vast and comprehensive knowledge of mankind and all of our silliness. If any being is capable of making snap and instant judgements, it would be God. It took him all of six days to create all of creation, he can probably judge us and send us all off before lunch."

"Truth be told, judging most of us is pretty easy as well. Very few of us can keep either the spirit or the letter of the ten commandments. Save for a few poets and saints, no one has lived a life free from the blot of sin. Covet thy neighbors goods? Covet thy neighbor's wife? Take the name of thy God in vain? Pride? Gluttony? Sloth? Thou shalt not kill?"

Mayhew paused.

"You don't need the vast power and omniscience of God to judge humanity. We know the verdict. We are all guilty. We are all bound for the dark and fiery place, with pitch forks and cloven hooves. Every one of us sins five times before breakfast and ten times after dinner. We wear clothes made by slaves. We eat food raised in the most inhumane way. We live amid phenomenal riches within a stone's throw of poverty, but we will not throw that stone. If we go back to those rules laid down in the Bible, none of us would escape whipping and Heaven would be very, very quiet."

Mayhew looked at his hand on the casket.

"I am a funny old man. I don't have much longer to travel out here and I will shortly be on the same short ride that David will take. As a result of a life fully lived and a death fully recognizable, I have come up with my own beliefs about God and the afterlife."

"I believe that God will judge us on Judgment Day. I believe that there will be an end of days, sometime far off in the future. Perhaps he will sit in some lifeguard chair and separate all of us into two long lines and send us off to wherever we will go. After our lives, in the intervening infinity of dust, WE don't wait for GOD to get HIS act together and judge us all in one fell swoop.

"Rather, GOD waits for US. Only one part of us dies and is placed in a box." Mayhew tapped the casket. "Another part of us, the soul, rises up to God. But the most important part of us, the most important essence, continues to echo down here on earth. The third part of us are our deeds. We live in the people we have touched. And those people keep a spark alive inside us. If we are good, and if we live a good life, this spark carries itself from person to person. That fire burns on and on through the wave-thundered darkness. A good man and his good deeds light the world for generations upon generations."

"My God is a merciful God. And that God waits until the end of days so that he can see the full extent of life. At the end of days, God listens to the last of the echoes and sees the last flame flicker out. The source of those flames that came guttering through the good deeds of the millennia, join him in his glorious house."

Mayhew's own voice had become hoarse.

"I never met this part of David Lowell. It is an odd feeling, for me, to say a few words over the body of a man that I never met, never spoke with, and never prayed with. There isn't much I can say honestly about this part of him. I can't tell you about the strength of his handshake or his great power or his fearsome look. I met him when he was less of a man and more of a name."

"But that part of him doesn't count for much, in the end. His deeds, like stones, have fallen into the pond, and the waves spread, redouble, and spread even further. Hold his good deeds in your mind.

Hold his best in front of you. Let that be your guide. Let that be your tribute. Let that be your prayer."

At this, Mayhew ceased.

In a matter of minutes, Elvis reached down for a handful of dirt and dropped it, clod by clod onto the casket.

Machinery hummed and the box began its descent.

The party was very nice. The caterers had taken control of the kitchen in the morning, assembled their hors d'oeuvres and finger foods, then built the serving stations and bars throughout the house. The one advantage to having thrown out much of the furniture is that you had plenty of room for a cocktail party.

When the guests arrived, they all said nice things about the view. And how lucky they were that the weather was so nice. October really is the best time of year out here, don't you think. Shannon does have the most wonderful taste, doesn't she? Yes, they said, I will have another scallop. Thank you very much.

The coaches hadn't come to the party. They made the necessary excuses and slipped away. Elvis sympathized. He missed Tillinghast and Palumbo, but he would rather be with them on the field than to have them with him in this yard, standing on the grass making small talk to Mr. and Mrs. Sandcrab. More guests had arrived for the party than had been either at the wake or the burial. Dreary depressing things, they said. Why not celebrate the dead? So, here they were.

He had found a story they liked and he retold it. He said that his father found out that he was sick and didn't have long to live, so he came here for his last days. He wanted to see his sister again. And he loved the island and his sister, so this was where he had to be….

After his sixth retelling of the story, Elvis gave up on the crowd. He slipped upstairs for a moment, lay down on his bed, closed his eyes and wished to fade away. No one, he thought, would miss him.

But he was missed. Maria had left her mother at the dessert table and was looking for Elvis. She did not find him, but she did find Nick Koch sitting on an Adirondack chair in the backyard and drinking a scotch.

She sat on the ground next to him.

"Afternoon."

"Howdy."

"What are you doing?"

"Heading into the deep end."

"Get there yet?"

"I think I might be close." He said. "Want to come swimming?"

"Not right now."

He glanced at her.

"Will you be my lifeguard?"

"Sure."

Nick took a deep drink, washed it from one side of his mouth to the other, then let it trickle down the back of his throat.

She knew Nick, slightly. There were a few parties and a class or two.

"Where's Elvis?" Maria asked.

"Memphis. In the Jungle Room."

"Funny."

"Do you ever think of the balls it took to name your baby "Elvis"?

"No."

"I mean, we are in "Boy named Sue" territory with that name. No way you can hide in the background if your name is Elvis."

"Not like Nick."

"Fuck, no." he sipped more whiskey. "Nicks and pricks are a dime a dozen. You can find us everywhere. Any gas station, donut shop, or detox ward has its share of Nicks and Pricks. But Elvis. You're not going to find too many of them."

"Unless you're in Memphis."

"And even then." He gestured. "The big guy is upstairs avoiding all of these people. And me. And you."

Maria blushed a little.

"You can't blame him." Drunk Nick continued. "His Dad is dead, he's stuck out here, and all of these crabs a scurrying around the dead body. And everyone wants to talk to him about his picture."

"Whiskey does great things to you."

"Don't it though." He finished off the last dregs in his glass. "What are you doing here?"

"I owe him a favor. Or two."

"Do you?" he said. "Don't we all?"

He sat up straighter in the chair. "I was about to get another drink. Can I get you something?"

"Nothing. Water."

"How about Vodka? It looks like water, but it has a kick."

"Just water."

"Suit yourself."

He tottered off for the open bar. Maria took the opportunity to steal his Adirondack chair. Her back, immediately, relaxed as if it exhaled all on its own. She would never leave it.

Nick came back with a red party cup full of scotch and ice. In his other hand, he had a small bottle of Poland Spring water.

"Chair thief." He smiled.

"I assumed that a gentleman like you gave it up for the lady."

He glared at her, then handed her the drinks. After a quick thirty-seconds, he found another Adirondack tucked around the side of the building. He dragged it over, leaving gouges in the grass. He set it up next to her, fell into it, then accepted his heavy glass of whiskey.

"You know why I am here?"

"To get drunk?"

"Done and done." He smiled. "I am here, because I love the guy. I love Elvis."

"You love him?"

"Absolutely. He can marry me. I will wear the dress." He smiled. "Let me tell you a story. This week, Monday, the big guy comes to practice. His Dad is in the hospital, his life has shit itself, he's in the papers everywhere, and he comes to a nothing practice. No pads, no nothing, just walk through and fuck off."

He continued. "So, your friends and mine, Billy and Jack, show up late and they start giving him a hard time. Now," boozily, he turned to her. "Jack, master of comedy, had pissed in the Big Man's locker last week. Elvis picked him up by his neck and bounced him against a wall. And he bitch-slapped Big Old Billy. Again...."

Nick faded out.

"So," he continued. "They were pissed. And those two lovely human beings take turns trying to take out Elvis' knees in this sprint drill. First time, they almost get him. Second time, he ducks out of the way, grabs Billy's face mask and almost twists his head off. So we break them up. No harm no foul."

"Except Billy is still talking trash. So Elvis takes his helmet and chucks it at him. Not a little toss, not an intentional miss, he aims for the kids head and nails him in the side of his ribs. He hits him so hard that you can see the screwheads in Billy's back. He threw to kill. Absolutely no doubt."

Maria felt cold.

Billy. Jack. Julian. The box on her chest opened up and she saw Julian with a knife.

Maria felt the afternoon disappear around her. She reached into her pocket to touch the gold coin.

Nick kept speaking. "The fucker has no fear. He didn't care what happened. He didn't care what those two could do. He just threw down."

Maria could barely hear him.

She stood up, went around the corner, and vomited.

CHAPTER THREE

At two in the morning, in the autumn fog and the first reds of a changing moors, Henry Coffin waited for a pickup truck. They had parked at the peak of Altar Rock, near the very center of the island. Through a trick of the fog, they couldn't see more than ten feet away.

The island of Nantucket is the furthest edge of the great Wisconsin glacier and, when the glacier melted, all the sand, dirt and trash that it carried got dropped. The North side of the island, under the far edge of the glacier, had little hills and valleys. The southern side had been washed flat by all of the melting water. Altar Rock was the largest pile of dirt left, even if it only rose 100 feet off the water's surface.

Danny knew that this piece of ground had been fought over by the Wampanoags for years. He knew that one of Coffin's far distant ancestors had bulled and buffaloed the great Chief Metacomet into leaving the island peacefully, and he knew that there was no more exposed and open place to meet on the island.

Danny didn't know why Graves had insisted on meeting here, but he didn't like it.

The Inspector, of course, was asleep.

Twenty minutes after two, a pair of lights comes bouncing over the path from the interior of the island. The truck leapt and heaved through the sandy road until it came to the base of the hill. Danny flipped his lights off and, in turn, the pick-up truck did as well.

It drove up the hill and parked next to the squad car.

Steven Graves stepped out of the driver's side, walked around to the passenger side and leaned against the door. Danny, at the head of the squad car, noted him. It was an odd position. There wasn't much he could do offensively or defensively. If shooting began, there would be no cover.

Not that there would be shooting.

Danny couldn't tell if anyone else was inside the pickup truck cab.

Coffin, now awake, stepped from the passenger side door of the police car and walked around to be face to face with Steven Graves.

Then, very slowly, a side window opened a crack.

Danny had his hand on his weapon.

"I don't like this, Henry."

"It's fine, Detective."

"We should leave, Henry."

"We'll be fine." The Inspector said. "Isn't that right, Steven?"

"Absolutely."

Detective Higginbotham stood on the far side of the squad car, with its body as a shield and watched the other men closely.

Henry looked at Steven.

"Sorry for that."

"It's okay."

"He looks out for me. He knows that someone will kill me someday."

"No, they won't."

"Someday." Coffin said. He looked at the young man, but was aware of the open window. "We don't know where Julian is."

Graves sighed. Coffin continued.

"What I believe isn't good. I believe that he was going to run away with Maria on that night"

Coffin had to pause while Stephen listened to whoever was inside the car. Stephen was speaking in a language that might have been Spanish and it might have been Portuguese.

Stephen looked up. "Please continue."

"I believe that they were to meet at a party and go to the boat from there. Two other boys tried to rape Maria, but Julian appeared and sliced one of them."

Coffin did not need a translator to understand what was going on inside the car.

"Maria saw him alive. He ran off, possibly on his bike, and the two boys may have attacked him again. I have a witness that says that they hurt him. We can't find him, however."

A torrent of words washed from the car window. Coffin understood none, but the grief was bitter, glass-edged, and familiar. The old man rested against the side of the squad car and felt the intimate edges of his old scar.

Steven regarded him oddly, as if Coffin had just landed a 12 foot shark and was watching it snap and twitch on the deck. He was surprised, awed, and a touch scared. Danny watched him and, slowly, put a hand back on his gun.

Graves leaned to the window, then looked at Henry.

"Do you know who hurt him?"

"No." he said. "We have suspects."

"Are you looking?"

"Of course."

"What happened to the girl?"

Coffin looked at Graves. "She is with her parents."

"Did you find any coins?"

"One." Coffin said. "Julian had given one to Maria."

"Yes." He answered absently as the conversation continued.

Graves leaned back to the window. He shook his head several times, but at the last shake, Coffin heard some quick hard words.

Steven smiled weakly.

"I am wondering if there is anything that I could offer you that would speed up the investigation. I am very interested to know who did this."

The Inspector looked at the young man.

"No." Coffin said. "We will find out who did this and we will bring those to justice ourselves."

"I am able to offer some considerable help." Graves was intensely pale as he spoke the words handed him from inside the cab.

"No," said Coffin. "I think it is best if I proceed as I always do."

More whispering.

Graves looked at the older man. "Would you excuse me for a second?"

Coffin nodded. Steven Graves opened the passenger door of the truck and sat inside. The smoked glass hid everything.

Coffin did not look at his partner. He did not look into the glass. Instead, he looked over the bed of the truck, over the hills and scrub pines, to the houses of Sconset and the distant rising stars from the Atlantic.

After several minutes, Steven returned. He held a purple lollipop in his hand.

"They would like to give you a gift."

"I don't need one."

"This one is just a lollipop."

"I don't eat lollipops."

"You shouldn't eat this one." Graves said. "But, if there is a time when you need help, for anything at all, the lollipop will get it for you."

Coffin stared at him.

"It is very rare and it is straight from Brazil. Keep it safe and it will help you. Sometime."

Graves handed the lollipop out. The Inspector thought of it, then took it.

"Keep it safe."

"I will, my brother."

"Really safe."

"I will. I promise."

"I have something else to tell you, but I don't want to."

There was a rap on the window.

"Ahab Cab." He blurted out. "Ask whoever is driving it if they know where Julian is."

"Why?"

"Just check them out."

Steven Graves was terrified. His eyes raced back and forth. Coffin noted this, but did not reach out to him.

Coffin nodded.

"Henry, let me know if anything happens. I am really, really sorry for Maria." Steve whispered.

"I am very sorry for Julian."

"Gook Luck, Henry."

"Peace."

Steven Graves, young, strong, and rich, scurried around the front of his car and got into the driver's seat. The truck lurched away.

CHAPTER FOUR

Elvis came downstairs at four in the morning. He listened for a moment in the main room until he realized that he was waiting for a sound that wasn't there. All the machines in his father's room were dark, silent, and still. Instead, Elvis listened to the silence.

He settled onto the new leather sofa.

The room rested one level above disastrous. The caterers had removed all of their platters and trays, then cleaned the kitchen. But the rest of the room had drifts of plastic cups, paper plates with shrimp tails, chicken bones, toothpicks, and half bitten brownies wrapped in napkins. Drinks had spilled on rugs and floors, Styrofoam coffee cups stacked up into towers, and Budweiser bottles mounded up in a cardboard box. The room had the stale sweet smell of rotting food and warming beer.

The death had its remnants too. Someone had stacked and arranged the funeral cards on a book shelf. A sweatshirt that his father had worn sat folded in a corner on a bench. His medicines and his foods remained in the kitchen. The doctor's appointments and the chemotherapy schedule remained written on the calendar, tallied long past hope.

All of this would go.

It would fall into large green trash bags. Pages on the calendar would change. Boxes would go to the Seconds Shop. The hospital would send a tactful older lady to collect the machinery that kept his father alive and comfortable for as long as he could stretch it out.

Then the house would revert to Aunt Shannon's. Neither Elvis, nor his father, had made much of a dent into her small world. A few nicks and scratches here and there. An odd bottle or two hid in the refrigerator. They hadn't left a book, a print, a chair, or even a good-sized stain to mark their time.

Out on the harbor, the boats of autumn swung at anchor. The very earliest tints of dawn lightened the eastern sky. Town was lit up, from the clock tower down to the wharves. Nothing moved: No cars, no pedestrians, no boats, no trucks. Everything waited for the next day to move forward.

This was the new day that his father had brought him to. This was the new world that they had moved into. He had been delivered to the island and left here, while the old man slipped across the sound.

It was the best he could do.

David Lowell didn't have a series of buildings he had designed. There was no shelf lined with his books, no gallery filled with his paintings, no bust in a hall of fame or name on a wall. He had made no more of a mark on the world than he had made on Aunt Shannon's house. A morning's worth of laundry, afternoon of mopping and three trash bags removed him from the planet.

Save one thing.

An hour later, Elvis waited out in the Marine Home Center parking lot. The air had become cooler and the young man wished that he had thought enough for a sweatshirt. His workout bag sat at his feet.

Two trucks passed him without recognizing him.

Tillinghast had slipped from his house in Monomoy at his habitual hour. In silence, he drove to the gym. Because he was lost in thought, he didn't go directly, but drove as if he would pick up the young man.

Of course he wouldn't be there.

When he saw Elvis, with both hands jammed into his pockets, rocking back and forth, the coach's eyes moistened.

Out of respect, he did not speak to Elvis on this morning. And Elvis, for his part, saw the tears in Tillinghast's eyes and let the old man be.

"It's going to be hard."
"I know."
"You are going to cry."
"I know, Mom."
'I don't really want you to go."
"I am not going to sit around this stupid house all day."

Well, Rosie could understand that.

She had promised Shannon that she would help clean up this morning. Rosie had already put the mops, sprays, and sponges into the car. The irony was not lost on her; her house was perhaps the messiest it had ever been, yet she had volunteered to clean someone else's.

Yet, she would not really be cleaning.

Oh, there would be vacuuming, washing, and mopping. For that, Maria would be useful. The cleaning Shannon wanted was for the dead. Rosie was going to help get rid of the clothes, the medicines, and the trappings and vestiges of David Lowell.

The survivors never wanted to do it. They never wanted to betray the faith. When they woke up in the morning, or when they glanced into the room, or if they just wished hard enough, they could imagine the dead would walk. They would want their clothes and their favorite coffee mugs.

So, she had walked into old people's houses with full sets of clothing hanging in the closet just as it was left. The book still had its bookmark, the Fresca was still in the fridge and the Fudge Ripple ice cream, with their last spoon mark, remained in the freezer.

It all had to go.

Hope was a thing with feathers. That needed to be caught, plucked, cooked, and eaten. Hope meant that you hadn't taken a good hard look at reality and accepted that the world would not become what you wanted it to be. You knew that he wouldn't call, that the test was positive, that the last slots were taken. For the survivors, hope kept them looking in the bedroom to see that familiar, breathing shape.

Today, Rosie would be killing Hope. It seemed, Maria would too.

Elvis said little during the workout.

After a long shower and a shave, Tillinghast drove the boy for a breakfast. They sat in a booth at the Downyflake, surrounded by tourists and a few old friends.

"Are you going to the game tomorrow?" the coach asked.

"Can I?"

"You can't play."

"I know." He said. "I haven't been to practice since Monday."

"I think it would be good for everyone if you went." Tillinghast said. "Jack and Billy are off the team."

"Oh." Elvis said. "That's a shame."

"Really?" The coach said. "Didn't you throw a helmet at one of them?"

"Jack is a good hitter. And Billy can block."

The old man looked at the boy.

"They weren't good for the team. You know that."

"It will be hard to win without them."

Tillinghast saw how hard the boy was trying to put it all in a box.

"I don't know how much this team has to win."

"They can still get to the playoffs?"

"Of course, but." The old man said. "You should start thinking about yourself."

"I haven't even played in a real game yet."

"I know." He said. "But you should think for a moment."

Their eggs and sausage arrived.

"What should I think about?"

"Should you remain on Nantucket?"

Elvis paused. "Why not?"

"Well, there are any number of private schools that could offer you better coaching, better facilities, and better teams than this one. You go off to Deerfield and the big college recruiters will find you faster. And you will get one hell of an education."

" And I won't get one here?"

"Compared to Hotchkiss, Phillips Andover, or Deerfield?" he said. "No."

Elvis was confused, tired, and sore.

"I don't understand." He said. "Are you going somewhere?"

"No." Tillinghast smiled. "Not for a while."

"So, why do you want me to go?"

"I don't." Tillinghast said. "Selfishly, I want you to stay. But…"

"But?"

"All of those prep schools are full of kids who have special gifts."

"And money." He sneered

"You have money, now." Tillinghast warned. "Your father saw that you had a lot of money."

Elvis fell silent.

"You go to Phillips Andover and you might have a roommate who is a virtuoso violinist. Down the hall might be a published poet. On your team might be future All-Americans in all sorts of sports. Some of the kids will just be rich and spoiled and connected, but many (and maybe even most) will have a special gift as you have. And that school will have a lot of experience teaching and training people like you."

"And Nantucket doesn't."

"No." Tillie said. "To be blunt, no." He had a bite of egg. "What we do is we teach kids, who don't have gifts, how to excel. It's a harder job, it's a more valuable job, but it isn't the job for you. I don't think."

Elvis was confused. He ate some egg.

"You want me to go?"

"No." Tillinghast said. "I want you to think about it very seriously and make up your own mind."

The boy shook his head.

"Look, Elvis." Tillinghast said. "You don't need to decide now. You don't need to decide in six months. But you do need to think about it. People are going to see you play and they are going to make promises and offers and you need to think about it."

"I don't know."

The older man lifted his head and rested it on his hands. His left hand gave a ghost of a shake.

"Elvis, do you know what the hardest question in the world is?"

"I don't know." He shrugged.

"What are you going to do now?"

CHAPTER FIVE

There was no Ahab Cab in the phone book.
There was no Ahab Cab listed at Visitor's Services.
There was no Ahab Cab on the list of hackney licenses.
But there was a white Chevy Minivan with an "Ahab Cab" light on its roof and a happy, spouting white whale on its doors. It was in the line-up at the airport at nine in the morning.
Henry Coffin was running on caffeine and good thoughts at this hour. Danny had dropped him off before he dropped off his daughter. The Detective had expressed his preference for police work over this random stuff, but he also wanted to keep his job, his mortgage, and his pension. Everything from last night smelled of unpleasantness and a new job search.
So, Danny told the Inspector that he would keep his phone near him and he would wait for his call. Then he went home, turned the phone up loud, and went to bed.
As a result, Henry stood sleepless and alone in the warm early October morning. A beautiful family of tennis players and skiers emerged from the terminal and selected A-1 Taxi. Ahab Cab pulled up into the first slot in front of the terminal and Coffin was moving before she put the car into park.
"Ride to town?"
"Sure." She said. "Anywhere in particular?"
"Police Station."
Andrea Murphy put the car in gear. She was a small woman who crested five feet only just barely. Andy was small, athletic, tough, and

endowed with the personality that high school boys admired. She looked hard at the old and dirty man in her backseat.

"Are you a lawyer?" She asked.

"No."

"Cop?"

"Not exactly."

She looked at him again.

"Just business?"

"At the station?" Coffin said. "Hope not."

Andrea nodded. He was looking out the window.

"So," he asked. "How do you know Julian?"

"I don't know a Julian."

"Little Brazilian guy?" he said. "About 18."

"Nope."

"How about a whole group of Brazilian guys?"

"I know a lot of South Americans. Give them rides everywhere."

"But no Julian?"

"I don't ask their names."

"I don't suppose they pay you in kruggerands, do they?"

Coffin held up Maria's coin. Andrea looked at the coin in the rear view mirror for a second too long.

"Nope."

"I suppose it would be hard to make change."

"I would think so."

Andrea steadied herself. She had been afraid of this for two weeks now. Since that night, she, and everyone else, just tried to act cool. Two Ton said there was a plan, and she had to believe him.

Andrea didn't believe that this gray and grubby man was part of that plan.

She touched the panic button. Everything in the car was now being broadcast and recorded. An unmarked State Police car would begin following her in a few minutes. Or it did when they ran the drill.

The gray man looked at her license.

"Andrea, my name is Henry Coffin. I am an Inspector for the police department here. Your cab isn't licensed with the town."

"I am just the driver. I don't own it."

"It's not listed in the phone book or at Visitor Services."

"I just drive."

"No, you don't."

"What else do I do?"

"I don't know, but I will make it my business to find out."

"Do you have a badge?"

"It's in my desk."

"How do I know you are who you say you are?"

"You don't. But I know you aren't who you say you are, Andrea."

The cab was traveling down lower Orange Street.

No cars were following them.

"I have no idea what you are talking about."

"Okay," he said. "Your rugs back here are very clean."

"So."

"Do you think there could still be some blood stains deep in the fabric."

She paused.

"I don't know what you are talking about."

A gray Ford LTD slipped in behind her. Her eyes went to the rear view mirror and noticed. Coffin saw her eyes and turned around. He waved.

"Curiouser and curiouser." Coffin said. "If you call the troopers behind you, I am sure that they can tell you who I am."

"I have no idea what you are talking about."

"Okay." Henry said. "Take me and the Statie to the police station."

Then he reached into his pocket, took out the lollipop and held it up in the mirror.

She stared at it, then braked quickly. There were no cars in front of her.

She said nothing for a moment. Then, aware that Two Ton and a whole bunch of armed men were waiting for her words, she said something.

"That's quite a lollipop."

Coffin grinned.

"It sure is."

At the police station, Coffin stepped from the car. He asked her if she would like to come inside, but she shook her head.

The trooper parked in front of a fire hydrant across the street.

Coffin walked inside.

Chief Bramden stood at the inner door as Coffin walked inside.

"My office."

"Sure."

The Chief was not angry. He was tired and annoyed. He was much cleaner and neater than Coffin was used to seeing, but he seldom got to the station during business hours. His hair was a-twirl, and his eyes had the look of beer and sleeplessness, but he resembled a man confronting a balky furnace. He knew the furnace would screw up. It wasn't a surprise to him.

"Henry, you know how to fuck things up, don't you?"

Coffin shrugged.

"You know what I am going to say, don't you?" he looked the Inspector.

"Sure."

"You know and still, I have to fuck with you." He said. "She is an undercover for the marshals."

Henry nodded.

"And now, you and I are the only ones who know that. In a few minutes you will forget."

"Sure about that marshall thing?" Coffin rubbed his eyes. "Doesn't look like a cop to me."

"Henry, do you know who I just spoke with?'

"No."

"Henry, the United States Marshal himself called me five minutes ago and he began yelling. He had been alerted to a problem three minutes before hand. Then, he called me from his office and alerted me to the problem. I got up from the desk, walked to the front door and now I am talking to the problem."

Inspector Coffin smiled.

"He knew you." Bramden said. "He did. He says to me.... Minutes ago, he says 'Keep the fucking Inspector out of this or he will get shot.' " The chief smiled.

"High praise."

"So, I figure this will be my time to finally fire you." Bramden spoke with some pleasure. "I know you. You will do something so stupid to whatever this undercover has going on that I will finally get to use that letter I have in my desk. This has to do with the phone and the woods, doesn't it? And the rape?"

Henry nodded.

"The phone is complete garbage." Bramden said. "And, unless I missed the paperwork, no one has filed any rape charges. Have they?"

Coffin spoke. "Not yet."

"Do we have a dead body?"

"No."

"Do we have a report of a missing boy?"

"No."

"So, you may have fucked up some super secret witness protection operation in order to do what, exactly?"

"There was a crime."

"Nobody commits a crime if the paperwork isn't done."

Henry crossed his arms.

The Chief raised his eyebrows. There was a pause, then he spoke. "Don't fuck this up. Let her work."

"We still have a murder."

"Of who?"

"Julian."

"Julian who?"

Coffin froze and realized that he didn't know the boy's name.

"No one called him in missing. No one has a body. No one even has a blood drop."

"It's in her car."

"No." the Chief said. "It isn't."

Coffin eyed the Chief.

"Are you going to let her do her work?"

Coffin made no move. The Chief took his silence for a "No."

CHAPTER SIX

Elvis stood near the bench in a sweatshirt. He jammed his hands in the center pocket, rocked on his feet and slowly felt his sanity slip away.

Because some kids wanted him to sign The Picture.

The team was losing. The mighty Whalers, in front of the home crowd, gave up a touchdown on the opening kickoff and just kept right on losing. After the first quarter, they were down two touchdowns. By halftime, they were down twenty-one points and the QB, Meyer, had picked a fight with his linemen.

The eyes of the crowd fell to the big freshmen. The team glanced at his huge bulk on the sidelines. To the boy, he was invisible, but to the island, he loomed.

In the middle of the third quarter, a running back for Blue Hills broke through the line and sprinted for the end zone. The new safety, Jack's replacement, bounced off the runner and rolled on the ground. The running back jogged into the end zone while the Mighty Whalers stood back at the line of scrimmage. Only Nick had tried to run down the field.

The crowd did not boo. Instead, they packed and insulated the air in silence. Palumbo, in agreement, pulled the starters from the game, inserted several squads of clean shirted, high numbered freshmen and sophomores, and declared the afternoon over.

Jack and Billy remained in the stands for the entire game. Stoned and happy, they traded a water bottle between them and soaked in the peak of their fame. No wins had ever been directly attributed to the pair, but this loss was awarded to them. They accepted the praise with grace, smiles, and a vodka salute.

Henry Coffin closed the front door of his house, patted Starbuck on the shoulder, and started to walk to the DeSalvo's.

He generally worked on Saturday nights. The week's dramas and comedies came to their cliffhanging climaxes right around one in the morning on a Saturday night. But with all the other excitement unfolding this week, and promising more for the week following, Henry felt that he could have a night with a head cold. Chief Bramden would celebrate and Danny would sleep easier.

The impertinent evening burned gently. The air brought Coffin back to Weston Field in Williamstown and tailgate parties followed by long walks through drying maple leaves and a cool evening in a his dorm room. There had been days then. He had been lucky, he had realized that he was living inside a museum of remarkable people and things. They all were charged full of potential, arrogance, and beer. It had been a time.

As there were neither colleges nor Maple trees on Nantucket, the reflected shame of his past and his potential faded. Instead, he passed through another museum of brick, cobblestone, and cedar shingle.

Starbuck crossed the street in front of him then nosed his way among the fallen leaves up Pleasant Street. The quiet disturbed him. It was an afternoon of hobbies and housework, underneath the summer blue of the late afternoon. Perhaps one more round of golf or one more trip to Great Point or one more slow walk around Sanford Farm. This time was ending. This time was fading slowly away and, with the unrushed efficiency of a checklist, would drain the pipes, seal the windows, empty the fridge, lock the doors, and move on to the next time and the next place with the implacable violence of the sun.

At the base of Mill Street, Henry turned and climbed the paved road up to the windmill. Already the Historical Association had put away the vanes and the sails, so that the windmill remained one rounded heap of shingles sprouting four wooden branches.

Starbuck and his master crossed behind the mill, again, then through the hedges to the DeSalvo's back porch. Starbuck, with dreams of cheese, was tail-whipping himself in anticipation.

Henry knocked on the door. Rosie rounded the corner, glanced at him and then pulled the door. Starbuck skidded to a stop in the kitchen and looked up in hope and faith that more cheese would be coming his way.

Rosie looked down at him, then opened the refrigerator door. She broke four slices of American in half, balanced them on his nose, waited a beat, and snapped "Go." The cheese vanished.

Henry sat at the table.

"Coffee?" she offered.

"Sure."

"Cream and sugar?"

"Both, if possible."

"Sure."

Rosie pulled the ceramic holders from the counter and placed them in front of the Inspector. Then she poured the two of them mugs of coffee.

"How are you doing?" Henry asked.

She waved her arm. "Fine."

"Really?"

"Well, what do you think, Henry?"

"Not fine."

"No." she said. "Not much."

"Where's Rick?"

"Working, I guess."

"Let's hope."

"I suppose." She said. "I don't see him much."

"I met him out at Paul Brody's house the other morning." Brody said. "He wanted Brody to help him kill those two boys."

She sipped her coffee.

"What did Paul say?"

"Well, he called me."

She looked at him. "So, I assume he said no."

"I think he would really like to." Coffin said.

"But…"

"You can't just kill two kids."

"Rick could do it."

"No, he couldn't."

"If he had the balls, he would."

"Living with compromise is a lot harder than dying with honor."

"Really."

"Sure."

She looked at the Inspector and wondered exactly how much of an expert he was on living with compromise.

"I would do it." Rosie said.

"How would you be able to live with it later?"

"No problems."

"Sure about that?" Henry eyed her.

"Ever had an abortion?"

"Can't say that I have." He admitted.

"Ever have a still birth?"

"No."

"If I can live with that blood, I can live with the blood of those two idiots."

"But now you have told me. You would be a suspect."

"I have." She said. "And if I killed them, I wouldn't be hard to find. I might be sitting next to the bodies, eating their hearts."

Coffin smiled.

"Where's James? Or Maria?"

"Out."

"Out?"

"They went for ice cream at the Juice Bar. It's going to close soon." She said. "I think they'll be fine."

"Okay."

She shrugged.

"What are you going to do?" Coffin asked her.

"About?"

"About Maria."

"We'll leave."

Coffin was surprised.

"Where?"

"I don't know. We are going out to see some schools sooner or later. She'll go to school and I will rent an apartment nearby."

"You could come back."

"She can't."

"She could."

"No, Henry. No, she can't. Half of those kids were at that party. They knew what was going on up in that room. They knew. Not a mystery. Just silence and shame."

Henry thought up words about acceptance and support and community, but they made no sense to him.

"She didn't do anything wrong."

"Doesn't really matter, does it?"

"It should. It will."

"No, it won't." Rosie said. "And you know it. The island doesn't think, it doesn't pause, and it doesn't forget."

"It is her home."

"Everybody has to leave home. Sooner or later."

James ordered a Watermelon Cream. Maria watched him hop with excitement until it finally came, then he began to work on it. After a momentary hesitation borne from the dieting days before her pregnancy, she ordered one as well. The two of them took their drinks across the street to a bench.

He had been here of course. Sitting with her.

It would always be like that. There would always be a ghost Julian standing with her on the street, at the beach, in the dark. He would always slip up behind her with his smile and his hungry eyes.

It seemed so strange, now. She felt as if she had lost a leg, but kept forgetting it was gone. She would stand and go to take a step before falling face first.

So it was with the ice cream, so it was with the bench, and so it was with the afternoon.

Maria handed the rest of her frappe to James. He finished it for her in one long slurp.

"Do you like it?" she asked.

He nodded.

"Are you going to make it through the winter without them?"

He looked at her.

She instantly recognized the mistake. "I can make it for you in the blender, if you would like."

"That would be nice."

Elaine slowly pulled up on the street. Maria noticed that the hammer hole remained in the hood of the car. She rolled down the window.

Inside, Elaine looked pale. "Maria!"

"How are you?"

"Okay. Can you talk?"

"Sure." Maria stood and walked over to the passenger side.

"You better come over here." Elaine said, motioning to the driver's side. She had not turned off the engine.

Maria looked to her little brother and circled the front of the car.

"How are you?" Elaine asked.

"Whatever."

"Are you okay?"

"No." Maria said. "You know I'm not okay."

The girl sighed. "I know, just…"

"It's nice to see you."

"You too." Elaine had tears building in her eyes. "I'm sorry."

"It's okay."

"No, I'm sorry."

Maria looked at her for a second, without the power of forgiveness. Yet she still spoke. "Thanks."

"I have to show you something." She reached for her phone.

Maria felt her stomach and lung drop. "Please, don't ..."

"It's not you."

Maria heard the shame in her friend's voice. And she also heard the unsaid, but Elaine held her phone closed.

"What is it?"

"James."

Elaine opened the phone to show a picture of her little brother sitting alone on a bench at the back of the elementary school. Maria didn't understand.

"How did you get this?"

"It got sent to me."

Maria still didn't understand why anyone would take a picture of her brother at recess.

"Who sent it?"

Elaine gave her the phone. At the top of the screen was the e-mail address for Jack.

She reached out with her ghost leg and felt the world spin again.

Rosie sat at the kitchen table and drank her second cup of coffee since midnight. She saw a dozen Rosies in all the windows, all sipping coffee, all calm, all answerless in the dark.

James slept in the TV room. She let him watch SpongeBob until he fell asleep. Then she left him there, with a blanket and a pillow, in front of a darkened screen. Rick had staggered into the house around eight. He silently climbed up to the unmade marriage bed and collapsed into it.

And Maria? Maria was also awake. Rosie was sure of it. The girl was too quiet, too still, too aware up in that room. She was a scared rabbit hiding from the wolf. Not scared enough, of course. A little more scared would have suited Rosie just fine. Preferably, if she could backdate that fear a few months.

Now, she sipped coffee.

Fear of the Lord, she had been told, was the beginning of Wisdom.

Rosie sighed. She could do with a little less wisdom right now.

She knew it would be like this.

All of her life, Rosie knew that she would be the one up in the middle of the night. When the Angels arrived with the terrible choices, she met them in single combat. Rick was for daylight and tomfoolery. Rick was for bluster and bravado and the hard negotiations that men do over trivia. How much will the land cost? How much for the truck? When will the plumbers come? He could wrestle clerks. But when the Angels came, Rosie stepped forward.

They stood silent before her now.

What would she do about the baby?

She sipped her coffee.

Well, it wasn't hers.

But it would be. The girl was too young to be a Mom although she was old enough to give birth. When that baby came, her brave and angry bitch of a daughter would hold the child out and ask for help. Then it would be the three of them for years.

There was a father.

No, there wasn't. Not if the Inspector was looming around. The boy was long gone or dead. Either way was much the same. He wasn't here. He left the gold coin and a lucky swimmer.

Maria would make a good mother.

She might. But she wouldn't make a good lawyer or a good doctor or a good Indian chief. For the seven years that the little one would take, Maria would slip back seven years from everyone else. By the time she drifted into the workforce she would be a decade behind and have a iron cuff on her ankle. When the law firm wanted her to spend 18 hours a day, she couldn't. She couldn't be a surgical resident. She might not even be a wife. When she cleared the dreams away from her eye, she saw her daughter turn thirty at the checkout counter. Her grandson would turn ten in a rented room with a drunken stepfather and a partial paycheck.

Rosie could raise it.

Yes, she could. And she knew how it would be when she first held the baby. She knew what she would feel when she saw the little ears, the little fingers and toes. She knew how she would be drawn into this life. But she had been raising babies since she was 25. When Maria was old enough to go to school, James came along. Now that James was old enough...

But it wouldn't be her baby. Rosie knew herself. She would be indulging in the warm nourishing martyr's bath of sacrifice and rectitude. Of course, she could do the feedings, the diapers, and the playtime that the baby needed. James' old crib and clothes were packed away up in the attic. They had to stay there. It had to be Maria's baby, even if Rosie would do a better job. Maria had to get up at three in the morning, Maria had to spoon the peas into the little mouth. Rosie would be the better mother, but it wasn't Rosie's baby.

If there was a baby.

It wasn't her body. It wasn't her choice.

Actually, yes it was. Yes, that little sixteen year old was wandering around in a body that had been clothed, nourished, treated, and loved by her mother. She had that body on loan. She was test driving it, while it was still under Mom's warrantee. She formed it in her uterus, she gave it life, and she brought it into the buxom and fertile adolescence. When Maria broke her arm, she came crying to Mommy. When she drove a nail through her foot, she came to Mommy. When she had a runny nose, a black eye, or a big whitehead, she came to Mommy. Mommy fixed it.

Well, now she has a plugged up uterus.

It wasn't her body.

No, she admitted, it wasn't. But it was her house.

Rosie sipped her coffee.

Julian.

Maria stared out the window. The windmill stood dark against the night sky. He had stood at the top of the mill once. He had put his arms over his head triumphant in the night.

It had only been a month ago.

Maria focused on that one good night when she had told him. It had been warm, it had been starry, and his hands were on her tummy. She put her hands over her belly, where his hands had been, and saw him again, on top of the mill.

There was another truth.

When she reached out with her heart, she didn't sense anything. She didn't feel that him. In the depth of her heart, she didn't hear him out there. Maria knew, in a place that had no words, that he hadn't been in the hospital.

She had seen him swim away.

All that was left of Julian was multiplying inside her.

Then she thought about James.

She had no computer. She had no phone. The only image was the one in her mind.

It made no sense for the longest time. James was sitting on the bench, in his khaki shorts and frog shirt. He was looking to his right, at other boys playing. Maybe he was having a time-out. Maybe it was part of the game. He was alone, but just for a second.

In that second, they had snapped a picture.

If they had used a phone, they were ten yards away from him.

In that second, they could lead him away. There was a game. There was a truck. Mom was waiting for you in the front office. And he would be gone.

They would do it.

She knew that. No one else would believe it, but she did. She knew it.

Maria was too tired to be angry or outraged. Too much had happened. Of course they would threaten him. Of course they would. They had the logic of sharks.

She had to do something. You couldn't run from the sharks. You couldn't hope they would swim away. You couldn't argue with them.

This time, she wouldn't leave him.

Maria rolled from the bed and wrapped herself in a polar fleece bathrobe. She knew her mother was downstairs and sitting at the table. There were things they could talk about and things they couldn't, but they certainly needed to talk.

She was no stranger to sneaking down the stairs in the middle of the night. The trick was to walk down the side of the riser, up against the wall. There, the boards wouldn't move and wouldn't, of course, squeak. But there was no need to go sneaking about this morning. There was no need to avoid her mother. Those days had gone.

Rosie looked up from the coffee. She set the mug down on the table.

"Look what the cat dragged in."

Maria did a small curtsy. "Late night?"

"Or early morning. I haven't figured out which."

Maria sat down at the table, in her usual spot.

"I'm sorry."

"I know. I'm sorry."

"I never thought…." The girl said.

Rosie lifted her hand. "Do we really need to go through all that?"

Maria stopped. Her mother looked at her with kind, but unblinking eyes. She had been at this table for hours. She was parked like some huge rock as wave after wave, visitor and visitor washed past. Rick. Maria. James. Coffin. Chaos and confusion swirled past and then drew out to sea. Still she sat at the table. Her face was calm, her eyes were tired, and her clothes were dirty.

Her mother continued.

"You've been through a nightmare. And you've put us through a nightmare." Her mother raised her hand again and stopped her daughter's words. "Of all the people who have been hurt in the last two weeks, your parents are the least injured."

"Mom…"

"That doesn't mean that you shouldn't be sorry and it doesn't mean that I don't accept it. That doesn't mean that Rick and I haven't taken some big hits. And it doesn't mean that we don't have to do some healing to do and it doesn't mean that we may not heal."

She sipped her coffee. Maria chose to say nothing.

"But I am not going to sit here at three in the morning and claim that we are the most injured. Not after what you have gone through. Not after Julian."

"We don't really know about Julian."

"Yeah we do." She said. "Honey, we know. He's dead. Either he's dead or he's dead to you. It's one and the same thing."

"That not true." Maria had, against her wishes, begun to tear up.

Rosie turned her face to her. She didn't reach out or embrace her daughter, but her look was kindly.

"Maria, I am sorry." She said. "I am sorry to have to say this to you, but you're a woman now and there is no need to keep things away from you. Is there?"

Maria didn't answer.

"Do you know what being a woman means? It doesn't have anything to do with sex or babies or clothes or Oprah. It means that you get a kitchen table." She sipped her coffee. "You get a kitchen table with four spots at it and your day, your life, is bounded by those four spots at the table. You can be a doctor, a lawyer, the head of a bank, or the leader of a Lesbian Biker Death Cult and you still have a kitchen table. Kids, husbands, lovers, parents, friends, they all take a turn sitting at your kitchen table. That's the thing about being a woman. There are always a bunch of people depending on you….or you are waiting for those people to come into your life. Then they are there and you worry about them. You serve them coffee or cereal or wine or cookies and you listen and you worry."

She paused.

"So, when you sit at your kitchen table, wherever it is, you need to know one thing. You can't lie to yourself. You can cry, you can yell, and you can bitch. But you can't lie to yourself. That is when you get into trouble."

Maria felt the life inside her. She shushed it. This was not the time or the place.

"So, he's dead." Rosie said.

Maria nodded. The tears began to drip down her face.

"The two of you were going off island. Do you still want to go?"

Maria looked at the table in front of her.

"I don't know."

"Do you want to run away?"

"I was never going to run away…"

Rosie held up her hand again. "Don't. Not now."

"What do you mean, don't?"

"Don't waste time with that."

"Who's wasting…"

"Maria." She spoke very deliberately and accented each syllable of her daughter's name. "Do you want to live with us or do you want to live away from us?"

"Do you mean on-island?"

"No. I mean do you want to live with us or away from us?"

"But we live here."

Rosie felt her patience slip. Her pregnant, raped, runaway daughter was trying to argue with her at three in the morning.

"Maria." She spoke slowly. "Nantucket is a town. Hyannis is a town. London is a town. Moscow is a town. Anyone can live in any town they want to live in. I don't care what fucking town we live in. I want to know if you want to live with us or away from us."

"I don't know."

The mother flexed her hands. "You ran away, didn't you?"

"Well…" more tears dripped.

"I am not upset about that right now. I just want to have some firm things that we can stand on."

Her daughter had her head down, looking into her lap, and the tears dripped onto her bathrobe.

"If you go to school off-island, you will still be with us. I will still be paying for you and you will keep coming back to this house."

"I want to live with you and Dad and James."

"Okay." Rosie put both her hands on the table. She knew what she wanted to say, but what she couldn't. Her daughter felt the same ties holding her back. But her daughter also felt the clockwork of that first decision start to move throughout the rest of her life.

"We have something else to talk about." Her mother continued.

"Okay." Maria felt her belly tighten.

"I don't think anything is going to happen to Billy and Jack." Rosie said. "Coffin was here earlier. There isn't anything he can arrest them for."

Maria looked out a window. She saw the picture of her brother. The Rage rose.

Rosie continued. She felt how absurd it all was. "Let's think about you. We need to think about where you are going to go to school."

"I am not going anywhere."

Rosie looked up. "We can send you to any number of great places. The education would be much better, they have…."

"I am going to stay right here. I am not going to let those two assholes get away with it."

Rosie said nothing.

"Don't you think," she started. "That you are giving them too much power and too much control? If you go somewhere else, you get a new start and a new life. Around here…." Rosie paused. "No one is going to forget."

"I don't want them to forget. I want them to remember for every day of the rest of their lives." She felt the rage build.

"Maria, think about what this means?" she said. "Think about what this is going to mean months from now."

Because Rosie was thinking about it. If she stayed on island, Rosie knew what would happen in the spring. She would have a new life, but it would shit its diapers on a schedule.

"I am not going to run away from them." Maria said.

"But you're letting them run your life. What are you going to do? Follow them around screaming for the next three years? What happens to you?"

"I don't care." The Rage splashed.

"I do."

Maria paused for a moment.

"Think about this." Her mother said. "Go to school Monday. It's going to be a fucking circus and a half, but go to school Monday and see what happens. If you feel comfortable, go back Tuesday. We'll take it a day at a time. Next Saturday, we re-assess."

Her daughter felt the rage ebb. Half-consciously, she put one hand on her waist.

She nodded.

"You've had a nightmare. An absolute, incredible nightmare." For all of her callous and heat, Rosie's heart still reached out. "and you need to deal with it as you want to. But here is the one thing you can't do. Here is the one thing I won't let you do while you sit at my table. You need to look forward. You need to do what is best for you and you need to look weeks, months, and years into the future."

Maria nodded. She knew exactly what her mother meant.

Rosie stood and left the kitchen, the table, and the morning to her daughter.

CHAPTER SEVEN

When Danny came in for work that Monday night, a man was waiting for him.

Two Ton Tommy was huge in an epic, cane using, and life threatening way. He sat on a metal chair, with his sandals and feet thrust out in front of his four hundred pound bulk. He breathed with great and loud difficulty, had bits of cheese powder on his sweatshirt and was the only man on island, in October, with a sweat.

Danny closed the door behind him.

The huge man heaved himself to his feet.

"Officer, I am Assistant U.S, Marshal Tommy Taracitino."

"Danny Higginbotham, sir."

"Detective Danny Higginbotham, from what I understand."

"Sure."

"And you work the night shift? You like that?"

"It's good for the family, sir."

"You have a family?"

"Wife and a little girl."

"Want more?"

"Pardon?"

"Do you want more kids?"

"We'll see."

The fat man eyed him.

"What is your little girl's name?"

"Hadley, sir..."

"She get conceived there?" The fat man smiled at his joke.

Danny smiled gently. "Not hardly."

"Do you have a picture?"

Danny looked at him oddly. The fat man continued. "I am curious, that's all."

Danny fished out an old picture from his wallet. It came from last year's school photos. She wore a blue dress.

"She is very pretty."

Danny nodded. Tommy put the picture on the table.

"Danny," he said. "You must be wondering why I am here?"

He said nothing.

"It takes a lot to get me out of Boston. It takes even more to put me on a boat and send me over here. More so, if you realized what I am in charge of." He paused. "I do the undercover work, Witness Protection, yet I am visible. People tend to remember me." He wheezed and smiled. "Somebody sees me in town, they figure that there must be an undercover working. So I have to be careful. And I rarely leave Boston."

"Sure."

"But here I am. I am came down here because I am worried. I am worried about you, I am worried about your partner, and I am worried about the Resource."

"The Resource, sir?"

"You've met her."

Danny recognized the deception. "Sure."

"She is in deep, y'know."

"No." Danny said. "I don't."

Tommy readjusted himself.

"Tell me about your partner."

Danny sat back.

"He is an odd man. He is a good cop."

"Good cop?"

"Sure."

"How would he do in Roxbury or Dorchester?"

"Probably pretty well."

"You think?"

Danny looked into the man's eyes. "Sure."

"I understand that he hasn't arrested anyone in a decade."

"I believe that's true."

"Doesn't carry a gun, doesn't carry a badge, doesn't wear a uniform."

"All true."

"He drinks a bit."

"So they say."

"He's a pacifist."

"True."

"He disobeys orders and is out of control."

Danny paused.

"Inspector Coffin is the finest policeman I have ever worked with." Danny said. "He is smart, he can sniff out a lie, and nobody ever messes with him. The next time he is wrong about a person will be the first time."

"But he will disobey orders, won't he?"

Danny looked at the big man. "Yes. Henry sees only one authority, and that is his own shit detector. And, as I said, I don't think I have seen him make a bad decision yet, sir."

"He doesn't show me the best discretion." He said. "We have a situation that requires some discretion."

"I'll leave that decision to him."

"His judgment may let a major international criminal disappear."

Danny looked right at the man.

"Danny," The Lieutenant Colonel picked up the photo of Hadley. "You have a bright future. You're smart, you're tough, you have made some good career decisions…."

"I'm black."

"That too." Tommy smiled. "You could have a bright future here or in the state."

Danny watched him. The big man pulled a business card from his shirt and pushed it across the table.

"Don't let Coffin screw it up for you." He said. "If you see him make a weird call or act in a way that might compromise the resource, I want you to call me. At that moment."

Danny looked at the card. He knew what it meant.

"Sir, I will talk to my partner. I will cuff my partner, I will lock him up in a jail cell, I will shoot him in the leg. The one thing I will never do is lie to him, sir."

Tommy looked at the man without surprise. Danny took the picture back.

"I will never do anything to hurt my family. You know my pressure point and I know it. The old man knows it as well. I will convince him to restrain himself, but…"

Danny stood and continued.

"Henry Coffin has no pressure points. If you threaten him, lie to him, or blow smoke rings up his ass, he will blow your precious resource all to hell."

"He's an arrogant fuck, is he?" Tommy commented.
Danny saw the calculation in the insult. He stood up.
Tommy continued. "You should talk to him."
"Goodbye sir." Danny turned his back on him.

"We have to talk."
"Sure."
The night was warm and wet. A damp drizzle had been falling on the island since noon and through the evening. Danny and the Inspector sat at a picnic table just off of the Milestone Road. They left the door open to the patrol car.
Both men had cups of coffee.
"So." Henry said.
"Lollipop."
"Who?"
"Remember your buddy, Steven Graves and his friend who gave you the lollipop"
"The guy you wanted to shoot."
"Yeah. Do you remember what Graves called him?"
"No."
"Lollipop."
"Okay." He said in a leading way. "Makes sense, doesn't it?"
The two of them stared out into the wet dark of the middle moors.
"I googled it." He said. "In Colombia, a lollipop is when they kill you, cut off your dick, and stick it in your mouth."
Coffin looked at him. "Well, that's nice."
"They have all these fucked up ways of killing people. Colombian Necktie is when they cut your throat and pull your tongue out, a Colombian t-shirt is when they cut your head and arms off, a Colombian Vase is when they cut your arms and legs off, stick your body in a trash can, and put your parts on top." He continued.
"You have got to stay off the internet."
"It's a fucked up world."
"I don't know anything about the world. This island is as good as I can do."
"It's a fucked up island."
"Sometimes."
They sipped coffee.
"So, you think Graves' employee and Julian's father, is a Colombian drug lord hiding out and mowing lawns." Henry said

"It's a thought."

"Sure."

"Helps explain why we have undercover marshals and Two Ton Tommy taking up space."

Henry didn't comment him immediately.

"Do you think Lollipop is an international criminal?" Henry asked.

"Makes a lot of sense."

"Only if you trust the Feds." Henry said. "This is what I know. Graves comes to us offering help with the Julian thing. Second time we see Graves, he has a guy in the car who offers us help."

"Offers you a bribe."

"I would have split it with you."

"Fuck you." He knew that, if the old man took a bribe, he would have shared it. Both things were possible.

"We know…" Coffin continued. "That Graves is scared of the guy and we know that the guy gave me a Brazilian Lollipop."

"So."

"One lollipop offered to a cop does not make someone a crime lord."

"What about our heavy duty friend?"

"He doesn't make crime lords either."

"What about the Andrea?"

Henry paused at that and looked into the darkness.

"Here's what I think. I think Andrea is a babysitter. I think she is here to watch out for Lollipop and make sure that he doesn't go anywhere or do anything, and nothing bad happens to him. So, all is well and good for a while. Then, his son, Julian, dies and someone panics. They would rather keep Lollipop in the dark than tell him the truth." Henry said.

Danny nodded.

"Which explains," the Inspector continued. "Why they are so interested in me."

"You might tell Lollipop the truth."

"I will." Henry said. "I believe he is the boy's father. I believe he should know the truth about his son."

"Which we don't know."

Coffin paused and nodded. "We don't?"

The two men looked out into the mist.

Coffin continued. "I think he is dead. The longer this goes on, the more I think it."

"You're not sure."

"How sure do I have to be?"

Danny adjusted himself. "Well, since it is my mortgage, my wife, my kid, and my pension, I would like to you be just. A. Hair. More. Sure."

"Message received."

They parked outside the Kelly house in Tom Nevers with their lights off. Inside the house, the lights were off as well.

Danny looked at the Inspector.

"Do we have to wake them up?"

"We know they are here."

"It's pointless."

"We could go back to the Lifesaving station, sleep the night through, and stop a speeder or two."

Danny looked at him. "As if we don't do that regularly."

Coffin got out of the car.

Danny followed him up the gravel to the front door. The inspector rang the bell twice and then waited.

They waited minutes past the point when Danny wanted to get back in the car. Finally, Mrs. Kelly opened the door. She wore the same purple sweatpants and shirt that she wore before. Otherwise, she appeared thinner, older, a hundred miles more tired.

"Inspector."

"Mrs. Kelly." He said. "How are you, my sister?"

She put her eyes onto his face.

"It's two in the morning, Inspector."

"I am sorry about that."

She said nothing.

"I am not waking him up. I am not waking up Mike, either."

Coffin looked at her. "Okay. Perhaps tomorrow."

"Probably not."

"We were hoping to ask Tommy some more questions."

"Inspector." She used each of the syllables with emphasis. "We are moving. I can't invite you in, because I have wrapped up the house. The movers come for the furniture in two days. And then we are going up to New Hampshire."

"I'm sorry…"

"Don't be. Don't be, it is for the best. Tommy needs a new start, Mike can come down and finish up the work he was doing, then start up again up there. Lots of work up there right now." She said. "It's a new start in a new place for all of us."

"The kids who did this to Mike…"

"Are still out here. And there isn't anything we are going to be able to do about that."

Coffin paused. Danny looked up at him from the path. He knew what would happen when he left the car. The Inspector had, as well. It was a measure of the old man that he tried anyway.

"Ginny, it has been hard. I know that." Coffin spoke softly. "It will continue to be hard. I can't guarantee that everything will work out for the best. But." He looked at her nose. "We have to speak the truth. We have to put it out there. If we reveal the truth and stand on it, no matter how hard it is, that makes a foundation. Your nightmare with these boys will be over soon, and you will have a new start, but without the truth, that start will always sputter. It's courage. One act of courage builds a chain."

At two in the morning, in the drizzle and cold of the approaching winter, Ginny Kelly looked at the two policemen.

"Henry," she said at last. "I am sorry for your loss."

"Thanks."

"I don't think I will see you again. You're a good man. You, too, Danny. Have a good night."

She closed the door.

Back in the car, Danny looked at his partner.

"Well, that went about as well as could be expected."

The old man looked a lot older.

"What did you expect?" Danny asked him.

Coffin looked at the dark house.

"More."

"People don't want to give more. They want to give less."

Danny started the car. Coffin continued to look out the window. "Well, now it can't be avoided."

"What can't?"

"We need to press on Lollipop."

Danny slowed the car.

Coffin continued. "If we could have gotten Tommy to press charges, then maybe we don't need Lollipop. But now…"

"Jesus, Henry. What if I buy you a drink?"

"Where is Julian?"

"I know, I know, I know." Danny repeated himself. "Can you try not to put Hadley on the list of victims?"

Milestone Road

They drove to Siasconset, pulled around the rotary and parked next to the NRTA bus stop. Behind the weathered, shingled shed, Henry pulled out his cell.

An answering machine picked up.

"Pick up the phone, Steven."

The machine timed out.

Henry dialed again. This time, a sleepy voice came on the phone.

"Steven."

"Yeah."

"Y'know who this is?"

"Inspector Coffin?"

"Right you are. Fifteen minutes from now, be on the Milestone Road."

"Um."

"By yourself."

"Okay."

"See you then."

Twenty minutes later, a new Ford 350 pulled out of the Tom Nevers Road and accelerated up to eighty. Danny stood on the accelerator and flashed the lights. The pick-up flashed his hazards and pulled over into the high grass. Danny pulled up behind him.

Henry opened the door.

"You know how much I don't like this." The black man said.

"Are you worried for me?"

"No. For me."

"If he is a drug lord, I'll take the bribe then."

"Just go."

Henry stepped out of the car and walked up the cab of the truck. Steven was in a sweatshirt and jeans. He had his license and registration ready.

"Put it away, Steven."

"Are you sure?"

"Let's keep the records clear for a while, okay?"

"Sure."

The older man leaned on the door to the new pickup.

"Steven, you know me, right?"

"Sure."

"You know how I am, my brother?"

"Sure."

"Be straight with me. Who are these guys who work for you?"
"I don't know."
Henry sighed.
"Henry, I swear, I don't know."
"You know something."
"I know that they work their asses off. I know that they don't go anywhere besides their house, the beach, and the job sites."
"And...."
'Nothing."
"Don't lie to me, my brother. We got all sorts of people asking all sorts of questions and they don't like the answers I give them. They don't know about you, but there is a lot of attention being paid."
"Henry, I don't know."
"Steven, look at me." The young man looked up. "Remember who you are talking to and where you are doing it. We aren't in the station, you don't have a lawyer, and the Staties aren't going through your stuff."
"Is that going to happen?"
"We'll see." Henry said. "But you have to trust me with the truth."
"I am telling the truth."
Henry looked at his face.
"Tell me some other truths, then." He said. "Tell me about the lollipop?"
"I don't..."
He paused and looked at the Inspector.
Then he sighed and let the story go. "There are ten guys and they came last March. One guy, about forty-five, he talks for the others. Julian is the youngest of the bunch. The others are hard looking, good workers."
"Julian was his son?"
"Yeah." Steven paused and looked forward. "He's ripped up over it."
"I understand."
The young man looked at him and remembered.
"They are odd guys." He continued, softly. "None of them use cell phones. Every illegal I have had, used a cellphone and a calling card. These guys don't call nobody. And pay? They like to get paid, but they don't do shit with it. Some rice, some beans, I get them some groceries and some beer and that's it. Every Sunday I take them to the beach for the day. Away from everybody else."
"So, tell me about the lollipop."
"It's a big deal. The head guy and the hard guys argued about it for a half hour before he brought it. Wouldn't tell me about it."

"Is it his chit?"

"His what?"

"His word. A get-out-of-jail card?"

"I don't know. I have never seen them. They like ice cream, not candy. None of them so much as touch lollipops."

Henry nodded.

"You're scared of these guys, aren't you?"

"They don't need me."

"I think they need you a great deal."

"Not to look at them."

"You had them for six months now."

"They work great and I don't have to do a thing. They don't cause any trouble at all."

"But you are scared."

"These are some hard looking guys. Ten of them."

Henry backed away from the window. He looked down the empty road.

Steven looked out from the window and watched the older man.

"What are you going to do?"

"I don't know. Nothing." Coffin said.

"Nothing?"

"I don't know" Henry said. "I need to talk to Danny. This guy Lollipop hasn't done anything bad on Nantucket, has he?"

"No."

"He hurt you?"

"No."

"So he hasn't broken any laws as far as I know, right?"

"Right."

Steven looked at him as if the Inspector was crazy.

For his part, the older man smiled. "Now, don't go speeding anymore."

Then he walked back to the squad car.

At the end of the shift, Henry met the fat man. Two Ton Tommy and Chief Bramden sat in the conference room. With the table pushed out of its normal spot so as to accommodate the fat man, Henry was jammed up against the far wall. Neither Bramden, nor Taracitino looked particularly well rested. The room held a hint of stale sweat and bad breath.

"Inspector, did you have fun?"

"When?"

"Was it fun? Did you like that?"

"You'll have to be more specific."

"Your ride in the cab?"

"I am investigating a murder."

"Bullshit." Two Ton Tommy barked.

Bramden interrupted. "Henry, I don't think you appreciate the situation here…"

"I guess not."

Two Ton Tommy looked at the Chief, but not the Inspector.

"Inspector," He continued in his guttural, buttery voice, "Andrea tells me you had a purple lollipop with you last night. Is this true?"

"Sure."

"Who gave you that lollipop?"

"A law abiding citizen."

"Citizen?"

"Would you prefer the word 'gentleman?'" Coffin countered.

"He's no gentleman."

"Was to me."

"What did he get in exchange for it?"

"Absolutely nothing."

"You're a liar." The sentence was said without emotion or emphasis.

Henry sat, folded his hands together, and rested them on the table. Tommy heaved his chest into grunts of breath.

"Inspector, you have found a way to get in the middle of a big operation we are running. There are, literally, thousands of people involved in this. All of them are…." He looked around for an analogy, and then plucked one from the air. "All of them are building a railroad. They have mapped out the route, bought or stolen the land, brought in the blacks and the Chinese to lay tracks and dynamite mountains. Thousands of people are laying track and you, by complete accident, are trying to stand in the way. You are like a big, fat bison waiting to be moved or shot." The irony was not lost on Henry, although it was on Two Ton. "So, I am the cowboy sent to either lead you out of the way, whip you into motion, or put a bullet in your head. Right now, I like the bullet."

Tommy was impressed with this speech and he savored it. Henry Coffin listened with amusement. Bramden was not amused. It was like watching someone threaten a truck.

"Inspector," The big man drew the syllables out. "I like firing people for harassment. The law is so much more flexible. All I need is to find someone you locked up, and get him to talk about an inappropriate word or touch, and you are gone. No pension, no health plan, no title. You have to go home to the Mrs. and the kids and deal with being called a pervert. I don't know anyone who could recover from that."

Bramden shot a glance at the Marshall, but the big man didn't catch it.

"So, that's where we are, my brother?" Henry said, in a low voice.

"I need you to come to Jesus." Tom oozed.

Bramden put a hand on his face. It would be a show.

"I already walk in the light." Coffin smiled.

Tommy waved his hand, as if he were pushing back a curtain. "I'm sure that Chief Bramden would accept his Inspector's resignation with regret."

Henry looked at the man. Bramden hadn't moved his hand.

Coffin put his cellphone on the table.

"Okay, so I resign. Then I call Marjorie at the Inquirer and Mirror and tell her about a murder off of Milestone Road and a rape-all of which the U.S. Marshals know about, have a witness for, but will do nothing about. Then, the fun begins when I hire a lawyer for wrongful termination."

Henry spun his cellphone.

"If anyone threatens Danny, it will happen. My brother."

He spun the phone again. And looked at the fat man. Tommy glanced at the Chief. The Chief shrugged.

"Do you know who I am?" the fat man whispered.

"No." Henry replied. "Do you know who I am?"

"You are the Inspector." He dragged the last syllable out. "Known throughout the state for his empty sack."

"I am a man with nothing to lose."

The roll of the trucks coming off the 8:15 ferry filled the silence.

Bramden finally took his hand of his face and spoke up. "Henry? Tom? Why don't we start this again?"

The big man rolled his eyes to the Chief.

Tommy looked at the Chief. "I just can't believe him. I can't. I don't trust him to blow the whole operation. I don't trust this guy. As a matter of fact, I want to lock him up."

"That won't help."

"It will make me feel good. Lock this guy up in Cedar Junction."

"On what charge…." Henry chimed in.

"I could find something."

"I'm afraid they will always let me use a phone…."

"Not if you're not in this country."

Bramden looked at his Inspector. "Henry, you are to have no contact with Andrea Murphy in the cab, no contact with Lollipop, and you are to do nothing in regards to the possible disappearance of Julian. Period. Full Stop."

Coffin stood up.

"Enjoy your freedom." Tommy grunted.

CHAPTER EIGHT

Elvis hung his hands on the shower head in his bathroom. The hot water steamed him. It coursed through his short hair, down his back and onto the floor.

"Let's go." Tillie shouted from the kitchen.

"What?"

"You've got school today."

Elvis looked up. With regret, he turned the handle off. He pulled the bath towel off of a hook and dried himself quickly.

Tillinghast stood in dress pants, button down shirt, rep tie, and blazer.

"I thought I might go later this week."

"No time like the present."

"I am not really ready."

Tillie looked at him. "Why not?"

Elvis, for his part, didn't have the words.

The Coach continued. "If you are going to play on Friday night, you have to make every practice this week. In order to go to practice, you have to go to school. If you play on Friday, we have a chance to win. If you play on Friday, you can give a couple scouts some reason to get you to Deerfield."

Elvis sighed, but did not put his feelings into words. He did not feel ready to let the world continue to move through the calendars and football games. Time should be set aside and stilled, while the grass had not yet sprouted on top of the mound of sandy dirt off of Joy Street. But it was football, and he knew how his father felt about football.

"Can I play?"

"I assume you remember."

"What about the helmet thing?"

"You got a one week suspension from team activities. One week is over. Let's go."

Elvis pulled on his sweatpants, wriggled into a t-shirt, then pushed his sockless feet into the basketball shoes. "I don't have the right clothes."

"You will be better dressed than three quarters of the other students. At least your pants are up around your waist."

"What about my books?"

"You've been doing homework?"

The boy shrugged.

"I think your teachers will give you a pass on that today. Enough with the excuses. Let's go."

They parked in front of the school. Next to the car was a spot reserved for the school nurse. The buses had already dropped off the few students who rode them and the first bell had rung. Tillie had asked him to wait. His suspicions, however, had grown.

"I want you to do me a favor today." He asked.

"Okay."

"I want you to shadow someone for most of the day. I want you to make sure nothing bad happens to her."

"Who?"

"It's Maria DeSalvo."

Elvis looked confused. Tillinghast realized, for a second, how far away the boy had been. "She was attacked last week."

Elvis looked confused. Last week remained a wound.

Tillinghast realized this after a moment. "Billy and Jack attacked her at a party after the scrimmage. They took pictures."

"They attacked her?"

"Raped."

Elvis looked out the window. "Oh."

"Her mother called me last night. She wanted you to be around today."

"To be a bodyguard."

"Something like that."

"Why doesn't she just stay home?"

Tillinghast looked at the boy. "You don't want to do this?"

"No." he said. "Absolutely not. It's just…"

Rosie's Explorer pulled into her parking space.

"There you go." Tillinghast said. "Don't do anything stupid."

"I don't understand." Elvis said.

"You don't have to. Just stay near her in the halls, have lunch, and everything will be fine." He said. "Meet me at practice this afternoon."

Still sore and with fresh bruises building, Elvis stepped from the car.

From inside the car, Maria looked out at the gigantic boy.

"Mom, what did you do?"

"I called in a favor."

"Is he going to be my boyfriend or something?"

"He can do whatever you ask him to do. I asked Tillinghast to bring him to school."

"Really?" she said.

Elvis was in his sweatpants, sneakers, and a t-shirt.

"Look," Rosie said. "You're doing a good thing for him. Otherwise he sits inside the house all day staring at his father's things. Now, he can start moving on."

"So, I am helping him?"

"I prefer to think you are helping each other."

Maria looked out at Elvis. He stood at the back of Tillinghast's car with his hands in his pockets.

Rosie continued. "I don't pretend that nothing will happen in school. I worry a lot more now."

Maria had to concede that she had a point. Especially when she thought of James.

The second bell rang.

"All right Mom, I'll see you after school."

"Be careful."

She stepped from the car and walked to the door. Elvis followed along behind. She opened the door and held it for him.

"Welcome back to the zoo." She said.

"Let's hope not."

"Oh, don't worry."

"I'm not worried." Elvis was a mutterer.

"You look worried."

"I'm not."

She looked up at him. The top of Maria's head came close to the center of Elvis' chest.

"You know this isn't a date?" she joked.

"Yeah."

"You can't kiss me."

"I know."

She looked up at him. "It's a joke, son."

"Oh."

The two of them walked under the skeleton of the whale. The hall was empty and the announcements echoed down around them. They climbed the stairs to the second floor and her locker.

The island saw them together. They were seen through the glass on the classroom doors and from the security monitors in the front office. When Maureen and Stephanie left Earth Science in order to go to the bathroom, they saw the two of them standing together. Kyle, coming back from the nurse and his Adderall, saw them too. And the word spread.

Maria opened her locker and a sheet of paper fell on the floor.

The picture of James.

Jack and Billy remained unimpressed. They stood together, attended (or skipped) their usual classes, and drifted through the halls and classrooms.

At lunch, Elvis and Maria sat together. Their table was watched, not just by the various concerned adults who knew the stories, but by the kids who just wanted to witness. Something would happen. There would be a fight. Jack had a knife. Billy had a chain. There was going to be a beat down. It was revenge for the helmet, for the locker room, for the fence.

But they weren't around. Only Elvis, like a great whale, swam among them.

"They are all staring at you." Maria said.

"Yeah." He said. "It happens."

For a moment, she wanted to claim they were staring at her, as if there was a contest to see who was the most notorious. Then she hesitated. "Is it always like this?"

"No. It will wear off in a week or so. Maybe after the game."

She paused. "Do you think they will ever stop staring at me?"

Elvis felt himself fall on his own ego. The history of the woman beside him opened itself up to him. Shame burned.

"I am sorry." He said. "I didn't think."

"It's fine." She replied, too fast. "It's fine."

"No." he said. "No, it isn't."

Their lives separated at that moment. Elvis would always be stared at and had always been stared at. He was a physical freak who was blessed in the world of high school. Everyone who saw him, saw riches and a professional future. Everyone who saw her, saw a victim, saw a wounded animal.

Soon, they would see a pregnant one.

She felt a shudder.

"Do you want to get out of here?" he asked.

"Sure."

He picked up her lunch tray with its fallen battalion of french fries, walked away to the trash, and dumped both of them. She let him. He felt awful and he didn't need to. He had done more for her than anyone in that room, and most of them had known her since kindergarten.

When he returned, she followed him outside to a low cement wall. His legs were longer than the wall: she needed to pull herself up onto it. Yet, when she sat there and he slouched, they were the same height.

"Tell me something," he asked. "Why did you come into school today?"

"I don't know." She lied. "It was better than sitting at home for another day."

"Was it that bad?"

"No." She pulled her knees up and balanced, somewhat precariously, on her heels and her tailbone. "I was getting to like Oprah." She smiled. "What about you?"

"I got told to come to school."

"Do you do what people tell you to do?"

"Well, not always. Tillinghast can be pretty persuasive."

Maria nodded. She only knew him as a social studies teacher whose hands would shake occasionally and who couldn't write on the board.

"He thinks I need to get back to football and then to play in the game on Friday."

"What do you think?"

"I don't know." He said. "I don't know anything right now."

His words struck her. They were honest and open and raw. She wanted to touch him, but she didn't.

"Do you miss him?" she asked.

"Yes." He answered. "No." he continued. "No, I don't. Because I think he is back in that house still. And he's not. I know he isn't, and he isn't coming back, but I don't really believe it."

She nodded and waited, but he didn't say anything else. After a moment, she reached into her back pocket and took out the sheet of paper that had James picture on it. She handed it to him.

"Who's that?"

"James, my little brother. He's the reason why I am in school today."

Elvis turned it over, looking for a message.

"The two fuck-ups stuck it in my locker this morning. They e-mailed the photo around last night. They're threatening him."

"Why?"

"Because I talked to the cops. Because it's what they do. It's how they work." She said. "So, I had to come in. I had to stand up."

He felt the rage rise up in him again.

"What are you going to do?" he asked.

"I don't know." She said. "But I am going to do something."

Elvis shook his head.

He walked her to class. Without a word, she left him at the door. Brody noticed him, but did not glance up or make any other acknowledgement. He stood outside in the hall until after the second bell rang. Jack and Billy came racing up the back stairs immediately after the bell and walked quickly to the door.

They looked at the big freshman.

Elvis felt his calling.

When they moved to him, he would take the two down. Jack would go first and hard into the lockers. Then it would be time for elbows, knees, holds, and throws.

They never moved to him. Instead, they opened the door to the classroom and sat down in their desks.

The moment lost, Elvis turned.

For a day, the classroom was repopulated. Jack and Billy took their usual seats on one side of the circle, Maria took hers on the other side. Tommy Kelly had not returned to the school, and would not. His desk remained empty and unremarked, as if he had been pulled under.

Brody sat in his chair in the center of the circle. His hair was greasy and his eyes glazed. He was slouched back in his chair, tipped back almost as far as it could go. His shirt was crisp, his pants had a sharp crease, but his skin and his eyes had the look of the deep sea. He knew that this was the last he would see of the two boys.

Billy was at once chipper and annoying. The message had come to them last period; they were going to be tutored at home. Pink had promised to challenge it, but they shooed him away. Staying at home with a tutor was much more their style right now.

"Let's look at Chapter 48."

A girl looked up. "We weren't supposed to read to there, were we?"

"Why not?"

"It's thirty chapters past where we are?"

Brody smiled. "No, that's fine. I just want to show you something. It will help."

No one in class was reading the book anymore. They pretended to and, if Brody chose to look at the homework, would show something between plot summary and bullshit. Brody had stopped really caring two weeks before.

"Well, here is who we have here. We have Pip, we have Jaggers, and we have Wemmick."

Brody enjoyed the last name. He slapped it around pleasantly. "Wemmick, Wemmick, Wemmick." He said. "Does anyone remember Wemmick?"

They all shook their heads.

"How about Pip?"

"He's the main character." Emily said. "He gets rich."

"Yes he does." Brody intoned. "And Jaggers?"

"He's the lawyer." She commented.

"And is he good?" His voice was swinging wildly. Emily looked surprised.

"What do you mean?"

"Is he a good lawyer?"

"Yes."

"How do you know?" He looked at Jack. "How do you know if someone is a good lawyer?"

"They drive a big car." Jack sensed that there was something else helping the teacher along.

"Not bad." Brody finished. "Good lawyers are rich lawyers, are they not?"

"Sure."

"Does Jaggers do good things or is he just good at being a lawyer?"

"He's just good at being a lawyer." Jack nodded.

"So, he isn't good?" Brody poked at him. "He isn't noble or a saint or anything. He is just a lawyer."

"You were a lawyer." Jack saw an opening to mock the man. "Were you good?"

"Do I drive a big car?"

"Sure. You drive that POS Blazer."

"So I must have been good." Said Brody. "But let's think of poor Wemmick. Wemmick. Wemmick." Brody started to fade, then he returned. "He is a clerk. He is a human photocopier. He lives with his father, the Aged One in a strange house called "Little Britain" that has a drawbridge and a miniature cannon. The love of his life, Miss Skiffins, dotes on him and they are to be married. What do you think of that?"

Brody swung his out-of-focus eyes onto Maria.

"I think that's great."

"Do you?"

"Sure."

"He doesn't have Great Expectations, does he?"

"No..."

"Simple boring life. Wakes up, helps his Dad, goes to work, copies stuff for the big man, comes home and has tea. Fires off his cannon."

Billy giggled.

Brody eyed him silently.

The class stopped moving for twenty seconds.

Brody's eyes focused.

"It's a good life, wouldn't you say?"

"Absolutely." Jack answered for his friend.

"What makes it good?" Brody flipped. "He doesn't have a big car, Miss Skiffins is dog faced and he has to take Jaggers' shit all day. What makes it good?"

No one answered. The teacher's tone had turned sharply. "He's a fucking clerk living with his Dad. What makes that good?"

No one answered. The teacher swung back to Maria.

"Do you still think it's great?"

Maria looked up at the teacher and at the boys beyond him.

"Sure. He's happy."

"Happy."

"Well, I haven't read it," she said. "But not everyone is going to change the world. Maybe if he just goes home everyday and has a cup of tea, that's pretty good."

"Y'know what." He said. "You should read it."

"All of it?" Billy asked.

"It's two whole pages. You can make it."

The class stared at him.

"Read it. Now." Brody barked.

Jack didn't read it. Billy didn't even glance at it. Maria skimmed the first page and was going to put it away when she read "If he should turn to, and beat her."

Her attention focused, she read the rest of the chapter.

Emily read everything that she saw in front of her. When she finished, she looked up as if she was finally pulling her face out of the water.

"What do you think?" Brody asked her.

"I don't know."

"Who is Bentley Drummle?" he asked her.

"Um. The guy who will marry Estella."

"And what will happen to them?"

"I don't know."

"He is going to beat her." Maria chimed in.

"Perhaps." Brody said. "Or what?"

"Or she is going to beat him."

"Billy!" Brody barked. "What does the word "Cringe" mean?"

"I don't know."

Brody took three quick steps and nearly backhanded the boy. Billy flinched. "That is what it means. It means to flinch in front of force."

"Or he might beat on your drunk ass." Jack chimed in.

Brody eyed him closely. "Yes, Jack, yes my jailbait, that is Bentley Drummle, he is either going to beat or get beaten. What do you think, Spider? What will happen to you? Beat or Cringe."

"Oh, I am a cringer." Jack stared at the teacher hard.

"Are you?"

The class froze for a moment.

"Emily," Brody whispered. "Who is Molly?"

Emily felt the violence build in the room like a tide. She tried to channel it. "She's the maid."

"You're right. What does Wemmick say about her?"

"Jaggers freed her."

"You're right."

Both Jack and Brody remained locked in a gaze. "Maria, what did Molly do?"

"She murdered someone. And she might have killed her child."

"But we know she didn't. We know her child is Estella."

Maria, who did not know this, agreed.

"But she had claw marks on her hand from the woman she killed, right?"

"Sure."

"Why isn't she in jail?"

"Because Jaggers got her off."

"And now she lives free, right."

"I guess so."

"That would be the value of a good lawyer."

The bell rang and Maria remained in her seat. Jack and Billy drifted around the other side of the classroom and filed out the door.

She didn't really know what had just happened. She had the picture of James in her hands, but she hadn't used it. Now the boys had left and the moment was gone. Brody was back in his chair, staring out at the harbor.

When she remained in her seat a moment after everyone had left, Brody glanced at her. Then Elvis appeared at the door and she left before he could say anything.

At practice, the coaches moved him up to the second row for stretching. No one had said anything to him, but his name was now on top of the depth chart at left tackle. Billy Trotter's name had disappeared.

In the locker room, no one mentioned his father. No one mentioned Maria DeSalvo, although he was clearly with her all day. No, the talk was about the horrific loss, the films they had to watch, and the smell of his old pads.

There were no copies of The Picture.

Nick out-sprinted him in warm-ups again. During his first full practice with the first team offense, he ran the wrong way twice. Each time, the quarterback picked up the dropped ball and bounced it off his helmet. Coach Palumbo pulled him by his face mask and called him an ignorant moose.

He never wanted practice to end.

CHAPTER NINE

Rosie pulled into her driveway to see her husband back in his wood shop. The air rushed back into her body. She parked the car and felt the weights lift from her hands and feet.

Maria, now silent, filed into the house. She was happy to be out of her mother's way.

He was back, finally, and Rosie felt some anger and some relief. She was angry in that deep, long standing, burning way that would heat up a branding iron for the next week or so. Of course, he was back and he was safe and there was that.

Rick was working the table saw in jeans and a tee shirt. From behind, he was the man she had always known. He was freakishly small and muscular; his waist and shoulders could belong to a high school linebacker. His head, of course, was gray haired, sun browned, and wind creased. She wondered, daily, what she had done to deserve him.

They had gone through some times and they had made some hard choices. When they found each other and started out, twenty years ago, her life was Algebra. To every problem, she had only to solve for X. After enough calculations, you could always eliminate the variables and find the solution…which was usually money. Now, from the vantage of years, her life had become calculus. Her family, her job, and her life were one large, irregular rotating spheroid of changing volume. Nothing was constant, everything changed, and the variables kept right on spinning. As they did right now.

She stepped from the car as the saw clicked off. Rick stacked the boards, and then propped them up against the door to his shop. He turned around to watch her arrive.

"How was school?"

"Fine."

"James is inside watching Blue's Clues."

"Good." She said. "Maria is inside She didn't go to school."

Rick nodded.

"So, is this how it is going to be?"

"How what is going to be?"

"You aren't going to say anything?"

"About what?"

"About last night."

Rick paused.

"Oh, sorry. I was out with Brody again."

"Were you high?"

"No, of course not."

"Did you forget our phone number?"

"Do I need to check in?"

"As a matter of fact, yes. Yes, you do." She said. "You've got a little boy and, let's see, a daughter who got raped. So, yeah, you need to check in."

"That's bullshit."

"No, that's my shit. My big, steaming, peanut filled shit." She said. "You leave your family at its worst moment so that you can go get high."

"Don't do that." He barked. "It's not fair. We didn't get high."

"Bullshit. It's what Brody does these days. Morphine in his tea. He's a heroin addict from the old school."

"We weren't high and I didn't abandon you."

"Well, then, what were you doing that was so important that you had to abandon your family without the courtesy of a fucking phone call."

"I am sorry about the call." He cooled down. "I should have called."

"What were you doing?"

"We were out."

"Bowling? Golfing? Jerking each other off?"

"Rosie, cut the shit."

"What were you doing?"

"Don't worry about it."

For a split second, she saw something she didn't like in his eye.

"What were you doing?"
"What I should. What I had to."
"What did you do?"
"I can't tell you." He said. "In truth, nothing happened."
"Bullshit." She snapped. "Do not lie to me. Do not do it. Do not do that."

He looked at her. Sorrow, remorse, and shame hung in his eyes. "Nothing happened."

"What might have happened?"
"Rosie," he said. "Nothing."

She took her school bag, swung it over her shoulders, and slammed it on the ground.

Something broke inside.

"James!"
He came stumbling out of the TV room. "Hi, Mom."
"Put your shoes on, we're going to the store."
"Can I get a matchbox?"
"Absolutely."
"Great!"
For the first time that day, Rosie felt her heart float.

Danny drove up Main Street with the Inspector in the passenger seat. The old man had showered, changed his clothes, did not smell of either bourbon or body odor.

"I heard the good news." Danny said. "No more Billy and Jack"
Coffin grunted.
"We're not done."
Danny let that statement sit.
"Henry, please."
"We're not done. We need to talk to two people."
"Are we done after that?"
"Maybe."

Detective Higginbotham drove silently. He preferred the old man drunk.

"So, we are still missing one boy and have the rape of one girl."
"Henry," Danny said. "For the love of God…"
Coffin thought of his partner and all of the issues that he wrestled with.

"Two conversations, Henry." He said. "Two conversations and I won't involve you in this anymore."

"Which isn't the same as saying you are out?"

"No." he said. "But I will leave you clear."

The black officer shook his head. He would never be clear.

"Where and who?"

"Essex Road and Pink."

"Who else?"

"You know."

He did.

The patrol car waited in a familiar driveway near the end of Essex Road. The spotters had long since seen him and cleared the street. Pink's Cab drove up the deserted street, made the left, and saw the squad car.

The cab didn't hesitate but kept going until he dropped off his fare. The young man looked decidedly sick. Coffin waved.

Pink, well aware of the current situation, drove the cab one mile to a well-lit elementary school parking lot. He was less than one hundred yards from where Jack and Billy had snapped a picture of young James DeSalvo. Danny parked the cruiser next to the cab. The Inspector opened his door, stepped out, then leaned against the closed door.

Pink unrolled his window. The notes of Stan Getz sambaed from the interior.

"Inspector."

"Counselor. How are you this evening?"

"Oh, I'm okay."

"Sorry about that fare."

"I imagine I will pick him up again in a moment or two."

Coffin smiled. He saw a glint of gold in a cup holder.

"Someone has been paying in gold, Pink?"

"No." he said. "It's just a coin I found."

"Can I see it?"

"No."

"The Secret Service is particularly interested in South African gold coins, Pink. They say that gold coins are used in many drug transactions."

"I wouldn't know anything about that."

"It is an unhealthy coin, Pink. You wouldn't want the wrong person to see it."

"Is that a threat, Inspector?"

"No." he said. "Just friendly advice."

"Glad to know you are so concerned" Pink said. "I spoke to the Assistant District Attorney, Ms. Davidson...."

"Yes."

"She said that the state police had taken over the investigation of that missing boy."

"They have."

"She was under the impression that there would be a lengthy and exhaustive procedure that could take many, many months."

"It might."

"They were going to re-visit your work. Sorry about that."

His smile was plain.

"Pink, how much do you think you can control those two bozos?"

"Not much. I don't have anything to do with them."

"Nothing?"

"Well, I represent them for the moment. I suggested that they might get other representation."

"You have another business connection."

"I am sure that I don't know what you are talking about." Pink said. "But it is true that I often gave them rides. I told them that I can't do that anymore either."

"You know that they are going to screw up."

"I know that you and everyone else are waiting for them to do it. I told them so."

"Then you cut them loose."

"Well, I believe you have been suggesting I do that for some time."

"I am sure I haven't been the only one. The folks on Essex Road probably aren't too thrilled with your friendship either."

"Who knows?"

"Pink." The Inspector wanted to end the verbal puppet show.

"Yes, Inspector."

"Whatever those two have done, it goes far deeper than boys will be boys."

Pink looked away from the Inspector and out over the steering wheel to the playground.

"Maybe they have, Inspector. I truly don't know. Truly, I don't. I do know that we live in a time when boys can't really be boys. You guys break up the bonfires and the beach parties. You make them stay in school all day instead of going off to the fields or the ocean or the army or anything else. There are no staff sergeants or top hands or even first mates to whip them into some sort of shape. Every boy needs a man to show him how its done, how life is to be lived. The boys need fathers. What do we give them? You've seen the two men involved here. You've seen the two fathers. What do you think?"

Coffin looked at him. "I think everyone does the best they can."

"I call bullshit to that, Inspector. I call bullshit. We let these boys grow up like wolves and we are surprised when they bite? The best we offer is football and what is that? Two hours an afternoon in the fall? What would Alexander have been without Aristotle? What would Achilles be without Menelaus?"

"You are laying it on a little thick here, Pink, aren't you? Jack and Billy aren't likely to be Alexander and Caesar. And you are no drug dealing Aristotle."

"No." he said. "No, probably not. But think about this. What does our society do with these boys?"

"Sooner or later, we will lock these two up." He said. "But, Pink, there are far worse things that can happen than jail."

"One hundred years ago, we sent them to sea or to war or to Alaska or even to the back forty. Now we send them to prison. It's not right."

"There are worst things than jail, Pink."

"Inspector, in ten years they will run for Selectman. They're good boys."

"They have to live that long."

"Don't we all?"

Coffin smiled again.

"Pink, take care of yourself," he said. "Really."

"You, too. Inspector. I would hate to have to break in a new cop on the night patrol."

Pink rolled up his window, the music of Stan Getz was stilled, and he backed away into the night for one last time.

Danny and Henry went to Altar Rock. Coffin was ready for his partner to try to talk sanity and clarity, but he didn't. Instead, he drummed his fingers on the wheel, flipped on his portable reading light, and submerged himself into his book.

The moon was bright enough so that the pickup truck ran without its lights on.

Coffin stepped out of the car. Danny stopped reading, but did not look up from the book. For a moment, he felt silly, as if he was an angry wife. Then he made peace with that anger. His engine was on. The glass was bullet proof.

The pick up truck slowed and stopped atop the small hill. Coffin knocked on the window and waved goodbye. Danny, long since being surprised, full of faith in the crazy Quaker, and aware that his next mortgage payment was due in a week, pulled away. He would call.

The front driver's side door opened and Stephen stepped out.

"Get everyone out, but the Dad." Coffin told him.

"They don't do that."

"They will."

"I want to talk to just him."

"He doesn't speak English."

"I am sure we can figure it out."

"Henry, really, these people…"

"Stephen, just do it."

He stuck his head inside. Within second, the rear doors to the club cab opened and three large Hispanic men stepped out. They scanned the horizon and then settled on the rumpled Inspector.

He did not look at them but stepped past, opened a door, and sat inside.

He was a small man resting in the center of the rear seat. When Coffin moved to sit in back with him, he slid himself over. The great criminal was a smaller man, dressed in flip-flops, dirty jeans, a tank top, and carefully oiled and styled hair. It swooped over the top of his forehead like a gray breaking wave, then ran out over his neck like an incoming stream.

He was, in short, a man like many others. He had his vanities, his pot belly, his bad teeth, and his hopes. Coffin recognized him as a man he had never recognized, a man who he had seen working or walking or standing in line. He was a middle-aged immigrant who pushed a lawn mower or stood in a bar with a beer.

Unlike other men, however, this one had had his left hand and several toes taken away sometime ago.

He did not look at the Inspector with the glance of command or the impatience of action. Rather, his eyes were sad. He knew what the meeting was for.

Coffin reached out his right hand. "Henry Coffin."

The man shook with his remaining hand. "Quinto Allende."

"I am sorry to meet you like this."

"As well." Quinto looked at him. "You think he is dead." His English was adequate for the task.

"I do."

"Ah."

He leaned forward on his knees and stared at the floor.

He remained this way for many minutes. Then he straightened with tears in his eyes.

Quinto looked at him. "You have lost a son."

"I have. My only son."

"Mine, too." Quinto said. "What sort of people would do this?"

"Kill him?"

"Lie to his father. What sort of people would do this?"

"Those without boys."

Quinto looked at him, clearly. "You are right. Those without boys. Anyone who has a small one would never do this."

The two men stood together on a hill and looked back into their pasts.

"I have been told, by this cabbie, Andrea, that he is alive and he is in a special hospital."

"Is she telling you the truth?" Coffin replied.

"What do you think?"

"No." The Inspector saw no hope.

"I agree."

Coffin sighed. "I have been taken off of the case. Others are in charge."

The Brazilian snorted, then the silence refilled the cab,

"Have you talked to his killers."

"Well, I have talked to the boys."

"And the girl"

"Yes."

"And you think the boys did it."

Coffin was aware, in that moment, of the stillness of the air. But he could not lie to the man. "Yes."

There was more in Coffin's mind. He saw Mike Kelly and Pink and the rest of the charade. He saw Rick playing killer and Brody.

"They told me that we would be safe. They told me that they could protect me. If I did this one thing, they said. They would protect me in the North. So I did that for them, and my boy and I and these others came north. And so we did. We left everything we knew and came here to lawnmowers and shovels and a quiet life. Then this happens."

"Who said?"

Quinto smiled. "The men with sunglasses. And their lawyers."

Coffin put a hand on the man's shoulders.

"He was a boy. He ran off with a girl." Coffin said. "My little boy ran off the end of a pier. He was with his mother in a crowd in the middle of the summer and he ran off a pier."

Quinto put a hand on Coffin's shoulders.

Both men had become sons to a cruel and unforgiving Father.

Eventually, the Brazilian sat up and wiped his eyes.

"Is she beautiful?"

"I am sure you have seen her."

He nodded.

"Do you think she is pregnant?"

"I don't know."

"What do you think, my brother?" The Brazilian asked. He was the first man to refer to him this way in some time.

"Why would you run away with a girl?"

"That's what I thought. Take money to her. Give it to her. Tell her it is for her child."

Coffin nodded. "What are you going to do?"

Quinto looked at the Quaker. "I cannot say."

Coffin nodded.

"What I can say," Lollipop continued. "Is that I will not be here much longer. They will move me. Or they will shoot me. It doesn't matter one way or the other." Coffin didn't interrupt him. "I would like to see my boy again. One more time."

Coffin nodded.

In that space, a great moment appeared. The depth and the danger opened up before the Inspector. If this man was who they said he was, he was capable and powerful enough to get what he wanted. But Coffin could not refuse this. Nor did he want to. It didn't matter what this man had done in the past, not to Coffin. He was another father of a cold son.

"Fair enough. It so happens I need a great deal of yard work done at my house. I live at 75 Main Street. You should visit."

"Perhaps, my brother. Perhaps."

After Coffin had stepped from the truck and the men had driven away, he called his partner. He made sure to clearly enunciate that Danny was, in fact, not with him at that moment so that who ever was listening would know.

It was the least he could do.

CHAPTER TEN

"Do you want to live?"

There was a knife at Jack's throat.

He nodded. There was a pinch at his neck when the needle went in.

They were sitting in the lee of a dune on the South shore. There had been some fun earlier up the beach at the victory bonfire. And there had even been some more fun a dune or two over with one of those freshmen. But now the two of them had taken a couple Percocets to come down off of all the coke and excitement. Billy was still descending, with his back to the sand and his eyes on the swirling stars.

Jack's hands were suddenly zip tied in front of him and his mouth was full of cloth. He had just enough time to think the word "Gag" when electricians tape sealed his mouth and he had to breathe out his nose. Then there were earphones in his ears and Twisted Sister blasting away and a hood over his head.

He thought, "I should have yelled."

"Stand up."

Jack was against it until the back of his hands were slashed. He felt the blood dripping from his fingers. He stood.

His pants fell to his ankles.

Then he got punched in the face. And fell over.

When Billy was also bound, Brody found Jack's cell phone and texted Pink.

"Pickup."

In the moments that the three of them waited in the darkness of the beach, Brody thought about writing the word "Remember" on both of their asses and taking a picture on Jack's phone.

He still had enough training in him to know how dangerous that would be.

And he was sure he would remember.

When Pink pulled into the beach parking lot, he saw both boys propped up against the trash cans. He saw the hoods over their heads and the white of their underwear.

So he stopped.

Pink stepped out of the cab and walked to the boys.

A hand held his arm from behind.

A voice said, "Do you think that it is time that we taught these boys a lesson, Pink?"

"Who are you?"

A point of a knife rested just below his right ear.

"Don't you think we should teach these boys a lesson?"

Pink nodded.

"We are going to bring them to the back of your cab."

"Okay."

Pink, however, did the work. He stood them both up and led them, shuffling, to the side door of the minivan. The man stood in the shadows.

Pink took the opportunity to whisper to them some words of encouragement. He didn't realize that their ears were filled with Dee Snyder singing "We're Not Going to Take It."

"Put them in the last row."

The boys shuffled onto the last bench.

"Now, get into the driver's seat."

Pink sat there.

A body moved right behind him and flicked the lights off.

"Hand me your phone."

"I am not..."

The knife touched below his ear. He unplugged it from the holder and handed it backwards.

"Take us to the public dock in Madaket. Please."

Pink put the cab in gear and started driving.

There was a hand on the back of his seat.

He knew who it was.

If it had been the Russians, they would all be dead. No one else would have gotten the drop on Jack and Billy that easily. He was taking care to be invisible to Pink. Pink couldn't say that he could identify him later.

Later.

The thought buoyed him up. There would be a later.

He drove past the Miacomet Golf Course and then, at direction, took the dirt road, Millbrook up to the Madaket Road. Their trip through the woods was solitary. Pink tried not to look in the rear view mirror.

Both boys leaned against each other.

Two cars drove into town while Pink headed out.

Plans and panic danced in his mind. He worked at convincing himself that this was just a scare to put into the boys. They would take them to Muskeget for the night. Drop them at the beach and let them chase birds and dodge seals for a few days. It was a good idea. It would scare the piss out of them. That was the plan, he decided.

When he pulled up to the public dock, he reversed the cab and backed it up. He could help out a little. He was a good sport.

The man with the knife said nothing.

It was quiet at three in the morning in Madaket. Two lights burned on the porch of the Admiralty, but every other house was dark. Overhead, the stars burned cold and bright. Two planets hung in the western sky while Orion began his climb in the East. The man opened the door and propped it open. He reached into the back and dragged the first boy, Jack out and sat him in the shadows of the pier. Then he came back and pulled the other boy out and sat him next to his friend.

"Okay, Pink. Out."

He couldn't use his hands or his feet.

He got the door open and half fell from his seat. Staggering, he propped himself up next to the car.

Another man, wearing a mask, walked off an older scallop boat. This one was a long Boston Whaler, with a large white table in the middle and, above it, metal scaffolding to support the metal drag nets that trail behind the boat. This one had two high horsepower motors bolted to the stern.

"Pink, carry Jack to the boat."

He slowly moved his feet over to the smaller boy. When he pulled the boy upright, he felt warm and alive. The other man came over and stood up Billy, then rolled him onto his shoulder as if he were a load of shingles. Pink rolled Jack on his shoulders and then, staggered down the dock.

The first man walked back up to the taxi, turned the engine off, and closed the doors.

He left the keys inside.

"Pink, be careful."

It was a familiar voice on the boat. He set the boy onto the dock and the two of them rolled him onto the boat.

The man with the knife walked up the dock.

"Step in the boat, Pink."

"But..."

"We still need you."

The other man had loosened the stern line.

Pink moved to protest but the man with the knife approached fast. The cabbie gingerly stepped onto the boat.

"Sit up front with the boys, would you?"

Pink nodded.

"Would you free that line, please?"

"Of course."

They would need three adults, of course. If the boys woke up, there might be problems. They couldn't just run the boat and drop the boys off. They might leave him on the island as well, but that would be ...a relief.

The engine started up and the boat slowly backed from the pier. The driver slipped the boat into first gear and it maneuvered up Hither Creek, past the final buoys and into the channel. Once clear of land, the driver opened both engines up and the nose of the boat started bouncing on the water.

Otherwise, the night was cool and clear. The lights on Tuckernuck glimmered, as did the channel markers. The spray was warm and a line of bioluminescence followed the curve of the boat.

Both of the men stood apart from Pink, behind the table. He slowly came to his feet and walked to the table in order to face them. The boat left the protection of Madaket harbor and bounced a bit more violently on the waves.

The driver throttled back slightly.

Pink braced himself against the forward edge of the table.

"So," he shouted over the engine noise. "What's the plan?"

In answer to that question, Paul Brody took his ski mask off. Rick DeSalvo hesitated, and then followed suit.

It took a moment for Pink to realize what had happened. It took another moment to comprehend the importance of seeing his future face to face.

"We're going to Muskeget." Brody said.

"What about me?"

"You're coming with us." He said. "Or you could jump right here."

"Well, then what?"

"It depends."

Brody pushed the boat faster and the front bounced two feet high in the chop. Pink felt himself float into the air, and then land.

He went back to the boys.

Their pants remained around their ankles. The skin of their thighs and their white underwear glowed in the starlight. Pink poked and prodded them. They were both very much alive and very much asleep. He gave up on waking them and watched the land slide by.

There had been chances. He could have jumped from the boat while it was in Hither Creek, he could have driven the car into a phone pole, he could have driven the car to the police station, he could have not answered the text at all.

Because this couldn't happen.

Tuckernuck slipped away and they crossed the channel between the two smaller islands. Muskeget was several hundred yards from Tuckernuck and several miles from the Vineyard. Fishermen swear that they have seen deer swim from Chappaquidick to these islands. At low tide, the sand bars are only under a very swift one or two feet of water. The flashing radio towers of Martha's Vineyard loomed in the night sky.

Tuckernuck had no power and no central sewerage, but it had a few dozen houses and even fewer people living there. Muskeget had last been inhabited by the Shore Patrol in 1900. After they left, the gulls and the seals took over.

Even now, he could hear the colony of seals rolling and slapping itself on shore.

DeSalvo swept the ocean with a flashlight until he found a buoy. Brody motored the boat slowly over to it and then tied it to its stern cleat.

After the roar of the engine and the constant wind, the sudden silence deafened.

"You can't do this." Pink said.

"Do what?"

"Leave us here."

"Why not?"

"It's murder."

"Yes," Brody said. "I am murdering you."

Rick looked pale.

"No, you can't."

Pink's arguments failed him. Brody and DeSalvo stood on the other side of the table and waited.

"Rick, you can't live with yourself after this. You will spend the rest of your life regretting this night. It will turn you into a monster. You know its wrong."

Rick opened his mouth, but Brody spoke for him. "What if it doesn't, Pink?" The teacher crossed his arms and looked at him. "What if, for the rest of his life, he knows he took some pain out of this world? He killed a few rats before they spread the plague. He eliminated a disease before it killed a million."

"You can't know that."

"I can make a guess."

"It's a lousy guess."

"What have they done so far?"

"Nothing. They're sixteen years old." Pink barked. "You don't know what they will become. Many great men started off poorly. Lots of them did things they regretted. Then, they repent, they contribute. Look at Moses."

"Moses is a story."

"He was a murderer."

Rick shrugged. "Which of these is Moses?"

"I don't know. You don't either."

"No, but I do know justice."

"No, you don't. This isn't justice. It's murder."

"Sometimes, justice is murder, Pink." Rick said. "Sometimes you see the hurt and the pain that they inflict, the barbarism and you say that it has to end. You say these two dirtbags need a chance. What about the good kids? Don't they need a chance to grow up without getting raped and assaulted? How many people have these little shits ripped apart?"

"I know one." Rick said.

"This isn't the answer." Pink pleaded.

"What kind of a father am I?" he asked. "What kind of a man am I if I know that I could stop the shit those two do and I don't?"

"Put them on the island! That would scare the shit out of them."

"These are the boys that ruined my daughter's life. They ruined my life."

"No, they didn't."

"They raped her and put the pictures on the internet."
"Her life is long. Your life is long. It's not ruined. "
"You're a father, Pink."
Pink stopped.
"You're a father. It could have been your daughter. It could have been your daughter's ass on the internet."
"It still could happen to her."
"But not from them."
Brody looked at the taxi driver. The night remained cold and dark. Beneath them, hundreds of animals swam back and forth, to and fro.
"Pink, how would you like to die?"

Later, the two men motored back to Hither Creek. Dawn bruised the eastern horizon. Rick looked at the empty space where the boys had been. Brody merely steered the boat.

On shore, he had one last duty. Rick drove Pink's Cab down to the Hy-Line dock. He dropped the cell phone into the harbor, put the keys in the ignition and found a tupperware container with twenty kruggerands in it.

He thought about tossing it into the harbor next to the phone, but he relented. Instead, he carried it back up to his house and buried it in the old screws and bolts of his workshop.

In his first morning as a murderer, he looked up at the dark, sleeping bedrooms of his children.

Milestone Five

CHAPTER ONE

Maria woke up and saw blood.

Panic flew from her and fluttered around the room. Slowly, she brought the bird back into her chest, lay back against her pink pillow and settled her heart.

Then she checked again.

It wasn't very much. It covered the tip of her finger and smelled like copper. It was, very definitely, blood.

Quietly, she slipped from her bed, wrapped herself in a bathrobe and padded silently to the bathroom. Her parent's room sounded remarkably silent; her mother was softly snoring.

With the door to the bathroom closed, she turned on a light and dropped her panties to the floor. In the narrows of her underwear was a stain of blood smaller than a quarter. She reached under the sink, pulled out a light days strip, and lined her underwear.

Then Maria walked back to her bedroom. Very slowly.

Lying down in her old bed, Maria stared up at the ceiling. She didn't feel any cramping, her stomach felt calm, she didn't think she had a fever. It was nothing.

And she was terrified of that nothing.

Maria lay there, sleepless, for the rest of the night. She knew that all she needed to do was to cross the hall to the nurse in the other bed and tell her what was going on.

And she didn't.

This nothing was all hers.

By the time her clock radio let loose with Mattie in the Morning Playing the Hits on WXKS, Maria had decided to skip school and go to the hospital. She had history first period and a study hall during second. No one took attendance until third period, at best. If she wasn't back after an hour and a half, then everything had gone down the shitter with wings and flippers.

There wasn't any more blood. She thought.

She dressed carefully and imitated the way she would dress if she was not about to die on an examining room bed. She checked herself in the mirror over her dresser and resisted the call of the make-up.

She breathed. She counted slowly and breathed again.

Okay.

In a way, she needn't have bothered. Her father hadn't come back until six in the morning, so everything was going off half-assed downstairs. Maria grabbed the initiative, dressed James in his favorite Elmo shirt and some sweatpants, made his lunch, and did all the get ready in the morning tasks that her father did.

Rosie was beside herself with concealed worry. In fact, the only person in the room who wasn't lying through teeth was her brother who didn't want to go to school because he had a tummy ache. The women knew how he felt.

By the time Rosie pulled up in front of the school, Maria was primed and fired up. She talked her body into the various moves necessary to get out of the car and across the parking lot as she had done for the last three weeks. After 24 steps, she opened the door, walked inside and finally gulped in the oxygen.

Her plan was simple. She would cross the corridors of the school all the way to the music suite, where she would hide out until the second bell. Then, she would leave the school, cross the street, and slip into the hospital.

"How are you feeling?" Elvis stood next to her.

"Wow." She felt the bird of panic escape. "Christ. Fuck. Christ."

"Are you okay?"

She had no idea what to do. He didn't either, but he was looking concerned. Her mother was crossing the same parking lot behind her.

"Come with me." She whispered.

He nodded and walked along behind. She moved quickly, but with the barest attempt at not running in a panic. When they rounded the corner, she slowed down.

"Elvis," she said. "I don't need you today."

"Why not?"

"Jack and Billy are staying home these days. They are getting tutored."

He looked at her.

"I heard that."

"Okay, so you're free."

"But those two could be anywhere."

"They're not going to be at school."

"Why not? You're here and they want to get at you."

"They won't be here."

He glanced at her with annoyance. Rage built in him.

"Look," Elvis said. "I get it. I am this huge, fat, freshman who is always feet away from you. I know it. You think I don't know what it's like? I am a big, heaving elephant in this place. I don't fucking belong here. Horton understands. You don't need to beat me over the head with it."

"No…" she said. Everything went sideways on her.

"But the thing is that I made a promise. I didn't make it to you and I didn't make it to your Mom or to my Dad or even to Tillinghast. I made it to myself. I am not letting you go."

"Look, Elvis. It's not like that."

"It's not like what? What isn't it like?"

For a moment she saw all three hundred pounds of him looming over her. She heard him speak, not quietly, and saw everyone stare at the two of them. They had plenty to stare at: he with his dead father and her with, well, everything.

She felt overwhelmed. And ridiculous.

"Come with me." She said.

She took off at a rapid clip. Elvis scurried to keep up.

"Look," she said. They crossed under the whale in the main corridor, then turned next to guidance. "I am in massive, massive trouble and I have to deal with it right now. I don't think you are an elephant or a freak or anything besides being a nice guy who got forced into being my bodyguard. I don't."

Elvis remembered, but did not remind her that she came to his father's wake and funeral.

"It's my problem and I have to deal with it. Alone." She said.

"Not today."
"I appreciate what you're doing…"
"No."
The second bell rang.
They stood outside the music suite.
"You're late." She said.
"They can call my Dad."
She felt the pain of his joke.
"Look…" she said.
"I don't care what the problem is," he barked. "I don't care what the trouble is. I am sticking with you. I am not letting you slip away."
"You can't."
"Go to a teacher then. Tell them I am stalking you." He snapped at her in the hall.
She looked up at him. Her eyes came to the middle of his chest. The arrogance of him.
"Or just go to history class and I'll get you afterward."
She thought she felt a drop of something wet.
"But you're not because you have to do something out there and I am going with you."
"You don't need…"
"You've made a lot of good decisions on your own recently?"
She slapped him. Hard.
"You have no idea what I have had to put up with." She barked. "You have no idea of the shit I have to live with. No idea."
He paused for a moment.
"No, I don't," he said. "But that doesn't matter right now because I am not going anywhere unless it is with you."
There was something wet. Not a lot. Just something.
She had no time.
"Fine." Maria snarled. "Here is the rule. You can't say anything. To anyone. Not to Nick, not to the football team, not to Tillinghast, and not to your dead Dad's grave."
"Fine."
She pushed open the door. He followed.
"We're going to the hospital. I'm pregnant."
The words dropped from her mouth like stones. She felt herself transformed by the pronunciation.

When they arrived, the waiting room was full of old people. They waited for blood tests, heart tests, physical therapy and a medical language to express all that hurt them.

Maria hung back for the first time this morning. To sign in with the nurse and to sit in the waiting room was to proclaim her pregnancy to everyone in the room. The nearly seven feet of freshman boy trailing her also would draw attention. The harmless lifeguarding of Nantucket life pushed her away. Someone would talk.

Elvis stood behind her. "Aren't we going in?"

"I'm trying to avoid the crowd."

"Isn't this an emergency?" he said. "They'll just whisk you into an examination room."

"They will probably make me wait."

"It is an emergency?"

"Fuck yeah."

Elvis looked at the crowd and didn't quite understand.

"Okay," he said. "Follow me."

He walked in, passed the entrance desk, and headed for the stairs. Either out of familiarity or fear, no one stepped in front of him. In two minutes, he stood in front of the Nurse's Station on the second floor. Maria had followed.

They were working and did not look up right away. From his father's long illness, he knew most of the women working there. For their parts, even though they knew his father had died, they were not alarmed at his presence.

Sherrie Higginbotham finished one folder of papers and looked up.

"Elvis, how can I help you?" She spoke to the boy, but looked at Maria. She remembered her from her previous stay.

"I need a favor."

"Okay."

"Can someone examine my friend?"

Sherrie was rapidly doing the math in her head. "Why don't we use one of these rooms?"

They stepped into an unused hospital room.

"Honey," Sherrie said. "What seems to be the problem?"

"I'm pregnant." Maria said. The words still held relief, and a new identity. "And I woke up this morning with some blood in my underwear."

"Let me see."

She kicked off her sneakers, unsnapped her belt and began unzipping her pants. Elvis, aware of the awkwardness, drifted out the door. Maria stopped undressing for a split second, then finished. She lifted her panties off the ground. The liner had one reddish spot on it.

Sherrie sighed.

They called and found Dr. Manning. Tupper had been sent home at one in the morning because he annoyed everyone and there was no work for him to do. The older women looked at Maria with the sad, professional knowledge that she knew she would see her again. But she had lived on-island long enough to know the virtue of tact and discretion, in particular when dealing with pregnant teenagers.

They brought her into the empty maternity ward. She lay on one of the beds and waited for the electronics to be brought in.

This would be the room that she would give birth in.

This would be the ceiling she would stare at in her pain. She may even be lying in this bed.

Sherrie returned with a portable ultrasound machine. Dr. Manning followed behind. Elvis Lowell remained outside; no one knew exactly what his status was, although the nursing station was willing to take a guess.

"Maria," Dr. Manning began. "We don't know why there is some blood. It isn't very much blood, so it might be nothing. Or it might be something fairly significant. Before we admit you to the hospital, let's do a quick ultrasound and see how everything is going inside there."

Sherrie looked at her. "Pull your shirt up, hon." Maria brought her shirt up just under her breasts. In a second, she squirted a cold green gel over her stomach. Manning fussed with the screen.

"Okay, let's see."

Manning swiped the plastic bar over her stomach pressing down and fussing. Her silence built.

"Okay," she said. "Here he is. And he is looking active."

Maria looked up onto the screen and saw a fog of static. Then, a bank of gray heaved and twitched. She started crying.

"He's okay. He's an active little guy, isn't he?"

The tears came hard and fast. She felt herself heave in sobs. Manning removed the bar from her stomach while she convulsed. The air couldn't come fast enough or hard enough.

Manning looked patient, but annoyed.

Sherrie looked down at her. "Is this your first ultrasound, honey?"

Maria nodded.

"Would you like to hear the heartbeat?"

Maria breathed slowly and calmly. She flattened her palms against the sheets on the mattress and nodded her head. Manning touch a button on the console, then pressed the bar against her lower stomach.

A rapid little heartbeat filled the room.

Lying very still, Maria resumed crying.

"I need to measure him, honey. Be still, if you could."

Maria nodded.

Only women bleed, she thought.

The Doctors decided that their opinion was that he was a healthy baby. But the Doctors thought that there were concerns. He was not as big as they would like, which isn't a bad thing. Just something to follow. As she was entering her second trimester, they weren't entirely happy with the thickness of the placenta. Again, it would be fine. Many mothers develop even thinner placentas and give birth to perfectly healthy babies.

Still, it was decided that she should check with the expert from Boston. He came down one Saturday a month. She should make an appointment.

It should be covered by her insurance. Or the hospital could put her on a relief list.

Dr. Manning, Sherrie, and another nurse all looked at her with professional and personal concern. When she reassembled her costume, Sherrie took a moment to say "Take care of yourself, okay?"

Maria and Elvis walked back across Surfside Road, slipped in the same door that they had left and then went to their fourth period classes.

Maria drifted through the rest of her day, with her mind clearly focused on her uterus and all that it contained. She kept listening to the heartbeat.

A small and shameful part of her had hoped that the quarter sized blood stain would lead to a painless and speedy miscarriage. Some cramps, some aspirin and the trouble went away.

But now the trouble has a heartbeat. And little fingers and toes. And a head. Her dark passenger couldn't be ignored and denied any longer.

After school, she walked with Elvis to the door of the locker room, as if she were some Labrador at the end of a clothesline. He was practically looking for a door handle to tie her too.

Which was unfair.

He had been silent and ten yards away through most of the day. He hadn't commented when she left the hospital doused in tears, nor had he pestered her with questions, nor had he transformed her into spun glass and ribbon candy. But he was vigilant and concerned.

With his hand on the leash.

After he disappeared into the locker room, she turned and started walking to her mother's office.

But not yet. Maria couldn't see her. There was a conversation coming that she had spent months avoiding that could wait another day or so. She didn't want to hand the leash to someone else. There were pains of solitude that felt a lot better than the pleasures of company.

Instead, she stood at the backdoor of the school unsure of the next few steps, the next few hours, and, really the rest of her life.

So after all of that, she walked to the football field, climbed the home stands up to the press box, and braced herself up against the wood.

Most of the players were still in the locker room, but the snappers and kickers were on the field for some quick practices. The field goal kicker, in particular, was laboring to send his somersaulting balls over the bar. She saw him practicing and another boy appeared to view, with his low booming kicks. She felt the tears build for him.

Then she heard the heartbeat again: thumpety thumpety thumpety thumpety thumpety thumpety thumpety.

Rosie waited for her daughter at her office. When the girl didn't show up five minutes after the final bell, she had her paged.

The panic spiked. After EVERYTHING that happened to her, she had to skip three periods this morning. And NOW she was nowhere to be seen.

She grabbed her bags, locked the door, and jogged as fast as she could out to the Explorer. She pulled out of the parking lot quickly, into the remnants of school traffic, and then, just as recklessly, pulled into the rear of the school. She drove against the traffic and parked near the football field.

Tillinghast saw her leave her car and start down the hill. He left the players and jogged up on an intercept path.

Rosie slowed when she saw that he look calm and even, slightly, amused.

"Easy, girl."

"Jesus Tillie, where is she?"

"Up on the stands."

Rosie stopped moving and scanned the aluminum bleachers. She saw her daughter huddled up against the press-box. "The fucking bitch."

"She's fine, Rosie. Elvis has bird-dogged her all day."

"Where was she when she skipped?"

"I don't know, but Elvis was with her. He skipped the first three as well."

"I'm going to kill her."

But she didn't move towards the girl.

"She's fine here, Rosie. Safest place for her to be these days. Those two wouldn't last long with this group."

Elvis jogged by at that moment. He ignored Rosie, but kept his eye on her daughter.

"I'm going crazy, Tillie. I swear to God I am going nuts."

"You've had a lot to work with recently."

"No shit."

"Look," he said. "I am no position to offer any sort of meaningful advice…"

"But," she interrupted.

"Let her stay with us. I will give her a ride home afterward."

"No. I want to kill her."

"Well, then she should really stay."

Rosie looked out over the field and to the empty stands.

"Okay." She sighed.

"You're sure?"

"Yeah." She said. "But take a good look at her. I might kill her myself tonight."

She waved to her daughter. Even though the girl was looking right at her, she didn't wave back.

Christ, what a mess.

As Rosie drove out of the parking lot, Elaine slipped from her car. The Golf had weathered Rick's onslaught reasonably well. She had put a cross of duct tape over the hole in the hood and ignored all of the other little dings and insults that had been hammered into her little car.

When her mother saw the damage, she was all in for the strongly worded letter with threats of legal action. Elaine knew that there was a debt that she owed that neither money nor auto-body could fix. She owed it, she knew it, and she could never pay it off; she was the friend who dropped the ball.

As the team began its warm-ups, she picked her way across the side of the hill to the stands. Maria saw her as soon as she put one foot on the rickety aluminum, but she didn't wave her away. She didn't beckon her forward or welcome her, either. Neutrality was a plus, at this point of the game.

"What's up?" she asked.

"Nothing." Maria said.

Elaine sat next to her in the lee of the press box. "Got cold fast, didn't it?"

"We were just in shorts and flip-flops."

"I know."

Neither of them spoke while they watched.

"You watching anyone in particular?" Elaine asked.

"No." Maria answered. "Well, yes. Elvis. But not really."

"Does he have a crush?"

"No, he's been assigned to me."

"This some new Rally Girl thing?"

"He's my bodyguard. Sort of."

Elaine nodded. The distance between them yawned. Maria continued.

"Y'know, in case Jack and Billy come back to school."

"Sure." Elaine nodded. She had no idea what to say. "I'm sorry." She added.

"It's okay."

"No, it isn't. Your Dad was right. It was my fault. I am sorry."

"I wanted to go down to the strip."

"No." Elaine said. "At the party. I should have known. I should have stopped it."

"You couldn't have done anything."

"Yes, I could. I'm sorry."

"It's okay."

Maria didn't want to forgive her, blame her, excuse her, or accuse her. She didn't even want to talk to her.

"How are you feeling?"

"Like?"

"With the baby?"

She sighed. She had to start thinking of it as a baby: diapers, onesies, pacifiers, sitters, and everything else.

"I'm all right."

"Do you know what you are going to do?"

"No." She drifted through the word. "I had a scare today."

"What?"
"I woke up to some blood?"
"How much?"
"Quarter sized spot."
"That's good sized." She said. "What did you do?"
"I went to the hospital."
"What did they say?"
"They said he was fine. They said I had to watch it and be careful."
"It's a boy?"
"I guess."
"So they did the ultrasound. Did they show you the pictures?"
"Yeah."
"Did you keep them?"
"No."
"Next time, ask if you can keep them."
Maria looked at her old friend. "I heard his heartbeat."
"What did you think?"
"It's cool."
"Yup." She said. "So, you made your decision, then?"
"Not yet."
"Yeah, you have."
"No." Maria was firm. "No, I haven't."
Elaine was quiet and held her tongue. Including her sister, she had five friends who had gotten pregnant in high school. The two who heard the heartbeat, kept the kids. The three who didn't, flew to New Bedford.
"Are you going to stay?"
"I don't know. I doubt it."
"Oh."
"I don't like being stared at all the time."
Elaine had to nod. "But, you would be away."
"I know. And what about the baby."
"Right." She nodded.
"It's a lot to think about."
"I don't know." Maria said. "I just hate being the girl who…."
"I know."
"It sucks."
"I believe you."

Yet, even then, Maria felt as if she were ten miles away. There was nothing else to talk about; she couldn't say anything about boyfriends, shoes, parties, or spoiled bitches.

Elaine didn't leave her. She sat beside her old friend and was ready to listen if she was ready to talk.

But she wasn't.

Coach Tillinghast felt his cellphone go off. He returned the call to Danny Higginbotham, then excused himself from practice. He called Maria down from the stands and took her back to her house, before he headed downtown to the police station.

CHAPTER TWO

In the minutes that Maria was being examined in the hospital, Henry Coffin was waking up. He heard the slow steps and quiet rake of someone in his backyard. Cautiously, he raised the edge of the blind and saw a one handed Hispanic man drag a rake underneath one of the hydrangea bushes.

Coffin's backyard had been sealed tightly one hundred years before. A six foot high white wooden fence circled it, with two doors. One entered into the house and the other out into another backyard. While he wasn't precisely invisible, Quinto was hidden from the traffic on the street. Were anyone to take the time and energy to come looking, all they would see is one more Brazilian cleaning up the backyard of a mansion.

Henry pulled on a pair of shorts and a t-shirt, then made his way to the kitchen and the door out into the back yard.

He pushed the door open.

Quinto leaned the rake against the side of the building, brushed his hand off on his pants, and walked inside.

Coffin's kitchen table was littered with crumbs, dirty glasses, books, newspapers, and miscellaneous crumpled balls of paper.

Coffin gestured him towards one of the seats and he took the other.

"Good morning, Quinto."

"Henry."

"I don't know if I have all that much to offer you here, I am afraid."

"That's fine, my friend." He said. "Do you have anything to drink?"

"Juice or coffee or something?"

Quinto eyed the dirty glasses. "How about something stronger?"

"I do have that." Coffin smiled.

In a moment, both men had ice and bourbon in glasses that were passably clean.

"To long life." Quinto toasted.

Henry agreed.

He didn't know why the man was here, precisely, although he had an idea. He knew he was in no danger from him. There was nothing he could take that Henry wouldn't give him.

"I like how you decorate." The Brazilian said.

"Well, it has been a while since this place has seen a woman's touch."

"Not that it needs it," he said. "Isn't that the truth of getting old? You just need a lot less. A bed. A dish. Something to eat. Something to drink."

"Friends." Henry added.

"Absolutely." The one handed man said. "And a son."

"Well..." Coffin said. "We can't all be lucky like that."

Quinto sipped his bourbon.

"The girl, Andrea, tells me that he is alive and in a special hospital. She tells me that they will take me to him when I do this thing for them."

"I think they are lying." Coffin said.

Quinto looked at him sadly. "I am not sure."

"I know."

Quinto was silent.

"What is it that they want you to do?"

"Nothing." He said. "Nothing. They want me to identify a former partner of mine. They have these planes with the cameras."

"Drones."

"Yes. They want me to point out this guy as he gets out of his car so they can blow him up."

"I see." Said Coffin.

"It is nothing." Quinto said.

"You'll be killing a man. Perhaps more than one. You might even kill families."

"It is what I must do."

Coffin gazed at the man.

"What if they don't have your son. Or if he is dead?"

"I don't know."

"Have you talked to him?"

"No. They say that he is sick and in a coma." He said. "Andrea showed me a picture of him in a hospital bed."

"What do you think of that?"

The one armed man shrugged. "It is a photo."

"They have his body, at least."

"Yes," Quinto said. Coffin heard the rest of the sentence, although he did not speak it.

"You will do this thing?" Coffin said.

Quinto sipped more bourbon. "I must."

"They are using you."

"Yes," he said. "Yes, of course. Yes," he said. "They have always done that. They have always known that they could get at me through him."

Coffin sighed and eased back into his chair.

"What father doesn't feel that way?"

"No one." He shook his head. The drink seemed to affect him quickly. "It's how they got me up here. Someone tried to blow up my boy on his way to school. Come with us, they said. Come with us and the two of you can be safe. And so I came."

Coffin thought of an old story. Julian seemed to have an appointment in Samarra. The Quaker smiled.

"Do you think this is funny?"

The quiet spread through the room like cool water.

"No." Coffin said. "I think it is tragic, my brother. No one should lose a son."

"No." he said. "Sons should lose fathers."

Coffin nodded. He poured the Brazilian more bourbon.

"I never thought I would live this long." Quinto said.

"Me neither."

"You weren't in my business."

"Well, in a way I am."

Quinto laughed. "I guess you are. I guess you are somehow connected to that long white river, aren't you?"

"Not quite as much as some, but I am." Coffin agreed.

"No one gets as old as I get in the business. The car blows up. The house blows up. The driver starts taking you in the wrong direction. They start shooting at you from windows." He sipped his drink. "I should be dead."

"I don't believe in 'should'." Coffin said. The effect of the long night and his second bourbon of the morning were starting to dawn.

"Things are or they aren't. People will do something or they won't. 'Should' is what other people want."

Quinto brought the glass to his lips again. He smiled.

"You aren't Catholic, are you?"

"No, my brother." Coffin said. "Quaker."

"Quaker?" Quinto smiled. "Is that the one with the special underwear or the outer space aliens?"

"No." He said. "We're the ones who believe that God is inside you, won't lie, and won't be violent."

He laughed.

"This doesn't sound like the sort of faith for a policeman."

"I like to think that I was a Quaker before I became a cop, rather than the other way round."

Quinto finished his second glass and reached for the bottle himself. "Tell me, brother. Do Quakers believe in hell?"

"No. Nor heaven."

"So, when this is all over, what happens to you?"

"Dirt. Ashes. Dust. Same as everyone else."

The Brazilian nodded. "No judgment."

"Not then, no."

"So what is left, then, after you go?"

Coffin looked out into the backyard. "Nothing, I suppose."

"It can't be nothing."

"It could."

"Did you believe that when your boy died."

Coffin sat silent.

When Petey died, he remembered falling and never crashing. He had stood at a wake and had gone to the church. There was something buried in a box out at Prospect Hill Cemetery. But he never imagined Petey in heaven. He was sure he wasn't on Nantucket. And that was it.

"When my son died," Coffin spoke. "I didn't believe in anything."

"And now?"

"Now?" Coffin said as he finished his second bourbon. He reached for the bottle. "Now, I believe I'll have another drink." He smiled and poured. "And, I believe in people. I try to."

Quinto raised his glass. "To people."

Coffin answered. "They will do the right thing after they have screwed up enough."

The Brazilian smiled.

"So," he said. "What do you think I should do?"

"You know how I feel about that word 'should'." Coffin said. "And you already know what you are going to do. You have already done it, I bet."

Quinto nodded.

"I have."

"Is she hurt?"

"No."

"Where is she?"

"My brother," Quinto said. "How I can I trust you?"

"How can you not?" Coffin said.

"You are the police."

Coffin shrugged. "Not everyone thinks so." He admitted. "But how can I trust you, if you can't trust me? Why would you even come into my yard if you hadn't already decided to trust me."

The Brazilian really looked deep into the other man's eyes. They stared back, bold and bored. He was an unusual man.

"You say you are a Quaker."

"I am."

"And you say that Quakers don't lie."

"I don't lie."

"Promise me that you will keep my secrets."

"Well," Coffin hedged. "Are you going to order Andrea killed?"

"No."

"Are you going to order anyone else killed?"

"You know that they are going to ask me to kill people back in Brazil." He said. "If they are going to give me my son back, I will happily pull that trigger. I will sacrifice thousands of lives to have my boy back."

Coffin was silent. The brutal mathematics lay in front of him. The sum was horrific, yet the equation was not yet complete. More could be done. The Quaker elders, however, would never agree to this deal.

"I know that." Coffin said. "I don't like it. I will however, keep your secrets."

"Your word?"

"My word." He said. "But you need to know that I don't want anyone else killed."

"I know." Quinto smiled. "My men have taken her to a house in New Bedford. When the time comes to let her go, I will send them a pizza from Domino's. Then they will put her back in a car and place her on the ferry. She will not be harmed, other than the narcotics."

"You want me to negotiate."

"Yes. With the fat man. I want my son back. He gets me my son back, I will give him back his agent."

"What if your son is dead?"

Quinto sighed. "I don't believe he is."

"He could be." Coffin said. "If he is dead, promise me that you won't order her killed. You will let her live."

"It's not an issue."

"But...."

"Yes, she will live. I already promised that." He grew impatient. "I don't want anyone else to die."

Quinto looked at him and wondered what else this man might know. "She will be sound and whole in two days. Just groggy."

"Good." Coffin said. "Here is what I will do. I will negotiate an exchange for your son. I cannot imagine that they are going to be terribly willing to talk to me about this."

"No."

"There will be a lot of pressure on the island."

"I know." Quinto said. "I was going to stay inside here."

Coffin nodded. He had suspected as much, as soon as he saw him in the backyard.

The two grieving fathers made their plans.

An hour later, the Inspector had showered, brushed his teeth, combed his hair and put on clean clothes. Then, he stepped from the front door and locked it.

The gray cover of autumn had settled onto the island. Many of the elms on Main Street had lost their leaves in the last heavy rain. The heavy canopy had thinned somewhat and the Inspector could, from his front step, see the town clock.

On a Tuesday morning, the cobblestones of Main Street carried trucks, pick-ups, and the occasional Escalade. Surfboards, kayaks, and fishing rods had left the roof racks and hid in closets and garages.

Coffin nodded to those that he knew, but he did not stop for conversation.

Before he came to the station, however, he ducked in Cy's. Miriam was standing in the center of the main bar, ringing out the registers. She looked up at him while the register chattered.

"Henry," she said. "Can I get you a drink?"

"Not right now, but I have a favor."

"Sure."

He handed her a sealed envelope. "Danny will probably come in here this afternoon. Would you see that he gets it?"

"Absolutely."

In his hotel room, Two Ton brooded. A carafe of coffee stood ready next to a cold plate of scrambled eggs and a forlorn cheese danish. The morning Boston Globe remained folded.

Two Ton sat on the edge of his bed, in his sweatpants and tank top. The weather channel flashed across his TV screen.

It was his first.

He had been lucky and he had been good. He had hired good people and he had listened to them very carefully. He knew when they would be okay and he knew when to bring them in. There had been close calls. There had been snipers and fire fighters and long trips to the hospital and to rehab. There had even been a relocation.

But no deaths. And no abductions.

He could always tell the recruits than no one had ever died with him.

Her phone clicked off at two in the morning. The green light on the computer screen winked out.

When he got the message, he sent the cars out to the last location. They found the phone sitting in her car at the airport. According to the records, she had been driving around all night. No one had spoken to her since midnight.

Nine hours ago.

Andrea was gone. Lollipop was gone.

As soon as he realized she was gone, he fired off the flare. He sealed off the airport and the ferries. He sent troopers to the boat wharves.

Everyone was coming now. They were coming from Langley, Quantico, Washington, and Boston. Hell, they probably sent up some operators from Fort Bragg. Knowing how much they wanted Lollipop, there were probably four satellites and two high altitude drones circling the island. They probably tagged the one handed man with some James Bond shit years ago. They would find him.

But Andrea?

She had a husband and a mother. Her mother lived in an apartment in Athol and worked as a Special Ed teacher in the middle school; a career born of divorce. Andrea's husband was a resident at Brigham and Women's. This was her last assignment, and then it was going to be a desk job and fat babies. When Two Ton had given it to her, they knew what it was. Six months of driving a cab on an island; safe and simple.

Now Andrea had disappeared.

Lollipop had disappeared.

His career had disappeared.

Only one man could recover them all.

The phone call came at nine in the morning.

"Marshal?"

"Yes."

"Sir, Inspector Henry Coffin has walked into the police station and he would like to talk to you."

The big man eased himself onto a chair in the conference room, then propped his cane against the wall. He placed his hands on the table, then checked his nails.

Coffin sat opposite.

"How do you feel?" The Assistant Marshal asked.

"Lousy."

"You look drunk."

"Do I?"

"You smell drunk."

"I just showered. Perhaps it is my shampoo."

"I fucking doubt it."

Henry eased back.

"Where is Julian?" Coffin asked.

"Who?"

"The boy. Quinto's kid. Where is Julian?"

"You talked to the old man?" Thomas was not surprised at the fact, but the admission.

"Of course I did." Coffin said. "You know I did."

"What did he say?"

"He wants to know where his son is."

"His son is in hell, keeping a chair warm for his old man."

Coffin looked at the big man without a fleck of emotion.

"Where is his body?"

"No idea." Two Ton threw off. "Where is Lollipop?"

"I can't tell you."

Tommy felt the room shift. He blazed at this old man.

"Can't."

"Yes, I am sorry. I can't tell you."

"Where is Andrea?"

"I am not sure." He said. "But she is safe."

"How do you know?"

"He gave me his word."

"You are a loon. Complete bat-shit loon. This guy has killed dozens of innocent people. This guy is known for stuffing cocks down a dying man's throat. And you believe. You think...." Two Ton barked. "That his word is good."

"Sure."

He shook his head, grabbed his cane, stood, and moved to the door. He opened it and called for the Chief. Bramden appeared in seconds.

"Chief, you gotta hear this from your ass-clown Inspector."

Bramden, already gray, turned to the Inspector.

"Good morning, James." Coffin said.

"Stuff it, Henry. What is it?"

"Lollipop wants to make a trade. He will trade Andrea for the body of his son."

The Chief, for his part, looked at the fat man. "Okay..."

"You know where Lollipop is?" Tommy barked.

"I can't tell you."

"You know where Andrea is?"

"I have an idea."

"But you won't tell me."

"No." Coffin said. "I want you to make the exchange."

"The balls you have, Inspector." Two Ton said. "The balls you have."

"It's your only play."

"No, I have another one."

"Henry," Chief Bramden interrupted. "Tell us where these people are. Let's save some lives here."

"Chief, I gave my word."

"Yeah, you did." Two Ton Tommy said. "And, for obstruction of justice, you are now under arrest."

Two hours later, after processing, photographs, and fingerprints, Henry Coffin lay on the bench in the only cell in the Nantucket station.

He would use his one call in a little bit, but he had seen this gambit before. As soon as the lawyers came in, everything got very serious and complicated. There would be time enough for that. Right now, Henry laced his fingers behind his head and fell to sleep.

On a video screen, Tommy watched the Inspector fall asleep. Rage burned at the margins of his mind, but he kept laboring deep inside. He turned to one of his troopers.

"Go get Danny Higginbotham."

At noon, Danny was pushing into his third hour of sleep. Curled into his side of the bed, with his pillow bunched up under him, he snored lightly through the morning.

One of the staties banged five times on his door.

The black man's eyes opened but nothing made sense in his blacked out room.

Five more slams hit the door.

He rolled himself out of bed, wrapped his blue bathrobe around himself, and opened the shade.

Two state police patrol cars, lights spinning and flashing, were parked in front of his house.

In the instant, an old anger rose in him. Lights spinning as he had done outside so many criminal's houses, now these cops stood outside his door. Would they have come for a white cop this way?

The mother-fuckers.

Which one brought the noose?

He stepped down the stairs and opened the door. Two young troopers stood before him, with another behind, carrying a shotgun.

"What do you want?"

"Are you Danny Higginbotham?"

"Detective Danny Higginbotham." He answered.

"Are you Danny Higginbotham."

He eyed the young man closely. "Yes, I am Detective Danny Higginbotham."

"We have orders to bring to the station immediately."

"You didn't think I would respond to a phone call?" he said. "You thought you would need a shotgun to bring me in?"

"I'm sorry sir, we have our orders."

"Your orders were to come to my door with a shotgun"?

"We have our protocols, sir."

"Am I under arrest?"

"No, sir." The young man said. "You are needed for questioning."

"Fine. I'll dress and drive down."

"No, sir." He said. "We are to accompany you."

"You have two cars. You can follow me."

"No sir."

The young officer had the full state trooper outfit, including the blond hair cut to a half inch and the goddam flat hat.

"Well, I am getting dressed."

"Sir, I am not to let you out of my sight."

"Boy," Danny used the word deliciously. "Do you have a warrant?"

"No."

"Do you see an emergency in this house?"

"No."

"Did I invite you in?"

"No."

"Then you stay right there."

"Sir, I...."

Danny turned his back on the men and walked upstairs.

The troopers looked at each other, but stayed outside.

In several long moments, Danny returned in jeans, a flannel shirt, and a polar fleece. Then, he wrote a brief note and left it on the stairs.

The rage in Two Ton's chest had not eased into embers. He sat without coffee, without breakfast, without so much as a glass of water.

Now, the black man sat across from him.

"Let's not fuck around." The fat man started. "Tell me where he is?"

"Who?"

"Lollipop."

"No idea."

"Did I mention that I am through fucking around?"

"You did. Then you sent three crackers with guns to wake me up and drag me in."

"Not fucking around..."

" And now you want to play whitey with a gun." Danny said. "Cut the shit."

"Consider it cut." Tommy said. He resettled himself on his chair. "We are starting a probe on sexual abuse in the Nantucket Police Force. It seems that one policeman would go and get blow jobs…" He said. "No, he would fuck girls in the ass while he was on duty. He told them that if they said anything he would come after them. Maybe a couple pictures of some girls and a few choice phone calls. Maybe someone in this stupid burg will figure out that Staties outside your door and some white girls sore assholes go together. How do you like that? Officially, no comment from an ongoing investigation."

As the rage built within him, Danny knew he was getting played. He took a breath.

"I don't think I need to talk to you anymore."

"All these God fearing white people would hear that there is an investigation, perhaps a leak, and those rumors. Well, how would a black man survive that?"

"You must be desperate."

"Yes." he said. "Because I am missing a good guy. Somewhere out here, Andrea Murphy is held against her will." He paused. "But I am about to saturate this island with real cops in search of Brazilians. With the two of you on leave…"

"You're nuts."

"Well, you have been with Inspector Confused for the last few years. I bet you know most of the people he meets. I know you can get me my man."

"So that's it."

"Yup."

Danny smiled. Always the same games. Divide and conquer.

"Doesn't look good for a black man on a white island." The marshal said.

"You don't know my partner."

Danny got up, turned around and left.

Detective Higginbotham got a cup of coffee on Main Street, sat on the bench and watched the cars drive by. The landscapers were hard at it. Their pick up trucks, complete with trailers, bounced over the cobblestones.

It was a miserable job. In the summer, at least, you rode around outside, mowed some grass, pruned some hedges and cleaned up the flowerbeds so you could fluff up your hours. In the fall, it was clean up. Raking, digging, fertilizing, rebuilding…dull, hard, and dirty work.

Someone had snatched the other cabbie, Ahab Cab. The shit was going to come down. Oh, yes it was. He felt bad for a moment.

Then that moment passed.

But the rage was there. Oh, my burning Christ, yes it was. Threats, shot guns, and fists on the door. They do know how to treat a black man.

"Danny?" A voice called to him from inside Cy's.

He got up, turned around, and stepped into the cool dark.

Miriam Gardner waited for him at the register. "The Inspector left this letter for you this morning."

Danny ran his finger underneath the flap, then read the letter.

He smiled.

"What is it?" Miriam asked.

"He is a strange old man."

"True,"

"He wants me to remember the Coopers."

He crumpled the note up, lit it on fire, and dropped it, burning, into one of her sinks. When it was all ash, he ran the water.

Thirty minutes later, he had pulled up a folding chair next to the Inspector. The older man continued to sleep. Danny reached inside the bars and pinched his ear. After ten seconds, Coffin's eyes fluttered open.

"How is the birdcage?"

"Roomy. Space for you."

"Let's hope not."

Coffin swung around and sat. He put his elbows on his knees.

"So," Danny asked. "What are you in for?"

"Obstruction."

"I got rape."

"Rape?"

"Easiest charge to lay on a black man is rape of a white woman."

"Not Mayella Ewell."

"Oh, they haven't picked out a victim for me yet."

"Probably someone dog-faced."

"Likely."

Henry sat looking at the cement.

"I saw Miriam this morning."

"How is she doing?"

"She's good."

Coffin's eyes flicked to the red flashing light on the camera on the wall.

"But you're ripped."

"Righteously. If he was on fire, I wouldn't piss on him. I would roast marshmallows."

"Get the big bag."

"Right."

His rage had subsided as it always did with the Quaker. The bars didn't confine the man much.

"So..." Danny asked. "What is our next play?"

Henry smiled.

"The fat man is going to try to ruin you." The Inspector said. "I am the only one who can get Lollipop and you are the only one who can get me. He can't walk away. Not now. He needs a scalp."

"Jack, Billy. Both of them have nice heads of hair."

"No, he needs to bring a big scalp back. And he will ruin you to get it."

"It's still sketchy..."

"He doesn't need to make a case. He just needs a scalp. That scalp. Lollipop gets flown off to Gitmo." Henry paused. "I would rather give him Lollipop than give him you."

"Well, that's mighty white of you."

"I don't have that many friends. I have to protect them."

"You have an odd way of showing it."

"Thanks."

Henry looked out through the bars at the cement wall.

Danny whispered. "What do we do about Jack and the rest?"

"I suspect they are past worrying."

Both men fell silent.

"So, how do you like jail?" The marshal waddled in, then placed his cane in front of him and leaned on it.

Coffin smiled. "What is that phrase from the poet: "I could be bounded in a walnut and declare myself the king of infinite space."

The fat man coughed. "I know where there are lots of cells waiting for old men who won't fight back in the shower."

"Dad show them to you?" Danny asked.

"Fuck you." The fat man snapped.

"Don't get upset, my brother." Henry said. "Tom, have you thought about my offer?"

"No deal."

"Look," the Inspector continued. "You have a bad hand here and you don't want to play it. I can help, but you've got to deal."

"That's it. You're going to Cedar Junction."

"No Lollipop for you." Henry said. "He'll disappear into the grass and never be seen again. As soon as I call a lawyer, I am out of this cell and drinking bourbon in my study. You go back to the mainland where you can explain to the CIA, the FBI and everyone else how you lost a cop and your target. Maybe I will write a letter as well." Coffin said. His tone dropped to quiet and serious. "Look at your cards, Tom."

"Are you threatening me?"

"I'm the guy in the jail cell. You are the Assistant U.S. Marshal. This entire mess disappears if you cut a simple deal."

"Or I can throw you in Cedar Junction, start the investigation on Kunta Kinte and see how long it takes to break you."

"You think Lollipop will give you that much time?"

"He can't leave."

"You don't know where he is." Henry said. "This guy has slipped out of tighter nets than this. And who are you looking for, exactly."

"Fine, sit here."

He waddled off and left.

Henry looked at his partner. "You better go get some rest."

"What if…"

"Remember the Coopers."

"Who are they?"

"Watch and learn, my brother." Henry said with a smile as he leaned back. "Watch and learn."

That afternoon, two Coast Guard helicopters practiced rescue maneuvers on the north and the south part of the island. Ten thousand feet up, two drones searched through a small grid. Their camera were accurate enough to count the leaves on the bushes and read the labels on the bikinis.

Nonetheless, aside from some large sharks that were swimming off of Muskeget and a squall of birds spinning near them, the remote pilots didn't see anything of note.

At the airport, next to a blue med-evac helicopter, six men relaxed with hand-held video games and books. They looked up only once, when a gray Lear Jet landed at three in the afternoon. Waiting is what Operators did, unfortunately.

At football practice that afternoon, no one paid any extra attention to the skies. There were always planes and helicopters going overhead. Instead, they practiced running sweeps and counters with their new left tackle. For his part, Elvis also happily submerged himself into the familiar routine of pads, helmets and collisions. He only wondered where Coach Tillinghast was.

Former Ambassador, former Undersecretary of State, former OSS Agent, and current member of the Massachusetts Bar, Attorney Tillinghast was on his way to the Nantucket Police Department to clean up another mess his government had made.

CHAPTER THREE

Tillinghast appeared at the police station; he wore his coaching shirt, carried a briefcase with a textbook in it, and dearly wanted to be on the practice field.

He knocked on the safety glass. One of the deputies came over. He did not recognize him.

"Name?"

"Tillinghast."

"What is your business?"

"I represent Inspector Coffin."

"Okay." The young man backed away from the microphone. He picked up the phone, spoke into it, and waited.

Tillinghast did not like this. He swung his briefcase in front of him and put both hands on the handle. After a moment, he dug out an old business card.

Assistant U.S. Marshall Tommy Taracitano huffed up the corridor with his cane. The deputy buzzed the door open and Two Ton emerged into the waiting room.

"How can I help you?"

"I am here to see my client, Inspector Henry Coffin."

"Mr. Coffin is currently helping us with an investigation. He hasn't been charged with a crime."

"Then it should be no problem to let me talk to him briefly."

"I am afraid he is working on a very sensitive project."

"Since you have taken some time to come out here and speak to me in the waiting room, I am sure that he could as well."

"I am afraid that he can't."

Chief Bramden appeared behind the glass.

"I am told that the Inspector is being held behind bars here, Marshal. Now, you are saying that I can't see him. Is that correct?"

"We are just at a sensitive point right now." He said. "Perhaps in a few hours."

Bramden appeared deeply pained, as if constipation had gone on for three days.

"Sir, if I walk out this door without talking to the Inspector, a lot of bad things will start to happen. The most minor of those is that I will be banging on doors up in Boston and getting a federal judge involved. You don't want that." He said. "Here is my card."

"I don't want your card."

Tillinghast smiled. "Why don't you take it, go inside for a moment, think, and then come back and we can talk?"

"I don't need to talk to you. We are in the middle of something very big."

Bramden knocked on the glass. Two Ton waved him away. Tillinghast stood with his card offered, as if it was a life preserver or a gift of money. Two Ton ignored that as well.

"Visiting hours start at 10 p.m.." The fat man turned on his heel and walked inside.

As it turned out, it took three phone calls for a federal judge to come on the line. However, this judge knew the old man distantly and fondly. He was stuck on the southeast expressway. So he took the call. After a day of tax fraud and corporate crime in its slipperiest, the chance to do one small piece of good appealed to him. So, after talking to dear old Tillie for a few minutes, he called the US Attorney. Then, for good measure, he called Two Ton directly. Nothing felt better than yelling at a cop while stuck on the highway.

In twenty minutes, the door buzzed and the young deputy ushered the coach into the holding cell. Coffin was reading. When he heard the door open, Henry sat up and looked at Tillie.

"This one's a prize, isn't he, Inspector?"

"He's not that bright."

"I should say not."

The lawyer shuffled to a chair. "So, why have you been denied your liberty?"

"The true place for a just man is a prison." He looked at the old lawyer and smiled.

Coffin stood. He hid his hand at chest level and pointed to the two cameras in the top corners of the room.

Tillie nodded.

"How is Elvis?" Coffin asked.

"He is doing about as well as can be expected." Tillie sighed. "He puts on a brave face, but I don't know if this is the right place for him. Deerfield is going to scout him on Friday."

"I wouldn't give up on the island right off."

"He has a lot of gifts that won't get met out here."

"There is more to life than football."

"That is my point, precisely."

The coach smiled. Here he was, locked up in his own police station and Henry was still defending the island.

"If you don't mind," Tillie said. "I have to go see a man about a horse."

The old coach stood and walked out the door. Bramden sat in his office, while the fat man worked the dispatcher's desk. He chose the Chief.

"Do you have a room where my client and I can talk privately?'

Bramden looked up with both annoyance and exhaustion. "Do you want my office?"

"Are we going to be recorded in any way?"

"I hope not."

"Really?"

"No, Tillie. It will be fine."

Bramden stepped across the hall into the holding cells. He unlocked the Inspector's cell.

"Your lawyer waits for you in my office."

"Thanks."

"Leave my liquor alone."

Coffin smiled.

Inside the small, cluttered office, Tillie had brought two chairs face to face. He sat in one, with a legal pad perched on his knee.

Coffin sat in the other chair. "Is this as private as we can get?"

"Pretty much. Where do you let the lawyers talk to their clients usually?"

"I don't think we have had too many inmates in the last few years." He said. "It hasn't been a problem."

"Does the plumbing work?"

"Works better than the locker room john." Coffin answered. "It's where most of the officers go."

Tillie smiled. Then he changed the topic.

"I have no idea why you asked for me. I haven't practiced real law in thirty years. I don't think I ever did a criminal complaint."

"I know."

"Don't you usually use Herman Lamb?"

"I needed you."

"I have no idea why."

"You are far too modest."

Tillinghast looked at his client and puzzled it out. "It's the resume, isn't it?"

"Yup."

"I don't see how that helps…"

"You don't really think Two Ton is calling all the shots, do you? Have you seen the helicopters circling, or the Coast Guard on patrol?"

Tillinghast had to admit that he hadn't even noticed the helicopters.

"Two Ton has a few hours to pull his fat from the fire and then someone in a suit flies in from Quantico or Langley. Herman Lamb may be a better and more practiced lawyer than you are, but he couldn't keep me from Guantanamo."

"They wouldn't send you there."

"They might."

Coffin, at that point, spoke truth and told him the whole story.

Paul Tillinghast wrote constantly and asked no questions. At the end, Henry asked him to make two phone calls. He agreed.

"You think this is going to be strange, don't you?"

"All things are possible." Henry said. "This might be the only time when it gets normal."

The two men smiled wearily.

"Okay, let me work."

Tillinghast stood, fussed with jacket and his notes, then left the office. In a moment, he returned with the Marshal. The fat man returned to his pose of leaning on the metal cane.

"Officer, Henry has told me everything that has occurred. Frankly, I am more than a little surprised that you have taken this turn."

"So."

Tillie grinned.

"When is my client due to be arraigned?"

"I don't know."

"Why wasn't he arraigned today?"

"Cut the shit."

"I am." He said. "I am also waiting on an arrest report."

"Keep waiting."

"Officer, your prisoner has representation, is protected by the laws of the country and the state, and must be treated fairly. Right now, it appears that you have tossed him in jail for little cause. And you, sir, are in jeopardy."

The fat man snorted.

Tillinghast continued. "Where is the Assistant D.A. on this? Has Jean been informed?"

The big man turned his head and focused on the lawyer. "The paperwork is on the way."

"But you can't give it to me?" Herman smiled. "I suggest you get Jean on the phone very soon or you might find yourself looking at some charges of your own."

"Oh, that's a threat?"

"Tom," The Inspector said. "I told you that you have a weak hand. And now I am showing it to you. Smarten up quick." Henry spoke slowly. "Here is your deal. I will arrange for Andrea's safe return in exchange for Quinto's son, either living or dead."

"If I don't..."

"Officer, I think others further up your chain of command, can explain in more depth, what happens if you lose either asset."

Tillinghast looked at the marshal. "I have taken the liberty of calling the Policeman's Union on the behalf of my client and his partner. They will want to discuss this matter with you tomorrow morning."

Tom eyed the old man. "You don't understand. This is a matter of national security."

"Luckily, we still have a Constitution. And this citizen has representation. And you have already begun using the state apparatus…"

"You don't have a choice, my brother." The Inspector added. "If you want Lollipop, you need to produce his son's body. Otherwise, Lollipop disappears. And Andrea as well."

"He can't go anywhere."

Henry looked at the fat man. Then, he shrugged and returned his glance to his attorney. "Well, then. You have your work, my brother."

Paul Tillinghast stood up and stuck out his hand to the fat man. "I'll be seeing you."

Tommy stared at it for a second, than reached out and shook it. The lawyer walked out the door.

Once the door to the hall had shut, the marshal turned on Henry.

"You think you are being smart with me, don't you?"

"Protecting myself, my brother."

"You will be doing a lot of that where I am sending you."

The Inspector sighed. "There is no use in threatening me. You can't send me anywhere without an arraignment."

"You think?"

"I am sure." He said. "Because this is blowing up. It's in your hands and it is blowing up."

Tommy smiled. "It's called an extraction. Just like with a diseased tooth. They do it with five men. Two will have weapons out and two will have tasers. They will each take a limb, immobilize you, then use plastic cinches on your wrists and ankles. Then, there is the gag, the hood, and the earphones. It's silent and over in fifteen seconds. Then you ride out to the airport and fly off in a lear jet. In six hours, you will tell every detail I need to know." He said. "Then, on the streets of Damascus, or Mogadishu, or Mosul or in a central European republic, they will let you walk away. Penniless white American who can't go to the embassy, has no passport, and can't speak the language."

"This is going to end badly for you." The Inspector said.

"I'm not staring out through bars."

"So, why can't you strike a deal?"

"Don't need to."

"If you could get Lollipop without me, you would have already. If you could recover Andrea on your own, you would have. And, unless I am mistaken, your replacement is on his way here."

"Have a nice flight."

He left the room with the three cells. Henry lay back on the cot and closed his eyes.

At nine o'clock that night, Chief Bramden came in with the deal.

In his dress white shirt, blue pants, shining black shoes, he unlocked the door into the room with the cells. He stepped up to Henry's cell and sat down on the folding chair near the Inspector's head. Coffin opened his eyes and swung his feet to the floor.

From the look of his Chief's jaw and the sounds outside the door, Henry guessed he was near the shift change.

"Henry, I have good news."

"Great."

"I have persuaded the marshals to let you go. It took some serious work, but it looks like they are going to drop charges. You can go home."

"Okay."

The Chief looked at the Inspector, as if the older man had forgotten his line and he waited for him to say it. Henry, however, remained silent.

"Julian is dead. They had him cremated. They will give you the ashes at ten tomorrow morning. You are to arrange the return of Andrea, alive and healthy, at the same time. After you give the ashes to Lollipop, they are going to arrest him."

"They will let him bury his son?"

"Where is he going to do that? Prospect Hill?"

"He talked about burying him in the ocean off of Sconset."

Bramden looked at him. "Henry, for God's sake, don't play any more games here."

Coffin shrugged. "It's what he wanted. I can't imagine it would be a problem. Sconset beach is secure. We can do it down by the Loran station."

"He wants to bury him in the ocean?"

"It's just ashes." Coffin said. "He didn't think that he would be able to visit the grave in the future."

The Chief nodded and smiled. "Probably true."

"Also, I would like Andrea to make a statement on Julian's death."

"You know she can't." Bramden said. "Julian never existed. Lollipop never existed."

"Quinto. His name is Quinto."

"His name might as well be Twinkie. He's about to disappear into the belly of this great country."

"Just the same."

The Chief was exhausted and annoyed. He rested his elbows on his knees and hung his head. He turned and looked at the Inspector.

"So..." Bramden said.

'You want me to make a call?"

"Please."

"The deal's good?"

"I'm sure it is."

Henry stood up. Chief Bramden removed a large brass key from his back pocket. He inserted it into the lock, then swung the cell door open. Then he lead the Inspector into his office. Henry, guilelessly, picked up the phone and dialed without looking up the numbers.

He called Tillinghast and relayed the details of the deal. He asked him to put a notice up on the door of the Hub.

Then he called Reverend Mayhew. Like other old men, Mayhew didn't sleep well. He agreed to meet at the Loran station at ten.

When Henry hung up the phone, Chief Bramden waited.

"Don't you have one more call?"
"To?"
"Danny will figure it out."
"Lollipop?"
"He'll see the card at the Hub."
"Are you sure?"
"It's likely."
The Chief chewed a thumbnail.
Henry smiled at the Chief. "If you don't mind, I would rather spend the night in the jail cell."
"Just go home."
"I think I would rather be here. In case there are developments." He said. "Besides, it's safer here."
"Henry…" The Chief looked exhausted.
"I'll get out if we need to house some real criminals."
"Henry, don't play any games."
"Perish the thought."
Without any other ideas, the Chief led him back to the cell and locked him in.

Danny Higginbotham came to visit him that night, before his shift started.
"Should I ask?"
"The bed's comfortable."
Danny looked at the stainless steel shelf and doubted it.
"Do you want another book?"
"No."
"They have a TV for in here."
"No thanks. I like the quiet."
"You realize," Danny said, "that I have to ride around with a Statie tonight."
"I thought they would do that."
"Probably bugged the car."
"No doubt." Coffin said. "But they cut the deal and they will be gone by tomorrow."
"What do you want to do?"
Coffin sat forward and looked down. "I don't know. Nothing."
Danny nodded.
"Where is Two-Ton Tommy?"
"They say he is asleep."

"In his van?"
"No. Jared Coffin House."
"Imagine the elevator."
Two officers walked by the door, laughing.
Danny looked at the Inspector.
"I know something that the staties don't."
"What's that?"
"I know you can't lie."
"That's true."
"So, what's the plan?"
Danny looked down at the man.
"Why are you asking me?"
"Do you think I would sell you out?"
"No." Henry didn't look at his partner. "Why are you asking?"
"I'm curious."
"I already told you."
He sighed.
Coffin smiled. "Remember the Coopers."

The officer was silent in the passenger seat. His hat rested on his lap. He did not look in any direction but forward. When Danny got into the car, the man introduced himself as Officer Pettigrew. After that, he said nothing.

Danny pulled the cruiser into the rest stop, midway up the Milestone Road. The engine ticked, the radar numbers glowed blue and the computer screen had only the vaguest hint of color.

"Officer?" Danny asked.
"Yes,"
"Where are you from?"
"Springfield barracks."
"You live out there?"
The young man looked over at him. "Let's just do our job."
"What is your job?"
The question hung.
"I am filling in for your partner."
"Uh-huh." He said. "Well, my partner doesn't carry a gun so I would prefer that you kept yours holstered."
"I'm sure it will be safe."
"I am not." Danny said.
The other cop merely stared.

"Friendly piece of advice, my brother," Danny said. "If you see something you're sure is wrong, don't be sure."

"And you, my brother." The man snarled. "If you see something you're sure is wrong, shoot it."

Danny smiled at the idiot.

"Do you know who the Coopers are?"

"No."

"Me, neither."

"Why?"

"Something my partner said to me. He told me to 'Remember the Coopers.'"

Pettigrew turned and looked out the windshield.

CHAPTER FOUR

Elvis left the locker room with his books and his sweaty clothes. He looked to the right among the few parked cars that were left, then to the left.

Nick leaned on the horn. Elvis came trotting over.

"Maria went home with Tillinghast at the beginning of practice."

"Oh." Elvis walked over to the car slowly. "I didn't know."

"Why should you?"

He shrugged.

"You haven't started passing notes and pulling pigtails"?

"It's not like that."

"No?"

"Not really." Elvis said.

"Not really isn't no."

"Tillinghast asked me to look out for her."

"Easy work for you."

"She's got her issues."

"Who doesn't?"

"Well, she has more than most." Elvis continued. "More issues, even, than you have." All of the morning's experiences washed over him.

"You don't know half of mine."

"You don't know a third of hers."

"I know she's cute." He said. "And she's into you."

"Not now."

Nick put the car into gear and drove the big freshman back to his Aunt's house. Nick asked him if he wanted to do anything later, but the big kid just waved him away.

Rosie had gone shopping.
Fuck them.
Rosie had taken the credit card and had gone to the Stop and Shop and bought a fifteen pound turkey breast. Then she bought stuffing in a box, mashed potatoes in a tub, green beans, apple pie, and lemon meringue. Then she bought candy.
And cashews.
Now, at five-thirty, Rosie stood in her kitchen, willing her oven onward.
Plus, she was making stuffing. She had gone all Barefoot Contessa on that as well. There was sausage, browned hamburger meat, fennel, marjoram, herb bread, grapes and some bizarre striped Hungarian spice that had been sitting in the back of the spice rack.
She loved stuffing.
Then, she was going to make green beans with onions on top.
She was celebrating. It was Thursday. Thanksgiving Thursday in October when the world was going to shit and no one would flush.
No one had set the table.
She slammed the door shut on the oven.
"Maria!" She yelled "Rick! Get down here now!"

Maria was in her room.
She was listening for the heart beat.
Thumpety-Thumpety-Thumpety-Thumpety-Thumpety-Thumpety-Thumpety-Thumpety-Thumpety-Thumpety.
But she heard nothing.
Julian was gone. She remembered the dream about him swimming. But she missed him. Terribly.
Maria went to the bathroom all day long. She really only had to drop a teaspoon of pee into the bowl. But while she was waiting for it to come out, she would talk to Julian. Very quietly and mostly in the privacy of her own mind, she had conversations inside the bathroom stall.
Mostly, they talked about the baby.
When her mother called, she was lying on her bed, both hands on her jeans while she spoke to Julian.

Maria rolled off the bed, stood (with a touch of dizziness) and then stepped downstairs.

Rick was in the workshop, watching the helicopters circle the island. He counted four. Two were old Bell and Howell copters from the eighties. They carried a huge electronic package on left skid, which he suspected to be an infrared recording and sensing system. The other two, however, were Blackhawks. They swooped along the South Shore out to Sconset, crossed to the north of the island, and then came in low over the South beaches again.

There had been police cars as well. Prospect Street was a busy street for most of the year; the squad cars routinely raced by. Today, they had been joined by several dark green vans with obscured windows.

Around noon, he had heard that they had found Pink's cab. It was stuck with a dead battery near A&P.

Nothing had happened, that's what Brody had said.

But…

He had seen Billy's father at Fast Forward that morning as he was getting coffee. They hadn't spoken and didn't speak as a general rule. Rick had thought about what he had done to his son.

Nothing had happened.

He heard his wife call a second time. He powered down the table saw, left his glasses, gloves, and hat, then walked up onto the back porch.

"Mom," Maria said. "What are you doing?"
"Making dinner."
"Why are you making Thanksgiving dinner?"
"Because I wanted to."
"I am not even hungry."
"So what?" she said. "That never stopped you before."
"The turkey isn't even done. It looks raw."
"It will be fine in a half hour. Set the table."
"It's covered in James' crap."
"Well, you better get used to cleaning up crap. Crap, blood, piss and jizz" She said. "It's what women do."

Maria caught the barb but didn't react.

"This is ridiculous." She said. "It's almost seven."
"You can use the protein." She said. "And call Elvis."
"Why?"

Rosie looked at her daughter. Hard.
"You owe him."
"Bullshit. He just follows me around."
"Like that is a blessing or something?"
"He wouldn't come here."
"Call him and invite his Aunt."
"For tonight?"
"Yes."
She shook her head.
Rick walked in the door. He saw all of the commotion his wife was in the middle of. Ten years of marriage and a graduate degree had taught him to keep his mouth shut. So he did.
"Rick," she said. "Are you staying here tonight?"
"Sure."
"You remember your son, James?"
"What do you want, Rosie?"
"Give James a bath."
"Will do."

James could run his own bath. He went bopping upstairs on his own, shed his clothes in the stair and starting running the hot water. Then, naked, he shuffled into his room and lay on his bed. The boy dug his Nintendo DS out from under his pillow and promptly gave Mario a goose around the mushroom kingdom.

Rick stood in the hall, holding his son's clothing and amazed at the wonder of his little boy. He had a hard little body made for playing and bouncing and splashing in the filling bathtub. Naked, he was face down on top of one of his sister's covers. The embroidered rainbow didn't threaten his nascent masculinity.

James had inherited his father's curly mop of hair and his thin shoulders and hips. Squirming on the bed in his game, the father recognized the writhing and twitching muscles that bunched and hid on the little one's back. He didn't see much of Rosie in him. Something to the eyes, perhaps. There were times when Rick could have had the boy himself.

The slides of the boy's life passed before his father. He remembered bringing him back to the house and having Maria hold him in her arms on the sofa. He remembered building the crib for him in the room, and then sitting next to the bouncing one year old for his afternoon nap. There were birthdays and Christmases and holidays and trips to the beach where he got sunburned dragging around a seven foot strip of seaweed and several long nights of sickness and fever. All the things that other boys do. Now, for this moment, he lay naked on his sister's bed cover, engrossed in Mario and waiting on a bath. Perhaps not tomorrow nor any day after that. But for tonight, yes. It was Mario time.

Rick left the boy in his room and entered the bathroom. He sat on the toilet and waited for the water to rise to its appropriate level.

He felt tears. He felt shame. He felt anger.

Then he called for his boy and he came.

Elvis was about to put a Hot Pocket in the microwave when the phone call came. Aunt Shannon was up in her room. The television was on and he suspected he may not see her again tonight. He stared at the phone and wished it to be silent, but it rang two more times. He picked it up.

"Hello?"

"Elvis?"

"Yes?"

"It's Maria."

"Oh." He said. "Hi."

"My mother has gone off the deep end and has decided to cook a Thanksgiving dinner this evening. She would like to invite you and Shannon to it."

"Oh." He said. "I don't know."

"It is a completely crackpot event. She is cooking a turkey and has pies and everything."

"Pie?"

"Apple and something else."

The big guy was quiet.

Maria spoke. "I understand if you don't want to come."

"Would you like me to come?" Elvis asked.

"Pardon me?"

"Would you like me to be there?"

"If you would like to…"

"But would you like me to?"

At her end, Maria pulled the phone from her ear and stared at it for a few seconds.

"Look," she said. "Let's not make a bigger deal out of this than it is. My Mom is going nuts and has filled our kitchen with food. We thought you would like to come up and eat it."

Maria looked out the window at the darkened windmill. She continued. "And, yes, I would like you to come up."

"We'll be there in a few minutes."

They ate at eight.

Rosie sat at the head of the table. She placed all the serving dishes on the counters, put the plates next to them, then served herself first. Rick sat to one side of her, Shannon to the other. Elvis sat next to Shannon and Maria next to her father. That left, regrettably, one empty chair at the end of the table. However, once Rosie settled into her chair, Maria became the serving wench. She poured wine for Shannon, gin for her mother, beer for her father, and she kept the dirty dishes on their way to the sink.

The vegetables were fine, albeit slightly chilled after all of their time waiting for the bird to finish. The turkey meat was white at the outside, but acquired a damp and pinkish look to the inside of the bird. Rick had performed the rituٰally carving with an electric knife that had been handed down to him. He did his best to leave the more questionable pink on the turkey's bones.

When everyone else had a full plate, Rick stopped his daughter and made her fill her own plate. She did, and then sat next to him.

Rosie reached out and held the hands of her two dining companions. They followed suit until the whole table was holding hands. Rick and Maria looked to her. They had never done this. And they had never had Thanksgiving dinner on Thursday night in October.

Rosie looked down at her food and she said nothing. The moment of grace spread to seconds and then to a full half minute. Rick was afraid that she might be crying into her food, yet she wasn't.

"I don't know what to say." She said. "I'm just glad you're here."

They nodded.

"To absent friends," she added.

They nodded again.

In a thunderous silence, the empty chair at the end of the table yawped.

The dead had risen and sat among them. They clustered the table as if they were huddled around a fire. Cousins, uncles, parents, grandparents: they came to warm up and enjoy the reflected light. In that light, Maria caught a glimpse of her lover in the reflection in the windows. His cheek shown for a second and was gone. Elvis saw a flash of light in his father's eyes. Rick was afraid to look for the drowned boys.

For a moment, the quiet ebbed into the room.

"Are you playing on Friday, Elvis?" Rick stepped on the silence. The plates and forks began in earnest.

"Yes, sir."

"What do you think of Blue Hills?"

"They're a good team, sir."

Maria chirped. "You don't need to call him, sir."

"I am sure he likes it." Rosie added. "Beats getting called shithead."

"Or late for supper." Shannon interjected.

Rick smiled at the old joke and ignored his wife. "I don't think I have ever been called "late for supper." He patted his thin waist. "But this is very nice Rosie. You outdid yourself."

"Thanks, Mrs. DeSalvo." Elvis added.

"Rosie, thanks for inviting us up here for this meal. It really is wonderful."

The compliments disarmed her and evaporated the pool of resentment she had been building. "Thank you." She said. "I just wanted to get everyone together."

"I thought maybe you just wanted stuffing." Maria said.

"Well, that too."

"Personally, I love turkey." Rick said. "We never have it, except for special occasions."

"That's because it is such a pain in the ass to cook." Rosie said.

"How did you cook this?" Shannon asked.

Under her polite guidance, the dinner slowly took flight. Aunt Shannon slowly tended to the bruised and battered egos and emotions of the table and clucked them into good cheer and polite humor. First they talked about the troubles of cooking a turkey properly and the value of basting bags, then to the upcoming football game, then to the approaching winter and the construction projects up in Dionis. Wine bottles fell, beer bottles toppled, and even the bottle of Tanqueray dipped. The evening soared on the updrafts of gossip, trivia, and compliments so that when Maria and Elvis emptied the table of plates, dishes and silverware, the kitchen clock stood at eleven. The pies had been cut and served, the ice cream had melted and, even, a pot of coffee had been drunk.

At the ending of a story out of school, Rosie exploded in a peal of laughter. The rest of the table joined her. Then a lone voice from above called out.

The table paused for a second, waiting for James to call it his wail again.

"Oh, now I've done it." Rosie said.

"I've got him." Maria moved to the stairs.

"No, that's okay." Rosie slowly stood.

"Mom, you've done enough today. I can take care of James."

Rosie, tired and tipsy, could only barely hold her tongue as she watched her daughter climb the stairs to a unsettled child.

Elvis, from the kitchen sink, thought about how different she was here, and how nice.

Maria opened the door to James room. She slipped in, shut the door behind her, and then slid into his little bed. He kept one light on in his room. His bed was littered with stuffed animals, books, clothes, and toys. Maria deposited as many of them as she could onto the floor.

"Hi James." She said.

"I'm scared." He said.

"I know. I heard you downstairs."

"I had a bad dream."

"You know its just a dream." She said. "It's not real."

He nodded. "It was sad."

"It wasn't scary"?

"No." he said.

Maria, for a split second, remembered the picture Jack had taken of James. The little shit had threatened him. As if he hadn't done enough. He was still out there, she thought. And still dangerous.

"What was it about?" she said.

"It was about the ocean," he said. "In my dream, the ocean was all around the house and we couldn't go anywhere because we didn't have a boat."

"Were you safe?"

He nodded.

"Were we all safe inside?"

He nodded.

"Okay." She said. "Then it's okay."

"We couldn't go anywhere." James said.

"We were safe, though, weren't we?"

He nodded.

"I am going stay here while you go back to sleep, cuddles. Okay."

He nodded again.

"Goodnight house." She said.

"Goodnight mouse." He answered. This was an old game that they had played when James was much, much smaller.

"Goodnight comb." Maria whispered

"Goodnight brush" he replied.

"Goodnight nobody."

"Goodnight mush"

"And goodnight to the old lady whispering hush."

James was quiet. She wasn't sure if he had forgotten the next line or if he had slipped off to sleep.

"Goodnight stars" he said, softly.

"Goodnight air." She answered.

"Goodnight noises everywhere."

She lay in the bed and waited for the boy to nod off.

Elvis and his Aunt left shortly after James woke up. Then Rosie and Rick got up, went to the TV room, and turned the sound up. Maria knew, from experience, that was how they argued.

It had been a day. There was another one waiting. In the quiet, she heard those noises everywhere. She heard the cars drive past and the TV buzz and the dishwasher cycle into a rinse mode. She heard the wind whistle over the roof and somewhere, just at the edge of hearing, the breakers rolled up the South shore. Underneath all of that, she heard the heartbeat.

She wanted to listen.

But, against her will and against a warm little boy, she fell asleep.

CHAPTER FIVE

She knew it when she woke up.
Everything that she had eaten the night before was lined up and ready to come spewing out. She stumbled out of her room, fell into the bathroom, cranked the cold water tap, and then voided herself into the toilet. At each moment when her stomach clenched, she felt a small spurt of pee escape into her panties.
The night was still. It was, at her best guess, four or so in the morning.
She was not doing well. She sat on the cold tile in her own, pee soaked panties. Next to her, was a bowl of her own sick. Her breasts hurt. Her hips hurt. Her feet had swollen up. They only fit into her sneakers; soon it would be flip flops. The big floral muumuu, the "baby on board" tee shirt, and the elastic waistband jeans weren't far away.
Eventually, she would have to stop hiding and pretending. Then there would be huge sweatshirts, special underwear, back supports and open sandals for her fat feet.
She would have to use special desks at school. She would travel on the elevator and carry a fat kid's cup of water around with her.
Then there would be the birth.
She flushed the toilet.
Her life was clear in the blueblack cold of Autumn.
Maria cleaned the flecks of vomit off the seat, dropped her underwear into the hamper, and washed out her mouth. Then she stepped, softly, back to her own bed.

It was one of those days for Mr. Brody. Maria saw it when she stepped in. He sat at his desk and looked out over the harbor. His eyes never left the water. The rest of the students had become used to this behavior, even as early as October. The stories were rich. Brody once spent an entire class silent, staring out over the sound. He nodded off in the middle of a film. He nodded off in the middle of a test. But, he was also intense, whip smart, and scared the piss out of everyone.

The TV was set up. Maria settled herself into her chair, organized her books, and tried not to think of waterfalls. By the second bell, the class was in their seats.

"Let's neaten up the group, shall we?" he said, still staring out the window.

"What do you mean?"

"Get rid of the empty desks. Everyone should sit next to someone on both sides."

Everyone looked at each other. No one would move fast.

"I don't think we will see Jack or Billy again."

"Don't they just have tutors at home?"

"Can't say." Brody continued to look out at the window. "Don't think you will be seeing them in here again. Let's get rid of their desks."

No one was willing to get up and move. Eyes flashed to other eyes.

"Well..." Brody turned and his voice rose. "Get rid of the desks!"

Three of the boys eased to their feet.

"This is not hard, fellas." The former Ranger turned, took three steps and flung Billy's former desk up against a book case. "Now, squeeze in."

The students quickly filled the space.

Brody, now in the center of the circle, kicked the other desk out. It teetered on two legs before it fell over with a thud.

The students quickly filled that space as well. The circle of desks had contracted quite a bit. While there were still fifteen students left, they were all intensely aware of each other.

Brody left the circle and lined up the two desks with three other spare desks he had. Now, the only remnant of the young men's existence in the class was blacked out in Brody's grade book.

Brody placed a stack of lined paper on Maria's desk. She took one sheet and passed the rest of the stack around the room.

"We are going to watch another scene from this book that you haven't read yet. I want you to know it as we continue to read about Pip being a silly little pimp in London. When he blows all of his money—hundreds of pounds--ALL of his money on stupid things for Estella, I want you to know about the bill. Everybody has to pay the bill for their stupidity."

Brody moved to the TV and pressed play on the DVD player. A black and white film swam into view.

Brody had used this same film twice before. Each time, Emily or someone else would whine about the lack of color. Today, they were all too scared.

Pip staggered across a street, was nearly hit by a horse, then stumbled up the stairs and into his room. His eyes opened up, with some difficulty, to find two gentlemen who were forcing him to sign something. Then, after a longer pause, the camera slowly revealed Joe to Pip's eyes. Pip found himself back in his old home and recovering in bed. Joe had paid his debts and whisked him out of London. The scene ended with Pip, Joe, and Biddy by the side of the river.

Then he froze the tape in the VCR. Joe had just said "What Larks!"

"What happened?" Brody looked at Emily, just to the right of Maria.

"I don't know. I haven't read that far."

"Think about it," he snapped. "What happened to the money?"

"Pip spent it."

"Is there any left?"

"Doesn't appear so."

"He's deep in debt." Brody barked. "He sold his furniture. He has to leave his apartment."

"Okay." She was scared.

"Where are his friends?" Brody barked at Jeff.

"I don't know."

"Where aren't they?"

He looked confused.

"Pip is destitute and sick. He has spent, according to Joe something like eight weeks in a coma. Right?"

"Right."

"So where is Jaggers? Where is Herbert Pocket? Where is Estella? Where is Miss Haversham? Where is Drummle? Where is Wemmick?"

"I don't know?"

"Where should they be?"

The room sloshed with silence and fear.

"With Pip." Maria said. "They should check in."

"Why don't they?"

"Because they aren't really his friends."

"Okay," he allowed. "Okay, Okay, Okay. What about Pip? What should happen to Pip?"

"I don't know."

"THINK!" he stormed. "What has Pip done?"

"He fucked up."

"YES!" Brody yelled. "Did he ever! He fucked up royally. He gave his money to his friends, he pissed more away going after a girl, and he made one last noble gesture for Magwitch. Fucking Stupid Yit." His voice was building again. "What happens to people in the big city who give up all their money, get abandoned by their friends, and then get massively ill?"

"They die."

"And they get eaten by the cats and the mice and the rats until the smell gets someone in the room." He said. "They are one nasty, smelly pool of blood, shit, and rat turds on a bed. That should have happened to Pip." Brody was still roving and ranting, but he seemed to be in a rhythm now. "But Joe saved his miserable life. He came in, he paid the debts, he hoisted his sick ass onto a carriage and brought him back out to the forge. Where did he get the money? He doesn't say."

Brody glanced at the clock.

"Any ideas?"

No one dared speak.

"Kelly," he snapped. "He needed to get thousands of pounds, tens of thousands of dollars to get Pip out of hock. How did he get it?"

"I don't know."

"How can one earn that kind of money? Not as a blacksmith."

"Maybe he made a deal with the devil."

Brody's eyes lit up.

"What do you think, Maria? Do you think Joe made a deal with the devil?"

"There's no devil. Not in this book, at least."

"It's his son." Brody snapped. "Does he make a deal with the devil to spare his son?"

Maria, pregnant and confused, nodded.

"But I think Dickens fucked this part of the novel up. I think he backed away from writing what he should have written. Think about Magwitch. Convict works for twenty years in Australia with sheep in order to set this kid up. Magwitch gives up his life for Pip. And Pip pisses it away. If I was Magwitch, I would have beat the snot out of the kid." He hammered a desktop. "You know what Joe should have said? He should have said. "You owe me. I am going to hell for you. I sold my soul for you. Your ass is mine and you owe Daddy. So, make it worthwhile. Make it valuable. You got your education, you got your connections, and now, you got your second chance. So go and make it worthwhile. I will burn in hell and rot for eternity and I will be watching and you best make all of my pain worthwhile."

Brody's eyes blazed at Maria.

Emily looked at the time. "What is for homework?" someone asked.

Brody snarled. "Figure it out."

After school, her mother hijacked her. She came to the last class, pulled her out before the bell rang and marched her to the car. Rosie got in, started it up, and got going. "Where are we going?"

"A little lunch."

"I had lunch."

"I didn't."

"Mom…"

"I think we need some girl time."

Maria stared out the window. "Okay." She surrendered.

Other mothers and other girls went to some of the nice restaurants where they slipped you some wine and the salad plates were chilled. Rosie liked a dump downtown. Cy's doubled as a tourist restaurant in the summer and a scalloper's rest home in the winter. It had big brass rails, thirty beers on tap, middle aged waitresses, and a wooden canoe suspended over the bar. Every single red-eye in the place turned to her when she walked in the door, then turned back to their dollar Budweiser bottles.

They sat in a booth in the back. Her mother ordered a Cisco Ale and a basket of Onion rings. The perverse imp in her mind wanted to order a Shirley Temple, but Maria settled on a Diet Coke.

"So," Rosie said. "How are you doing?"

"Just great."

"How was the rest of the day?"

"Fine."

"How is Elaine?"

"Good."

"She looked nice today."

"Yeah, she did."

"Anything going on?"

"I think she wants to fuck Mr. Brody."

"Well, he's good looking."

Both women had grown accustomed to sharp changes in direction. Conversations darted about like tag on roller blades.

"How are you doing?"

"I'm fine."

"Well, that's just great."

"Really, I'm fine."

"You're going to make this hard, aren't you?"

"Make what hard?"

"Look at me, Maria." Rosie took one of her daughters hands and held it. "Look at me carefully, and decide if you want to fuck around any more."

"What?"

"Because I am 100% done. Done, done, done. I am done with the bullshit and the lies."

Maria tried to look confused. She felt her stomach fall.

The beer and the onion rings arrived. Maria's Diet Coke got replaced.

Rosie dropped a half cup of ketchup in the basket of onion rings. She smeared it like a pool of blood. She picked up a thick one, dragged it around in the red mess, than chomped on it.

"You are a sick, sick girl." Rosie said. "I thought of this the other night. When you were in your room and your father was God knows where." She said. "Here you are, raped and drugged at a party." Maria opened her mouth. " I saw the picture. I know what fucking happened so don't try lying to me."

Maria looked around. All of the booths were full around them. Anyone could hear.

"And your boyfriend is dead. Coffin comes up to tell us himself that the boy is dead. But you don't react to that, either."

Maria was still. She felt the oxygen seep from the room.

"Then I keep hearing these little steps in the night that go pitter-patter-puke. And I see my girl start to grow in ways that I know well. The tits, the hips, the hair. Oh, I know that shit well. Take a good look at what pregnancy gets you, little girl. Take a good look at what your genes have in store for you."

Maria made a face, but said nothing. She wasn't sure her lungs were actually still working.

"So, I lie awake at night and I think about my little girl who got raped, whose boyfriend is dead, and who is pregnant. Then she wants to return to school."

Rosie looked at her daughter. The mother was not angry or upset. Instead, she was coating the onion rings with ketchup and eating them, slowly.

"And I decided that you are sick."

"I'm not sick."

"But you are pregnant."

"I'm not pregnant." At the pronunciation of the word, she heard the rapid little heartbeat again in her head.

"Don't lie to me. Here is the first rule of being knocked up. Don't lie to your Mom because she mother-fucking knows better."

"I'm not."

"Yeah, well. Time will certainly tell, won't it?" Rosie looked at her with an impish glance. "Wait here."

She got up, walked to the bar and returned with a tall glass of champagne.

"So, if you aren't pregnant, you would drink the champagne, wouldn't you? It won't make you sick and it certainly wouldn't hurt the baby. Because there isn't one."

"I don't drink."

"Horseshit." Her mother chuckled. "Have I mentioned that I am through with bullshit? Have I mentioned that?"

Maria crossed her arms. The heartbeat had speeded up. She saw the little boy, in his fluid, spinning about. She saw little fingers and little toes and that pumping beat.

Rosie took the glass and held it up. "I drink to your abortion."

"You're disgusting." The first tear dropped from an eye. With a path made, the rest of the tears flowed. She did not sob and she did not whine; Maria merely wept.

Rosie sipped for a long moment, then set the glass down.

Maria stood up.

"You can leave, but I don't know where you are going to go."

"Are you throwing me out?"

"You wish I would."

Rosie hadn't moved. Maria stood at the end of the table, ready to stomp out. Her tears traced her cheek and fell to her jawline.

"Do you know what being a mother means?"

Maria just stared at her. She heard the heartbeat. She had an idea.

Rosie continued. "It means you can't leave."

She began preparing another onion ring. She hung it off her fork, again. "Husbands, boy friends, baby-daddys...they can all leave. As a matter of fact , it is often a lot easier if they do. Children eventually leave. That was my hope for you. But, honey, mothers never leave. I'm staying right here and maybe you will too."

Rosie picked up a whole, bloody ring and held it so it formed a loose zero at the end of her fingers.

Maria stood at the end of the table. The tears had eased and she felt herself slip back into that warm, floating place.

"You might as well sit." Rosie said. "Like I said, where are you going to go?"

Maria looked out the door. Her mother had something up her sleeve. And Maria was right.

"So," Rosie said. "Let's just pretend like you might be pregnant. You would have two basic choices: Do I keep it or do I toss it back."

"Mom..."

"Now, if you decide to keep the baby, you would need a place to raise it, keep it warm, let it sleep, feed it, get a job, get daycare, and all the rest. So, you would have to stay home with your dear old Mother. Think about that."

Rosie helped herself to a smaller onion ring.

"Think about spending the next twenty years of your life with me. We, you and I, would raise the baby together. Imagine how much fun it would be to be with me until you are almost forty and I will be...almost seventy.. You can go work at the Stop and Shop or Wee Whalers or something, so long as you can be with your baby. Because I ain't doing that."

Maria made a face. The child moved within her.

"Your father will be so thrilled to have you, with a baby, for the next twenty years. Neither of us is getting younger, so having you around to help out around the house, clean, do errands and take care of us as we get older. The more I think about it, the better I feel. You could be my bitch. Your little boy could help out your father at work."

"I am not pregnant, Mom." The lie singed her gently. The word, and its power, dropped from her tongue heavily.

"Good, because when you get pregnant, you tend to blow up like me. Those are your genes, girl. You could even wear my clothes."

Rosie finished her beer.

"Again, it's not like you have a choice. The baby's father is dead, isn't he?"

Maria face didn't change.

"So you guys can't move in together and get married. We can't have a wedding reception with the Daddy's Little Girl dance, now can we? We can't have a lovely little baby shower with cute presents and cupcakes. Worse, you have no skills and no degrees. No happy little nursing degree or PhD in Art History or even a god damned high school diploma. You can't even be the night manager at McDonald's."

The waiter came and brought Rosie another beer.

"So, you know how you feel right now? Pissed off and trapped. Enjoy it. Get nice and fucking comfortable. Because that is your life, bunny-my-honey. That is your life."

"Mom, can you stop?"

"Sure, tell me the truth."

Maria looked at her. She had to go to the bathroom, her back hurt, and her breasts were sore again. But she hated the blimp so much. She had no tears now, she had no safe warm floating or gentle heart beats. Just rising, burning anger.

"You're not speaking." Rosie said. "Which means that you can't say the truth."

"Well, I got raised right."

"You'll get a chance to do a better job than I did. Real fucking soon."

"What do you want, Mom?"

She ate the last onion ring.

"I wanted a white wedding without a fucking ring bearer. I wanted to go to a nice restaurant in Cambridge after you got your degree. I missed that, didn't I?" she said. "Failing that, I wanted the truth. Didn't get that, either."

"Mom, I told you the truth…"

Rosie reached into a purse and pulled out an envelope. She placed it on the table in front of her daughter and then, quick, she took hold of the girl's hand.

"This is the paperwork for your admittance to MacLean Hospital in Belmont. You are going to get admitted, have an abortion, and then spend as much time as you need to rebuild the lego set in your head… It has my signature, a check, your medical records, and everything else they need."

Maria shook her head. "You are not locking me up."

"The hell I'm not." Rosie drank down deep. "You have two choices, little girl. One, you can get the scrape and shrink, then come back here, graduate, go to college, become a chef and an investment banker with a pony for the weekend or you can do the jelly donut dance and spend the rest of your life locked down on Nantucket cleaning the shit out of my toilet."

She handed her daughter the envelope and laid it on her hands. "Your call."

"So, you're done?"

"Yup."

Maria stood up. "Fuck you." She stormed out of the restaurant.

Rosie smiled. Her girl took the envelope with her.

The tears washed down with each step she took. She felt them shake free when she stepped down from the curb and saw them land on the cobblestones like four rain drops.

She knew she was crying and she knew she must look like a mess, but Maria was just going to keep going. It fell like rain; nothing she could do, nothing she could say, and it wouldn't stop her from going.

Maria held onto the kruggerand. She had slipped it out of her pocket and into her palm when she left Cy's; although she had taken to carrying it for weeks now. Aside from the baby, it was the only thing she had left of him.

He was beside her now. He loped along, hands shuffling along, out of rhythm with his feet just slightly. He had nothing to say, of course. But he was there and he was concerned and she smiled at him, gently and painfully.

If only they had made it.

It would have been a mess, but he would have been with her each night. It would have been some back bedroom of someone else's house. They would probably eat take-out and lie on the bed. Maybe he would talk about his day or perhaps they would just watch TV so he could work on his English. He would touch her belly constantly. It would drive her nuts to be fondled so often, so polished.

He was dead.

Maria's pace had slowed. She was halfway up Union Street, walking on the brick sidewalk between the picket fence and the parked cars. The air had cooled, but the sky remained bright and cloudless. The elms with their remaining yellow leaves rattled against the October sky.

She didn't know where to go. The bitch was right about that.

Union Street joined up with Water Street and began to follow the reeds and eel grass of the shoreline. The pick up trucks and Volvos passed more quickly here. She would be recognized.

Robert P. Barsanti

Maria paused before the ducks at Consue Springs. She crossed the street, found the bench near the willow, and sat. She had become tired with all the crying and walking. Her feet breathed for a moment, but her back had begun to tighten. The bench was only a temporary answer.

The ducks clustered around her, but she had no bread for them. They quacked, looked, turned, and waddled back down the bank and into the water. Where do the ducks go in the winter? They stay right here and eat bread. The become island pets.

The bitch was right. She was right and she was wrong. Maria knew that she had been pushing the decision off. It wasn't as if she had forgotten she was pregnant-her morning bathroom runs kept the idea fresh in her mind. It was nice to retreat inside to that bright warm spot. And it was nice to just have the secret. She could go through her day with that golden secret. But the bitch was right. She wouldn't be pregnant forever and it wouldn't be a secret much longer.

And then what?

She had no one. Elaine was useless for anything but a cigarette and a ride to the party. Her Mom had already voted. She felt the envelope in her back pocket. There were other kids, other adults. All equally useless. No one would make the decision for her.

Check that. Her mother had made a decision.

No one, Maria said, was telling her to keep the baby. No one was thinking up names for him and buying him clothes and touching her belly and waiting for a kick.

Because that one was dead.

The tears returned. She descended in great gulping torrents. They burned her cheek and dropped onto her blouse and kept on coming. She couldn't breathe, she couldn't see, and she couldn't stop crying. Hidden inside the willow, beside two hundred swimming ducks, the stab of Julian's death finally reached her heart and sliced it, over and over again. She cried and sobbed so hard she felt dizzy. Her bladder pushed on her at each sob and a drop trickled out. And she couldn't stop herself.

She forced herself to think of him alive. She brought the image of him climbing the steering arm at the old mill, and then standing atop the roof. Lean, balanced, feline he ran up the old wooden pole and stood against the stars. That was who he was. It was who he had been.

She couldn't have his child. Because it would be her child. She had no money, she had no job, she had no baby-daddy or even a husband, she had no prospects, she had no chance. The rest of her life would be yoked to her parents; even if she had her own apartment and a job, she still would be tied in tight. There would be no college. There would be no career, other than that of waitress or cabdriver out here. She would be her mother, without the house, or the husband or the job.

Julian was dead. His child would be too.

And she would live.

She cried harder.

An hour later, she walked on to the only place where she could go. Her underwear was wet, her legs were chafing, her feet hurt and she was dying for a nap.

"Is Elvis home?"

She showered, she ate a little, and she napped for two hours. Shannon called her mother to let her know where the girl was. Rosie packed a paper bag with clothes for her and dropped them off. In the kitchen, with her daughter sleeping in the guest bedroom, she saw the envelope on the counter. Rosie had no doubt that Shannon had read it.

That was fine. She was beyond that.

Truth be told, Shannon was helping her out.

Rosie thanked her, nodded to Elvis, and walked away.

Later, when Maria woke up, Elvis was sitting by her bedside. He had sat beside this bed for a long time before. He was familiar with it.

"Hello." Maria said.

"Hi."

"I'm sorry." She said. "I didn't know where else I could go."

"It's okay." He said. "I'm glad you're here."

"I have to ask you for a favor."

"Okay."

"Can you drive?"

"Yes." He was unsure of this.

"Can you take me to Belmont tomorrow?" she said. "My Mom has a car on the other side."

"Don't you want your folks to go?"

"No." she said. "I need you. It can't be them."

Elvis was silent.

"Do they know?"

"Yes."

"Why are you going?"

"Does it matter?" she said. "I really, really need your help, Elvis."

The boy sat back and decided that it didn't matter.

"Yes," he said, "But there is this thing I have to do for Coach in the morning."

She smiled. "Of course."

CHAPTER SIX

October faded slowly during its final days. The unofficial start of winter comes at Halloween. Both of the winter bars, the Chicken Box and the Muse, throw big parties and all the drunks come out as their favorite fantasy. Time and sexual energy gets invested into the costumes until they become a tapestry of art and desperation.

By the end of October, the tourist numbers have dwindled to nothing. The foliage, such as it is, has turned and fallen in these last few weeks, the sky turned to slate, and the white caps regain their winter look of gray, implacable permanence.

On Halloween, Main Street closes at four o'clock and all the preschoolers, with attending parents, parade up to the Methodist Church. Almost all of the shops, even those closed for the winter, open their front doors for witches, Elmo, and goblins.

Coffin and Higginbotham drew the crowd control duty and stood by a squad car near the opening to Orange Street. Both men watched the hundreds of parents and children move slowly up the cobblestones to the Methodist Church and candy. Somewhere in the crowd, Danny's wife and his daughter Hadley moved. Hadley had decided to be a princess this year, which was absolutely no surprise to either of her parents.

Rosie had brought James down this year. After several hours of his mother's digging through the basement and hunting for the right clothes, she surrendered and bought him the "Blue's Clues" outfit that he had wanted. The boy loved the floppy dog ears and he whipped them back and forth on his head. Maria had taken him to Halloween in the past, but she was sick and in the hospital. James had called her earlier and sent her a picture of what he looked like. She had told him that he liked it very much.

This year, Halloween fell on the night of the Old Colony game. The coaches had sent the team, in uniform, down to Main Street two hours before the game, at five in the afternoon. The little kids were thrilled to see their older brothers walking up and down the bricks, handing out Charleston Chews and Snickers bars. Many of the little boys who played PeeWee football at the Boy's Club dressed up in their uniforms as a costume. Other little boys wore the numbers and uniforms of their favorite professionals.

Elvis was a huge hit among the little ghosts, goblins, and Green Bay Packers. He emptied his bag of Reese's Cups the fastest and posed with stacks and piles of little boys. They asked him to perch on his shoulders or his head. He, gently, obliged. They all took pictures.

Later than evening, in his second start as a Varsity player, the Whalers defeated the Crusaders by forty four points. A sophomore running back ran for two hundred yards behind the big left tackle. Afterwards, he spoke with a reporter.

Nick took him out for a six pack after the game. They drove to Miacomet Beach, with the rest of their players and their fans, and had a bonfire.

Before Coffin and Higginbotham went to break up the bonfire, they were called to a fight at the Chicken Box. But by the time Danny drove the squad car up Dave Street, the fight crowd had dissipated. One man sat bloody and bruised on a bench, tended to by two friends and an angry woman.

When Coffin approached, he saw that the beaten man was Bud Mitchell, Jack's father.

"What's the trouble, Bud?"

"No trouble." He said.

The woman started yelling about the goddam Mexican assholes that were taking over the island, but Coffin shushed her.

"Can I take you home, Bud?"

"Sure."

"Do you think you need to go to the hospital?"

"No, I think I am fine."

"Can you guys take care for yourselves?" He looked at the rest of the support crew. The three of them had been well medicated. They nodded.

He walked Bud to the squad car and eased him in the back seat.

Milestone Road

Danny glanced at the man in the rear view mirror and flickered with recognition. He put the car into gear, let the lights flash until they were on Pleasant Street and headed to the Cape on Somerset.

Coffin turned around.

"Did you get yourself into trouble back there?"

"No, no trouble," he muttered. "I was asking if they had seen Jack"?

Coffin nodded. "Had they?"

"No." Bud smiled. "But he must have pissed a bunch of them off."

Coffin spoke. "I imagine so."

Danny looked to him. "Do you think he went off-island?"

"I don't know." He said. "He and Billy must have gone somewhere." The beaten man looked out the window "But he usually calls. He always wants me to take care of his cat, Mr. Puddles. He always calls about Mr. Puddles."

Coffin nodded.

The beaten man turned to the two policemen. "It's like I lost him somewhere?"

Danny looked at the addict in the rear view mirror and felt his soul tear.

ABOUT THE AUTHOR

Bob Barsanti lived on Nantucket for twenty years. He taught in the schools, lost golf balls on all of the island's courses, and has eaten in all of the island's restaurants. In the summer, he is often at the beach with two charming boys. Currently, he is living and teaching in the Berkshires.

He has two other works. He has collected his essays on teaching in "Rolling in the Surf" and his essays on Nantucket in "Sand in My Shoes." He writes regularly for Yesterday's Island.

Made in the USA
Charleston, SC
11 June 2012